MW00624212

REVENGE

of the

BARBARY

Ghost

Books by Victoria Hamilton

A Gentlewoman's Guide to Murder

Lady Anne Addison Mysteries

Lady Anne and the Howl in the Dark
Revenge of the Barbary Ghost
Curse of the Gypsy

Vintage Kitchen Mysteries

A Deadly Grind
Bowled Over
Freezer I'll Shoot
No Mallets Intended
White Colander Crime
Leave It to Cleaver
No Grater Danger
Breaking the Mould

Merry Muffin Mysteries

Bran New Death
Muffin But Murder
Death of an English Muffin
Much Ado About Muffin
Muffin to Fear
Muffin But Trouble

REVENGE
of the
BARBARY
Ghost

VICTORIA HAMILTON

BEYOND THE PAGE
PUBLISHING

Beyond the Page Books
are published by
Beyond the Page Publishing
www.beyondthepagepub.com

This book was originally published under the name Donna Lea Simpson, copyright © 2012 by Donna Lea Simpson.
Cover design and illustration by Dar Albert, Wicked Smart Designs.

ISBN: 978-1-950461-22-6

All rights reserved under International and Pan-American Copyright Conventions. By payment of required fees, you have been granted the non-exclusive, non-transferable right to access and read the text of this book. No part of this text may be reproduced, transmitted, downloaded, decompiled, reverse engineered, or stored in or introduced into any information storage and retrieval system, in any form or by any means, whether electronic or mechanical, now known or hereinafter invented without the express written permission of both the copyright holder and the publisher.

This is a work of fiction. Names, characters, places, and incidents either are the product of the author's imagination or are used fictiously, and any resemblance to actual persons, living or dead, business establishments, events or locales is entirely coincidental. The publisher does not have any control over and does not assume any responsibility for author or third-party websites or their content.

The scanning, uploading, and distribution of this book via the Internet or via any other means without the permission of the publisher is illegal and punishable by law. Your support of the author's rights is appreciated.

REVENGE

of the

BARBARY

Ghost

One

How should a lady go about forgetting an utterly unforgettable man?

Lady Anne Addison huddled in the dark on the grassy lip of a cliff overlooking a Cornish cove, watching the moonlight dance on the waves that broke on the gleaming beach, many fathoms below. The tide was rising, and the sound was a hushed susurration, a whisper that blended with the rustle of the long grass around her. It reminded her of a husky voice whispering in her ear, a wicked, devastatingly masculine voice, familiar to her and ever-present in her dreams.

Lord Darkefell.

Two weeks before, she had fled from Yorkshire to this lovely spot in Cornwall to enjoy time with Pamela and Marcus St. James, effervescent brother and sister, friends since Anne's disastrous Season many years before. But if she was to be honest, her flight had been prompted by a need to get away from the infuriating, impenetrable, exasperating and completely dazzling Marquess of Darkefell, the man who had inexplicably proposed to her moments after saving her life. She had teetered on the brink of oblivion, shoved to the edge of a cliff above a waterfall by a murderous madman; the marquess risked his life to save her, then bellowed that she had to marry him.

As spring blossomed in gaudy profusion in the Cornish sunshine, she had begun to wonder why she had run away. Not that she believed she should have accepted Darkefell's proposal. They barely knew each other. Shared kisses, as breathtaking as they were, were not a sturdy base upon which to build a union that would last many years and see as much sorrow as joy. She had only *begun* to take the marquess's measure when he shouted at her that she must marry him.

Must. Marry. Him. The words taken separately did not threaten, but together . . . oh, the overwhelming panic! She fancied herself courageous, but it was fear that had sent her scuttling south away from a fearsome urge to throw herself into the marquess's arms and shout yes.

Her cowardice was not a welcome revelation. She put her chin on her knees and stared at the moon, but a noise below on the shore made her peek over the edge of the cliff again. She couldn't see a thing, and so returned her gaze to the waning full moon above.

If not for that idiotic proposal and her odd reaction to it, she reflected, she would not have departed from Yorkshire so hastily. It wasn't that she couldn't see herself married to Darkefell—Tony, as he was known to his intimates—it was that she feared she would too easily become entranced, then infatuated, and finally sucked into a swirling vortex of adoration. He was intelligent, forceful, handsome, a skilled seducer, and maddeningly, *infuriatingly* fascinating. His kisses suffocated her with strange desires she knew not how to defeat. And his wretched proposal, as infuriating as it was, had threatened to undermine her determination to delay marriage until she knew her own mind on the subject.

He was a dangerous man.

She sighed and stared up at the blanket of gleaming stars, idly picking out constellations her father had shown her through the lens of a telescope many years before, as she pondered her marital prospects. It seemed the longer she remained a spinster, the more difficult it was to imagine being married. She had been her own woman for so long and now, at the age of twenty-four, did not want to become a mere appendage, a burden, a moral obligation to any man. Some would argue she already was her father's burden, and too long a weight on his purse, since she had not deigned to yoke herself with a man in holy wedlock. But her father, the Earl of Harecross, abstracted, scholarly and buried in his ancient Greeks and Macedonians, his language studies and cultural research, never made her feel that she was a encumbrance, legal or otherwise.

She stretched out on the ground, cradling her head in her bent arm, and lazily played with the long grass, weaving it in and out of her fingers as she contemplated her mixed feelings toward the marquess. While Darkefell kissed her she could think of nothing but how she wished it would go on forever. But when he released her, he was still the same commanding, wretchedly stubborn man! Preposterous to think that marriage to him, apart from the obvious physical delights he could offer and the wicked pleasures he would no doubt teach her, would be anything less than a parade of exasperating arguments and endless aggravation.

But lying out on a moonlit cliff in Cornwall in the middle of the night while her cat, Irusan, played with the toads and rodents, would solve nothing. She should go in and sleep. The next day promised another round of visits with new acquaintances in the seaside village of St. Wyllow, on the north coast of Cornwall: flirtation with Marcus St. James, shopping with Pamela and perhaps a fete or party with the officers of St. James's regiment, billeted in nearby St. Ives.

She heaved a sigh, weary at the thought of it, and began to rise, brushing dried grass from her full skirts and petticoat. "Come along, Irusan," she called out, softly. As she stood, a movement on the water caught her eye. And on the beach! She hunkered back down and stared over the cliff through the curtain of dancing grass. Irusan returned to her side and rubbed against her legs.

"What is that, puss, on the beach?" Anne whispered, squinting. He answered with an inquisitive "mrow?"

Moonglow caught the movement and lit it from above like a chandelier above a theater stage. She watched men on the beach, creeping out from the shadow of the cliff, and spotted a boat approaching, oars swishing through the choppy water. Anne frowned and stared as she put one staying hand on Irusan's thick mane of fur. The moonlight path delineated a boat lumbering low in the water and manned by many oarsmen. A cresting wave carried the boat forward and it surged onto the sand. The men on the beach dashed forward to pull it up further, and the activity became frenetic. An oilskin cover was thrown back, then barrels and boxes were plucked from the laden boat and passed along a line of dark-clad men. Some slung rope-tied tubs over their shoulders and beetled up the shore to a dray with a draft horse hitched. One figure stood out, alone, waving a cutlass and directing the activity with bold motions.

Smugglers! There was no other explanation, and Anne shivered; she was familiar with sordid tales of the brutal tribe, so-called free traders, near her Kentish home. Wondering what she should do—stay down in the grass to avoid detection, or depart to the safe confines of the house—she watched, breath held.

Cliff House, Pamela's rented home, was a good ways back from the cliff from which it took its name. A rocky cut divided the bluff where she huddled from another prominence beyond, which jutted above the sandy beach at an equal height. As she glanced toward that other cliff, she noted movement in the moonlight, something more than the tall grass rustling in the quickening breeze. Several men stood, suddenly, and with a shout surged toward the rocky path along the cut, down to the beach.

But another figure appeared that same moment, floating impossibly in midair beyond the cliff's edge where Anne crouched. She fell back on her rump in the long grass and scuttled, crablike, backward. It was a black-bearded, turban-clad man, dressed in a banyan made of rich, glowing fabrics, and ballooning white pantaloons; he slashed a scimitar through the air with one hand while holding a lantern in the other. His mouth opened as if he shouted, but no sound came out, and the men who had been moving down toward the smugglers halted in the rocky cut, the whites of their eyes gleaming in the moonlight, faces bleached with fear. The Mussulman — for that is what the specter appeared to Anne to be, though she had only oriental portraits to go by — gestured wildly, then, with one grand motion, produced smoke. The men fell back and Anne, trembling, put one hand to her mouth to keep from crying out.

An explosion accompanied by a brilliant shower of sparks shattered the quietude and echoed in the sheltered bay. Another crack of sound down on the beach echoed against the cliff wall, and sand arced up, bright lights lit the night sky; the zinging sound of fireworks followed the explosion. Anne stumbled to her feet and cried out, staggering further backward from the cliff edge as some of the other group of men retreated in a panicked scramble of movement, back up to the far prominence. Irusan had already streaked away, back toward the house.

Anne's only thought was to escape and she ran quite a way, but turned back toward the cliff as the smoke cleared, and saw that the Mussulman, or Mohammedan, as she had also heard them named, was gone. But to where? Curiosity, her fatal flaw, would not allow her to just return to the house without knowing all. She crept back and looked over the cliff edge; the beach below was deserted! The remaining revenue men on the other side of the cut — preventative men was what Anne surmised they *must* be, and fortunately they had not seen her — stood as still as she and stared, agape. Then they again clambered down to the beach, with shouts and angry howls of disbelief.

Anne, grateful for the moonlight, hastened through the long grass away from the cliff, down the slope, back toward the protected garden of Pamela and Marcus St. James's house. What had she just witnessed? Smugglers, to be sure, but who or what was the Mussulman—a ghost? an apparition?—and where had the smugglers gone after his fantastical performance?

She had been bored with the frivolous parade of life in Cornwall, and was wishing for something more interesting to help her forget Lord Tony Darkefell. As so seldom happens in life, it seemed that her wish had been granted. She entered the gate at the bottom of Cliff House's garden, and, with Irusan dashing beside her, bustled to the terrace, then in the door and up the servants' stairs to her third-floor suite.

"Where were you, milady?" Mary, Anne's maid, ghostly in her plain shift and nightcap, cried, rushing to her as she entered the bedchamber. "I was that turned aboot with fright! I haird weird noises, popping and clattering, thought to ask you what it was, and found you gone."

"Mary," Anne said, grasping her harried maid by the upper arms. "I have seen the most monstrous thing!" Pacing in the narrow confines of her room, a small white-papered chamber with slanted ceilings, she described the scene, her suspicion of smugglers, and the appearance of the Mussulman specter. She stopped and stared, sketching the scene in the air with her hands. "He rose from beyond the cliff like . . . like nothing I have ever seen. And he floated! I'm going to Pamela to see if she has ever seen the specter."

Her maid shuddered. "Oh, milady," she said, keeping her voice down, for her son, Wee Robbie, was asleep in the attached dressing room, where Mary and her boy had a cot. "I dinna wish to know more. If it's smugglers, they're a desperate lot of cutthroats, and the less said, the better."

"You've been with me long enough to have heard the tales at Harecross Hall," Anne said of her home near the Kentish shore, and rumors of smugglers along the coast of the channel. "Smugglers I will avoid speaking of, but I *do* wish to know more about the *specter*. What can it be? I'd go back out now to look, but it disappeared, and won't be back this night, I've no doubt. I wish to explore the cliff edge tomorrow, though."

"But ye won't go out again tonight, will you? Promise me?"

"No, Mary. I'm just going down the hall to speak with Pamela, and then I'll return to my bed like the proper spinster I'm supposed to be."

The maid gazed at her for a long moment and then said, "Perhaps Miss St. James knows all about the smugglers' use of the beach below."

"Pamela would *never* countenance those brutes using her beach! No, as a tenant in this house she has a right to know what I've seen. I'm going to tell her."

"Aye, but perhaps you're just carryin' water to the well."

"Don't be ridiculous. I'll be back in a few minutes."

After two weeks at Cliff House, she knew her way along the dark and narrow halls. The house had all the appearance of airiness and roominess from the outside, but inside it was a warren of ill-conceived dimness and antiquated notions of lighting. It was a very old house, and many times in the last weeks Anne had heard strange sounds emanating from downstairs, only to find, when she went to investigate, that the noises had stopped. She'd heard creaking from above, too, in the attic, but the house was not particularly well kept and Anne thought it was likely what her maid called wee beasties. Mary feared that the house was haunted, but Anne thought it was just poorly ventilated and draughty, and probably overrun with mice.

Pamela's room was not far, though further than Anne would have thought practical. Why had Pam not put her in the suite next to hers? It certainly would have been easier for the maid, Lynn, who came in daily to make up fires, haul ashes, clean slops and change linens. Anne tapped on her friend's door. "Pamela, are you awake?" She entered, to find her dark-haired, blue-eyed friend sitting up with a candle and reading a novel.

"What is it?" Pam said.

Anne climbed up on the end of the bed, sweeping the poofed skirts of her *robe à la polonaise* aside, and tucked her feet underneath her. She said, "Pam, the most amazing thing. Did you not hear fireworks a short time ago?"

"Fireworks? What are you talking about?" Pam asked, her pretty face wrinkled in a puzzled frown, laying her book facedown on the covers.

Anne repeated her story, with the appropriate interjections from her friend.

When she was done, Pam leaned forward, her dark eyes sparkling, and said, "You've just seen the Barbary Ghost!"

"I beg your pardon?"

"My dear, you've been here almost two weeks. Have you not noticed the small inn down the road a ways? We pass it every time we walk to St. Wyllow."

"I've seen the inn, but why do you speak of it?"

"Anne, it's called the Barbary Ghost."

Not wishing to admit that her normal perspicacity was lacking these days, so wrapped up were her thoughts and efforts in supposedly forgetting a certain dark-eyed marquess from Yorkshire, she merely said, "Tell me about the Barbary Ghost!"

Pam settled back against her pillow. "Cornwall, being a peninsular arm thrust out into the sea, was thought by some to be particularly vulnerable, and many years ago a Barbary ship entered these waters. The Barbary pirates are notorious slavers, my dear, and have a wicked taste for northern ladies to take off to their pasha's harems, where the pale-skinned girls become highly prized concubines."

"I have heard of Barbary pirates, my dear, and their ransom demands."

"Yes, well, the captives who do not bring ransom money are kept in harems and subjected to the most shocking treatment! Anyway, this particular pirate ship anchored near St. Wyllow, and it is said that a landing party ended up right on the beach below this house!"

"Really?" Anne said, clasping her hands together. "When did this happen?"

"I don't know the exact date," Pam said, waving one hand in the air in a dismissive gesture. "Trust you, my practical friend, to wish for a time schedule. It was years ago . . . perhaps as much as an hundred. Anyway, one particular Barbary pirate came ashore in search of a certain girl, one whom he had seen from afar, and with whom he had fallen in love."

"Seen from afar?" Anne cocked her head to one side. "How was that possible for a man on a sailing ship to see all the way to this house? Or do you mean she walked on the shore, or the bluff?" Her practicality would not stand such a piece of nonsense.

"Shush, Anne, dear," Pam admonished, with a humorous glint in her lovely eyes. She closed her book and tossed it aside. "You'll take all the whimsy out of this with your pragmatism. So this Barbary pirate landed ashore with his terrible crew, but while the others plundered and robbed and pillaged—"

"All the usual piratical occupations, of course," Anne drily interjected.

"Exactly. He, this particular Barbary pirate—"

"Let us call him George for short," Anne said.

Pam laughed. "All right, George, then. George climbs up the cliff and finds—"

"Arabella," Anne said. "Why not? Give the imaginary maiden a fitting name."

"Right. Arabella, the fairest maid in St. Wyllow!" Pam said, dramatically, clasping her hands to her bosom. "Legend has it that she lived in this very house, maybe even in your room, or mine. Imagine! So, George kidnaps Arabella and carries her off to the ship, and the successful pirates leave and begin to sail back to the Mediterranean."

"But," Anne added, with a quizzical lift to her brow. "There must be a 'but,' my dear, or there would be no further story, for if there is a Barbary Ghost, there must be a dead Barbary pirate somewhere, and I sadly conclude that the ghost is of our darling, romantic George."

"How clever you are!" Pamela exclaimed. "True. Arabella was dreadfully sad, and George couldn't bear to see her wasting away day after day, pining for her home and family as they sailed south."

"A pirate with a conscience," Anne said, a satirical edge to her voice. "How novel."

"Yes, well, he couldn't bear it, and he knew when he returned to the pasha, his overlord, that Arabella would become his master's concubine. He wouldn't even be able to keep the girl he loved! So, he escaped with his darling Arabella, on a ship heading north. Thus, he returned her to her family, in this very house."

"But?"

"Of course, another 'but'! *But* . . . Arabella's angry father and brothers turned out in force and slew George before Arabella could say that she owed her life to the gentle Barbary pirate."

"And ever after he haunts your cove?"

"You have it!" Pam cried, with a delighted laugh. "And you have seen this fellow?"

"George? Well, I did see something in the guise of a Barbary pirate, certainly, though it looked fearfully solid for a specter, and put on a fireworks spectacular, too! He appeared rather ferocious." Her smiled died and her eyes widened as she leaned forward and clasped her friend's folded hands. "But more importantly, Pam, my dear, you have smugglers!" she said, in much the same way one might say, "You have mice."

"Oh?" Pam's expression blanked, and the color fled from her cheek.

"Yes, smugglers, below, on your beach. What shall we do?"

"Do? Good heavens, Anne, what do you expect?" Pamela said in a trembling voice. "That I should march out there and arrest them? I'm going to do what every good Cornwall resident does at this time of night, if they suspect smugglers are abroad; I am going to turn my face to the wall and sleep." She tossed the book to the floor, blew out her candle and snuggled under her covers. "Good night, my dear," she said in the sudden darkness. "Go to bed, and don't venture forth at night."

• • •

Earlier that same day . . .

Anthony, Marquess of Darkefell, was in Bath accompanied by his secretary, Mr. Osei Boatin. Mr. Boatin's lineage was exotic. A Fante prince from the interior of an African nation, he was captured by a warring Ashanti tribe and sold to an English slaver, and shipped toward Jamaica. But he became gravely ill, as did many others in the crowded, filthy hold of the slave ship. Ordered to dispose of the sickly humans as if they were spoiled cargo, in an effort to cut losses, the crew began throwing those closest to death overboard into the frigid Atlantic waters. Osei was rescued from certain death at the hands of his captors by the marquess himself, who was on another ship in the convoy; Darkefell and his twin brother, Lord Julius Bestwick, leaped into the ocean and rescued Osei and as many others as they could manage before the cold or drowning defeated them.

Mr. Boatin was grateful to his employer, but the feeling went beyond mere gratitude to a selfless devotion. He had been given another chance at life, and *not* a life as a slave, but as a free man. He swiftly learned English, both spoken and written, and gained an education mostly due to his own perseverance, intelligence and determination, then became the marquess's secretary. Lord Darkefell trusted Osei to depths seldom seen in such a dependent relationship. The African, though logic and reason were no mystery to him, had also shown a valuable ability to understand the English with whom he worked in a more penetrating fashion than his employer, and so Darkefell relied upon him, deferring to him on occasion when logic failed and human insight was needed. It was a relationship unique in many ways, but no more exceptional than were the two men.

The marquess and his secretary entered the vestibule of the Bath residence of the dowager Viscountess Everingham and handed his visiting card to the elderly butler. Truffle, the butler, bowed and bore the card before him on a silver tray, slowly ascending the steps and treading creakily down a hall.

As he disappeared, Osei said to his employer, "Do you wish me to accompany you, my lord?"

"Into the lion's den, you mean? Or should I say, the lioness's den? No. Stay here and see if you can ingratiate yourself with any of the staff. If I am unlucky in finding out where Anne has gone, perhaps you will have more luck."

"If they'll speak to me. Some of the serving class seem to fear that the color of my skin indicates an inability to speak English or comport myself as a gentleman ought."

"You will find Bath more cosmopolitan, Osei, more like London than Yorkshire."

Truffle, above, had finally entered an overly warm sitting room, crossed the carpeted floor and handed the card to the viscountess, who owned the Bath townhouse.

She squinted at it, her rheumy blue eyes small within folds of weary flesh. "I can't make this out. Barbara," she said to her middle-aged daughter, who sat on a sofa near the window with a book on her lap, though the page had not been turned for an hour. "Can you make out who this is?"

Truffle bore it on a tray across the room to the other woman. Lady Harecross took it and read it. "My goodness; Mother, do you know the Marquess of Darkefell?"

"Darkefell?" the viscountess said, her wavery voice thin and crabby. "No. Should I?"

"I don't know him either. But I do know *of* him. My goodness. Truffle," she said. "Show the marquess up." She stood and smoothed her silk chemise dress, straightening the pink silk bow at the waist and hoping she looked as slim as she once did. "Mother," she said, her tone stern, "do behave, please. At least until we find out what the marquess wishes. My goodness, but this is vastly more entertaining than discussing the evils of the chambermaid and cook's kitchen mutiny."

A few moments later a darkly handsome man strode into the room, and both women felt that visceral thrill experienced when in the presence of a truly compelling man, one of those few who seem to live in a more vivid sense than others. He was the kind of man for whom women sat straighter and unconsciously primped, and both ladies wished they were wearing more fashionable garb, and were several years younger.

Truffle doddered in after him and wheezed, "Lord Anthony, Marquess of Darkefell, miladies." He bowed and exited.

"Good afternoon," Lady Everingham said from her chair, past the age where she would rise for any man or woman short of King George or Queen Charlotte.

"Good afternoon, Lady Everingham," he said, crossing the room and taking her hand, kissing the air a judicious inch above the back of it.

"This is my daughter," the viscountess said, waving her hand, "the Countess of Harecross."

Barbara stared at the young man avidly. Very handsome! The kind of compelling younger fellow some of her friends sought out for their *affaires d'amour*, not that she would ever consider such a thing, despite her estrangement from the earl. But it did one no harm to gaze at a handsome face, she thought, as he bent low over her hand.

"To what do we owe the honor of this visit?" her mother said, quavery voice stronger now, with her interest piqued.

He directed his remarks to the younger woman. "I believe I am acquainted with your daughter, Lady Harecross; Lady Anne Addison?"

Barbara flapped her mouth for a moment. "Yes! Yes, of course. She was north, in Yorkshire, visiting her little friend . . . what is the child's name? Mother," she gabbled, "that newly married one, sister to Anne's late fiancé? What *is* her name?" She was flustered, and that had not happened for many a day.

"Lydia Moore she was, now Lady John Bestwick." Lady Everingham raised her glass and peered at the marquess. "Of course! You are Lydia's brother-in-law, the current marquess. Involved in some havey-cavey nonsense sometime ago."

His handsome face hardened to the tensile strength of granite.

Barbara hastened to soften the other woman's bluntness. "What my mother means, is, you were the innocent object of unkind gossip, Lord Darkefell."

His unexpected grin was devastatingly flawless as he said, "Is there *kind* gossip, my lady? And if there is, does anyone listen to it? I am in Bath looking for a residence to rent for the summer for my brother and sister-in-law. They are to be the recipients of a happy surprise in seven months or so, and she's nervous, it being her first such arrival. Lady Anne was so kind as to suggest a doctor here, Dr. Haggerty, your own physician, I believe, ma'am?" he asked the countess.

"Dr. Haggarty . . . of course! He was most helpful with my *accouchements*."

The viscountess asked Lord Darkefell to stay for tea, and he proved to be the most charming and interesting guest they had had for many a day. They would dine out on this conversation for weeks to come, for both women swiftly remembered all the tales told of the marquess; there was mystery there, and tragedy. His estate was cursed, some said, and Darkefell was an elusive guest, though sought after. How intriguing!

But he had not come to charm *them*, Barbara thought, as she poured him tea and slipped something stronger into it. Several times he had, in a roundaboutation way, asked after Anne. Was Lady Anne in Bath? No. Then more conversation. Was Lady Anne at home in Kent? No. More conversation. Was Lady Anne expected any time soon in Bath? No, for she disliked Bath intensely. She was coming to visit her mother and grandmother in two months' time, but she would not arrive a moment before she had to.

He appeared frustrated, his jawline jutting and harsh.

The elderly viscountess slyly asked, finally, when it seemed that they had exhausted every other bit of news or gossip, "So, Darkefell, do you wish us to *tell* you where my adventurous granddaughter is right now, or do you wish to go another round of questions first?"

He grinned, a lopsided and charming expression that brought a sparkle to his brown eyes. "Ah, questions; it was the very theme of my brief friendship with Lady Anne, ending with a particularly interesting one for which I have never received an answer. I would be grateful, ma'am, if you would tell me where she is. I feel sure she would like to hear how Lydia is doing, for she left in . . . a bit of a hurry."

The mother and daughter exchanged significant looks at his pause.

"My granddaughter is in Cornwall," the viscountess said, her lorgnette raised as she openly eyed him. "We last heard she was staying at the home of her friend, Miss Penelope St. James, in a village called . . . er, St. Wyllow, I believe. West of St. Ives on the north coast of the county. Miss St. James has an impecunious brother who has oft pursued my granddaughter."

A dark expression that flicked across the marquess's handsome face told the mother and daughter more than an hour of idle chat. Soon after, Lord Darkefell excused himself, and left.

The countess and viscountess immediately conferred.

"From viscount to earl to marquess in three generations; we do exceedingly well, Barbara," the elderly woman said, her voice grating with excitement.

"So handsome! And a marquess!" Lady Harecross said, clapping her hands together. She leaped to her feet and swept about the room in an excess of high spirits. She whirled and faced the older woman. "It could not have passed your notice, Mama, what he said about a particular question to which she had not given an answer. Could he have proposed marriage already, after such a short acquaintance?" She shook her head. "No, I'll not believe my daughter so foolish as to reject a man of such caliber. Vast estates, wealthy . . . what can Anne have been thinking, to leave Yorkshire when she had such a man on her hook? And what, oh *what*, can he see in my wayward daughter?"

"You have always undervalued Anne's charms," Lady Evering-ham stated, her voice gruff. "She is intelligent, and some men like that, as I tried to tell you in her come-out year. But you wouldn't listen to me! You *would* go about things the way you caught Harecross, with fluff and flattery, simpering and stupidity. *You* would have been content if she had married Sir Reginald, a mere baronet! How fortunate he died."

It was an old argument, and one in which Barbara would not engage. "Well, perhaps the best thing she did was leave Yorkshire," Lady Barbara said, one finger on her chin. "For see how it has caused Darkefell to scurry south, he who will hardly be seen in London, even at parliamentary season! He refuses all invitations but those he cannot evade."

"Anne has intrigued him."

"But Mama, we must get Lolly!" Barbara said to her mother, her tone urgent. "It didn't matter that Anne was living with that sly, insinuating young woman and her raffish brother, while she was meeting no one of importance, but for Darkefell to find her thus? If he truly has offered for her, we have him hooked. I'll not let my daughter throw away such an opportunity. We must dispatch Lolly immediately! There must be no whiff of impropriety surrounding Anne."

As little as they agreed in other areas, the mother and daughter were united on that. They summoned Truffle, and had him send the potboy out to rooms in a poorer part of Bath, to one Miss Louisa Eleanor Broomhall. That woman, existing on the fringe of society as she did, gathering crumbs from the tables of the prosperous, never let a moment lapse between an invitation and her acquiescence; she hurried to the stately town home of the Viscountess Everingham.

"What do you wish, my dear cousins?" she asked, sighing contentedly as she licked the last smear of cream cake off her fingers and dusted crumbs from her ancient dress, the best she had, now twenty years out of fashion. She washed the cake down with liberal gulps of splendid strong tea, a luxury she had not been able to afford in months.

"Louisa, Anne is in need of your services," the elderly viscountess said. She was one of the few who would not call the woman Lolly, saying it was an infantile reminder of Anne's childhood; the young Lady Anne could not say "Cousin Louisa Eleanor," and so affectionately named her Lolly. "Now listen closely because you must leave this afternoon on the post for Cornwall. This is your task."

That afternoon, Miss Lolly Broomhall, with her modest luggage, cheerfully set off on the post carriage to St. Wyllow, Cornwall, and her favorite second cousin, Lady Anne Addison, a *darling* girl upon whom she had doted since the young lady was born. Her orders were, first, to try to get Anne to return to Bath so a proper courtship between her and the Marquess of Darkefell could be conducted under the watchful eyes of her mama and grandmama. But if that did not seem possible, then she was to stick like glue to Anne, so no hint of impropriety would accompany what must surely be a foregone conclusion with such a man as the marquess. If he had truly made up his mind to wed Anne, then they would make sure he got his wish. It would be an engagement worthy of a wedding at St. George, Hanover Square, London.

The countess and viscountess had begun to plan the wedding even before Lolly left them, for a successful conclusion was sure to follow. Lord Darkefell had as good as revealed his intentions to them, and such a bold gentleman must achieve success in whatever endeavor he set himself to accomplish.

Two

"St. James, you are intolerably dull today," Anne complained, the next afternoon, as she and Pam walked with the captain along the high street in St. Wyllow, where they had by arrangement met him. Both were on his arm, his sister on his right, Anne on his left. "I was particularly sure you, who are interested in all manner of oddities, would be entertained by my story, and wish to help me understand what I saw."

"You saw a ghost, my dearest Anne," Captain Marcus St. James said, bowing to an acquaintance across the street. "But that only shows that a lady such as yourself should not be out in the night air damaging her lungs in such a dreadful way. I'm sure those prevention men are fully occupied without worrying about a gently bred lady becoming mired in difficulties."

She examined her military friend, Pamela's handsome older brother, from under the brim of her straw bonnet. He was a captain in the Light Dragoons, and wore his uniform well; his boots gleamed, no dust smudged his beautifully cut crimson coat, and his white breeches were spotless. Fairer than his sister, his hair was flawlessly powdered and coiffed, and Anne knew he scrimped in other areas to purchase the best in creams, powders and pomades. He was the perfect military dandy.

And on this occasion, mindlessly obtuse. "But the Barbary pirate specter, St. James," she said impatiently, tugging his arm. "What was it? I'm a skeptic, and do not believe in ghosts, nor spirits of any kind. Therefore this was an illusion, a mere parlor magician's trick, but how? I want to know."

"Did you see the Turk in London two years ago?" he asked, nodding to another acquaintance while a group of young ladies clustered in front of the millinery shop watched him, and giggled together. He eyed them and winked, sending the giddiest girls into fits of gleeful chatter.

Anne rolled her eyes and shook her head over another of St. James's continual non sequiturs. "What in heaven's name — or who, I suppose — is the Turk?"

"It is an automaton that plays chess, and wins every game! I would give a year's wages to figure out how that works!" He smiled down at her, his mobile mouth twisted in a self-mocking smile. "I am not one who can look at a trick and tell how it was done." His blue eyes were bright with mockery.

Anne squinted at him, wondering if he was laughing at her, or merely being truthful, as Pamela tripped lightly away from her brother to the shop windows.

"My dear," Pamela said, tapping Anne's free arm, "do you think I should buy that new bonnet I have been admiring, or wait for the new shipment from London?" They paused before the diamond-paned window of the milliner's shop, where the wares were temptingly displayed for distaff shoppers to ponder. The group of chattering girls had moved on.

"I would advise waiting," Anne replied, dropping St. James's arm. She did not want to draw out the afternoon with an endless discussion over fashion. As much as she appreciated fine clothes, fans and frippery, there was too much else to think of that moment.

"But I do think it would so suit my green sarcenet," she said, pointing to the chip straw bonnet. It was adorned with died plumes of an olive tint and gold silk ribbon. "You know I plan to wear that this afternoon at the officers' luncheon to welcome the new regiment colonel, Sir Henry Withington."

"Buy it, then," Anne said impatiently, and turned back to Marcus. "St. James, if it is not a real ghost—and my skepticism is firm—then there must be some apparatus to raise and lower the jokester, and fireworks are involved, for the smoke and explosions were meant to conceal his disappearance, I feel sure. Is it something to do with the smugglers? Is it to aid them, or halt them?"

"Pam," St. James said, eyeing his sister with a significant look, "talk to her!"

Anne puzzled, looked from the captain to her friend.

"You have no interest in shopping, Anne," Pamela said with a pout. "What good is having my best friend staying with me, if she shows no interest in normal affairs?"

"Ah, there is Carleton," St. James said, gesturing toward another red-coated officer on the opposite side of the narrow street. "I must ask him about . . ." The rest of his comment was lost in a mumble as he sprinted across the cobbled road, halting for a dray carrying a load of barrels, then joining his fellow officer.

"What is wrong with him?" Anne asked Pamela, watching the two talking. A freshening breeze tumbled up the steep street, and she raised one hand to hold her bonnet, watching a gull circle and wheel in the sky above them. In the manner of many seaside villages, St. Wyllow's high street descended from the highland toward the sea, where walks along the shingle were considered gentle enough even for a lady. Anne had walked the shore many times in the last two weeks, though only so far as the bathing machines, which were not in commission this early in the Season. Pam had not answered, and Anne glanced over at her. "Am I annoying you both?" she asked, with a trace of acerbity that she could not restrain.

Pamela sighed. "Have you ever thought, Anne, that Marcus, as an officer in the King's army, cannot say all that he knows?" she asked, with a direct look. "Perhaps there is some raid planned on the smugglers. I don't pry into such things and keep my own counsel. There are surely things he cannot divulge, and he would not be impolite, not to someone for whom he cares as much as you."

Stricken, Anne mumbled, "I hadn't thought of that."

"And really, *no* one here speaks openly of smuggling," Pamela whispered, looking up and down the narrow street. It was relatively deserted, but there were still some ladies enjoying the morning air. "It's considered poor form."

Another officer had joined St. James and his friend, Captain Carleton, and all strode back across the street to join Pamela and Anne. The usual flirtatious nonsense went on, much directed toward Pam, as the most familiar to them of the two ladies, but Anne had her fair share of banter, too. It was decided that the gentlemen would walk the ladies back to Cliff House and take tea with them.

Anne, with an officer on either side of her, strolled along the dusty road away from the village. The road followed the coast, and the sea, a smooth glassy surface in the distance, glinted beyond the farmer's fields and grassy countryside from the sun overhead. It was warmer than usual for May, but that was often the way in Cornwall, Anne had been told. She freed her arms and fanned herself, letting the gentlemen's banter roll over her until she heard a key word. "I beg your pardon, Lieutenant Briggs?" she said, turning to the older of the two men. "Did you just say something about smugglers?"

"Aye, ma'am," he said, his cheery round face wreathed in a sly smile. "Now, trust that! I've been tryin' all kinds of flattery with you, and nothing worked until a discussion of the fuss last night."

"What fuss was that?" she asked, casting a look ahead to Pamela and St. James, who had been joined by another friend, a major. Pam walked between the two red-coated men, a slim, blue-gowned accent to the crimson wool. Anne deliberately slowed her pace and fanned herself with her free hand. "Has something happened?" she asked, keeping her tone languid, so as to not appear knowledgeable or too interested. She had plenty of practice in her life at that, for in London, it was socially perilous to appear interested or interesting. Cultivating an air of insipidity was considered a sign of good breeding by her mother and those of the same way of thinking. When he didn't continue, Anne said, "You did mention smuggling, didn't you, sir?"

"What Briggs refers to, my lady," the other fellow, a tall, thin lanky youth with a soft manner, said, "is a raid last night, unsuccessful as it turns out. The prevention men again tried to capture some sly smuggling devils, but a fracas of some sort broke out, and the smugglers disappeared."

"How could they disappear?" Anne's whole attention was riveted, but she deliberately kept her expression placid, playing with the fingertips of her gloves.

"The whole cliff area is riddled with caves, ma'am."

"But surely all it takes is to follow the smugglers?"

"'Tis not so simple, for *they* – the smugglers – know where they're going, while the revenue officers are just guessing, and guessing wrong means a fruitless hunt in the dark. They've tried searching the caves in the light of day, but have found little to guide them."

"This is an old problem, is it not?" Anne asked, glancing from gentleman to gentleman, forgetting to appear uninterested. "Ever since the government imposed heavy duties."

"Taxes that they require for the protection of our country," Lieutenant Briggs said, his cheeks going red and his brow furrowed.

Anne shied from any political discussion of the merit of such taxes, and what they were truly being used for. She had heard much about the subject, and knew that in many people's estimation corruption, royal profligacy and war in Europe had drained the country's coffers. More revenue was being raised on the backs of those who could least afford it through excise tax, supposedly on luxury items. But were tea and tobacco really luxuries when for some, they were the only pleasures to be had at the end of a long day of labor? Instead of making her true opinion known—and restraining it was a great sacrifice for an outspoken woman—she kept her mind focused on the subject about which she was truly curious. "I've heard something about a local ghost."

"Ah, yes," the lanky fellow, Captain Carleton, said, "and here we are, the Barbary Ghost." He indicated an inn, past which they were strolling.

Anne looked up at the sign, and laughed. It was adorned with an exaggerated image of the fellow she had seen the night before, a fellow with a dark beard, turban and ballooning pantaloons, waving a scimitar. Though she had been past the inn a half dozen times in the last two weeks, she had never paid heed to the sign, a woeful example of her preoccupation of late, due to a certain arrogant marquess, whose imperfect excellence lingered in her mind like a haunting melody. Or rather, malady. Distance from him was supposed to be her cure, but the fever still burned.

She turned her mind away from Darkefell. Confessing what she saw the night before to the two officers was out of the question, for it would be tantamount to admitting she was wandering alone in the night; even *her* spotless reputation could not stand such an assault. To do something shocking was one thing; to have that something laid bare for all the world to know about and comment upon, entirely different. "How vivid that depiction," she said with a light laugh, and gestured back to the sign they had passed. "Has anyone seen such a creature, really? And how is this related to the smugglers?"

Her companions then told her how the prevention men had witnessed just such an apparition the night before, and not for the first time. In the last few months the ghastly vision, wielding a scimitar and fearful firepower, had several times threatened the excise men. While many thought it a true specter—local farmers refused the revenue officers right-of-way across their land in fear of the apparition coming to get them, for it only seemed to appear when the King's agents were about—its most recent appearances, sensible folks agreed, had to do with the increase of smuggling accomplished by a particularly clever band of cutthroats known locally as the St. Wyllow Whips.

They had walked on toward Cliff House. Anne fell silent, listening to the two men ramble. She longed for some free time and for Pamela to be busy, because she was intent on scaling the steep pathway down to the sea—the rocky cleft between two bluffs was called a cut in local parlance—to examine the cliff face. There must be some apparatus that hoisted the "ghost," for she did not for one moment believe in a visible spirit that could float. Pam's resolute refusal to speak of the smugglers or the ghost, other than her relation of the story of its origins, was disappointing, as was her lack of interest in walking along their own beach. Boring, she said, and too difficult a climb down to the shore for a lady.

Watching the blue-gowned figure strolling ahead of her, Anne reflected that Pamela St. James had altered significantly in the last few years. Pam had visited Anne at Harecross Hall a year before, but had been wan and ailing, recovering from a difficult period of fever. Now she seemed in reasonable health, but infirmity had changed her. She was thinner than before, and indolent. She cared more about bonnets and clothing and flirtation with the officers than she ever had, though, to be fair, Pamela St. James had always enjoyed the art of flirtation. But now her skill had a harder edge, a more desperate flavor.

Did she need to marry? Was she in financial trouble? It had not passed Anne's notice that Pam and Marcus St. James were as impecunious as ever, not a feather to fly on. Though she had never pried, Anne had always assumed that there was some family money, enough to eke out an existence, but not enough to live comfortably. Marcus's wages as an officer in the British army would be almost completely offset by his expenses.

The very next day—market day in St. Wyllow—Anne had already decided she'd take steps to add to the household, instead of detract, by purchasing supplies, and ordering necessities, wine, coal, food. It was only fair, for she had more than enough funds and would not see them suffer for her extended visit and the burden of herself, her maid and Wee Robbie.

They approached Cliff House. Marcus and Pam's rented house was closer to the road than the ocean, but due to the peculiarities of the landscape, the lane to it ambled downhill and around, so the roof of Cliff House was the only part visible from the highway. But as they neared the house, Anne spied a feminine figure sitting on a trunk alongside the highway by the turnoff to the lane descent. Pamela and her officer escorts, some distance ahead of Anne and her attendants, greeted the humble visitor.

Anne shook her head in some dismay, but was not especially surprised. She had expected this arrival at least a week earlier. Hastening her step, she called out, in a cheerful tone, "Darling Lolly . . . Mama and Grandmama have dispatched you to keep their collective eye on me, have they?"

"Well, my dearest Anne," Lolly said cheerily, offering her soft cheek for a kiss, "you must have expected they would, did you not?"

Anne straightened after giving her distant cousin the expected affectionate greeting. "I knew it could happen, but thought from the curt tone of Mama's reply to my letter informing her of my stay here in Cornwall that she was sufficiently put out by my behavior to ignore me completely for a time. Did she give you any marching orders, beyond coming to Cliff House?"

"Now, my dear, enough time to talk later," Lolly said, bright-eyed, as she dusted off her traveling dress and stood. She glanced around at the officers. "Please introduce me to your charming companions. I do so take pleasure in uniformed gentlemen, and think no man as handsome as those with epaulettes and gold braid."

• • •

The inn was promising in its tidiness, Darkefell decided as he dismounted and handed the reins to a speedy young fellow who had circled the building from the rear, where the stable yard would be. Throwing him a coin, and commanding that his horse, Sunny, be well cared for, the marquess looked up at the garish sign—a Mussulman pirate, for God's sake—and entered the Barbary Ghost, a low-ceilinged inn like most. He loitered in the taproom, listening to the men jawing over tankards of bitter.

"They 'spect me t'catch the damned fellows, but won't give me the men to do't!" a bent and bewhiskered fellow said, puffing on a pipe between words.

"Nouw, Puddicombe," another fellow said after a long pull on his tankard, wiping froth from his lips with the sleeve of his stained jacket. "T'smugglers are joost gettin' too clever, ain't they?"

"Eh, the buggers runned away at a coupla bangs and pops last e'en. T'other excise men get troops; I get farmers wi' cudgels and scythes." He shook his head and sprawled in the low-ceilinged inglenook near the fire, smoking and quaffing. "No troops, nor a cutter, nor anything but farmers. Might joost as well face 'em alone."

"Aye, but you've caught some of 'em!" one fellow said.

"Not them the folks hereabouts call the St. Wyllow Whips, and that bastard leader o' theirs, Lord Brag, or whatever the 'ell they calls 'im."

Laughter broke out. Some unintelligible jokes were flung back and forth, something about a ghost, and fireworks. Puddicombe's face got redder and redder, and when he whirled in his seat to yell for more beer, he caught sight of Darkefell and bashed one of his pals on the shoulder. All the men turned, then, and stared, and the remarkable conversation stopped.

When talk resumed, the topic was farming, and they chatted of sowing and reaping. Darkefell glanced around. At that moment a barrel-chested man that he recognized came through to the taproom from a back stockroom.

"Quintrell!" the marquess called.

The man turned and stared at him in the murky taproom. The grimy diamond-paned windows offered only dim light, but enough to recognize the marquess, it seemed, for a smile broadened the publican's face. "Master Anthony! Or should I say, Milord Darke-fell!" He wiped his hands on a bar rag, tossed it aside and bowed to the marquess.

"I remembered that you bought an inn somewhere near St. Ives, and here you are! I hit it right on just my first try. But before we get into proper greetings, do you have a room I might rent from you?"

"Oh, aye, milord," he said, a smile wreathing his round face. "I've a grand room that'll be yours, if you just give me an hour."

Once they got the formalities out of the way, and Darkefell had announced that his valet was not to join him, for his secretary would be following to act as his factotum, they settled down to a drink together in the tavernkeeper's office, a tiny room off the taproom. Quintrell relaxed as it became clear that the marquess was not on his high horse and was just going to be one of the lads for now.

Joseph Quintrell had been, many years before, the late marquess's equerry on his Cornish estate, some miles away nearer Launceston, close to the Devonshire border. When Darkefell's father died, he left a generous bequeathal in his will to Quintrell, and with it, the man and his wife bought an inn near her home village of St. Wyllow. It appeared to be a success. The two men spoke of friends departed, and Darkefell offered Quintrell sympathy on his wife's death some years before. They spoke of the pride of Quintrell's heart, his son Johnny, now twenty-one, and working for his father.

Then Darkefell got down to the matter of business he wished to discuss, the tenants of Cliff House and their visitor, Lady Anne Addison. Quintrell knew little about the tenants, except that it was a brother and sister, Captain Marcus and Miss Pamela St. James, the captain billeted with his regiment near St. Ives, but was in St. Wyllow every free moment, staying at Cliff House when he had leave.

"This Captain St. James . . . he married?"

"No," Quintrell said with a sparkle in his eye, "in fact, quite the opposite. He's the kind 'oo's cut a wide swath through the females o' this village."

"What do you mean?" Darkefell asked, feeling a knot of anxiety building in his stomach.

"He's just that type, y'know, the kind the ladies swoon over. Fair-haired dandyish feller, good-looking, or so I'm told, not bein' a judge o' that sort o' thing. A red coat improves any fellow's look, I'm told."

"And he spends much of his time at Cliff House." The knot of anxiety froze into a lump of dread. His Anne was passionate by nature, a fact he knew, even if she would not acknowledge it. His fear was that the spark of passion he had awoken with a multitude of kisses—every kind from chaste pecks on the cheek to amorous assaults on her luscious mouth—would leap to a flame with another man's fanning. She had run from his offer of marriage, but it was a rude and belligerent wooing, he now admitted, hasty because of his state of anxiety at the moment.

He had just watched her teeter on the edge of a cliff, almost losing her life to a madman's crazed attack, and it had hit him in that moment what pain he would feel if he lost her forever. Another woman may have been swept away by his passionate proposal, but Anne viewed it as a startling bit of lunacy, and departed Yorkshire.

Still, he had followed her to Cornwall because he had every confidence that a renewal of his suit would receive a more favorable reply, now that she had had time to think about what she had rejected. Her mother and grandmother's gratifying response to him in Bath had shown him there would certainly be no family objection, not that he had expected there would be.

"Who is this lass, milord, the lady you seek?" Quintrell asked.

With a sigh, Darkefell said, "A woman of extraordinary intelligence and the poor taste to refuse my offer of marriage." He sat back in his chair and stuck his booted feet out in front of him.

Quintrell raised his bushy eyebrows. "Refuse a marquess? Begging yer pardon, milord, but that don't seem too intelligent to me."

With a sharp bark of laughter, Darkefell snorted, "Nor to me, Quintrell. But I have not given up hope. She is a lady worth winning, I have decided."

"And yer like yer father, milord, if ya don't mind me sayin'. He was niver one t'take no fer an answer, neither."

"It's not the first time I've been compared to my father, but in this, at least, I do not mind resembling him."

"He were a better man than many thought, sir, an' I'm one has cause to know." Quintrell rose from their table and bowed. "'Scuse me, milord, while I make sure t'lass is gettin' your room ready."

Left alone, the marquess pondered. First, he decided, he'd find out what he could about this dashing captain. His Anne had, perhaps, a fondness for regimental red after her late fiancé's unfortunate death several years before, but he was not about to purchase a captaincy just for that sake. Then he would go about making Anne see that his proposal was not well phrased, perhaps, nor particularly well timed, but it was serious. She would listen to his proposal and consider it properly, for he would not be dismissed like some cow-handed sprig of a boy.

And that was that.

Three

The next day dawned bright and sunny, another lovely day in Cornwall. Anne was crabby, though, and snapped at everyone, not her usual demeanor. She couldn't think what was wrong with her! Lolly had arrived, yes, one more proof that her mother would never leave her alone to live her life, but Anne dearly loved Lolly, and by now knew many ways to circumvent her "companion" when it was inconvenient that she should be around.

In fact, the night before, while Pamela was in St. Ives at the rout to welcome her brother's new regimental colonel—for Lolly's sake, knowing her companion would be weary after such a trip in the Royal Post carriage, Anne had remained at Cliff House for the evening—Anne had been a little overly generous in pouring the blackberry wine, and Lolly had nodded off quite early, while it was still twilight. Taking advantage of her companion's drowsiness, Anne slipped out to the cliff to see if the smugglers or ghost appeared, but she was disappointed.

Those few pointless hours spent watching and waiting must be what was causing her dissatisfaction, Anne reflected, as she pulled on her gloves preparatory to their walk to the village. It had been too dark to explore, for she didn't relish falling off the cliff, and boredom had set in after a while. That had to be the source of her miserable mood, she decided, as they set out to St. Wyllow market day. She was just miffed at her disappointing ghost hunt.

But self-knowledge would not let her pacify herself with such delusions. In truth, it was the dream that still haunted her. As the three of them strolled to the village, dust rising up from their progress, Lolly kept up a constant stream of nonsense to Pamela, leaving Anne to recall her vivid dream. It featured the powerfully built Marquess of Darkefell. He stalked her, following her wherever she went, and finally he confronted her, taking her in his arms and holding her close to his body. Trapped, her arms pinned to her sides, she had felt helpless, and the wicked look on his face showed that he knew it.

What were his intentions? What did he want of her? She had struggled and twisted, but there was no getting away from him. She had awoken in the gloom of the early hours, just before dawn, to find herself helplessly bundled up in her sheets.

She couldn't imagine why the dream upset her so, for she had dreamt of men before. There was a passionate side to her character that she'd had her share of unrequited passions, daydreams, one-sided fascinations, generally with very unsuitable men: a good-looking footman, a roughly handsome stableboy when she was very young. But never before had she experienced such intense and entirely improper physical yearning mingled with fury and a sense of helplessness that was not wholly unpleasant, as she had in her dream, in the arms of the far-too-suitable Marquess of Darkefell.

"Far too suitable." Her eyes widened as she understood why that phrase occurred to her in a description of the man. Lord Darkefell was an eminently appropriate suitor to Anne in title, wealth, age, and every other little necessity of character and position. If her intention was to remain heart-whole and unmarried, she was in danger. Her *tendres* for unsuitable men stayed in her imagination, pleasant fantasies to while away the hours. But Darkefell was doubly dangerous. She was fascinated by him, for one thing, and she feared if she allowed herself, she could become wholly consumed in love.

He was an honorable man, and despite an air of rakishness, he was really rather circumspect, as far as his affairs went, from what little she had been able to glean while resident on his estate. Fear of ravishment, then, was not behind the dread that had permeated her dreaming self while in his arms. In truth, she desperately feared that she would be inveigled into marriage with him, when she did not yet know what she wanted from life.

But that was ridiculous. No one could make her do anything she didn't want. She stiffened her spine and strode on. Putting those thoughts out of her mind, she set herself to being entertaining to Lolly and Pam as they strolled toward St. Wyllow. Pamela had been accommodating about Lolly turning up unannounced, and even more than before, Anne knew she had to find a way to repay her friend's generosity. Market day was her opportunity.

The sea breeze was light, the walk refreshing, and St. Wyllow bustling in comparison to the normally quiet morning. Market day; was there ever a better day to see a village? On the common, locals had their stalls set up: fresh new greens, paper sacks of mushrooms, butter and cheese and eggs in bowls, strings of herbs, pots of preserves, pies and cakes, live chickens and geese in wooden boxes, strings of trout, and even a bucket of oysters. It was a feast to the eyes and nose, the scent of sage and mint mingling with the yeasty fragrance of fresh-baked bread.

Even the sounds were such as to make her hungry, for a chicken's contented cluck made her think of fresh eggs poached and served on a bed of sautéed mushrooms and the garden greens presented for sale. Anne, always an enthusiastic gourmand, glanced around. Where to start? She must have the soul of a housewife, she thought, to enjoy the sight of fish and eggs and vegetables so much.

Not that she had eaten much good food since coming to visit at Cliff House. Pamela's "cook" was a surly local woman who came in to "do" for the brother and sister, but did not live in. Her eldest daughter cleaned, she cooked, and they returned to their own home in time for dinner with her family. It was a novel arrangement for Anne, to not have a cook living in, one that she could see had its benefits and drawbacks.

Such a way of living was less expensive than keeping a cook and chambermaid available at all times, but on the other hand, Pamela's lady's maid, Alice, also had to answer the door and show in guests, as well as look after Pamela's clothing and hairdressing. Alice was a local girl, too, and did not seem to mind her extensive other duties, which included emptying slops on occasion, dusting and waiting on the table, and helping cook clear the dinner dishes. In deference to the cook's need to get home to her own family at a reasonable time, they dined very early at Cliff House, while the sun was still up in most cases, unless they were willing to eat a cold supper of cheese and meat.

Mary was scandalized at Anne's easy acceptance of the situation. It wasn't fitting, her maid fumed, for the daughter of an earl to live in such disarray. The house was dirty, the slops were not cleaned as often nor as carefully as they should, the fires were not swept daily, the front step was never scrubbed, and there was no order in the household. Anne thought it gave a peculiar holiday atmosphere to the whole adventure, and Robbie thrived in the disordered household. Irusan was growing fat from the number of rodents he was catching.

Was dirt really so dangerous a thing, then? Mary thought so, but

Anne was surprised at her own capacity for ignoring the dust and cobwebs.

Anne looked about, her foul temper evaporating. The village green, where the market was set, was a large open triangular space at the top of the village, just below the church, a Tudor chapel of excessive quaintness. Lolly enthused over every pretty child she saw, especially the red-cheeked farm children, brought to market day by their enterprising parents, who sold their goods on the green. Anne encouraged her companion's amusement, which was simply talking to the prettiest children, and even bought her a large bag of boiled sweets to hand out. Her only stricture in providing of the treat was an admonition to Lolly to give some sweets to the ugly children as well.

Lolly swiftly became a popular attraction. Deposited on a bench in the middle of the green with her bag of sweeties on her lap, she had children clustered around her like bees on a hive.

"Pam," Anne said, glancing over at her friend as they strolled from farmer's cart to stall to barrow, "I am so sorry Lolly was dropped on us in this manner. It was unconscionable of my mother and grandmother to behave in such a high-handed manner."

"Darling heart, Lolly is a sweet old biddy," Pamela said with a smile, while she turned a length of lace over in her hand. Noting the price attached, she gently laid it down and turned away. "How could I ever frown about her presence?"

"Nonetheless," Anne said carefully, knowing her friend's pride, "it does increase the load upon your household, and I absolutely *insist* on contributing to the expense of putting the two of us and Mary and Wee Robbie up for this delightful holiday. I will not take any negative, so you must just say, *thank you, Anne, dearest, give me whatever you think fair.*"

Despite Anne's jocular tone, Pam froze up briefly, her expression holding a flash of prideful disdain, but then she grinned and said, elegant brows raised in the shade of her broad-brimmed straw hat, "My dear, I am not without resources. Knowing how I love gossip, your best currency to repay me my extravagant hospitality would be information. Tell me what sent you scurrying away from Yorkshire and darling *dizzy* Lydia's side, when you had just discovered she was with child? I know you, Anne; you are the soul of helpfulness, and it seems to me you would not depart at such an interesting time without compelling reason. You've been here two weeks and have said not a word, you sly boots! I've been circumspect until now, but am perishing for gossip or scandal."

Anne was silent, consciousness burning in her cheeks as she examined a stall with ribbons. "How about this hue?" she finally said, holding up a chartreuse grosgrain.

"Not with your coloring, darling, it makes you look feverish. Or is that just because I am inquiring too closely into events in Yorkshire?" She leaned closer, her stiff silk gown rustling. "There was a man, I know it, and if you don't tell me all the details I shall set Marcus on you, and you know he can winkle out any secret."

With the haunting memory of the dream of Darkefell upon her, Anne muttered, "There was a man, Pam, I cannot lie. But such a man! I've never met anyone like him." She stopped dead and stared blankly. "Why? Why did he keep kissing me?"

"He kissed you?" Pam clapped her hands together, eyes sparkling. She grabbed Anne's wrist and tugged her away from other shoppers. "You must tell me all about him!"

Anne tried to brush off further questions, but Pam was resolute. So while they observed a game of battledore on an open part of the village green, she briefly told Pam some of her encounters with the marquess, and related her dream from the night before, and how it had brought back to her vividly the feel of Darkefell's lips pressed against hers.

"My dear, I do think you had better marry, and quickly," Pamela said with an odd, pensive expression.

"What do you mean?"

"Never mind what I mean. But do consider marriage. The man sounds like a catch. Oh, there is Marcus!" Pam said, waving to her brother, who was bent over Lolly, laughing.

He added another sack of sweets to Lolly's booty. That lady was now teaching the children a song, while engaging the youngest in a rousing game of peek-a-boo.

"Darling Lolly," Marcus said indulgently as he approached, circling the part of the green where the battledore game was being played and bowing to the combatants, a couple of young ladies who smiled and curtseyed at his notice. "So simple are her joys. Can she really be as transparently sweet as she seems, and so enormously empty-headed?"

"Marcus," Anne admonished, as Pam dawdled behind them at a stall selling candles. "Lolly has suffered much in her life. Her parents died leaving her very poorly off, and the suitor who was supposed to save her from penury proved unworthy and took what was left of the family wealth in the form of silver plate, before disappearing back to Ireland."

She watched Lolly for a moment. An elderly man with a cane now sat beside her, and the two chatted while she doled out sweets. "She lives on the knife edge of destitution, and makes shift with rooms in Bath, when as a countrywoman, she would much rather live in a seaside village like this. With all that, she still manages to maintain an admirably sunny outlook. I admire her."

"I beg your pardon, Anne, my dearest. Once again you have shown me," he declaimed, hand over his chest and hat swept off, his powdered hair exquisitely curled, "with your excellent heart, why I need you as a wife. Will you marry me? I feel sure you would make me over anew if you would just say yes! Come, make me into a man worthy of my last name?"

Anne laughed. "St. James, how droll you are! I cannot stay angry at you."

"And *another* reason why marriage to me would be a good match," he murmured into her ear, bending over her. "We will never stay angry."

"I wish you could find a way to make your sister as hardheaded about finance as you," she said, obliquely referring to what she believed was his primary motive for proposing, her very good income. "I am trying to offer her some recompense for my drain on your household, and she freezes up."

"I will handle her, dearest lady," he said softly, straightening. "Do what you will, and I will *make* her accept your aid."

"Thank you," Anne said with heartfelt meaning. Sometimes St. James's pragmatism was helpful.

An attractive older woman, with a bountiful display of bosom, dropped an enormous strawberry on the grass, and St. James stooped to pick it up, brushing it off and presenting it to the woman. Anne, her attention caught, watched; a look was exchanged, and, she thought, a note, with the fruit. She was not surprised when Marcus disappeared a few minutes later, and the lady was absent, too. Men would always have complaisant women as lovers, she thought, single or married. Marcus and his lover had likely met by design, and slipped away to be alone.

She forgot all about him as she strolled on to another stall.

Pamela and Anne spoke desultorily, as they looked over the wares. Pam asked her a question, but Anne had stopped dead and stared; could it be? No, it couldn't possibly . . . but, yes! She felt the color flood her face even more as she stared across the market green at the most handsome man in England, Lord Anthony Darkefell.

Pam followed her gaze and exclaimed, "Well, what a dashing fellow!"

Darkefell's gaze met Anne's, and she knew in an instant that as amazed as *she* might be, *he* was not surprised to find her there. She turned away, but in another moment, she was not surprised to see a pair of highly polished riding boots before her downcast gaze.

"My Lady Anne, how pleasant to find you here. How are you? You look extraordinarily well."

The words trickled through her hearing, competing with an odd buzzing. She looked up, blinking rapidly, and stared into his handsome dark eyes, fringed in sooty lashes; the dream streamed through her, the feel of his arms, the sense of his hard chest against her soft bosom, forgotten sensations of suffocating desire thumping in her chest. Her cheeks burned red—she could feel them flame—and a hundred thoughts and sensations rattled through her. Why had he come to Cornwall? Was it for her sake?

And what if it was?

All this time she had thought him safely in Yorkshire, when day by day he had been getting closer and closer to her. Nearer with each step—her dream the night before; had she known he was near, perhaps even in St. Wyllow already?

Pamela was casting her puzzled looks, and waiting for an introduction. Anne stumbled through it, she knew not how—the dawning knowledge on Pam's pretty face flustered her even worse, coming so close after her revelation to her friend about the kisses shared—and then, gratefully, he explained his presence equally to them both.

He had come south, he said, to see about renting a house for Lydia and John in Bath. While there he *happened* to meet Anne's mother and grandmother, and they *happened* to mention her whereabouts, and since he *happened* to be traveling to Cornwall to see to some renovations to their house near Launceston, and since an old former worker of theirs *happened* to own the Barbary Ghost Inn, he thought he'd take a couple of days for a riding tour.

"That is a lot of *happen*stance," Anne commented, acidly, pleased to hear her own voice without a waver or a crack.

He grinned. "Indeed. I delight in happenstance. You will be pleased to learn that a friend of yours, Osei Boatin, accompanies me — he has been held up a day or two — and looks forward to reanimating the acquaintance."

"I shall be delighted to see Mr. Boatin again," Anne said.

"But not me? I'm shocked." He turned to Pam. "Lady Anne is my most severe critic, Miss St. James. She loves to find fault in me."

"I love any simple pleasure, sir, as you know," Anne said.

He chuckled and raised his expressive brow at her.

St. James approached just then, and with a broad grin said to his sister, "Look at my new acquisition, Pam, a jeweled snuff box. With my initials! Ain't it perfection?"

"Marcus, lovely!" Pam said, eyeing the trinket with a frown. But she smoothed her worried scowl and said, "Do say hello to a conquest of Anne's, Lord Anthony Darkefell from . . . Yorkshire, isn't it, my lord?"

"Pam, do stop fooling," Anne said, her voice trembling. "He is no conquest of mine. How ridiculous."

Marcus had gone still and eyed Darkefell with concern, while the other man stared him down.

Uneasy at the sudden crackle of tension in the air, Anne said, "We should collect Lolly before she makes the entire village population of children bilious. And I need a cup of tea."

"Wonderful idea, Anne, darling!" Pamela said. "Come along! St. James, walk with Anne and darling Lolly while I monopolize the marquess. Lord Darkefell," she said, taking his arm, "you must come back to Cliff House with us and have luncheon. Anne has told me so little about your adventure in Yorkshire, and I am positively *perishing* for more information. She told me some nonsense about a werewolf she unmasked! Do talk to me."

• • •

The back terrace of Cliff House had a pretty view out to sea, but to Darkefell's practical eye it was crumbling, in awful condition, the masonry undermined by the damp salt air. The whole house had that air of raffish disrepair, like an elderly roué, almost blind and crippled, but still flirting with every woman available. He half listened to Miss Pamela St. James prattle while he watched the fair-haired captain bend his head to Anne, intently listening. She, damned by Darkefell's brother, his sister-in-law and his mother as worse than plain, was actually much prettier than the marquess remembered, or was that just the effect of her sparkling conversation with that twit, Marcus St. James? The smartly uniformed fellow was courtly toward Anne, dusting off the bench upon which she sat, but he was an army captain; were they not renowned for their chivalrous behavior to the fair sex? Perhaps the captain's behavior meant nothing. Or perhaps it meant he was wooing Anne with pretty words and promises.

Darkefell decided he must know some things, and would before he left Cliff House that day. First, was Marcus St. James living at Cliff House, under the same roof as Anne? Second, did she blush when he spoke to her, as he remember her doing on occasion with him? And third and fourth and fifth . . . did she tremble when he touched her? Did she sigh when he kissed her? Was Marcus St. James wooing Anne? He kept a tight control on his jealousy, clamping down on it with gritted teeth and clenched fist.

He set himself to think of anything but his frustrated wooing of Lady Anne. Cliff House was a ramshackle three-floor stone dwelling, with overgrown gardens and an air of reckless charm, much like the mistress, Miss Pamela St. James. The sitting room was too dark on such a lovely day, she had airily proclaimed as they arrived, leading them around the house and down to the terrace by way of a stone path and steps, so they would sit and have a picnic luncheon. Darkefell suspected she was not too sure of the cleanliness and order of the interior.

"Miss St. James," Darkefell said, strolling to the edge of the uneven flagstone terrace and gazing toward the sea, "you have a charming view here." Cliff House overlooked the ocean, in a sense, though it was well back from the water. The terrace gave way to the garden, and the garden sloped down to some scrubby shrubs and a wind-warped apple tree hard against a stone fence. Beyond the wooden gate the property sloped upward again, opening onto a long, high bluff of rocky outcroppings and unkempt grass, beyond which the blue ocean sparkled and puffy clouds danced along the horizon.

"I am fortunate that the view is free, my lord, for I could not afford it if the landlord charged what that beauty is worth."

He looked back at her, surprised by her refreshing honesty. She was beautiful, he admitted. A little older than Anne, perhaps, with dark hair and eyes, an intriguing dimple in her chin, and an excellent figure, if tending a little toward gaunt cheeks. He glanced over at Anne, who was engaged in a lively discussion on some topic with Captain St. James. She was feverish in her intensity, leaning toward the man, her hands working to describe as they did when she was quite unconscious about it. *There* was the difference between the two ladies: fire. Miss St. James was a lovely woman, but there was an absence in her that he could not quite describe to himself. She might well have a heart to rival Anne's, but he had no desire to find out if it was so.

A slovenly serving woman in a dirty apron and gown, led by Anne's enormous cat, Irusan, brought out a tray laden with a teapot, cups, and plates of cheese, ham, bread and cakes, and thumped it down on a wrought iron table, then turned and stumped away. The puss made its way immediately toward Anne, but stopped at St. James and rubbed against the officer's leg. He bent down and picked the cat up as they continued talking.

Damned cat, Darkefell thought. All it ever did to *him* was growl.

"Mrs. Quintrell," Pamela said pleadingly, as the woman slumped back toward the door to the kitchen, "could you please bring out the decanter of port in the sitting room for the gentlemen? And some glasses?"

The woman glared at Miss St. James, and Darkefell tamped down an urge to bark an order, instead, mildly saying, "Quintrell? You aren't any relation to Joseph Quintrell, are you?"

"Aye, me husband is his brother," she said grudgingly.

Pamela made a swift introduction, giving Darkefell his entire due, and the change in demeanor was instant. The cook bustled back in the house and soon came back out accompanied by her daughter, carrying a tray of crystal goblets and the decanter of port. Unfortunate, from Darkefell's aspect, since he despised port, but Mrs. Quintrell's improved attitude toward Miss St. James was worth drinking a glass of the awful stuff.

Once she was gone, Miss St. James laid one hand on his jacket sleeve and said, "You are quite the knight in shining armor."

Anne glanced over just then, and so Darkefell put his free hand over hers and caressed her slender fingers. "I hope I was able to be of some small service in rendering Mrs. Quintrell's attitude more amenable to direction. They are a stubborn family, by and large, and proud."

But Anne simply returned to her conversation with the red-coated captain. So, jealousy was not to work, though she could not have designed a better way to agitate *him* than her intimate conversation with the blond-haired, slim-figured and elegant Captain St. James. He was a dandyish fellow, the kind beloved by ladies everywhere, and his uniform just added to his air of dash. The damned cat was now, at least, sitting on the stone bench between them, being petted by both Anne and her companion as they talked.

Miss Lolly Broomhall, who had been inside for a time, returned to the terrace to take luncheon with them, and conversation became more general. She managed to talk even while consuming an adequate tea, expounding on the children of St. Wyllow and relating the very interesting conversation she had with an old man who knew the town well. He had kept her entertained, apparently, with all manner of fascinating stories of bygone years.

They ate lunch, and drank tea and port. St. James gracefully attended every whim of Anne's, supplying her with some of the leaden cake, taking her dirty plate away, refilling her teacup. It was obvious to Darkefell by then that he courted her, and a fiery pit of jealousy burned in his stomach, charring the heavy luncheon he had not really wanted.

Darkefell stood. "My dear Lady Anne," he said loudly, talking over some of the captain's prattle, "would you walk with me toward that interesting cliff beyond the garden? I can bring you up to date with all of those at Ivy Lodge, since I'm sure you have not yet had the opportunity to receive news from Lydia and John."

He was flattered, if surprised, by the alacrity with which she jumped up from the bench. Irusan followed, but Anne put out one staying hand when it appeared that the captain was about to follow them, too.

"No, St. James; there is nothing more tedious than a conversation about people with whom you are not acquainted. The marquess and I will be back in half an hour, and you may gaze longingly after me from the terrace, if you are so forlorn."

Her joking tone took the sting out of her refusal of his company, Darkefell thought, but the captain looked put out anyway. Small victories, he thought, small victories. He had come to St. Wyllow solely to find out the state of her affections, and he would not leave until he was sure she returned his regard.

Four

Darkefell took her arm. Anne, garbed in a lilac gown and contrasting gray caraco, with a jaunty bonnet perched on her thick, intricately coiffed dark hair, kept glancing sideways at him as they walked down the garden and out the rickety wooden gate, followed closely by Irusan. She pointed out the best path, as she was well acquainted with the bluff, and they ascended. Finally, as they strolled across the scrubby grass toward the escarpment, she turned to him and said, "I was surprised to see you at the market, but I had a feeling you were not surprised to see me."

"You're correct. I knew you were here, Anne." He crossed his arms over his chest and planted his feet in a wide stance, watching her. "And I'm not sure you were really surprised. You must have known I would follow, for you clearly intended it."

She glared at him. "I beg your pardon?" she said, her tone cold. She meant him to understand that she was displeased by such presumption.

The wind lifted the dark lock of hair that always trailed over his high, pale forehead. He swept it away and smiled, an undeniably attractive expression on one so handsome. "Oh, come, Anne, after what we've shared, you knew I would follow you. You intended it. Don't be coy; it ill suits you." He reached out, and with lingering fingers brushed back a stray, wind-tossed lock of her hair from her cheek as he leaned toward her.

Ignoring the jolt of pleasure his light touch sent through her, she stepped back, and gained a small measure of mean satisfaction that he lost his balance. Irusan sat staring up at him with ill-disguised hostility. Darkefell righted himself and frowned, appearing somewhat less sure of himself, which was all to the good in a man so supremely overconfident.

"How is Lydia?" she asked.

"She's well. I have engaged a house in Bath for her and John beginning in the middle of July."

"And how are my mother and grandmama?" she said with a hard tone in her voice that she fully intended he understand. Words alone could not express her displeasure at him seeking them out. He *meant* her to think that he had simply come across her kin at a fete or party, but Grandmama never went out; people came to her. He must have visited with no invitation, a breach in courtesy that her mother and grandmother would overlook in someone of his elevated stature.

But he was not discomfited by her ire, chuckling as he said, "They seem very well, both of them; completely charming, I must say. Lady Everingham and Lady Harecross both send affectionate greetings."

"Oh, they sent more than that," she murmured, now understanding the timing of Lolly's arrival. Her companion was to be a watchdog, but also, no doubt, she was to further the match between Anne and Darkefell at every opportunity. Anne knew her mother well. Could she blame her, really, when a marquess satisfied every requirement of a husband for the daughter of an earl?

But Anne was willing to set aside his presumption, as she had more interesting things to think about. "Word from Lydia and my family is not the reason I agreed to walk with you here."

"Really?" he said with an appreciative gleam in his dark eyes. He moved toward her and put his arm around her waist. "I knew there was more."

"Don't be an idiot," she said, pulling out of his grasp, battling a desperate wish to throw herself back into his arms.

Irusan growled threateningly.

Darkefell must never know about her dreams, Anne resolved, and how she still remembered every kiss between them. She couldn't think rationally when he caressed her as he did, and if she was to ever consider marriage with him, she would need every ounce of her rational thought, every bit of brain power, to figure him out, and decide if she could live with such a rogue for the rest of her life.

But she still could not quite believe that he was serious about courting her with an eye toward marriage, and felt sure he had some ulterior motive she could not yet fathom.

"You never did answer me, Anne. I asked you a question the last time I saw you, and you did not answer."

He referred, or course, to his proposal, hurled at her as a command or challenge.

"I believe my leaving the next morning was all the answer that should be required of such an absurd question, if you can even call it that," she said, and was surprised by a pained look that flitted across his face.

"Very well," he said grudgingly, "for now. But we will speak of it again."

"As I said, I had another reason for walking with you here." She strode to the cliff edge and he followed, grabbing her arm as if he was afraid she would go over. "Isn't the view breathtaking?"

"Yes, but come away from the cliff edge, if you please."

She was surprised by his tone, and when she looked at his face, the unease amply displayed in his expression. "What is it, Darkefell?"

"I don't wish you to be quite so close to obliteration, that's all."

"Oh, pish tush!" she cried, and spun away from him, doing a turn on the cliff edge. "I won't fall. I'm very surefooted, and have an excellent head for heights. If you remember, I climbed the tower folly at your estate and felt no unease. Or, well, a little shakiness in the ankles on those dreadful stairs, but nothing more."

"*Please*, Anne, come away from the cliff edge."

"Oh, all right," she said, eyeing him, noting a tightness around his generous mouth. Did he really care for her so deeply, or was it just his own anxiety over the height? It occurred to her that the last time they had been together, she had almost tumbled off a cliff of similar height. Perhaps that explained his unease. "But there is a reason for being here," she insisted. "Look out . . . what do you see?"

He relaxed as she stopped edging toward oblivion, and turned his gaze to sea. "Water. Sky. The sun. Clouds."

"And?" she asked.

The bluff was high and had a grand view of the shoreline for miles. To the west the property sloped gradually, trailing downward for about a half mile toward a scythe-shaped slice of beach in the distance. Directly below the bluff upon which they stood was a sand beach that was broad at low tide, but that virtually disappeared at high tide. To the east was a jagged cut, a deep V that sloped up, with high-walled sides of rock and a floor of sand disrupted with rocky outcroppings, like broken black teeth jutting through the sandy slope.

The marquess held his hand up to shade his eyes and surveyed it all, then turned back toward Anne. "Am I missing something?" Darkefell asked. "What the devil else is there to see?"

"No, you're absolutely correct," she said, returning to stand in front of him. "There is nothing else to see. Except," she said, coming closer to him, "I saw, night before last, a Mussulman pirate hovering just beyond the cliff edge in the middle of the air!"

He stared into her eyes, then burst into laughter. Sobering, he said, "Really, Anne, you had me believing you were serious for a moment."

"But I did see it!" she insisted, feeling the irritation he always seemed to inspire within her. "I saw the famous local specter, the Barbary Ghost!"

"And this was in the middle of the night? What were you doing out here at that time? And alone? Anne," he said, taking both her shoulders in his big hands, "promise me you won't venture out in the night again. Promise me!" He shook her slightly.

"Don't be ridiculous, Darkefell," she said, twisting her shoulders out of his hands. Of course he had missed her point, or was ignoring it, which amounted to the same thing. "There's more . . . listen!" She leaned into him, excited even at the memory of the spectacle. "Before I saw the Barbary Ghost, I saw smugglers gathering on the beach, welcoming a rowboat, and transferring smuggled goods to a dray on the beach!"

"This is too much!" he growled. "You're no fool, or at least I didn't judge you to be one. If there are smugglers involved, then this is even more dangerous than some tomfoolery with a ghost. You must never come out at night, Anne, for those who witness smuggling often pay with their lives. They're a cutthroat tribe, and would not hesitate even though you're a woman."

"I'm no fool, Darkefell," she said coldly, disappointed in his prosaic reaction. She had thought him adventurous.

"Exactly what I said. But you have proven to be *reckless* in the past."

She watched his eyes. He was genuinely concerned for her safety, and she understood that, but still, he could not expect to tell her what to do. "Darkefell, I don't suppose you really understand a woman's life." She examined his face, and saw the quick frown of incomprehension, but she would get to her point soon enough. "I have been watched and guarded my whole life. While the young men I knew in my youth went to sea, traveled to Italy and beyond, studied at Oxford, and spent their years gambling, drinking, and roaming the world, I took dancing lessons, learned to play the pianoforte, and spent my hours netting purses, learning the fine art of directing a household of servants, and entertaining the vicar and his wife."

He sighed. "I understand your wish for excitement, Anne, but engaging in hazardous . . . no, worse than hazardous, *thoughtless* activities will only end in an early death and heartbreak for those who care for you."

"By your judgment, but why should I substitute *your* judgment of unsuitability for my own?"

"Because I know better than you, that's why!" he said, balling his hands into fists at his side. "I'll not have my wife—"

"Darkefell, I am *not* your wife, not now, nor in the future; if you had set out to design a means of reminding me why I could never accept your proposal, you could not do better than this!" She glared at him, trying to ignore the rapid pulse in his temple and throat, the signs of agitation she knew well in him. Next, his cheeks would suffuse with red, and the color would sink to his neck. Male temper; it had been used to successfully bully women for millennia, Anne suspected.

Yet he did not speak.

Deliberately, coldly, hoping to chill his ire, she said, "I will *not* be confined or constrained, my every move approved or censured. My mother and I have parted over this, and though I am no fool, and am reasonably careful for my reputation—I have no desire to be notorious, my lord—neither will I hand over every iota of control to a coterie of servants, companions, parents and then, when I am so desperately bored I can no longer think of anything beyond the next assembly, a husband who will own me body and soul."

He was speechless, staring into her eyes.

Would he not speak, not protest her declaration of a right to self-determination? She had expected him to spout a litany of reasons for feminine subjugation. After all, religion, tradition, even nature conspired to keep women dependent upon men. She thrust her face toward his. "Do you understand what it is to be a woman? Any man I marry would be able to decide where I live and how. He would even have command over my body, his to take pleasure in . . . or not.

I am *not* a thoughtless chit. I have pondered long and hard and careful on this, Darkefell, and I will live as I see fit . . ." She paused, then in a lower tone said, "Or not live at all."

Doubt clouded his dark eyes, and she thought, *There, now he will take me in disgust and leave with some vague excuse. I'll never see him again.*

But he grabbed her shoulders, jerked her into his arms, and bent his head, claiming her lips in a kiss so fierce and long that she could not breathe and beat at his shoulder, gasping for air, as she made smothered cries for him to cease. Irusan, who had been off hunting mice in the long grass, came pelting back and hurled himself at Darkefell's leg, yowling in fury. The marquess released Anne and cried out, shaking the cat off his leg.

"Irusan, behave!" Anne yelled. The cat slunk away with a grumble. She put a trembling hand to her mouth.

Darkefell's face was red. "I suppose I deserved that," he said, touching his leg, blood beginning to show through the buff breeches of his riding costume, "but I think both you and your cat, madam, have given your opinion of me in ways more eloquent than words." He whirled and stalked away, back to the house.

Pamela was still on the terrace, staring toward them. Even from a distance Anne could see concern in her friend's stance. She waved one hand to her friend and turned back to the ocean to regain her composure. Anne had been about to tell Darkefell of her plan to investigate the cliff face and ask if he wanted to help; they had solved a murder together in Yorkshire, and she *had* felt that she would trust no one so well as him when it came to an adventure. But she was wrong.

Darkefell was gone by the time she got back to Cliff House, and Pamela was tactful enough to remain silent. St. James, who had fortunately not witnessed Darkefell's rough embrace, kissed her cheek gently, and said he would see her on the morrow, but he had to get back to his regiment. He reminded them both that they were to meet the next night at an assembly in St. Ives.

Pam did not comment on what she saw, and Anne was grateful; she had no wish to talk about the scene she had just experienced. Mingled in her breast were warring emotions: fury at Darkefell's attempt to dominate, thrill at his skillful kiss, overlaid by an ache at the knowledge that he could not change, nor could she, so they must stay apart. She would live under no man's thumb.

Far better, for her, she realized, would be a husband like Marcus St. James, an indolent wastrel. Once she married, her family would finally leave her alone to manage her own affairs, and Marcus was an easy, controllable sort of fellow, only wanting to live pleasantly. One word from her would bring a serious proposal of marriage from the captain, and she was old enough that she did not require her parents' consent.

It was certainly a thought to make her pause.

• • •

Osei Boatin had arrived at the Barbary Ghost Inn by the time Darkefell returned, and had his employer's clothes tidied properly, the traveling desk set up on a table near the low window, and his own gear stowed. Though he was the marquess's secretary, he would act as valet while they traveled.

Studious, intelligent and reserved, it was painful to Osei to deal with the stares of strangers, but given his skin color, his demeanor, even his perfect elocution, he knew himself to be somewhat of a rarity. There were many Africans in England, but they were mostly servants and laborers, not given the opportunity to learn and better themselves. The few who were not in that class were viewed as aberrations, thus his own singularity. With a reticent manner, he still drew attention wherever he went.

He was aware of the marquess's reason for traveling to Cornwall, but kept his own counsel on how effective he thought the journey would be with a woman as proud and stubborn as Lady Anne Addison. Darkefell's shrewd rationale for bringing Osei with him to Cornwall had in part been the secretary's warm friendship with the lady. Darkefell, limping from the cat's attack, told him all that had occurred, even Anne's story of the Barbary Ghost and smuggler sighting, up to the moment when he had clasped her to his heart and kissed her on the cliff.

After a pause, Osei diplomatically said, "I do not think, sir, that it was a propitious moment to press your suit, when the lady had just declared her independence."

"I know, I know," Darkefell said, throwing himself on the lumpy bed and passing one hand over his face, grimy from the wind. "But she looked so damned wonderful to me. She's magnificent, and I handle her completely wrong. Still, I know she's attracted to me. Why does she not just accept her feelings and marry me?"

Osei turned from the desk by the low window, where he was organizing some papers that required the marquess's signature. "Perhaps," he said diffidently, "she has rashly responded to a proposal before and regretted it?"

"Or she's still weeping for her damned red-coated fiancé from five years ago. Women have a capacity for mourning that escapes men." He stood and straightened his jacket. "I'm going down to speak to Quintrell, and try to get to the bottom of this smuggling near Cliff House. If Anne is truly in danger, I will carry her away from here even if I have to kidnap her to do it."

"Oh, I am sure that is the perfect way to win her heart, sir," Osei said, his dark eyes glinting with humor behind his gold-rimmed spectacles.

Darkefell grimaced. "Don't be insolent." But he softened his words with a snort of laughter and a shake of his head.

The landlord was in his stockroom, a plump, pretty serving girl told the marquess, and he followed her directions. He tapped on the door and entered, glancing around the dark room, with its stacks of barrels and crates of goods.

"Let me buy you an ale," Darkefell said, after some desultory talk about the weather. Quintrell agreed.

They talked for a while and drank, and finally Darkefell broached the subject of the smugglers, though he didn't divulge that he had heard about them from Anne, or anyone at Cliff House. His questions opened a floodgate of information from Quintrell, who appeared genuinely troubled about the gang that had, in the past year, begun business along the shore near St. Wyllow. There had been many smugglers, but this gang was well organized and steadfast. Quintrell shook his head over it all; he was concerned that their success would bring imitators, and there would be a kind of war among the smuggling gangs. It had happened before, in other places. That settled one question Darkefell had. Quintrell would surely not be so effusive if he were a party to the lawbreakers.

Quintrell finally fell silent, but then looked up into the marquess's face, and asked, "Milord, I need counsel from someone not connected to St. Wyllow. Might I tell you somethin' on the hush?"

"Of course."

"No, sir," he said, his pouchy face lined with worry, "I mean this not lightly. You'll not tell the authorities, even though it may be something illegal I must confess?"

Darkefell hesitated. He was no friend to crime, and if there had been some violence, or some connection Quintrell was now regretting, what should he do? He took a deep breath; he trusted the steadiness of his father's old equerry. Quintrell was a sober, honest man. If he'd made a mistake, it was just that, a mistake he now regretted and would not repeat. "You can tell me anything," he said finally.

With relief, the fellow began to talk. At first, he just spoke about his happiness when they first bought the Barbary Ghost Inn, and how his wife and he had some good years. Her passing was a very dark time, for he had loved her dearly, and ever since, he said, it felt like he had been missing from some parts of his life, one of those being his son, Johnny. "I just haven't bin here. Not in the ways that matter, anyhow. Still, 'e's a good boy, is Johnny . . . most of the time." He fell silent, a brooding expression on his lined and scarred face.

"But?" Darkefell urged, feeling that they were finally coming to the crux of the matter.

The man stared down at the scarred tabletop. "I've coom to the part o' the story, sir, where I must confess what ill suits my wish that you think well o' me." He didn't pause, though, launching right into the rest of the story. "There's a fellow by the name of Sam Micklethwaite. 'E's a local man, owns a lugger an' a cutter. Does some honest shipping, good business. But a year or so ago, 'e come to me with some ankers o' gin to get rid of. Says he found 'em offshore. Now, that happens, right enough. Many a fisherman has found smuggled barrels—ankers, half ankers—sunk offshore to hide 'em. Nothing wrong with rescuing such goods, I say; it's not like 'e smuggled 'em, 'e just found them. I bought 'em, and sold the gin in the taproom."

He stopped. Darkefell was about to speak after a long silence, to say he didn't think there was any cause for alarm, but Quintrell spoke again, staring steadily out the cloudy window toward the livery stable behind the inn.

"I thought nothin' about it, 'til Micklethwaite came with more, another time. I bought them from him, but the *next* time I questioned him. He was cheeky about it, saying yes, they was smuggled goods. Didn't I want to profit? I turned 'im down, milord, that day. But then he dropped it on me; said my Johnny 'ad been working for him, and if I didn't want him turned in, I'd keep me mouth shut and buy some gin."

"Turned in? To the excise men?" Darkefell asked.

"Aye. If it's true, if Johnny's bound to those smugglers, and Micklethwaite dropped a secret word to th' excise men . . ." He trailed off and shook his head, mournfully. "Milord, that revenue man—Puddicombe is his name—e's saying the government's talkin' about transportation for smugglers, to the ends of the earth, Van Dieman's Land! Lord, I'd never see my boy again."

"Have you told Johnny to stop working for Micklethwaite?"

"We haven't spoke about it. 'E don't confide in me no more, so I'm not dead sure, y'see. We've had our troubles, have Johnny and I since his mother died. He blames me, y'see, sayin' she worked herself to death. She weren't well, and that's a fact, but I tried to keep her abed. Made her feel useless, she said, and she wouldn't stop, but 'e don't see it that way."

"What can I do to help?"

A sweep of relief covered the older man's face, and Darkefell realized that until that moment, Quintrell had been tense, waiting to see if his risk in telling the marquess would result in disaster.

"Find out," he said, his voice rough with emotion. "Find out how my Johnny's involved, what 'e does for Micklethwaite, and mebbe how we can get 'im out."

Darkefell thought about Anne's spying on the smugglers. This gave him an added reason to find out what was going on, and put a stop to this smuggling gang and the danger to young Johnny Quintrell. Quintrell had not worked for his family for many years now, but still . . . Darkefell's opinion was that loyalty ran both ways with him and his. He clapped the other man on the shoulder and said, "Stop worrying. I'll do whatever I can to extricate your son. If he's anything like you, he's a good fellow at heart, though perhaps in a little over his head."

Tears welled in Quintrell's eyes and he nodded, but Darkefell uneasily considered that he had no idea how he was going to do it, or even if he could. His own motives for watching the smugglers were in line with Quintrell's fatherly concern, though, and he had full confidence that he could help.

Starting that very night.

Five

Anne was muddled and angry, unable to even think about bed. She paced her bedroom floor, and as it was a small room, that required much turning; her long dark hair was unbound and swung out at each turn, frizzing wildly in the damp sea air. Ever since Darkefell had left, she had been working herself up into a stew at his presumption in first trying to tell her what to do, and then kissing her in the open like that! Once Marcus had left to join his regiment, Pamela had demanded answers. All afternoon, and through a quiet dinner, she asked questions about the marquess, and even through the evening as they sat quietly, mending their spring bonnets.

Lolly, sitting with them and sewing, had listened with wide eyes but an amazingly closed mouth. Perhaps Anne shouldn't have confessed so much about her relationship with the marquess in front of her companion, but even if her mother did find out how far the relationship had gone, she could not force Anne to marry the man.

Though she'd probably try.

And now Anne was so worked up she couldn't sleep, regretting saying so much, frustrated by her life, feeling hemmed in on every side by her mother, her grandmother, her companion and society.

Mary came in to Anne's bedchamber from the attached dressing room, where she and her son slept, and closed the door quietly behind her. "That is one weary wee boy," she said softly, making her way around the room, tidying as she went, her full skirts softly rustling. "He spent all day on the seashore, and bathing too, even though the water was dreadful cold," she said, dusting some spilled powder from the dressing table and then cleaning hair from a brush. "I was that worrit aboot him, dashing in and oot o' the waves like he does. I didna take my eyes off him for one second. Your puss is curled up in his bed; it's a precious sight."

"What does he mean by following me here, Mary? Why is he plaguing me so?" Anne, still pacing, did not need to say who or what she meant, for they had already spoken of the marquess at some length.

As she put away some sheets of paper into Anne's traveling desk and closed the lid, Mary gently said, "A man in love will do many a strange thing, milady."

"He's not in love with me," Anne declared, contemptuously, though her maid's words sent an odd thrill through her. "He doesn't even know me," she insisted. "And a man in love would not promptly try to change everything about the object of his affections, as Darkefell is trying to do to me."

Mary paused in her tidying. She hesitated for a long moment, but then said, watching Anne, "I think it would be well for you, milady, to lairn more about the man, before tossing him aside. P'raps he's just such a one as you *should* marry."

Anne gave a snort of derision, but a sound outside drew her attention; she leaned on the windowsill and stared out. From her window, though, she could only see a small portion of the back garden, and none of the sea. A moving shadow angled across Pamela's terrace. "Who is that?" she gasped. "And what are they up to, creeping around outside the house like that?"

With the imperious marquess's commands fresh in her mind and heart, Anne impetuously decided to do the opposite of everything he said. Even as she made the quick decision, she felt how foolish it was to be guided by negation, but an anxious trembling within her would not let her stay still. She did not want to think of what Mary had just said, that she should give serious thought to marrying Darkefell.

"I want to know what, or who, that is," Anne said, retrieving her cape, and heading for the bedroom door.

"You'll not go without me, milady," Mary said as she followed, throwing a shawl over her shoulders.

As Anne unlatched the garden door, feeling the rush of cool sea air on her face, she murmured, "Cliff House is certainly easier to leave than Ivy Lodge was." She referred to the dower house of the marquess's Yorkshire estate, where she had stayed while visiting Lydia; it was a much larger house with a regiment of servants and variety of locked doors.

She led the way out onto the terrace and paused, glancing around, her heart pounding in agitation. Whatever or whomever the shadow belonged to, it was gone now. Who could it have been? "Stay here, Mary," she whispered, putting out one hand and touching her maid's cloaked arm. "I'm just going up to the cliff to see if anything is going on."

"I'm not letting you go alone," Mary insisted, following her.

Anne crept down the garden in the moonlight, through the rickety gate and up the grassy slope to the bluff, huffing and puffing by the time she got there. She crouched and urged Mary to do the same, as they crept closer to the edge, near a stunted and twisted tree that clung to the edge of the cliff and shadowed the lip. It was too dark to see anything other than an impression of movement below. But when a lantern flashed for a moment, Anne could see that the beach was full of men.

But seconds later both Anne and Mary reared back in amazement as, out of the murky void on the cloudy night, a figure rose from beyond the edge of the cliff. It was the Barbary Ghost, so close they could almost reach out and touch it, if it truly was a substantial being! Mary shrieked in terror and started up. The ghost whirled, howled in rage and drifted closer to them, the air between them lit up with fireworks, smoke and flame blazing.

Mary grabbed Anne's arm and yanked her back from the cliff edge, but Anne pulled away and strode closer, just in time to see the ghost flailing, men below on the beach scuttling away from a rowboat, as on the cliff opposite Anne and Mary—the bluff that topped the other side of the deep cut—men rose from the shadowy murk and swarmed down toward the beach.

"Milady, come away, please!" cried Mary, her voice a thin wail of terror.

"No, I have to see—" Anne's words were drowned out by a burst of gunfire, then more fireworks. She tottered close to the edge, but the ghost was gone, disappeared in the drift of smoke that the sea breeze tugged and pulled, this way and that, particles glinting in the faint moonlight that peeped from behind a cloud.

"No more, milady," Mary gasped, as some more shots rang out, and shouting alerted them to a tussle on the beach. "We've got to go back. Please!"

"Where did that ghost go? Did you see anything?"

"Nooo!" Mary wailed. "Please, milady, come away!"

At the bottom of the cut, Darkefell had been lurking in the shadows of the scrubby shrubs at the base of the cliff. Above him explosions crackled, echoing off the cliff face, while beyond him, in the open, the smugglers beetled up the shore, abandoning wooden crates, dumping whatever they carried in their haste to get away.

He had followed Johnny Quintrell as the young man snuck from the inn that night, and this was his destination, directly below the St. James's rented house, if he judged correctly. That answered Joseph's questions about his son's involvement. Darkefell was looking for an opportunity to snatch the boy back before the revenue men, who swarmed out of the cut, got to him and arrested him.

But shots rang out again, and when he looked up in a flash of light from some explosive, it was to see Anne — *his* Anne — tottering on the edge of the cliff! After he had told her to stay out of it! That made his decision simple. Johnny would have to fend for himself; Darkefell was for rescuing Anne.

He slunk into the shadows and up the jagged cut, struggling against the wet sand, willing himself to not break out into the open. He was aware of men just to his left who were working their way down, likely the revenue men in a pitched battle with the smugglers. Shouts and confusion surrounded him, but he went unnoticed in the fray. There was only one direction for him, and that was up, toward Anne.

He finally topped the cliff face, and saw Anne, not alone, he was happy to see, but with her faithful maid, Mary. He raced to her, pulling her down. "What the devil are you doing out here?" he growled.

"Darkefell?" she cried.

He put his hand over her mouth, "For God's sake, madam, keep your voice down. Mary, go back to the house," he said, for in the ghostly light of the rising moon that slanted its pearly rays across the surface of the ocean, he could see that the Scottish maid was frightened out of her wits.

"Aye, milord," she said and scuttled away. But then she paused, looked back and said, "Take care of her, milord, please!"

"You know I will." Once Mary was gone he pulled Anne down to the ground, and whispered in her ear, "I'm going to let go of your mouth, but keep quiet!" He took his hand away.

"If I didn't know better," she hissed, gulping in air, "I would think you were trying to smother me."

In answer, he pulled her toward him and fastened his mouth over hers, grimly determined to silence her. He half expected her to bite his lip—she had done *that* before—but instead she returned the kiss, pushing him onto his back. The dormant sensuality he kept ruthlessly subdued roared to life as he felt her long hair streaming about him, and her warm, soft body covering his hard angularity. The sensation of her full lips pressed to his raised his heart rate to pounding. Hungry for more, he grabbed her hips and pulled her close, but she resisted.

"Happy?" she gasped. "Now, *let me go*." She pushed out of his grasp and rolled away from him, then slithered to the edge of the cliff on her elbows and knees.

He rolled onto his side and cupped himself, adjusting, trying to make himself more comfortable, but to no avail. Trying to ignore the physical discomfort her passionate kisses and voluptuous body had ignited, he crept to her side and collapsed.

"Darkefell, I saw it again, the Barbary Ghost," she muttered. "Then Mary shrieked, and I swear, the ghost stared right at us and howled!"

The scramble below was dissipating, but a shot rang out, and Darkefell pulled Anne back from the lip of the cliff. Holding her close, he murmured, "Do you think Mary's scream alerted the smugglers to the revenue men?"

"I don't know," Anne whispered, in his ear.

His eyes rolled back at the intimate feel of her warm breath on his neck and ear, the murmur of her beautiful voice, and he supposed he unconsciously dug his fingers into her arm; she protested. He forced himself to relax. "I . . . I beg your pardon, my dearest Anne." He nuzzled her thick veil of hair. "I had no idea your hair was so long," he whispered, tangling his fingers in it, his voice oddly gruff. "And it smells so lovely." He put his hand on her back and stroked, down to her bottom.

"Darkefell, stop!" she said, swatting at his hand. "What are you doing here, anyhow?"

He rolled away from her, cleared his throat and summoned coolness. "I was down on the beach watching the smugglers," he said, deciding not to divulge his reason for being there yet. He pushed himself up on his elbows and looked over the cliff edge. The beach below appeared deserted, from what could be sensed with the wan moonlight. There could be a battalion of men hugging the cliff, in the shadows, though. "Then I heard an altercation," he whispered, "then the fireworks, and the excise men came swarming down from the cliff opposite here, on the other side of the cut. I saw you flailing about on the cliff's edge, and began up the cut, staying in the shadows."

"I wondered where you came from."

"You were tottering about on the edge of the cliff, so I came up to make you heed common sense."

He thought she would retort angrily, but her tone was thoughtful when she said, "I hope no one was hurt."

He remembered Johnny Quintrell, and fervently said, "I hope that, too. But what the devil were you doing out? I specifically told you to *stay in*." Even as he said it, he knew it was wrong; would he never learn that to command her was to alienate her? Or did he just enjoy being censured by her?

But again, she reacted coolly. "And I told you I had no intention of being bullied into doing what you think is suitable. Are you going to help me discover what this ghost is all about, or not?"

He made a quick decision. "I am indeed going to help you." *To stay out of trouble*, he finished in his mind.

"But we can do nothing right now," she said. She peered over the edge of the cliff. "All's quiet. They're gone, I think, but it's too dark right now to detect. I do hope no one was hurt." Anne got to her feet and dusted off her dress. "Come back tomorrow, Darkefell. I want to have a look at this cliff side, and figure out how the ghost does his disappearing act. Then I want to find out what—or who—it is, and what his game is."

"Kiss me," the marquess said, taking her arm, "and I will agree to anything."

So she did.

• • •

"But dear, I don't understand what you mean to do," Lolly said the next afternoon, wringing her hands together.

Anne, with Mary's help, dressed appropriately for clambering about on the beach and rocky cliff. Luckily Pamela had some business she could not avoid that day, and would be gone until dinner, after which they were going to the assembly at the regimental mess. "I told you, Lolly dear . . . the marquess and I are going for a walk. Given what must be on Mother and Grandmother's minds, you are merely fulfilling your duty by promoting such an endeavor."

She looked doubtful. "I'm going with you."

"No, Lolly!" Anne turned and gazed at her companion.

Lolly Broomhall was an untidy, pudgy woman with a pouchy, pale face. Her clothes were out of style, and though carefully mended, were sadly frowsy. But that very moment, her lips pursed in an unusually firm line, she appeared dignified and every inch the lady she was born. "I won't be any trouble," she insisted. "But I would be dreadfully remiss if I didn't accompany you."

Anne sighed and turned back to the glass. "Mary, can you make just a few wisps of hair dangle? It softens my angularity."

"And why wouldya be worryin' about that?" Mary asked, with a sly smile.

Anne caught a glance between her maid and companion. So, the two women were cohorts in the effort to get her leg-locked (as she had heard marriage termed by a male friend) to the marquess. "No reason."

"You will be careful, milady," Mary said anxiously, leaning in and working on her mistress's recalcitrant hair.

Anne nodded, soberly. "Yes, after what Mrs. Quintrell said this morning, I certainly shall be careful."

That morning the cook had, with great relish, talked about the skirmish the night before, and the death by shooting of one of the excise officer's hired men. Anne had had a terrible moment when she considered that Darkefell had been down there in that scuffle, and could have been the one to take a stray bullet if he had not scrambled up to tackle her. Then she had another few terrible moments when she realized that she could no longer imagine her life without Darkefell in it. That, however, must be a passing feeling brought on by the intimacy of their last moments together. The last kisses as he walked her back to Cliff House had been spectacularly lovely. He had held her close for a long few minutes, kissing her ears and neck, a sensation she found was particularly sweet. She had dreamt of him all night, but this time when she awoke she did not feel angry or irritated.

An hour later, as the afternoon sun climbed the sky, arching over through the blue dome, she met the marquess on the bluff beyond Cliff House, and tried to ignore the way her heart skipped a beat when she saw him. She was prey to an insidious attraction to the handsome marquess; his looks seemed designed to delight the female heart and mind, she thought, gazing at him as he politely greeted Lolly, bowing over her hand as the woman twittered a drawn-out greeting. He was dark-haired, broad-shouldered, dark-eyed, and with sensuous lips and a muscular torso.

She, on the other hand, was too tall, too plain, and too independent. His pursuit of her was some kind of strange quirk in an otherwise perfect male. She was not being silly about it, nor falsely modest; she was intelligent, and some men might like that. She was wealthy in her own right, with an inheritance over which she had complete control because of her scholarly father's lackadaisical attitude toward finance. Not wishing to be bothered about it, he had made sure his banker gave Anne liberal access to her own funds. Many men would like her affluence.

And there was the crux of her problem with marriage: What would she gain by marrying? Any man who would marry her for money was not worth considering. (Did that mean she should really *not* consider Marcus as a possible husband? Would she despise him before long? She wasn't yet sure.) But any man she married would expect to have full control over her finances. In fact, her money would become his. And her time, and her body.

She felt the flush of attraction mount her cheeks as Darkefell turned to her and took her hand, smiling into her eyes.

"Are you well, Anne?" he asked, anxiously, squeezing her hand and gazing steadily into her eyes.

"You've heard about last night? About the excise man killed?"

"Yes. Quintrell, the owner of the Barbary Ghost Inn—he was my father's equerry many years ago—told me all about it this morning." His lips tightened. "It is a terrible turn of affairs. If it was a purposeful killing, then it signals how desperate are these smugglers, and how dangerous."

She waited, but he did not again command her not to go near the cliff or beach at night. "Let's begin. Lolly," she said, turning to her companion, "please stay up here. I need you as a lookout, for I do not want it to be too obvious that I am examining the cliff face. I'll look up to you occasionally; wave if all is well."

Lolly reluctantly agreed, and as Anne and Darkefell made their way down the steep, rocky cut, he chuckled.

"What are you giggling about?" she asked, clinging to his hand as she clambered over a rocky outcropping.

"You are a managing woman, aren't you?"

"I come by it honestly," she said, putting her free hand out, and steadying herself on the rocky spike. A stiff breeze came up from the beach, and she was grateful that she had not worn a hat. The wind tugged at her hair, pulling it down from her careful hairstyle. She glanced back at him. "You've met my mother and grandmother. Do you not think I favor them?"

His expression was serious when he said, "No, not in the slightest."

Her heart pounding wildly—just the exercise, she told herself— she turned back and recommenced scaling down the cut, dropping his hand and relying on her own perfect balance. Why should her heart pound so, at such an answer? Did he mean she did not have the opulent beauty of her mother, faded though it was? Or was his reference to something in her personality? She daren't ask him.

"I don't really understand you, Darkefell," she said in a conversational tone, glad her flaming face was turned away from him.

"Anne, women always say that about men, but we're really very simple creatures."

She didn't respond. They got down to the beach, and she turned to the rock wall, trying to catch her breath. She examined the sheer rock face, looking for any indication of some mechanism. She resolutely did not believe in ghosts, and especially one dressed in Barbary gear who exploded fireworks.

But what, then, was the creature? The face was human, not that of a doll or dummy, and the floating was most often graceful, but last night, when startled, the ghost had become jerky. She shared her thoughts with Darkefell, who had joined her.

"Look," she suddenly exclaimed, pointing to a spot about a third of the way up the wall. "That appears to be a kind of cave, or deep crevice. Let's go up there."

"In those skirts? No, *I'll* go and report back to you."

Like hell you will, she thought, but did not say. Curse words were the province of a weak mind. Instead of answering, she hiked up the skirts of her cream and pink *robe polonaise,* the most suitable gown for such work, as the skirt was already tucked up somewhat, and began to clamber up the rock face. Luckily, it was not completely sheer, and had foothold and handholds a good ways up. She was red-faced from exertion, and panting, but was gratified that Darkefell, following her, seemed to be faring no better.

The crevice was just above her now, and there was a rocky outcropping at it. She pulled herself up as far as she could go but was in a dreadful predicament; she clung to the rock face, her skirts preventing her from getting her leg up to the rock shelf to mount it. Nor could she reposition herself. "I believe that skirts are a device of men to keep women from exploring a full range of movement," she grunted, frozen in place.

"Oh, certainly," Darkefell said, his tone one of irritation, as he pulled himself up to the rock shelf. "And we deliberately manip- ulated nature to make women the childbearers, so they would be tied to the home, and would therefore need men."

He put down his hand and she reached up, grasping it tightly. With one massive pull he raised her up to the rock ledge with him. She stumbled close to him.

"Don't be ridiculous," she said breathlessly.

"Are you all right down there?" came Lolly's twittering voice. "Is everything all right? I can't see you, Anne, and I'm afraid to get close to the edge."

"I'm fine, Lolly, dear," Anne called, releasing Darkefell's hand and clinging more closely to the rock face. She wasted not another moment, sidling toward the cave, but when she looked back, Darkefell was not following. "What is it?" she asked.

He shook his head. "We've never found Hiram Grover's body, Anne," he said, staring into her eyes.

She felt a jolt of anxiety and her stomach clenched; just a reflex from the recent past, she told herself. After all, that was only a few weeks ago. Hiram Grover was a killer who had plunged to his death off a rocky escarpment, after trying to kill Anne.

Still, she didn't get the connection, nor what had prompted him to say that just then, until she looked at the cave. The last time they had been in a cave, Darkefell had found the murder weapon Grover had used to kill Lydia's lady's maid, Cecilia Wainwright, a young woman who had done no harm to anyone. "I'm sure his body will turn up somewhere," she said, keeping her tone neutral. She turned her mind away from the awful thought of what weeks in a river would do to a man's body. "It *must* turn up sometime!"

"We searched and searched." He shook his head and leaned back against the rock face, closing his eyes. "I traveled south in part to tell Grover's son what I had done to find his body. It was grim. Theo tried not to blame me, as a good Christian, but it was there in his pained expression." He opened his eyes and met her gaze.

"Darkefell," she said, looking into his dark, haunted eyes. Seeing the pain there, she sidled closer to him and put one hand on his sleeve. "Tony," she said more gently, "he tried to end my life, and you saved me. What else could you have done?"

He grinned unexpectedly, and took in a deep breath, putting his hand over hers. "Will you call me Tony from now on? Always? I do like the sound of my name on your tongue."

Stiffly, she said, "I cannot do that when we are in company, but—"

"But when we're alone."

"All right. Let's look into this cave, then get back up to Lolly before she suffers an apoplectic fit." Holding firmly on to a rocky outcropping, she crept into the mouth of the crevice, to find it was only a few feet deep. But it was certainly worth looking within. There, in a pile on the cave floor, was a coil of rope, and an oilcloth sack. Anne darted forward and from the sack pulled out pantaloons, a white shirt and . . . she turned, holding up her prize discovery.

"What the devil is that?" Darkefell exclaimed.

She shook the hairy handful. "The Barbary Ghost's beard and wig!"

They left the pile where it was; there was no point in depriving the ghost of his costume until they knew who it was. They climbed back down to the beach and did a little more searching around, but Anne confessed her weariness, and they climbed back up the cut. Once they were on the bluff once more, Lolly collapsed to her knees and closed her eyes, muttering what Anne suspected were prayers of thanksgiving for her safe return. But Anne strode directly toward the gnarled, hovering tree over the cliff face. Darkefell raced after her and grabbed her arm.

"Slowly, my dear," he murmured, his mouth twisted in anxiety.

"Darkefell, don't be tiresome, I'll be careful." She neared the cliff edge, while the marquess stayed well back. "This is it!" she crowed. "Darkefell, you must come closer and look!"

When he edged forward she pointed up into the thick piney depths. There, nestled against the trunk and secured with a thick chain, was a pulley, and a coiled rope.

"Part of the mechanism for elevating the pirate ghost. This is how the trick of the floating phantom was done!"

Six

Pamela was pensive, after her daylong excursion. Dinner around the small oak table was subdued without Marcus's bright banter to enliven it, but he had his duties to his regiment. Lolly did her best to keep a flow of conversation going in the cramped dining room off the sitting room, but it seemed stiff and forced. For her own part, Anne was lost in thought, but her contemplation had little to do with the Barbary Ghost. She was having trouble remembering her objections to Darkefell and his proposal.

After discovering the floating ghost mechanism, she and the marquess had walked and talked, while Lolly returned to Cliff House, needing a restorative pot of tea after such an agitating morning. Darkefell had repeated to Anne his apprehension that Hiram Grover was not dead. The man, who had owned a neighboring estate to Darkefell's, though he was in the act of selling to the marquess, had been accused of the murder of Cecilia Wainwright, Lydia's maid. He was seized, but escaped the magistrate's custody and tried to kill Anne. It was Darkefell who saved her, and in so doing inadvertently sent Grover over the precipice to his doom, in the swirling waters of Staungill Force, a high waterfall on the marquess's land.

Anne had dismissed his concern at first, but when she looked over at him and saw his furrowed brow, she took it more seriously. They talked at length, and ultimately concluded that if Grover had not died in the fall, he must have been so badly hurt that he would have succumbed to his injuries. There was no proof he was alive, but it would have been gratifying to have positive proof that he was dead.

But any conversation with the marquess left her contemplative. Darkefell had been a puzzle to Anne since the first moment they met. Every time she tried to dismiss him as high-handed or arrogant, he would reveal a side that was unexpectedly thoughtful or sensitive. It was not that she wanted a weeping suitor, or the kind of gentle, poetical lad her friends swooned over. However, if she was ever to marry, her husband must talk to her as a rational human being, and on many occasions, Darkefell did just that. It was unnerving. Just when she decided he could never be the kind of man she should wed, he would do something that showed him in a different light, as one who would suit her in every detail.

The scrape of a knife on china brought her back to the present and the dinner table. Lolly was gazing down at her plate with genteel disgust on her softly wrinkled face.

Pushing an overcooked carrot around her plate, Lolly said, "Miss St. James, I wonder if it would be too much to ask if I could dabble in the kitchen on occasion?"

"Whatever for?" Pamela asked, mechanically sawing through a tough piece of lamb.

"Cooking, you see. I have become accustomed to cooking for myself and others," she said, "for in my rooms in Bath, we share kitchen facilities."

Anne felt an arrow of guilt dart into her heart. Lolly had been raised in gentility, and to be sunk to such an extremity as cooking for herself must mean her funds were very low indeed. She dropped her fork. "Oh, Lolly, I didn't know you were so—" she began.

But Lolly forestalled her, raising one hand and saying, "Shush, Anne, dear, I have found that I quite enjoy cooking, and I'm rather accomplished, if I may say such a thing without sounding too puffed up with conceit. It is immeasurably more pleasing to provide for oneself than to be at the mercy of such a servant as I could afford, some horrid, dirty little drudge who knows nothing of food, nor even rudimentary cleanliness!"

Anne could understand Lolly's wish to provide food for herself. Mrs. Quintrell's cooking showed how inept hired cooks could be. Her skills were far below the standards one would expect, and her dishes were barely edible, and then only as a necessity. Even the fresh bounty Anne had ordered delivered to the Cliff House kitchen from local farmers had been so poorly cooked it was nearly inedible. It was a crime against the fresh food. Anne also suspected Mrs. Quintrell took the choice bits home for her family, leaving the rest for Pamela and Marcus. If it was her own household, Anne and Mrs. Quintrell would have had it out, but it was not her place to reprimand the serving staff.

"Satisfy yourself, Miss Broomhall," Pamela said with a little worried frown that created two vertical lines between her brows, "but please, *please* do not offend Mrs. Quintrell! She's quite capable of leaving in a huff, and I could not do without her and her daughter."

Kitchen politics, Anne thought, a woman's province. While men decided international diplomacy, women placated ill-tempered cooks, even ones as slovenly and incompetent as that woman.

"I am very tactful, my dear, and shall tread carefully." Lolly finally laid her cutlery down, gently, on her plate, a tacit sign that she could not bear to eat another morsel of such ill-cooked provender.

After some preparation, Pamela, Anne and Lolly set out in Anne's carriage for the evening's entertainment. Anne's coach, horse and Sanderson, her surly driver, were stabled and kept in St. Wyllow, while Anne stayed with Pamela, for Cliff House had no suitable carriage house, and the stable was the merest shed, a shamble of a building that tipped sideways. Sanderson had been sent a message that his services would be required that night to take them to the structure just outside of St. Ives, where the officers' assembly for the town would be held.

Anne and Pamela had already attended some parties and fetes at the regimental headquarters, in the past two weeks, so Anne knew what to expect, however, the hall was, this night, crowded. It was not a building intended for such a throng, being constructed of wood, with a humble step and rather dirty aspect. However, judging from the brilliance of the light shining from within, and the sound, which was a chatter of conversation and high spirits as Anne had never expected to see in such a place, it was enough to cause her some doubt as to what could have drawn so many.

As Sanderson handed them down from the carriage, Anne settled the skirts of her second-best gown, a lovely dark blue French serge fabric with bows of stiff silver lace, and asked, "Did they invite every soul in Cornwall, and Devon too? Are they all here to greet the new colonel?" It appeared, as they entered the hall, that every mother and daughter, and most of the men, from miles around were in attendance. Red coats, usually in the vast majority, made up only a part of the jacket hues, and the ladies were decked in best style, with a jewel-like profusion of colors in glittering array, and even some diamond and ruby necklaces and bracelets in evidence. It made Anne's blue silk lustring *robe anglaise* seem too casual for the affair, but Anne knew it was she who was gowned appropriately, and the other ladies who were overdressed.

They stood at the top of the stairs, overlooking the crowded ballroom floor, searching for St. James, until an anxious person pushed them from behind. Anne turned, giving a cold look to the belligerent soul. A slim, angry woman stared boldly at her and said, with a flick of her fan, "Get along with you, now! Move on, I say!" She then turned to a younger girl, whose wrist she firmly held. "Becky, remember your manners. You're to meet a real live marquess tonight, probably your one and only chance; you must not stammer, you must not tread on his feet, and you must not let your nose dribble unbecomingly. I'll beat you thoroughly if you disgrace me."

Pamela bit her lip, the first sign of good humor she had evinced all day. Anne, though happy to see that, murmured, "Darkefell has managed an invitation! How did he do it, and how has his attendance become such common knowledge?"

With great composure, Pamela said, "As I passed by the regimental office today, I stopped and spoke to Colonel Withington, suggesting that as the Marquess of Darkefell was in residence at St. Wyllow it would do the regiment honor to invite him. The colonel is apparently acquainted with the marquess, and thought it a grand notion. Darkefell's your friend, Anne; I thought it would be only polite."

Anne glanced grimly around at the company. "Well, that explains the horde of husband-hunting mamas, shelved spinsters, and green girls."

"I didn't think you'd mind, Anne," her friend said with an anxious glance. "He seems such a good man, and terribly handsome."

"He's overbearing, imperious and stubborn," she said, though in the wake of their conversation that day her conscience prickled.

"Aren't all men? But he's also rich as Croesus." Pamela surged forward with the crowd.

Startled, Anne watched her friend descend to the ballroom floor. She had assumed Pam had Darkefell invited for *her* sake, but was she really setting her cap at him herself? A twinge of something uncomfortably like jealousy bolted through her. Anne ensured that Lolly was happily settled in a chaperone's chair, chatting with other middle-aged, lace-capped, gossiping ladies, and caught up with Pamela, who had found her brother.

The military band got up a spritely tune, and Anne and Pam both were beset with requests for dances from officers. Finally paired with Marcus, Anne relaxed, and reflected that just because Darkefell was invited did not mean he would come. He had never seemed, to her, the kind of man who would enjoy a crush like this.

But why did his possible attendance unnerve her so? She had become inured to his presence, she thought, and having spent several hours with him earlier that day, she should be completely uncaring of whether he came or not. But Darkefell could be quite intimidating in his best attire, and with his formal manners in place. It was not that he was forbidding, but the opposite. He was seductively beckoning, enticingly attractive. Would she ever stop noticing his looks? It irritated her that he was so good-looking and she so plain. They were unmatched, like a thoroughbred and a farm horse. Teamed up, they would make a ridiculous sight.

Perhaps that was one of the stumbling blocks to considering his proposal of marriage. As much as she wished it were not so, she feared the ridicule that would inevitably follow if she, a plain woman, were hitched in the matrimonial harness with the gorgeous Marquess of Darkefell. And did she fear his gaze would inevitably wander to the fresh specimens of loveliness that each year were introduced to society? She couldn't bear it, she just couldn't bear it, if she wed him and he wandered!

Oh. She took in a deep, shuddering breath. That was a new knot in her tangled feelings toward the Marquess of Darkefell.

"You haven't heard a word I've said," her dancing partner complained, tweaking her cheek as they came together in the pattern of the dance.

"I beg your pardon." The dance continued. "St. James," she said as they came together once more and began a walking portion of the dance, "when you marry, what shall you be looking for in a wife?"

"Oh-ho, do you mean you are considering my constant offer of marriage, my dear girl? I'm pleased beyond anything. In fact I'm walking on clouds this minute, for you embody the very essence of—"

"Don't go on like that, St. James," she said crossly. "I mean exactly what I say; what are you seeking in a wife?"

"Honestly?"

"Honestly."

"Well, I would like a wife with a sense of humor. An adequate purse, a sense of style, good manners." He smiled down at her. "And she should *adore* me above all others, and forgive me my peccadilloes."

"Do looks not enter into it?"

"My darling," he said with a soft smile, "you are much more attractive than you consider yourself. You're far too modest."

Irritated that she was so transparent, she said nothing as they parted in the figure of the dance. When they came together again, she changed the subject. "I've been transfixed by all of this turmoil over the smugglers, and the poor excise officer who was killed last night. Did you hear about it?"

"Indeed I did, poor fellow. I hope he didn't have a young family. Still, it's the risk any man takes in the pursuit of his duty."

"I suppose. Women and men have their separate spheres of risk, for women have childbirth, and that is a risky business in itself."

They parted once more in the pattern of the dance, and Anne glanced around as she lightly touched hands with all the gentlemen down the line. Many of the young women, doomed to be without partners—the dearth of young men was monumental in the face of such a large female presence—stood along the wall staring disconsolately toward the door. It was among them that she first saw the stir. Mechanically floating through her part in the country dance, as she advanced down the line toward him, she spotted Darkefell at the top of the steps that descended into the ballroom; he was stunningly handsome in dark blue silk with a froth of exquisite lace at his throat. But also, she was overjoyed to see, he was accompanied by Mr. Osei Boatin, who stood just behind him, his dark face and glinting glasses giving him away, even though he tried to stay in the shadow of his employer.

The mayor of St. Ives rushed up to the marquess and made his obeisance, then with a sweeping gesture, seemed to offer to introduce him to some of the company. As if in pantomime, Anne could see Darkefell decline, and indicate with a negligent wave someone in the offing.

It was Colonel Sir Henry Withington who finally greeted Darkefell properly, and introduced him around the room. The dance ended, and Anne, suffocating in the crowded warmth of the ballroom, was led back to Lolly by St. James, who stayed to chat with them both.

But Anne could not attend. Where was Darkefell? Would he seek her out? And why did she care so much? She searched her heart. She liked him very much, and it pleased her vanity that he seemed to like her, and had followed her all the way to Cornwall.

He was intent on marriage. There was a part of her that shrieked that she was ungrateful. To have her hand sought by such an eligible man: handsome, wealthy, titled, but beyond that, with a heart worth having, brains, and a troubled goodness that she found intriguing. How could she ever do better than that, if marriage was to be her eventual fate anyway? If she tossed him away, she would never find a suitor so perfect, in the eyes of the world. And perhaps for her own heart.

She set those thoughts away, and greeted Pamela, who, her cheeks warm from the dance, approached, followed by her partner, Captain Carleton. They chatted, the topic of their conversation the raid of the previous night, and the fact that an excise officer being killed might lead to the army being called in to aid the customs officer, Mr. Puddicombe.

"Puddicombe's here," Carleton said with a gesture toward a stalwart fellow watching a young girl, who spoke with a half circle of attentive red-coated officers. "That pretty girl he's watching is his daughter. It's said that he's trying to marry her off to one of the officers. Ever since his wife died a few years ago, he's been at loose ends what to do with the chit. He even took her to London, it's rumored. She's *well* known among the officers, I may say," Carleton said with a smirk.

Pamela laughed, lightly. Her voice brittle, she said, "Where would a man like that get the price of a London Season?"

But Anne gazed at the officer in shock. It was impolite to speak thus of a girl, to say the least—his implication had been sly, but quite clear—and she had judged him more of a gentleman than that. Frostily she said, "I think, sir, that concerning a young girl who may have only her reputation of which to be proud, you should keep such gossip and implication to yourself, if you would show the colors of a true gentleman."

His cheeks flamed slightly, and he bowed, silent.

"Ah, you've been caught out, Carleton, for the dog you are," St. James said.

"You're one to speak, St. James," the fellow said. "There is your little shadow, the brewer's daughter."

St. James glanced around, and made eye contact with a young woman who stood with an amply proportioned lady of middle years. He bowed and smiled. The richly gowned lady looked familiar to Anne, and she realized that it was the woman with whom St. James had shared a look in the market. As St. James excused himself, Anne asked Pamela, "Who are they?"

Pam glanced in the direction Anne indicated. "Ah, Miss Julia Lovell, daughter of the brewer."

"But who is the woman with her?"

"Her aunt, the wife of a local baronet, Lady something-or-other. Lady Foakes, I think? She's chaperoning Miss Lovell, I've heard."

St. James had approached and was talking to them both, then he took Miss Lovell's hand and led her away while the older lady watched, a look of ill-disguised longing on her face. But Anne's attention was pulled away by the dark, furious expression on the face of another young man, who stood watching Miss Lovell and St. James as they strolled around the perimeter of the room. "And who is that?" Anne asked, about the young man, but Pamela had gone off somewhere.

Darkefell, weary already of the crush, did his duty, chatting and listening, being introduced to more people than he would ever remember as he followed his host around the room. Colonel Withington was a Yorkshire man, and they were acquainted, though not closely so. He accompanied the colonel to meet his wife and daughter, then more of the officers. But all the while he had watched Anne dance, laugh, flirt, and then saw her go pensive as she watched St. James stroll away with a pretty young girl.

Was she jealous, then, of St. James's regard?

Never one to delve into his own emotions or examine his feelings, he *had* wondered if he was just pursuing Anne because it was a novelty to be so roundly rejected. But no, in the moment when he saw her above, on the escarpment the night before, and with bullets flying, he had felt a visceral fear that she would be hurt. Like it or not, she had a protector and knight in tarnished armor. He cared for her deeply, and jealousy ripped into his gut at the thought that she was, perhaps, in unrequited love with St. James. If she rejected him forever, he would not easily forget her. He'd never met a lady like her, and didn't expect to again.

When he finally was able to excuse himself from the colonel's company, he made his way around the room, hoping to find Anne unaccompanied. The assembly room was built with a gallery above, from which the smoking, card and supper rooms could be reached. The gallery overhung the ballroom, a shadowed alcove along one side, and in the darkness many a young couple would retreat for a few moments of unrestrained courtship. But it puzzled him when he saw Miss Pamela St. James in those shadows, and with Mr. Puddicombe, the local excise officer he had seen in the taproom of the Barbary Ghost Inn.

She slipped away from the fellow in that moment, but the conversation had appeared intimate, secretive. And faintly threatening. Odd. He did not like to think any friend of Anne's was in difficulty.

He found Anne and watched her from a distance. He remembered thinking her plain when first they met, and had criticized her protruding nose, her long face, and lips too full for fashion. But he couldn't see it now. Why? Did not appearance remain the same, no matter what your relationship was? How was it that now, when he looked at her, he saw her sparkling gray eyes, and wanted only to press his lips to hers. Fear of losing her haunted him. The desire to carry her away as his own made him restless and fervently eager. Desire that she alone could satisfy had already invaded his nocturnal brain, leading to indecent dreams, and was beginning to infect his thoughts every time she was near.

He'd gone about everything all wrong, he feared. It seemed that it was his fate, when all around him young ladies were being offered to him for his delectation, that he wanted the one woman who seemed unimpressed by his eminence, and even less by his character. Perhaps that was part of her charm, for what thinking man could bear to be adored every minute of the day? Such empty adoration must eventually give way to dissatisfaction when his faults became apparent, but clear-sighted Anne had no illusions about him. If she could love him, it would be a steadfast, lasting love, that would carry them through their lives and into dotage.

Unable to bear watching Anne from afar, he was just about to go to her when a commotion broke out under the gallery. He looked back, fearing for Miss St. James, but it was her brother who was in trouble. A young fellow had him by the collar of his smart red coat, and was threatening him.

"Stay away from my Julia if you want to live, you oily bastard!"

"John!" a girl cried, pulling at the young man's sleeve. Her tone was agonized, her pretty face twisted in anguish. "Leave the captain alone, *please!*"

The melee was stopped very quickly, as Colonel Withington pulled the young man away from St. James and hauled him off away by the scruff of his neck.

St. James, looking huffy, straightened his jacket as his fellow officers jeered at him.

Darkefell went on and finally, at long last, greeted Anne. She wore a blue-purpley colored gown of some fine fabric, and looked, in his estimation, head and shoulders above every other woman there. She greeted him kindly, but in his reflective frame of mind, he was perhaps quieter than usual. She gave him a puzzled look.

She was already promised for the supper dance, so, rather than be on the outskirts of her circle, only able to watch her while she was escorted by another man, he went to the smoking room, though it was a habit he had never acquired. One did not smoke because one wanted to, he knew, but because it was fashionable and social. Nonetheless, he did not smoke, but merely strolled, thinking.

He lingered along the periphery of the smoky oak-paneled room, watching, listening, wondering how long he should stay in Cornwall. It struck him that his best avenue to success with Anne might be to get to know those around her, and to that end, he strolled toward St. James's group. As little as he liked the captain, he ought to learn all he could about his rival.

Captain Marcus St. James, his fair hair brushed back from his high forehead and heavily powdered, was regaling the other officers with a humorous story about the young man who had attacked him, a certain John Netherton, who was besotted with Miss Julia Lovell, but who could not court her as long as her family hoped St. James might come up to snuff. He ridiculed the pretensions of the young man, who was a simple barrister's apprentice, with no hope of a proper income for a few years to come. Miss Lovell, on the other hand, was the daughter of a well-to-do brewer and had a sizable dowry, which St. James was eyeing with some musing as to whether it was worth the leg-lock to be able to sell his commission and live in leisure.

Then Darkefell heard Anne's name raised, by one of the other officers. He drifted closer.

"She's a *very* wealthy lady," St. James said casually, downing a brandy.

"Long beaked, though, eh, St. James? Plain as ditchwater, compared to the lovely little heiress, Miss Lovell."

"That she is, lad," St. James said expansively, easing back in his chair and puffing on a cigar. "But I think I can get Anne to marry me. Her money's many times the Lovell dowry, and will spend quite prettily. She's a fine woman behind the beakiness and big mouth, though she's awfully opinionated. Plain and plain-spoken!" That garnered a laugh from the drunkest of the officers. "Y'know," St. James continued, "as plain as she is, still, I don't have to see her to give her a poke in the dark and get her with child."

More uproarious laughter greeted his cruel, crude wit.

A red tide of fury surged in Darkefell's brain, and he shoved fellows aside. In one fluid motion he pulled St. James up by the collar and punched him, hard, sending the slimmer man flying across the room onto the floor.

"Hey there!" one of the captain's friends said. "Not right, old man, to catch him unawares!"

"He's aware now," Darkefell said, waiting for St. James to right himself. "Let him come at me." He cracked his bloodstained knuckles and waited, crouched.

"You poncy bastard," St. James roared. He wiped the blood from his nose, removed his jacket, handing it to a friend, then put up his fists. "*Now,* I dare you!"

Deep in his gut Darkefell was gratified. He'd been wanting to do violence to St. James since the moment he met him, and now he had the invitation and ample reason. He launched himself at the other man with no hesitation, feeling flesh beneath his fists.

Anne, in the supper room, frowned at the noise coming from the men's smoking room, next door. "What on earth is that?" she asked, about the roaring voices. Lolly, enjoying a splendid cream tea, with scones, clotted cream, honey, jam and all manners of lovely provender, merely shrugged her shoulders. Captain Carleton was off getting another plate of cakes for Lolly, but Anne couldn't wait to find out, her curiosity piqued at the shouts, the sound of tumbling and the yelling.

She followed the surge of others out the door and along the gallery, pushed and shoved and doing her own share of pushing and shoving, and heard some young girls excitedly chattering about a fight. To her horror, she heard Darkefell's name, and then St. James's! She shouldered her way through and saw the two men wrestling on the floor, but it was soon clear that Darkefell was destined to be the victor. He pummeled St. James ferociously, and blood streamed from the slimmer man's ears and nose, and a cut along his eye was dripping. His powdered hair was limp and hanging in his eyes, the powder soaking up blood and turning his blond hair red.

"Stop it! Stop it, Darkefell, *this minute!*" she shouted, scrambling forward and jerking the collar of his coat; miracle of miracles, the marquess stopped.

He got up off St. James. "Lady Anne," he said, his tone formal, as he settled his shirt down on his brawny shoulders, and pulled his soiled cravat off. "I'm sorry you had to witness this, but—"

"Shut up!" Anne shouted, pushing past him. She knelt by St. James. "Marcus, are you all right?" she cried, then looked up at his military friends, who stood gawking. "Help him, some of you! Help him to the cloak room. And send for a doctor."

She accompanied Marcus as he was carried down the stairs to a cloakroom. Behind her, she could hear some commotion break out, but didn't spare even a look backward. In the cloakroom, as the physician bandaged his wounds and Anne bathed his cuts with a cold cloth, St. James looked up, chagrined.

"I had so hoped to be your hero, my dearest Anne," he said with a crooked grin. "Oh, that hurts even to smile!" He touched his chin, gingerly.

"What happened?"

He shook his head, his pale eyes gleaming in the dim candlelight, but then said, "Well, you will hear of it eventually, and it might as well be from me. I hate to say it but that bloody marquess insulted you, my dear, and I could not bear it."

"What? Darkefell insulted me?" Anne felt a sickness deep in the pit of her stomach.

Marcus looked grim, his face shadowed in pain. "It's true. I shouldn't tell, but I won't have you spoken of that way, not by anyone. He spoke lightly of your . . . your virtue, my dear. He was bragging about having kissed you repeatedly, and insinuated that you had gone, perhaps, further than was strictly to your credit. All that in front of the others!" He reached up and touched her cheek, gently.

Anne choked back a sob. She had been prepared for a misunderstanding, some kind of joke gone wrong, but this? Darkefell, telling what they had done, revealing their most private moments? She had told no one about the kisses they had shared, the intimate moments—no one but Pamela and Mary.

How could Darkefell have done something so dastardly? If it had not been that circumstance, if it had not been about those kisses, she would not have believed Darkefell would say anything. But she saw how it was. In his jealousy over St. James, he had probably wished to stake his claim to her, for kisses, in their world, were as good as promises. "I'm so sorry you had to hear that, and from him!"

"I wouldn't have him speak of you that way, Anne, darling," he said, catching her hand to his chest. "I'd rather die. I punched him, but he's a madman. I'm sorry!"

"No, you did what you could. You defended my honor. I thank you for that. You are a true gentleman."

Seven

Marcus's military friends assured Anne that they would take care of the wounded captain, so Anne left the ball directly, unwilling to give the gossips fuel for their speculation. The evening had turned chilly, and Anne wound her Kashmir shawl around her, reflecting bitterly on the events of the evening. As Sanderson took her arm to hand her up into her carriage, where Lolly and Pamela already waited, Anne heard a voice call her name. Turning, she saw that it was Osei Boatin. She took one step away from the carriage.

He bowed, formally, but his expression, in the flickering lamplight outside of the regimental assembly hall, was one of troubled inquisitiveness. "And so you are leaving, and without a single word for Lord Darkefell, my lady?"

The lamplight flickered on his glasses, and she couldn't see the expression in his dark eyes, but it didn't matter. "I have nothing to say to him."

"My lady, I feel you must have misunderstood the altercation between Captain St. James and Lord Darkefell."

"I hardly think that is likely, Mr. Boatin, as I heard the truth of the quarrel from Captain St. James himself," Anne said, her tone flinty. She liked the secretary, but understood that he had been sent by Darkefell to make up to Anne. There was nothing that could make up for exposing her so, and in such a place!

"What did the captain say? It is possible you misunderstood, or—"

"No, Mr. Boatin, I did *not* misunderstand. You're loyal to your employer; that is admirable and understandable. But I will not stand by silently and accept that he has seen fit to expose our most . . . our intimate . . ." She broke off, shook her head, but then continued: ". . . exposed some of our *conversations* to the world at large. It will not do!"

A breeze heightened the flames from the flambeaux that flanked the assembly hall entrance, and with the light from her carriage lamps, Anne could see Osei's expression, conflicted and somewhat puzzled, but she dismissed it as his uncertainty over what to do to improve his employer's position with her. She stepped up into the carriage and took a seat, but then let down the window and leaned out, saying, "Good evening, Mr. Boatin. I hope you enjoy your stay

74

in Cornwall. But tell the marquess that he may as well go back to Yorkshire, for I don't intend to see him again." She rapped on the side of the carriage, and called, "Go, Sanderson!"

• • •

A sleepless night and a pounding headache left Anne feeling shaky the next morning. She had no appetite — unusual for her — but Lolly cajoled her into consuming a coddled egg and toast. Pamela, Mrs. Quintrell told them, had departed first thing on her way to St. Ives to visit her brother in the infirmary, leaving a message for Anne not to wait for her before deciding her schedule for the day.

Having eaten her egg and toast and drunk a cup of tea, Anne sat, gazing absently out at the cloudy day.

"Anne, dear," Lolly said tentatively, rearranging the flower vase on the table in the gloomy dining room.

Anne turned from the window at her quavering voice. "Yes?"

"May I ask you something?" She nervously smoothed her stomacher, the tatty satin embroidery and drooping ribbon bows the worse for age.

"Of course; what is it?" Anne replied.

"Could we go to St. Wyllow this afternoon and perhaps buy a leg of lamb? Ever since Mrs. Quintrell's awful . . ." She broke off and glanced toward the door that let directly on to the kitchen, then continued in a whisper, sitting down by Anne and leaning toward her, "I shouldn't really say it so bluntly, but that lamb, it was rather tough, and lamb should *never* be tough, my dear." She shook her head sadly, making a sound between her teeth. "I have wanted for some time now to try my hand at a good roast lamb, with a sauce I have been working on."

"You don't need my permission," Anne said, examining Lolly's pale face, lines where she hadn't noticed them before, her cheeks sagging and pouchy. "It's Pamela's home, and she's already given permission to use the kitchen, and you may do whatever you want with your time, you know that. Mother is your employer, not I."

Lolly's cheeks turned pink at Anne's forthright speech. She stared down at her hands, folded in her lap, both thumbs rubbing a piece of limp ribbon. "But . . . well, I do not like to ask, but lamb . . .

a whole leg, my dear, would be costly, and . . ." She drifted off, and then shook her head. "No matter, my dear. I'm sure whatever Mrs. Quintrell wishes to make for dinner will be adequate."

Finally Anne caught what Lolly was asking, in her roundabout way. She leaped to her feet and bent over, kissing her companion's forehead. How had she been so blind, so intolerably self-involved? Her companion was tired, Anne could see that, and worried. It was the cost of the meat that concerned her, for Lolly had no money of her own for such a thing as a whole leg of lamb, and disliked asking for what she insisted on viewing as charity. Her pride was too tender an accessory for one so poor.

"I need something to do or I shall go mad," Anne said. "I shall take Mary and Robbie into the village, order a good lamb quarter, and some other things. Have Mrs. Quintrell prepare a list, and I'll take care of it. If I do it while Pamela is occupied, she cannot worry about my purchases. Though I've already ordered wine and coal, I've been trying to find a way to contribute more to the household budget without anyone squirming, and this is the perfect opportunity."

Lolly sniffed, tears standing in her eyes. "You're so good to me, my dear!"

"Nonsense!" Anne said bracingly, with the uneasy feeling she was exactly the opposite. How long had poor Lolly been trying to work up the courage to ask for a joint of meat? "If you make us a good lamb supper then you are the one doing us a favor. What Mrs. Quintrell does to perfectly good food is a grave offense."

It was a relief to walk to the village with Mary and Robbie, for they both kept up a swift pace, unlike Lolly, who could not, it seemed, walk and talk at the same time. And since she liked to talk a great deal, she walked excruciatingly slowly. Robbie was interested in everything, bright-eyed, inquisitive and fractious, like a puppy. Oddly, Irusan had decided to join them; he did that back home in Kent, when Anne went for a walk, but only seldom in other places. He kept pace alongside his mistress.

Her tasks in town were quickly accomplished. The butcher promised to send the lamb immediately, and Anne summoned Sanderson and informed him of the other items she had purchased. He would deliver them himself to Cliff House, carry them inside and consult with Lolly about their dispersal, as well as speaking to a coal merchant for her. Anne was free, then, to stroll around the village with her thoughts, as Mary went to a local barber for help with a toothache and Robbie stayed with Sanderson to help fetch and carry.

St. Wyllow was quiet, but the dreary emptiness suited Anne, as did the low ceiling of clouds overhead and distant rumbling of thunder, for she was in a meditative mood. Solitude was a rare treat away from Harecross Hall, for a young lady was expected to be accompanied everywhere, as if the world was a dangerous place. At that moment the only danger she was in, she thought, strolling the sloped high street with Irusan by her side, feeling the scudding wind tug at her bonnet, was from the wound to her heart. Darkefell must have wormed his way in deeper than she had expected, because his betrayal ached.

Humiliation was a part of the sting, but more painful was imagining what prompted such behavior. There had been no care for her in revealing their most intimate moments, it was his manner of staking his claim to her. In her dark mood, she wondered why he was intent on marrying her. Perhaps the Darkefell family coffers were emptier than they seemed, and it was her dowry and inheritance that was the attraction. He would not be the first marquess to marry a less than desirable woman for love of his estate.

She walked on, until she realized her faithful feline was no longer at her side. She looked back and saw the big tabby sitting and staring down an alley she had passed a few moments before. She returned to him, glanced down the narrow lane, and saw a female form bustling down the side street; from the back, it looked just like Pamela, with the same dress she had on when she left that morning. But her friend was supposed to be out at St. James's military encampment all day making sure her brother was all right. That couldn't be her, could it?

Curiosity piqued, Anne picked up her skirts and followed, Irusan trotting at her side. Now, where had the woman gone? After a few minutes of walking down alleyways, one not too fragrant, with slops running in a foul stream down the sloping center, she caught sight of Pamela talking intensely to a man. As she approached, becoming alarmed at the aggressive stance of the man—he had Pamela by the wrist—she heard her friend cry, "I can't do it,

Puddicombe . . . please, just leave me alone. Isn't money enough?"

"Pamela, what's wrong?" Anne asked, striding down the alley, swiftly followed by Irusan. "Is this man bothering you?"

"Anne!" Pamela cried as she whirled around, her pale face stained by tears. "No, no, it's just a misunderstanding!"

The man—Anne remembered seeing him at the ball the night before—touched his cap and bowed, having released Pamela's wrist at Anne's outcry. "I beg your pardon, Miss St. James, milady."

He sidled past them and scuttled down the alleyway toward the street, watched by Anne. She turned to her friend. "Pam, if you're having trouble, let me help."

"It's nothing really. Please, just leave it alone," she cried, wiping the tears from her cheek.

"Pam," Anne started, and grabbed her friend's arm.

But Pamela shook her off, and with a pleading expression said, "I'm going home. I have a terrible headache. Please, Anne, just let me go." And she walked away.

Anne, baffled by the whole affair, let her go. "Come along, Irusan. Let's go back to the village green." She decided to sit on a bench on the green while she waited for Mary to come away from the barber's.

Five children were chasing a piglet that had gotten loose from a neighbor's pen, but having more fun in the chase than they would if they caught it quickly. But though she would normally have laughed along with the children, Anne couldn't shake a sense of desolation. A deep sense of loneliness invaded her, even as Irusan butted his head at her leg and stayed close by. She was being ridiculous, she thought, for the only thing that had changed in her life since the day before was the betrayal of Darkefell. As she pondered that, tears welled in her eyes, and she thought perhaps she had begun to care for him in ways other than the purely physical.

She choked back her tears as she noted an elderly man shuffling along the pathway that bisected the village green. Cane in hand, he slowly made his way toward her bench. It wasn't until he almost sat in her lap that she realized he was blind, and didn't see her. She scooted out of the way, and once he sat, said gently, "Good afternoon, sir. This must be your regular seat; I hope you don't mind my sharing it."

He didn't start at all at her voice, but gave a wide, gap-toothed smile that split his seamed face in two. His dark eyes were marbled, Anne could see, the cataracts in both clouding them completely. Blindness darkened his life; his smile despite such a bleak fate humbled her, when she considered her own perfect health, wealth and dismal mood.

"I sit here most fine afternoons," he said gently.

His voice had a faint accent, or perhaps a dimension she felt was familiar somehow, the cadence and inflection ones she had heard before.

"It's cloudy today," he continued, "but fine, still, after a long damp winter. Any day it doesn't rain, in Cornwall, is considered fine, you know."

They chatted for a while, and she learned all about him. Mr. Abraham Goldsmith was from Kent, her part of the world — he heard something in her voice, he said, that told him so — but had moved to St. Wyllow when his blindness progressed until he could see nothing beyond shade and light. His only relative, a widowed niece, Mrs. Rebecca Miller, lived here and cared for him. He held up his walking stick, a fine piece of carving, and said, blind as he was, he still did woodworking, and sold what he could for his living.

Anne examined it. "It's beautiful!" she said, awed. The top knob was a deeply carved tree, intricate and handsome, and below the tree were circles of symbols. "The tree of life," she said softly.

"It is! How did you know?" he asked.

"I'm familiar with the symbolism, sir. Do you make walking sticks for other people?" she asked.

"I do on occasion," he answered.

"My father suffers from gout, but will not admit it hobbles him, and so sits in his library more than is good for him. If he had a stick to lean on, I might encourage him to walk with me over the estate. Will you craft one for me?"

She was rewarded by a wide grin and a softly spoken thanks, and they discussed the design of the stick. Anne wanted to incorporate Irusan, and so picked him up, placing him on the bench between them. The gentleman felt the giant, shaggy tabby, saying yes, the fellow's massive bushy head would make a fine ornament for the top of a walking stick. Anne's father loved the cat, and Irusan returned the sentiment, following the earl from room to room and sitting atop his piles of books long into the night, as her father read and studied. Irusan was to be immortalized on the head of the cane, and his eyes would be inset chunks of emerald. Dignified and haughty, Irusan seemed to take the honor in stride. He crept onto the old gentleman's lap, purring in his deep, throaty way, while he allowed himself to be petted, a rare reaction to a stranger.

As Anne and her new acquaintance talked, about nothing and everything, she felt a deep sense of peace pervade her. Perhaps she had lost Darkefell's friendship—it had never occurred to her before that she valued it at all—but she was still a fortunate lady, with wealth and health and more choice than any young woman she knew. Life progressed. She would forget the marquess in time. He was not worthy of her regard, if he could do such a thing as destroy her reputation without a thought.

• • •

"Johnny, you *will* talk to me. I know what you've been up to," Darkefell said for the third time. He had cornered the lad in the storeroom of the Barbary Ghost Inn, and was determined to get to the bottom of things. After the night before and Anne's incomprehensible message, sent via Osei, he knew he should be trying to find out what was going on with her, but he was angry. Someone had told her lies—he suspected Marcus St. James—but she knew him at least well enough that she should have come to him first, before believing them.

"Milord, I ain't got nothin' to say." The young fellow's hands were shaking as he carved a piece of cork to act as a stopper for a flask of ale.

Darkefell sat on a barrel and examined the young man. At twenty-one, Johnny was stout, strong, with the powerful frame of a fighter. He would be the ideal sort for a smuggler to hire, a fellow who could tote ankers of gin, and fight excise men at the same time.

"Your father is worried, Johnny," he said, switching tactics. "Ever since your mother died, he knows he's not been himself, but he wants you to know he will do anything to help you, if you will just break free of the villains. I won't turn you in if you tell me the truth. I only want the best for you and your father."

The mulish expression melted from his broad face, and Johnny said, "There's nothin' I can do, milord," he said, shrugging hopelessly. "Micklethwaite's got me. If I try to say no, he'll have someone kill me da, he said it! I can't let 'im do it. Poor da don't deserve that. I just gotta keep goin'."

So it was as Quintrell feared; his son had gotten in deep and didn't know how to extricate himself from the situation. "But if you are arrested and transported, that will kill your father more surely than any smuggler's ruffian."

Johnny shrugged and grunted, "Can't do anything now."

"At least let me try to help," the marquess said.

The fellow gave grudging assent.

An hour later, after much questioning, Darkefell left the interview with a little information, all the young man dared tell him about future plans. Micklethwaite's lugger was expected on the next good night in the cove below Pamela St. James's house. Darkefell swore to help the young man get out of the trap he was in, but Johnny did not seem to hold out any hope of deliverance from the marquess's aid.

"Why is the landing scheduled for that exact spot again?" Darkefell finally asked, but Johnny just shrugged. He didn't know, and couldn't guess.

Darkefell walked into St. Wyllow, intent on finding the excise man, Puddicombe, to see if the crown would ever make a deal in exchange for turning over evidence and information. If the boy would provide all he knew in exchange for not being charged, Darkefell could send the lad north for a time, to protect him. But he couldn't protect Joseph Quintrell from possible reprisals from the smuggling captain, if it got out that Johnny had turned traitor. That was a problem the marquess hadn't figured out yet.

Distracted by his thoughts, he heard her voice before he saw her. Anne. He whirled around, searching, and saw her sitting on a bench in the village green with an elderly man, talking. Just . . . talking, as if there was nothing wrong in her world. Anger bit into him.

There was a lot wrong in *his* world, and she was going to know about it as she explained what the hell she meant by the message Osei had been reluctant to share, that Darkefell should just go home, that she didn't intend to see him ever again. He strode through the village green to the bench and was pleased when she appeared apprehensive.

"My lady," he said, greeting her, frostily. "How are you today? How pleasant to see you, after the *charming* message you sent me by Mr. Boatin last night!"

"That is no tone to use with a lady, young fellow," the old man, sitting beside her on the bench, said. "You have no right to speak to her so angrily."

Darkefell, shocked at the temerity of the villager, when most quailed before his displeasure, gaped, speechless.

Irusan leaped down and stalked toward the marquess, while Anne put her hand over the old man's, where it rested on his carved cane. "It's all right, Mr. Goldsmith, this angry fellow is an acquaintance, and harmless for all his bluster." She stood, smoothed down her full skirts, and said gently, to her bench companion, "I will come by your cousin's home and purchase that stick in the pattern we spoke of, if you will make it."

The man put out his hand, and it was then that Darkefell realized he was blind. He took Anne's hand and said, "Thank you, miss. I have so few opportunities to help my cousin, who has been so kind to me. Your purchase will allow me to repay some of her kindness."

"The pleasure is mine, sir, for I seldom know what to purchase for my father. This has been fortuitous. Shalom, chaver." She turned to Darkefell, and with a haughty look, she said, "I will speak with you in private, sir."

She walked a ways, and he followed, with Irusan keeping pace.

"How do you know Hebrew?" he said, examining her with interest.

"I don't know Hebrew. I can stutter a few words. There is a vast difference." She paused, then added, "My uncle's second wife is a Jewess."

"How did your family react to that marriage?"

"My uncle said he married the first time to please his family. He married the second time to *spite* them. I don't think that's completely true, because I can see that he loves Sarah deeply. But my mother—his sister—will not speak to him except through someone else, and to my grandmother, her son is dead." She paused, but a smile tugged at the edge of her mouth. "I spend as much time with them as I can."

He laughed out loud and strolled with her, gazing off down the road, the steep slant toward the sea. He had been furious with Anne just minutes before, but now . . . he shook his head in wonder. Just being in her company calmed him, even when she was the one at whom he was angry. It made no sense at all, and yet it made exquisite sense, summarizing the contradiction that was his relationship with Lady Anne. He glanced over at her, but swiftly looked away. The thought of what she believed about him was too painful to consider, for the moment.

The view down the sloping high street was squarely presented at the end, like a vignette in motion framed by the still life of the surrounding buildings; the ocean was dark gray and choppy, with curling white caps. A sailing ship approached the St. Wyllow dock. He hadn't spent a lot of time in seaside villages, but he could see the charm of the ever-changing scenery of the ocean.

Irusan dashed down an alley after a mouse, cornering it behind a pile of wooden crates. They stopped to wait for the hunter. Calmer than he thought he'd be, he glanced over at his companion and asked, "Anne, what in God's name did you mean by that odd message you sent me through Osei, that I might as well go home, because you wouldn't see me again?"

"I think you know very well what I mean, my lord."

She was back to "my lording" him again. He thought they were long past that. Tamping down the flare of anger he felt, he said, "I think you ought to reiterate, for me, what I am supposed to have done beyond defending your honor?"

She turned to stare at him. "Defending my honor?" she cried. She bundled her shawl around her and crossed her arms over her chest. "By exposing me . . ." She trailed off and glanced around. There were a sufficient number of people out strolling that she stepped closer to him, stared up at him and said in an angry hiss, "Defending my honor? Is that what you call exposing every little detail of what we have done, of the kisses . . . in short, of the intolerable license you have taken with me, and in such a crowded place as that ballroom last night? My reputation, which *does* matter to me, is obliterated among the officers of the Light Dragoons. And all by your licentious mouth, my lord."

He saw then his difficult situation, and what must have occurred. St. James, the cad, had gotten to her first and poured poison in

Anne's ear. He wasn't sure how the fellow knew about the kisses and intimacies they had shared, but it was likely through revelations Anne would naturally have made to her intimate friend, Pamela. Regardless of how it had happened that the captain had such information, Darkefell couldn't tell her the truth of what began the fight without hurting her intolerably. St. James's words had such a cutting cruelty to them that he would never repeat them to her, not even to blacken the name of a man he must regard as a serious threat in his quest for Anne's hand in marriage.

"And for you to have implied that we did more," she continued, "beyond kisses . . . Darkefell, I would not have suspected it of you! I can only think you did it to damage my reputation with St. James, who you must view as a rival."

He shook his head, bewildered. How to extricate himself? For he would not let her dwell in such an illusion. It would not be honorable to let her think him a cur, only to have her go straight into the arms of a man who would marry her for her wealth and make her miserable for the rest of her days. "Anne," he said gently, putting his hands on her shoulders, "do you not know me better than that? Better than to think I would do such a thing as destroy your reputation?"

She gazed up at him and shook her head, a sad expression in her fine gray eyes. "I have known you less than a month. How can I know of what you are capable?"

"You are the most intelligent woman I have ever met, and a good judge of character. I place myself utterly in your hands. What do you *believe* of me, then?" Their eyes locked, and he held her gaze, his fingers clutching her shoulders. He wanted to shake her, to yell, to make her believe him, but those things would only hurt his case, and he restrained himself. He must learn patience.

Finally she sighed. "What am I to think of what St. James said?" she mused. "Why else did he attack you? Did you slight Pamela? Or insult him?"

"I don't really wish to discuss it, Anne."

"No, Darkefell," she said earnestly, "you cannot just refuse to tell me what you said to make him attack you. That's not fair. I've known St. James for these last six years, and never known him to be anything but equable."

Darkefell stared down the street, feeling as storm-tossed as the approaching ship. "What if I told you that he did not attack me, but I him?" he said, gazing at her again, longing to touch her, to kiss her, but knowing that to be impossible in such a public place.

"Well, I suppose I would believe that, for you do have a dangerous temper," she said tartly. "I would still want to know the genesis of your disagreement."

He thrust his chin up in the air. "I will never repeat what he said, but I was, indeed, defending you. What was said by Captain St. James was hurtful, but did not damage your reputation, you can rest assured of that, except in the manner any scurrilous words damage a lady." He gentled his tone and said, as he gazed into her gray eyes, "Anne, believe me; no one beyond your circle knows about the kisses we shared. I would imagine you must have said something to Miss St. James, and she, probably in all innocence, told her brother, and so he used that to excuse his execrable conduct."

"I'm confused!" she cried, turning away and gazing down the long hill toward the dockyard.

"But you acquit me of licentiousness, or of taking your honorable name in vain?" He touched her shoulder and she turned around to face him. "I would never hurt you, Anne."

She took in a long, tremulous breath and let it out. "I think I believe you, Tony," she said softly, meeting his gaze.

Tony; she only used that name when they were intimate. He let out a deep breath. It was enough for that moment, and in a public place, but he vowed he would kiss her again before long. "Let's walk back up along the high street, for you said you were waiting for your maidservant."

"Where is my cat?" she asked, looking up and down the slanted street.

Irusan trotted out of an alley just then, down the street to them, and deposited at Anne's feet a large, gray, dead mouse. He sat and looked up at her with a triumphant expression in his green eyes.

"Why, thank you, King Irusan," she said in jest, at the mythical origin of his name. "Dinner!"

Eight

Darkefell had some kind of errand he needed to perform, so they parted, Anne collected Mary, and they walked back to Cliff House. Mary went upstairs to rest; her tooth had been extracted and she was wan with pain. Lolly volunteered to care for Robbie for the afternoon. She'd given him a task, she said, and he seemed excited about helping "Miss Lolly" with some "secret" project. Pamela was resting, after coming back from St. Wyllow a half hour before Anne had, apparently, and the whole house felt oddly empty.

Mrs. Quintrell, in a huff over Lolly's intent to cook dinner and her steadfast refusal to allow the hired woman to "help," had accused Lolly of insulting her, a ridiculous accusation, and likely a ploy to raise her wages. Lynn, her daughter, who did all of the maid work in the house, left with her mother. Fortunately, she had already emptied the slops, swept the fireplaces, and changed linens.

Alice, a pale, quiet girl who was Pamela's maid, and was completely devoted to her, busied herself with the other chores. Compared to the noisy Quintrells she was ghostly, flitting from room to room but disturbing no one, as she swept and polished.

Anne would bribe the mother and daughter to come back to work the next day, she told Lolly, so that poor woman must not worry. Grateful to be left alone to think, Anne sat with her traveling desk open on the table near the window in her room and began a letter to her father. Talking to Mr. Goldsmith had reminded her how much she missed his gentle good sense and unfailing geniality. But the letter was doomed to be unfinished. She stared out the window over the distant bluff toward the gray, tossing ocean and looming sky.

Who was she to believe concerning the contretemps of the night before? She had known Marcus St. James for six years, and he had been unfailingly kind, gentle, polite, even courtly toward her. She had known Darkefell for just a few weeks, and he had been unfailingly irritating, commanding, dark, incomprehensible and overwhelmingly, *lavishly* seductive. And yet the marquess would have her believe that St. James had said something so hurtful about her that Darkefell had not only taken offense and beaten the captain to a pulp, but he would not repeat it.

And she was inclined to believe him. She tapped her fingernails on the fine mahogany finish of her traveling desk. Was that the power of his kisses, or just the honesty and pain in his eyes?

Knowing she'd not finish the letter that afternoon and looking for a little fresh air and outdoor solace, Anne folded it up, put it away in her desk and retreated to the garden. But what she found there was St. James, sleeping on a padded bench in a protected alcove. His face was swollen and bruised, and one of his eyes looked like it would be shut until healing diminished the swelling. That brought her back to her dilemma; did she believe Darkefell, or St. James?

She sat down on a bench nearby, at an angle with the captain's, and huddled in her warmest shawl. She waited, watching Lolly and Robbie, who were out on the broad open bluff picking something. Irusan had joined them and leaped around after grasshoppers, making the boy laugh and shout. If only she could recapture that lovely peaceful feeling she had experienced on the St. Wyllow green, in Mr. Goldsmith's company.

"Where have *you* been all afternoon?" St. James asked, staring at her out of his one good eye.

His tone was distinctly petulant.

She frowned. "I was in St. Wyllow, shopping. I thought you were at your regimental infirmary, and I thought Pam had gone to visit you for the day. Did she not tell you I saw her in the village?"

"I didn't see her come home. Must have been sleeping. If she went to St. Ives, she had a wasted trip, for they let me go for a few days. Said my face was disreputable, and hurt the regiment's reputation." He stretched and sat up, moving a little stiffly.

He wasn't wearing his uniform, and Anne noted that his clothes, though impeccable as always, looked a little threadbare. She wondered once again whether the brother and sister were still solvent. It was expensive to be a captain in the Light Dragoons, for one was expected to pay for meals on a rotating basis, linen, a washerwoman, cleaning services and a soldier-servant, who would do his valeting. If he was also contributing to the rent on Cliff House, it would stretch his pay beyond the breaking point.

He hadn't spoken of Darkefell, and Anne found that odd. Was he not going to complain? Surely, if he was innocent of any wrongdoing, he should be trying to elicit her sympathy. It was something he did for every slight, real or imagined.

"I spoke to the marquess in St. Wyllow," she said, watching him.

He stiffened momentarily, but then shrugged and gloomily stared off at Lolly and Robbie.

"St. James, tell me the truth," Anne said, leaning forward and staring him in his one good eye, his right. "What really happened between you? He told me that you didn't attack him, but rather *he* was the aggressor."

"Did he say why?"

There was something about the odd alertness of his tension, how his eyes—or rather eye—was hooded, secretive, and something about his tone . . . she suspected that what Darkefell said was the truth. "St. James, I cannot abide people lying to me. I would rather hear any unpalatable truth than be soothed with a lie."

"Women always say that, but they never mean it," he replied, with an attempt at his normal, charming smile. "Ow!" he moaned, and touched his split lip. It oozed a little blood, which welled over the crusted scab.

"I mean it. Take me at my word and tell me the truth. What did you say that caused Darkefell to hit you?"

But he was silent. Finally she cast her gaze toward the sea, and watched a boat bobbing on the horizon, probably a fishing vessel. On it, men would be hauling in nets, casting a worried eye to the sky, hoping they could make it back to harbor before the looming storm hit. All the other lives unknown, she mused, and it would all remain unknown to her. Most of life, most of the *world*, would remain unknown to her.

For the last six months or so she had been feeling a restlessness, a desire to experience new things. If she were a man, she would take up exploring, go to sea, or make a new life in Canada. To do any of that as a woman would require a complete break from everyone and everything she loved, for a woman who did those things would be shunned by society, her reputation irrevocably ruined, while a man would be celebrated for a similar boldness.

Something bright glittered near the horizon, on the boat. "St. James, did you see that?" she asked, putting one hand up to shade her eyes. Even though it was not sunny, the bright daylight made it hard to see so far. "There it is again!"

"What?"

"Like . . . like a mirror, or something . . . shining on the horizon, near or on that boat."

"Probably someone holding up a spyglass, watching the weather," he said negligently. "I'm going in for a nap. Your friend has given me enough bruises and cuts that I shall need to heal for several days. I'll see you at dinner."

· · ·

Lolly was the only bright spot at the dining table. The dinner was wonderful; roast lamb with wild thyme, a salad of baby greens—sorrel, salad burnet, cress and dandelion—tender young carrots and new potatoes. The salad was Lolly and Robbie's surprise, the greens wild ones she had identified on the open bluff and the bitter watercress from a stream a half mile away.

However, Pamela had no appetite and St. James's mouth hurt too much for him to eat properly. Anne, though, was surprised, given how upsetting a day it had been, how much she enjoyed the food. "Lolly, dear, you are a genius," she said.

"I'm only sorry Mrs. Quintrell was so . . . that she left so hastily. I should visit her, apologize . . ." She drifted off and stared down at her plate. Her lined face was drawn down in a worried frown.

"Nonsense. I'll take care of it," Anne replied, easily. "That is, if you do not mind me interfering, Pamela?"

Her friend, sunk in her own thoughts, just nodded as she picked at her salad. The rest of the meal was consumed—or not consumed by most—in silence.

After dinner, Anne sought Pamela out in her sitting room, reclined on a brocade sofa by the window.

"Pam, I've been a wretched friend so far," she said, sitting on a stool near her. She examined her friend's face in the dim lamplight, but her expression was blank. "I'll not let that go any further. Something is deeply worrying you. You told me you were going to see St. James today, but you were really in St. Wyllow with that dreadful man, that Puddicombe fellow. What was that about? Why were you talking to him? Is there anything I can do? Are . . ." She trailed off, not sure how to broach the subject. "Are you in *any* kind of difficulty?"

Pamela met her gaze and smiled, weakly. "I'm fine, my dear. I told you, it was just a misunderstanding! Please don't let anything worry you."

Anne examined her face. Though Pamela St. James was only a few years her senior, already the first signs of age were upon her. Lines bracketed her mouth and creased her forehead, and as lovely as her eyes were, they held an indefinable air of sadness. A couple of years before, Pamela had written Anne that she was to be married, but the fellow tragically died, and since then she did not seem to have recovered from the sorrow. She had declined into ill health, and now was prematurely aging.

Pamela closed her eyes and leaned her head back.

Anne took that as a hint. "I'll let you rest for now. But please, think about talking to me. If you are in any kind of difficulty, I want to help."

Anne quietly exited the room. Here she was with two of her best friends, and she had not told either of them about her and Darkefell's discovery yet, along the cliff. However, with them both under the weather, now was not the time. There were clearly other priorities. Tomorrow, if St. James was feeling better, she would make him accompany her to have a look at the Barbary pirate costume and rigging off their cliff. It was unthinkable that someone was using their property to launch such a venture, for Anne suspected that the pirate ghost was a ruse to distract the excise officers and delay them from their capture of the smugglers.

The long, emotional day had taken its toll, though, and as evening crept in upon them and a steady wind buffeted the ancient house, she felt tired and out of sorts. An hour to finish her letter to her father, and then she'd go to bed.

• • •

Darkefell and Osei watched from the marquess's open window. A thin yellow lamplight chased away the darkest of shadows in the stable yard and courtyard below them. The marquess, alert and watchful, heard steps on the flagstone path below, behind the inn, a path he knew led along the cliffs toward the cut between Barbary Ghost Inn property and that of Cliff House.

"There," Osei said, pointing to a figure slipping along the path, keeping to the shadows.

"That'll be Johnny," the marquess said. "And that means there is more of the shipment coming ashore. I suspected the debacle of the other night meant not everything was unloaded." Darkefell pushed himself out of his chair and launched toward the door, with his secretary behind him.

"No!" Darkefell said, turning and putting out one staying hand. "Osei, stay here. If I end up in trouble, or arrested by accident as one of the smugglers, I need you free to help me."

He looked disappointed, and Darkefell almost laughed at his scholarly secretary appearing so downhearted and pensive, at missing the adventures of the night. "Don't worry," the marquess said, clapping the younger man on the shoulder. "I have a feeling you will see some action before we are done dismantling this smuggling gang and getting Johnny out of trouble."

• • •

After finishing a long, detailed letter to her father, Anne had a burst of energy. There would only be a few more nights of low tide occurring at the right time, Anne thought, rummaging in her wardrobe for her darkest cloak. After the last botched landing, she had to assume the smugglers would continue to try to unload the cargo, and if they were counting on their pirate ghost to distract, then they would use the cove below Cliff House again.

And she was going to be there. How many times had she crept from Ivy Lodge, the dower house of Darkefell's estate in Yorkshire, as she sought an answer to the werewolf mystery, and the deaths of three young women? One had been solved, certainly—Hiram Grover, a local landowner with a grudge against the Darkefell family, was the killer—but the other two, to her thinking, were still mysteries. An accident and suicide explained the other two young ladies' deaths, Darkefell had said, but she was still not sure. And Hiram Grover's dead body still not found! That, though, was not her mystery to solve. This was.

Anne slipped from the house completely alone, with just the faint glimmer of a lamp to guide her steps, for she was not going to disturb Mary for such a trifling walk, not when the maid was still suffering pain from her pulled tooth. Anne was just going to the cliff at the end of the bluff to observe, not a dangerous operation. If the Barbary Ghost showed up, then all the better, so she could, now that she had seen the rigging, judge for herself who it was and how they did it. She had no intention of interfering with the smuggling, nor of being seen by anyone.

She did wonder, briefly, if she had become too attached to the thrill of stealing about in the dark, and making discoveries. It was one of the terribly unladylike characteristics for which her mother and grandmother would surely condemn her, if they only knew. She sent them a smirking grin in her mind; *let* them condemn her. She would never go back to living as they thought appropriate.

At the cliff's edge she concealed herself behind a barricade of brush that she had composed earlier in the day, when no one was watching, and extinguished her lantern. The night was quiet but for the hushed wash of waves on the beach. It was so dark only the faintest differentiations told her where the tree was on the precipice.

But her ears told her when someone else approached, swishing through the lush grass. She could faintly see the outline of a man, moving slowly. He cautiously felt his way along the cliff, until he was well beyond the tree where the rigging was mounted, then he appeared to kneel, and Anne could hear a faint, rhythmic scrape of sound; it seemed, to her, that he was pulling something up from the cliff with a rope.

Excitement built in her stomach. Tonight she would learn the secret; who was the ghost, and how did he perform his magic?

Her hearing, sharpened by the darkness, picked up the faint scrape of a flint being struck, and a tiny pinpoint of light sparked, then leaped into a flame; it just as quickly disappeared, except for a faint halo of light. An enclosed lamp, perhaps?

In rapid succession she translated sounds; the huff of a man working hard, the squeak of a pulley, the creak of a tree branch bearing weight. She came out of her blind and crept forward, toward the tree, then to the cliff edge. She peeked over, and there was her

Barbary Ghost, but to her astonishment, since the ghost did not have his beard affixed yet, she recognized him even from above.

"St. James!" she cried out.

Marcus St. James looked up at her and by the light of his veiled lamp, she saw the almost closed eye, and the bruises and cut lip.

"Anne," he muttered. "What the devil are you doing out here?"

"So *you* are the Barbary Ghost! I should have known." She fell back, holding her sides and laughing. She clapped her hand over her mouth, intent on staying silent.

Over the lip of the cliff rose St. James, pulling on his rope and pulley mechanism. He grasped the cliff edge with one hand and held up the lantern with the other, steadying himself where he dangled. "Don't give me away, Anne, please!"

"I wouldn't dream of it," she said, delighted to see that the scoundrel was her ghost.

"Do you swear it?" he begged. "That reflection you saw this afternoon was a signal to do my act tonight. I must move into place and be ready to give those idiot excise men the fight of their lives." With a wicked grin, warped by his swollen chin, he added, "I have a new explosive I've worked on. Stole some powder from the regiment battery. It ought to scare the religion into those cowards."

She sobered and crept closer to him along the grassy cliff edge. "St. James," she muttered, "if you are caught it could mean hanging, to be aiding the smugglers as you do."

"I know," he said. "But it is only for a time or two more."

"Are you getting paid?" she whispered.

"Of course. The money is for Pamela," he said. "I can't let the dear girl exist in penury, when it's all my fault."

"What do you mean, *your fault*," Anne asked, but he shook his head and swung away from the cliff, sticking his beard on haphazardly. She assumed he was reacting to some signal from below, for just then a rowboat splashed to shore, and shadowy figures set to work unloading and moving the goods.

• • •

Darkefell hung back in the shadows, watching Johnny go to work with the others, transferring ankers of gin or rum from the deep hull of a rowboat up the beach to a waiting dray. There was one fellow, a smaller man, who appeared to be in charge, and he directed them all with the wave of his cutlass and gruffly shouted instructions. A second rowboat slid into shore, and he waved some waiting men to pull it higher, and start unloading.

Had the excise men heard of this night's landing? Would they be raided?

And then it began. The hoot of an owl, a shout, and men came rushing down the cut, and this time, though they looked up and saw the Barbary pirate go into his elaborate act, fear of the "ghost" did nothing to deter the revenue men. But the smuggling gang leader valiantly directed his "army" just as well as any military man. He sent the strongest, stoutest fellows into pitched battle, and they wielded their weapons, mostly just cudgels and poles.

And Johnny Quintrell was in the middle of it all! No cudgel would protect him from an excise officer's musket. Darkefell would not let poor Joseph lose his only consolation in life, his son, not if he could do a single thing about it!

Shouts, and turmoil, guns flashing, explosions rocketing around them from the Barbary Ghost, presumably, for that specter was clearly visible at times, and at others concealed by smoke and bursts of fire, a cannon shot from a lugger out at sea: it all contributed to the tumult on the wet sand. Darkefell darted through the crowd, sliding on seaweed, choking on smoke from the gunpowder, buffeted and bashed by the men scrambling with the ankers over their shoulders. The huge draft horse whinnied and reared at the commotion, the dray toppling sideways in the gloom. A man cried out in pain, perhaps hit by a musket ball or the slashing hooves of the terrified beast. Every time the flash of gunpowder lit the air, Darkefell used the light to find his way.

And there was Johnny, standing like a perfect target among the seething crowd, his expression one of petrified indecision. Darkefell dashed to him and seized him, but the boy struggled and cried out.

"Shut up," Darkefell growled in his ear, "and come with me to safety. I'll not let you die, Johnny; I'm your friend, whether you want one or not."

"Milord," the young fellow whispered. "What's a'goin' on? We was supposed to be safe tonight, perfectly safe. An' . . . an' I saw some feller—I think it were Mr. Puddicombe up on the rise—an' he was shootin' at the *ghost*. Why was he shootin' at the ghost? I don't understand."

"Never mind any of that," grunted Darkefell. "Let's get you out of here!"

After that the boy didn't struggle and followed eagerly enough, shedding the ankers of liquid strapped to his bulky shoulders. Not willing to implicate the inhabitants of Cliff House, Darkefell pulled the younger man away, up the cut, in the shadowed lip of the cliff, and away from the St. James house, but it plagued him; how did whoever performed the Barbary Ghost stunt manage to do so from so close to the home, unless . . . was it with the knowledge of the owners, or even Pamela, who rented the house? Was she receiving money to turn a blind eye? It was something he would need to take up with Anne the next day, for he would not allow her to stay in a place of such danger.

• • •

Anne scurried back from the cliff edge as the firefight broke out. St. James was an experienced military man, and could look after himself, but she had to admit she was frightened. She hoped that St. James, seeing it as a losing battle, would abandon his post. As she retreated, she spotted St. James, without his pirate beard and part of his costume, hunched over and running, tripping and stumbling, toward her.

"Get back to the house and go upstairs," he grunted, gasping for breath. "Things have gone badly. Not even my ghost frightened the excise men away this time."

"What are you going to do?" she asked.

"I'm coming in, in a few minutes; I just want to get . . . to be sure no one is hurt."

She guessed that he must know some of the participants, and honored his care for his comrades. "All right," she said. She had no wish to get a musket ball in her shoulder or any other place, so she went in. She stayed awake a long time, but when she heard someone creeping down the hall and went to see who it was, thinking it was St. James, it was just Pamela.

"What are you doing up, Pam?" Anne asked.

"I woke up; had a bad dream, I think," she said, one shaky hand to her forehead.

"You look feverish," Anne said, putting one hand to Pam's forehead and feeling it damp with perspiration.

"I'm not feeling well. Something awoke me and I couldn't get back to sleep," she said. "I was just going down to the kitchen to get a glass of buttermilk from the larder to settle my stomach."

"Let me get it for you." Anne was relieved when Pamela agreed with no demur. It must have been the clash below on the beach that awoke her, but Anne did not want Pamela to catch her brother coming in, for she wasn't completely sure Pam knew about St. James's nocturnal occupation.

Anne took her friend the buttermilk, then returned to her own room, but even though she wanted to see St. James when he came in, she was exhausted and couldn't keep her eyes open. She fell fast asleep and didn't hear another thing.

Nine

Darkefell had successfully returned to the Barbary Ghost Inn with Johnny Quintrell, and sent him to bed, telling him they'd talk in the morning. Osei, who was, of course, awake and waiting in one of their cramped pair of rooms, heard the whole story.

"So the Barbary Ghost made an appearance," Osei said as he knelt to help Darkefell off with his boots.

The marquess leaned back on his elbows on the bed, while his secretary pulled on the stubborn footwear. "I begin to wonder how this can happen without the knowledge of Miss Pamela St. James, at the very least."

"You speculate that the lady may receive some recompense for turning a blind eye to the ghostly 'haunting'?"

"Perhaps," Darkefell answered, grimly, removing his jacket and pulling his shirt off over his head. He handed the apparel to Osei and scratched his bare chest, then smoothed the wiry chest hair down. "Or perhaps the brother and sister are even more deeply involved."

"From what I have heard, in the talk around this inn, nearly everyone in these parts is involved in some way with the smugglers. Farmers will loan horses or equipment, drays, wagons, for if they do not, they will find their barns vandalized or their livestock dead."

"And many more do it for the goods they may receive as payment," Darkefell speculated. "What else have you heard? And why do they speak so openly in front of you, when they hush the moment I enter a room?"

The younger man smiled, slyly, an unusual expression for him, solemn as he usually was. "These people at the inn *may* have the impression that I, a simple savage, do not understand them, or perhaps that my faculties are not . . . acute."

Darkefell grinned and pulled off his breeches, tossing them to his secretary. "You, my friend, are a trickster, a Loki, a mountebank!"

"I take exception to that characterization, my lord," Osei said, returning to his customary gravity, and presenting his employer with a nightshirt. "I have had to become many things since coming to this country, some of them not natural to me, but I am not responsible if people make assumptions without reference to reality."

"The person responsible for the Barbary Ghost would agree with you, for once you see beyond the frightening appearance, it really is just a magician's trickery you witness. What else have you heard?"

Osei sat, while Darkefell performed his evening ablutions, and talked. The suspected smuggler was a local man, Micklethwaite, and he owned not one, but two ships, a lugger and a cutter. He kept them both busy and professed to be a legitimate importer of goods from the Low Countries: cheese, lace, fabric, chocolate, coffee and other goods, upon which he paid the excise. No tampering with goods, either by using false-bottomed barrels or dried-out tobacco, had tainted his day-to-day performance as a shipper.

Some shippers attempted to avoid paying excise taxes by using specially constructed barrels with false bottoms; while the top contents were merely water for sailors, sections at the side were illegally shipped brandy. Or they dried the tobacco they carried, which meant that the tax they paid was on a lighter weight. When the tobacco was sold, though, it was rehydrated to give a higher weight. It was a game with ever-changing rules. However, cheating the taxation officers with such ruses was a different and less dangerous game than evading tax by smuggling goods.

So Micklethwaite had avoided any taint of cheating so far, but it was becoming more widely suspected that he smuggled. He transported goods from Ireland with his smaller ship, it was claimed, and occasionally hired out his services to ferry furnishings or other items, but there was a lot of time between legitimate shipments. That was when he apparently plied his smuggling trade, accepting, it was suspected, loads of goods from larger Dutch and French ships, which he would then sell or trade to English buyers. He was either, Osei said, extraordinarily lucky in never being caught, despite gossip about his role in the trade, or he was paying the right people to turn a blind eye.

"Including the local excise officer, Puddicombe? I've heard the man complaining loudly that the crown has not seen fit to give him aid from the Light Dragoons at St. Ives, those gallants so ably represented by that lot at the regimental assembly the other night."

"However," Osei said, leaning forward, lamplight gleaming in his spectacles, "Mr. Puddicombe was offered some men by the last colonel of the Light Dragoons, but he took offense, saying he and his local fellows could do the job better than any vain captain."

"Interesting." Darkefell then told Osei about his evening's adventures and his rescue of young Johnny Quintrell. "I'll speak to him in the morning and try to get him to see it would be better to help the crown than end up in a pitched battle with the excise men, and have his life's blood drain onto the sand. As much as we suspected Puddicombe of complicity in the free trade, I would not guess that from last night. Unless I am mistaken, that represented a new fervor in the revenue men's attempts to shut down the St. Wyllow smuggling gang. Why now? Why is he trying so hard to catch them now, when at least two other times he and his men were forced back by nothing more than smoke and gunpowder?"

"That, indeed, is the question, my lord."

• • •

Mary, appearing to feel much better, awoke Anne the next morning to tell her that Mrs. Quintrell had come back with no prompting, and so breakfast was ready. As Anne descended the creaky stairs, the scents of laundry and soup and beeswax polish indicated that cleaning and food preparation were indeed going on. Pamela was already in the dining room, but not eating. She stood at a window and gazed out.

"How are you this morning?" Anne asked, going to her friend.

Pam merely shrugged. Anne gently brushed away a trace of cobweb clinging to her friend's hair. Lynn Quintrell's housemaid duties were certainly not performed with any degree of enthusiasm or ability! The home was getting dirtier by the day. Even though she had filled in for the absent Lynn Quintrell the day before, Pamela's lady's maid, Alice, a local girl, didn't seem to do her job properly either, for Anne rarely saw her.

Mary claimed the young maid didn't seem to know the proper way to do anything, apart from the rudiments of hairstyling. Sewing, millinery, spot removal: all were mysteries to Alice. But then, Pamela likely could not afford better on her limited income. Incompetent help was better than no help at all. "Are you recovered from your poor health yesterday?" Anne asked, watching Pamela.

"I'm fine, really, Anne," she said with a slight smile on her perfect bow lips.

Anne took some of the eggs that sat on a sideboard, but looked askance at the other items, some of them unidentifiable blackish lumps. Mrs. Quintrell might be back, but she was in no good mood, if the state of her cooking was any evidence. "Where is St. James?"

"I haven't seen him this morning; I suppose he's gone back to his regiment," Pam said with a frown.

Anne felt a momentary qualm. Perhaps he had gone back to his regiment early, but why? The easiest way to find out would be to see if his horse was still in the small stable just beyond the house and outbuildings. She could hardly eat breakfast, she was so anxious. Since Pamela employed no groom and kept no carriage, the stable was usually empty. St. James looked after his own horse when he was there, feeding and grooming Pilot, as the gelding was named.

She slipped from the house out the front door, followed the crushed stone path around it to the stable, a rickety, leaning building — the stable was in worse shape than the other out-buildings — and tried the door. It was unlocked. She pushed it open, the creak of the hinges shuddering through her ears, and found what she did not want to find. Pilot huffed and stamped, and anxiously looked over the low stall wall at her in the gloom, rolling his eyes.

Anne swallowed hard, her stomach churning. This did not necessarily mean a thing, she thought. Not a thing! St. James was not the most responsible of fellows, and he may have gone for a walk without feeding his horse or tending him. She returned to the house and sent Robbie down to the stable to do what was necessary for the poor animal, feeding, watering, grooming and turning him out into the tiny enclosure next to the stable. The boy was excited about being given such an important chore. "Just be careful of his hooves, Robbie," Anne warned. "He's a well-trained fellow, but a fidgety boy might unnerve him."

She retreated to her room to ready herself for the day, and since she had no secrets from Mary, told her everything that had occurred the night before.

"Fancy the captain being the ghost all along!" the maid marveled, coiling Anne's long hair into an acceptable style for day. "Never would I have thought of it!"

"But where is he now?" She twisted her head, looking at her reflection in the wavery glass of the mirror, and nodded. When one was not a beauty, it simplified things; tidiness and economy of time were the two guiding principles of her daily regimen. "That'll do," she said about the style. "At least you've tamed it. In this dampness, it wants to frizz and puff out into a cloud of hair." She rose and sighed. "Marcus didn't sleep in his room, Mary, I checked on my way back up. Lynn Quintrell is still helping her mother in the kitchen, doing dishes and pans, I suppose, from Lolly's meal last night, so she's not been upstairs to make up the beds, and his has not been disturbed." Anne paced and then stopped to gaze out the window toward the cliff. "He was going back to make sure the others were safe, I think. But *what* others? Who, in particular, was he concerned about?"

"I dinna know, milady. But the captain can take care o' himself, I'm sure."

"Something was different last night from what I witnessed before. Seeing the Barbary Ghost impeded the excise officers little. They came better prepared for a fight. I need to find out what has gone on in past months. I hope to heaven St. James is just out walking after a sleepless night."

But waiting patiently for something to happen, or for Marcus to show up, or for the tide to retreat so she could go down to the water, was not in her character. Instead, she thought of easing her curiosity on some other points. For weeks, she had heard strange noises at night, some from the attic, some from the lower levels of the house. The attic, she had discovered early, was just a storage spot, and the noises must have been from rats or other small animals sheltering from the wind or rain. Perhaps the noises from the cellar were animals too, but she did wonder how large an animal would make a noise in the cellar loud enough to drift all the way up to her second-floor room.

She was going to find out if there was any way into the house through the cellar that did not involve the main level of the house, she decided. And perhaps Marcus was down there, working on one of his mechanical toys, projects she had known to consume hours of his time in years gone by, without him being aware that people were waiting for him.

She hoped that was the solution, as she slipped through the kitchen while Mrs. Quintrell was in the crude cold pantry, and found the basement steps on the other side of a plank door. She quietly pulled the cellar door closed behind her, and crept down the stairs, appreciating the weak light from the candle she had thought to bring.

The basement was a warren of room after room after room, and it took her a few minutes to figure out where she was. The foundation was old stone and crumbling in some spots, dirt tumbling in through cracks. She walked through the whole string of rooms immediately one after the other and saw nothing but crates, barrels, and shelves of jarred preserves. Cobwebs stuck to her hair and clung to her dress as she poked her nose into corners.

But eventually she found a door she had not yet opened. Perhaps it led to the outside.

She held up her candle and examined the latch. It was shiny, without the patina of age or any rust from the damp sea air, but it had no padlock. She lifted the latch and pushed open the door; no creak or whine gave away its movement. Holding the candle up, she stepped into the room, some kind of work space.

It was, unlike the rest of the dusty stone-foundation cellar, immaculately tidy. A bench lined one wall, and under it were kegs. Anne frowned. This space had the definite mark of St. James; he was much neater in his habits and more organized than his sister. He had for years amused himself with clockwork automatons, card tricks and magician's illusions (a fact that should have made her twig to the identity of the Barbary Ghost) as well as the more serious branches of scientific study, and wherever they lived, he had a workshop. Above the bench were shelves with tools neatly stowed and a row of small pottery globes with neat cork stoppers, as well as small wooden casks labeled "potassium nitrate" and various other elements in Marcus's neat script.

She set the candle on a nearby barrel and looked around, wondering why the workshop was in a secret part of the house. In the past he had demanded large windows and bright light for his work space. Then she glanced down at the keg; printed on it in stenciled letters was the word "gunpowder." Hastily, she snatched her candle up and backed away. So *that* was why he had this hidden;

this room was the center of his Barbary Ghost fireworks illusions.

She exited the room and latched the door, then ascended the stairs, for there was nothing else to see in the cellar. Marcus was still not back, and in fact never did return.

Pamela didn't even try to conceal her agitation. Anne decided to share what she knew with her friend, and was relieved to find that at least Pamela was aware her brother was the Barbary Ghost. "How long have you known?" she asked her friend, as they sat on the terrace. They had decided to walk down to the beach as soon as they judged the tide would have rolled out, to see if there would be any reminders of the melee the night before, or any clue as to where St. James had gone.

"I've known all along. St. Ives is only three miles from here, and he was able to slip out at night from his regimental billet easily. You know what St. James is like," Pamela said with a faint attempt at a smile. "He loves excitement, and he's always dabbled in hocus pocus. The Barbary Ghost was his idea, and I think he would have done it even if Captain Micklethwaite had not approached him."

"Micklethwaite?"

"He . . . he's apparently a ship captain who uses his vessels for the free trade, as those fellows call it."

They were silent for a while, but finally Pamela stood and paced to the edge of the terrace, looking out to sea. She turned back to Anne, wringing her hands together. "I can't wait any longer; I want to look down on the beach, just see what went on, if there is any sign of what he has gotten up to. Perhaps Marcus got caught in his cave by the tide. He cannot swim at all, you know, and has a dreadful fear of the water."

Anne felt sure that the small crevice she had found, though above the tidewater, would not be a viable place to spend a night. It wasn't deep enough, nor secret enough. But she could not take away her friend's suggestions. As for herself, she feared that St. James had been arrested the night before. If so, they would hear about him soon; she didn't want to imagine what would happen to him after that. For an officer in the army to take part in such illegal activity could be possibly treasonous, for all she knew of the law. She did know that treason was a hanging offense.

Though Robbie insisted on accompanying Anne and Pamela

down to the beach, Anne sent Mary to St. Wyllow for Sanderson. She wasn't quite sure why, but she wanted her sturdy driver at Cliff House, if only to take them to St. Ives to see if St. James had, for some odd reason, decided to walk back to his regiment.

Or in case he had been arrested and they had him in a military jail.

They clambered awkwardly down the cut toward the beach, dresses and shawls making the climb difficult. Pamela, not as energetic as Anne, needed to pause after the climb and sat on a rocky outcropping for a long moment. The tide had receded, leaving behind, on the wet sand, a line of seaweed and detritus. Anne could see that the smugglers had not had the opportunity to retrieve their missing booty, as ankers and half ankers and wooden crates littered the beach, jumbled by the tide.

Pamela recovered, and she and Anne walked toward the slice of shore below Cliff House to try to see up to the crevice in the rock, but once there it was evident that whatever had happened the night before, St. James was not there now. "We may as well go back to the house," Pamela said, her tone listless.

Anne shook her head. "You can go ahead, but I want to look around a little more."

"I'll wait for you, then," she said with a sigh.

Anne eyed her with a worried frown; Pamela did not seem to be herself lately, or had she been this way for longer than Anne had bothered to notice? Her high spirits were more occasional now than they had been, but was that just a natural mellowing with time? Anne turned back and scanned the rock wall, and then gazed down the beach. A jot of color beyond a rock caught her eye; perhaps a bolt of smuggled cloth, or a flag, or some such thing, flapping in the wind?

Robbie, his pockets full of shells, bounced after her, but as Anne began to clamber over the rocky outcropping near the base of the cliff she put up one hand; some foreknowledge quivered within her at what she would see, and she was not going to have that little boy scarred by the sight, if it should prove to be unfortunate. "Robbie," she said, her voice trembling, as she turned and looked back at him. "Go back to Miss Pamela, if you would."

"But—"

"Robbie, now!" She took in a long shaky breath and turned her gaze back to the flapping piece of cloth.

He retreated and she put out one hand to steady herself, then climbed over the rock. She gasped in horror, a sick sound gurgling in her throat. St. James's dead eyes, crusted with sand and seaweed, stared at her, his flesh white and pasty, wrinkled from saturation from the tide. But he did not drown; oh, no . . . his throat had been cruelly cut, and his flesh hung open, the tidewater having scrubbed him clean, leaving behind a pale, waterlogged appearance, with more seaweed tangled in his hair and across the ferocious wound.

"Oh!" she cried, then clamped a hand over her mouth. She glanced back, her vision blurred by tears. Pamela and Robbie were down at the water's edge, the woman watching while the boy used a piece of plank to dig in the sand. Anne swiftly clambered back over the rock intent on one thing: She would *make* Pamela go back up to Cliff House, where she would tell her what had happened to her beloved older brother.

But things rarely work out as expected. When Anne spotted Darkefell striding purposefully down the beach toward her she ran to him and threw herself into his arms.

"Anne, Anne, what is it?" he asked, holding her close.

For one long moment she surrendered to the delicious warmth of his arms, putting her head against his chest. His steadily thudding heart, racing from the climb down, his warmth, the growing familiarity of his scent: it all comforted her, and the tears came.

"Tony, oh, Tony!" she groaned, looking up at him. "It's St. James; he's dead, his throat slashed! He's been *murdered*!" She pushed away from him, staggered sideways, and lost her breakfast on the wet sand.

Ten

Anne quickly recovered and pointed out where the captain's body was, indicated by a piece of fluttering cloth behind a rocky outcropping. She then went directly to her friend, murmuring to Darkefell that she must break the tragic news to the dead captain's sister. He watched the pantomime of horror; Pamela shrieked in dismay, putting out her hands as if to push away the truth, then dissolved in tears, covering her face, her sobs carried away on the ocean breeze.

Hugging her friend in a close embrace, Anne rocked Miss St. James and patted her back while the young lad, Robbie, stood silently watching. As tender as Anne's sensibilities clearly were, Darkefell reflected, her strength was asserted by her immediate recovery, after her brief illness, and her determination to offer her friend the comfort and support she needed in this awful moment. Though some would call Anne's strength unwomanly, he saw it differently. No matter what life threw at her, she could accept it or overcome it. It seemed to him that women often had that role, of forbearance and fortitude. To call such inner fortitude unfeminine was to dismiss what ladies had to bear their whole lives long in childbirth, marriage and mourning.

But a grim task awaited him. Darkefell turned away from the scene of such sorrow, and bent down to examine St. James's body. The captain had been murdered, certainly, as Anne had said, for his throat was slit with great precision and expertise, the flaps of waterlogged skin pallid and horrible. Whomever had killed him had murdered before in the same way, for the cut was appallingly precise, one deadly slash with a saber or cutlass. St. James had certainly died *before* he was in the water, judging by how the wound was scoured clean, and from the amount of ocean sand imbedded in it. If not for the tangle of rocks at the base of the cliff, his body may have been swept out to sea. Perhaps that's what his murderer expected to happen.

The captain was dressed in just breeches and a shirt, pink-stained from blood, but it was impossible to tell if that was what he had been wearing when he died. Crouching by the body, the marquess glanced up and around, over to Anne, who held the weeping Pamela in her arms, still anxiously watched by young Robbie.

What should he do about the body and the ladies? He was grateful that he was there, and able to spare Miss Pamela some grief, perhaps, though there would be no assuaging ultimately the terrible anguish she must still suffer. As he tried to decide how to convey St. James's body up to Cliff House, he reflected that he must remember to thank Anne's clever maid, Mary, who had paused at the inn on her way into the village, to ask that he go to her mistress. Her Scottish blood was sure something was wrong, she said, and how right she was. He would not have wanted Anne to have to handle this on her own, even though he was sure she could have.

His glance slewed up to the cut in time to see Sanderson, Anne's bulky driver, striding toward the frozen tableau. Darkefell motioned for him to come over, and the man obeyed instantly. "There has been a tragedy here," the marquess said, standing, "and I wish to avoid upsetting the ladies by confronting them with the corpse of Captain St. James. Carry him up to Cliff House, concealing his state from Miss Pamela St. James as much as possible."

He paused and looked down at the wide, staring eyes, then bent over and closed them as much as he could. "I don't want her to see the wound, if it can be avoided," he muttered. "Explain to the housekeeper, or whoever is there, and do not let them deter you from taking the body up to a spare room, or his own chamber, if you can establish which it is."

Sanderson grunted his assent, bending to his somber task, and Darkefell clambered over the rocky outcropping and slid across the wet sand to the pair of women, shielding their view of the driver's occupation as much as he could, but he was impressed, as always, by Anne's stoic resolve. She held her friend's head against her shoulder and spoke soothing words, but the despair in her eyes as she looked up at Darkefell made him wish he could be *her* comforter.

He put one hand on her shoulder, and spoke quietly, being as matter-of-fact as he could. "Sanderson is taking Captain St. James up to the house. Who is the magistrate for this parish?"

"Magistrate?" Miss St. James asked, wiping her tears with the back of one trembling hand. She looked up at Darkefell. "Why do you want the magistrate?"

Darkefell darted a look at Anne; did the other woman not know the state of her brother, and how he died? Anne shook her head, as if reading his thoughts. "Never mind, for now," he said. Sanderson had strode ahead with his tragic burden. "Let us go back up to your house, Miss St. James. Are you all right to walk, or do you require assistance?"

She could walk, it seemed, but he supported her on one side, with Anne on the other, and the little boy, Robbie, just ahead; they made their way slowly back up to the house.

The next few hours were a tumult of emotion and difficult decisions. Anne sent word to St. James's regiment, while Darkefell insisted on locating the magistrate. It wasn't that Anne didn't think they needed the magistrate—it was clear to her that St. James had been murdered—but having to explain it all to Pamela was heart-rending.

They were in Pamela's room; her maid, Alice, had been sent downstairs to help Mrs. Quintrell and her daughter, for the household was in an uproar.

"Who would want to kill St. James?" Pamela cried, for the third time since Anne had explained why the magistrate was necessary. "Marcus didn't have an enemy in the world."

Anne returned to her friend's side from the window, where she had been looking out to wait for Darkefell's return with the local official. "What about this smuggling business? You knew about St. James's part in it . . . is there anything else I should know? Did you know when there was to be a landing, every time?"

Pamela, tears trailing down her cheeks, covered her face with her hands. "What does any of this matter?" she said, her voice muffled. "I'd like to be alone for a while."

"Pam, I—"

"Anne, please! Just let me be."

So Anne left the room, pausing outside the door. It broke her heart when she heard her friend burst into anguished sobs, but perhaps Pamela needed just to cry it out. That was a woman's prerogative, after all, and no refuge for weakness, but a path through sorrow, toward strength. Muttering a prayer out loud as she passed the room where Marcus's poor body lay, Anne descended to find Lolly rearranging the sitting room and directing Alice where to dust.

Anne had thought Lolly would be shattered by the tragedy, but she looked up as Anne entered the room and said, "There you are, dear, just in time. If we are to have a number of gentlemen—the marquess, the magistrate and perhaps someone from Captain St. James's regiment—I thought I would take the liberty of arranging the furniture a little better. Men dislike being crowded, in my experience, and we cannot make them sit outside, for it is increasingly damp."

Glancing around, Anne could see the practicality of Lolly's improvements, which was to take Pamela's artistic furniture arrangement and push everything against the wall, leaving adequate room for booted gentlemen. She was about to comment favorably when she heard a noise outside. She glided to the window overlooking the gravel drive. Darkefell and another gentleman were dismounting their horses, and both handed the reins to Mr. Osei Boatin, who accompanied them. As they were moving toward the house, Anne recognized her own carriage pull up, and a gentleman in a regimental uniform, red cutaway coat faced in white and trimmed heavily in gold braid, stiffly got down: Colonel Sir Henry Withington.

The men greeted each other in the hale and hearty male pattern, handshakes, bows, claps on the back. No falling on each other's necks in a time of sorrow, as women do. Anne felt a tug of humor at the picture that would make, if they but behaved as ladies would in such a circumstance, but pushed away the thought. This was no time for levity; poor, dear Marcus was dead. She straightened her stomacher, patting her full, dark skirts into place. This was a house of mourning, and the formal patterns must be observed. Soberly, she greeted the gentlemen, while Lolly, eerily calm and organized in the face of tragedy, trotted out to the kitchen to order the obligatory refreshments.

Darkefell leaned close to Anne and murmured, brief and to the point, "I've made free with your driver and carriage; Sanderson is going off to fetch the local vicar, a Mr. Barkley. He'll return with him directly." He then straightened and said, "Lady Anne Addison, may I introduce to you Mr. Alexander Rokeby Twynam, the magistrate of this parish. And you've already met Colonel Sir Henry Withington, an old acquaintance of mine and Captain St. James's regimental colonel." The men made appropriate obeisance, and sat where directed, uncomfortably filling the small, gloomy room.

Colonel Withington was the first to speak, as he removed his sword from his hip, laying it across his lap. "Lady Anne, this is a terrible occurrence. St. James, from my brief acquaintance with him, seemed charming and a credit to the uniform. Is Miss St. James going to join us? I would like to express my sympathy."

"She is indisposed, as you can well imagine," Anne answered, gravely. "I am acting in her stead, gentlemen, and have her permission to speak for her in matters concerning her brother."

Mr. Twynam, a large, heavy gentleman dressed in an enormous embroidered frock coat and wearing an impeccable wig, leaned forward, the chair beneath him creaking ominously, and said, "My lady, I *will* require a few minutes with Miss St. James today. I've got some concerns about what has been happening with this smuggling gang, and Mr. Puddicombe, the local excise officer, has made some rather grave accusations."

"What kind of accusations?" Anne said, her tone shrill, her stomach churning. Puddicombe . . . that was the fellow Anne had seen Pamela with in the alley the day before, the one with whom she was arguing.

"I should perhaps not call them 'accusations,' my lady; more like questions he has raised. Nothing with which to concern yourself, but I will need to speak with Miss St. James just to clear things up. And my lord," he said, turning to the marquess. "I was told by my son, who is a lieutenant in the Light Dragoons, that you and Captain St. James had a rather vicious bout of fisticuffs at the regimental assembly a few nights past. The captain sustained the worst of the scrap, I hear. What was the quarrel about?"

Darkefell turned crimson, the telltale vein pulsing in his temple. Anne watched him, wondering if he would confess what St. James had said to make him so angry.

"I think if you wish to know what it concerned," he said, his jaw square and his teeth clenched, "some of St. James's intimates in the regiment will be able to tell you. Many of them were standing about and heard the captain."

"Would it not be simpler if you just told me?"

"No," Darkefell said and did not elaborate.

The magistrate eyed him, his brow furrowed in thought, but said nothing further.

Lolly flitted in just then and was introduced. The magistrate bowed deeply over her hand and she twittered a greeting, her pale eyes wide as she curtseyed. But the older woman swiftly excused herself and gestured to Anne to follow her. When they got out to the hall at the bottom of the staircase, Lolly breathlessly said, "Miss St. James is distraught . . . almost hysterical. I cannot calm her, Anne."

"I'll go up, then," Anne said, casting her gaze up the stairs. She could hear Pamela's voice, becoming louder and more shrill. She was not going to let her friend be subjected to any kind of male brow-beating, so she swiftly went back into the sitting room and said, as the men all stood, "You will have to excuse me, gentlemen. Poor Miss St. James is suffering acutely, as you can imagine, and I must go to her."

"Of course, my lady," the magistrate said, bowing, a ponderous action in one so large. "I *will* need to speak with her, though."

"Mr. Twynam," Colonel Withington said, irritation in his tone, "I'm sure you can excuse Miss St. James for a couple of days."

"No, I cannot. If the lady wishes us to find out who killed her brother, she alone can provide information about his most intimate conversations and thoughts. I *will* see her."

Anne understood his insistence, and felt it best to placate him. "If you'll just allow her to speak with the vicar first, about services for her brother, I think it will make her calmer and give her time to compose her thoughts. The vicar is on his way even now, I believe."

He bowed again. "That is eminently sensible, Lady Anne. You are doubtlessly a most valuable friend for Miss St. James to have in this tragic circumstance."

Anne excused herself and rushed up the stairs. Pamela turned to her as she entered the room while Alice, the maid, escaped, and said, "It's my fault! It's my fault St. James was murdered. I have been thinking of it for hours and cannot escape the conclusion. It's *all* my fault."

"Calm yourself, Pam," Anne said, glancing back to the door. "There is no time for hysterics. We must talk about what you will tell those men about St. James's activities last night."

• • •

Darkefell took the two men to see St. James's body, where it had been laid, in his room. He described the body's position on the rocks, and how it appeared likely that the high tide had swept it there, leading to the inescapable conclusion that the captain had been killed the night before. Twynam frowned down at St. James, and expressed his determination to search the beach where the captain had been found.

Looking down at the pale dead body of Marcus St. James, Darkefell experienced an odd moment of self-knowledge; he was not particularly sorry that the captain was dead, except in the sense that the fellow was far too young to return to his Maker. He didn't know him well enough to be sorry, perhaps, but he hadn't liked him. The fellow was intolerably rude about Anne, an unforgivable slight, particularly as he was a serious competitor for Anne's hand. Darkefell acknowledged a deep, dark part of himself that was glad to have his competition swept aside. St. James would not have made Anne happy. He had concluded that only *he* could do that, and though perhaps that was an overinflated opinion of his worth, he believed it firmly. Anne deserved better than Captain Marcus St. James, wastrel and roué; she deserved the Marquess of Darkefell.

But . . . he sighed, watching Twynam examine the captain's sodden clothes. Anne had cared for the man. As much as Darkefell thought St. James must have had something to do with the smuggling, he was not about to expose him, and so ruin his reputation when there was no opportunity for him to redeem it. Not yet, at least.

Twynam stood, finally, in the middle of the room, looking around. He stepped over to the window and looked out, the view of the cliff and the sea beyond it, then turned slowly, his expression set in a frown. "Why was the captain down on the beach? Does anyone know?"

"Not to my knowledge," Darkefell answered.

"I believe this murder happened before high tide last night, and his body was swept up onto the rocks by the water."

"I think you are right, Twynam," Darkefell agreed.

Colonel Withington, his pleasant face set in a sad expression, said, "Good god, men, must you so coldly speak of such matter in this room, near the body?" He knelt by the bed and bowed his head, murmuring a prayer.

"I think Captain St. James's spirit would wish, if he is here in this room, that we make every effort to find his killer," the magistrate said.

Darkefell agreed, and watched Twynam, thinking what a contrast this fellow, as local magistrate, was to his own area magistrate, Sir Trevor Pomfroy. Pomfroy, pompous and stupid, a deadly combination, would have leapt to some conclusion, but Twynam did not seem about to do anything rash. It confirmed for Darkefell what he had been thinking for some years; as the most powerful man in his parish, and indeed in his part of Yorkshire, it was time to replace his inadequate magistrate in favor of someone with more modern thoughts and opinions.

Twynam nodded as he turned, surveying the room, then he met the marquess's gaze. "I must see Miss St. James before I leave, and I do not think I can await the arrival of the vicar. He may not be available, after all, or may be out on a parish call. Would you see if the young lady is now available, my lord?"

He was not going to let that go, quite clearly, and to do his job effectively, that was only to be expected. Darkefell made a swift decision, nodded, and exited to the hall, pausing as he surveyed the rooms. He tapped on the first one, and Anne's maid, Mary, came to the door and directed him to one at the farthest end of the hall.

He tapped on that door. Anne, pale but composed, peeked out.

"Twynam really does need to speak with Miss St. James, Anne. He just wants to find the killer, and I think he's a good man to do it. Could she speak with him?"

"Let me ask her," Anne said and closed the door.

He could hear them murmur to each other, and finally, she came back.

"If Mr. Twynam would visit her in her room, she will answer what she can. But I won't leave her alone, Tony, not when she's like this. She's . . . fragile."

Darkefell, feeling utterly like an errand boy, fetched Twynam and guided him to the young woman's chamber, leaving Colonel Withington with the captain's body. Pamela St. James reclined on a sofa by the window, her lovely face ravaged by grief and tears, her eyes swollen and her hair disarrayed. She pressed a stained kerchief to her eyes, blotting her tears. Not sure whether to go or stay, Darkefell lingered at the door, until Anne beckoned him in. He sat on a chair by a dressing table, while the enormous Twynam crouched by Miss St. James.

The magistrate asked her a few questions about St. James, and about herself, why they had settled in Cornwall. She answered calmly enough; since St. James's regiment was stationed near St. Ives, Pamela had decided to locate nearby.

"Now, yesterday, Captain St. James was . . . er, convalescing from an injury he had sustained in a quarrel."

The man glanced over at Darkefell, who felt his face flush and that damned vein in his neck throbbed.

"My lord, this is where you join the tale, I believe?" Twynam said in a deceptively calm tone. When no one said a word, he looked around. "Come now, you all were there, at the regimental assembly. Does anyone care to tell me what the marquess and the captain had to quarrel about?"

"Miss St. James and I were at the assembly, sir, but the altercation took place in the smoking room. We were not present." Anne glanced over at Darkefell, and raised one eyebrow.

"I cannot believe that Captain St. James did not tell anyone what the quarrel was over," Twynam said.

Anne stayed silent. Darkefell knew that she could not repeat the story St. James had told her, about his supposed revelation of their intimacy. Even though it was what Marcus had told her the quarrel was about, and even if she had questions still about its truth or falseness, confessing it would not do her own credit any good. Nor would it help in discovering who killed St. James.

But Twynam let the question hang and glanced from face to face until Anne, her cheeks pale, took in a trembling breath and seemed about to speak.

Darkefell said, "I will speak with you in private, Twynam. It is not a story for ladies."

"All right," Twynam said genially. He stood, groaning a little and rubbing his knee. The floor creaked as he shifted his weight from foot to foot. "Miss St. James," he said, as if it was an afterthought, "where were you last night when the smuggling clash was going on below Cliff House?"

"She was in her room, sir, of course!" Anne said, outraged by the question.

"I asked Miss St. James, my lady." He kept his gaze steady on Pamela.

"I was in my room," she said. Her pale hand fluttered to her forehead. "I awoke . . . perhaps from the noise . . . and did not feel well. I was going to get myself a glass of buttermilk, but Anne offered to get it for me. She did, and I returned to bed."

"And you, my lady? Why were you out of your room, as you must have been if you offered to fetch buttermilk for Miss St. James?" Twynam said, turning toward Anne.

"Of course she was abed as well, Twynam, by Miss St. James's own word!" Darkefell said.

"Do none of you answer your own questions?" the man asked, looking from one to the other of the three younger folk. "You each seem loath to answer questions about your own movements and eager to answer for each other."

"I heard a noise outside my room, sir, and found Pamela in the hall heading downstairs, so I went to the larder for buttermilk for her. She appeared feverish, Mr. Twynam. She has suffered from that complaint before, and I worried about a recurrence."

"Good. That is all I wished to know . . . for now." He headed toward the door. "My lord, if you will precede me?"

Darkefell exited, but Twynam paused in the door. "One more thing; I have heard wild tales of some ghost that hovers off the cliff and frightens the more suggestible of the excise officer's crew. Do either of you know of what I speak?"

"That is the infamous Barbary Ghost, sir," Pamela said with a faint smile, brushing back a stray lock of hair on her cheek. "If you believe in such things. The old tale is about a pirate who stole a young lady from this very house. As you say, the more suggestible of the men may have seen something, but I know nothing about it."

"Good day, Miss St. James, Lady Anne. I will see you again, very soon."

It did not escape Anne's notice that the man had not followed up on his assertion that Puddicombe had made some kind of accusations, or allegations. About what, she wondered? What did the excise officer know, and what was he browbeating Pamela about the day before? And why had Twynam put off speaking about it?

Eleven

Pamela broke down in tears and sobbed, her face cradled in her arms, as the men left the room and descended the stairs, the wooden steps creaking under Twynam's weight.

Anne felt so useless. To try to take her friend's mind off her tragedy, she hunched down by the sofa and softly said, "You were going to tell me something earlier, my dear." When Pamela first made the comment, it was not a good time for the discussion; she had wanted to ready her friend for the questioning she knew was going to come, and so had not pursued Pamela's "confession." She had been hysterical and didn't make a lot of sense. "You were saying it was all your fault, St. James's death. I don't understand; whatever did you mean?"

With a last choked sob, Pamela took the handkerchief Anne offered—her own was sodden and stained beyond use—and dried her swollen eyes. She looked up at her friend. "Marcus was alive and well after the skirmish last night. I saw him."

"*You* saw him?" Anne stared at her.

"When you met me in the hall, I had just come upstairs."

"But you were in your nightgown!"

"I had my shift on under, um . . . other clothes," she admitted.

"So you were down on the beach," Anne said, trying to figure out what Pamela was saying. It came to her then that Marcus's dead body had not been wearing his pirate gear; some time between when she last saw him and when he was murdered, he must have taken off his ghost costume. "Why?"

Pamela didn't directly answer, saying, "I was down on the beach during the melee, and Marcus came to get me; he was worried about my safety, and helped me get up the cut almost to the house. But then he went back down. I don't know why!" She sobbed, tears welling up in her eyes. "Marcus only got involved in the smuggling because I had already made a deal with Micklethwaite," she said, her tone leaden. Holding Anne's handkerchief to her mouth, she bravely choked back more tears.

"Micklethwaite . . . the ship captain." Anne rose and paced to the window, methodically working through her thoughts. This just could not mean what it sounded like it meant, she thought, resolutely determined not to jump to conclusions. She turned and stared at Pam. "So you *knew* about the smugglers landing goods on your beach," she said, reiterating the facts. "But why were you down there last night?"

Pamela hesitated. Her glance flicked up to Anne's eyes and then away. "It's more than just knowing about the smuggling, Anne. I organize the landings and direct the dispersal of smuggled goods. Micklethwaite and I are partners in the enterprise. I am Lord Brag, the smuggling leader."

She should have thought of the possibility, Anne admitted to herself, but who, looking at Pamela St. James, prim, fashionable and pretty, would ever have expected her to be Lord Brag, the smuggler? Certainly not Anne, and she had been living there, under the same roof, for weeks. "But why . . . ?" She trailed off, staring at her friend. There were no words.

At that moment Lolly tapped on the door and ducked her head in the room. "I do so dislike intruding, but Mr. Barkley, the vicar, is here."

Pamela stood and took Anne's hands in her own. "Please, Anne, will you trust in me and order your driver to come for us tomorrow morning, early? I know it's the Sabbath, but . . . but I just couldn't face the congregation tomorrow, and I have someplace else I must go. I'd like you to go with me."

Anne, still trying to digest what she had learned, agreed. Pamela would not divulge any more, merely saying that all would be revealed on the morrow. For now, she was going to do one last thing for her beloved brother, and see the vicar to order his funeral. His regiment would take care of most of the arrangements, and the regiment's chaplain would perform the ceremony, but Pamela had some things concerning which she needed to speak to the vicar. She asked if Anne would come with her to speak to the man, and Anne acquiesced.

While Pamela and Anne met with the vicar in the study, a dark little room off the staircase landing, and Darkefell saw the magistrate and colonel off, Osei had set himself to be useful around the house. Lolly Broomhall had taken a liking to the marquess's quiet secretary, but when Darkefell came back in the house, she gave the younger man a stern look and asked for a moment alone with the marquess. Osei bowed and said he would ready their horses.

Darkefell faced the softly rounded little lady. "May I be of some assistance, madam?"

"You may," she said. She sat down in a chair in the sitting room and indicated that he was to sit opposite her. "Lord Darkefell, you are a Yorkshire man, I understand?"

"I am." And for the next ten minutes, Darkefell found himself being grilled on his home and family. There was nothing that he was not prepared to answer, so he was forthright, amused by her pointed line of questioning. Was he prepared to marry? Yes, he answered. When the time and the lady was right, he would do his duty to his title and birthright with alacrity. Did he consider his family home to be ready for a lady? Yes, he said, he had taken considerable pains in renovating it, and the results were pleasing, in his own estimation. Even Lady Anne, whose opinion he esteemed, he said, had seen the work he had done to make the castle more comfortable, and approved it.

Miss Broomhall paused, her lips pursed, and looked down at her locked hands. Then she looked up again. "And what are your intentions toward Lady Anne, young man?"

This was where it ended. He was not about to announce his intentions to this lady, though she had every right to ask as Anne's nominal chaperone. But if he had learned anything about Anne, it was that she was independent, and suspicious of his methods in attaching her interest. The slightest hint that he was securing the good offices of her companion might be enough to doom his suit, for a while at least. He did not intend that *anything* would keep her from accepting his hand in marriage ultimately, but in a battle for a woman's heart—or at least a woman as stubborn as his Anne— subterfuge was a necessary part of his arsenal.

"Intentions, Miss Broomhall?" he said airily, sitting back in the creaky chair. "My intention is to be her friend."

Lolly Broomhall gazed at him steadily, her dour expression sitting poorly on such an apple-dumpling face. But he could not laugh at her while she was so serious, and for such a good cause; she clearly cared for Anne a great deal, and Darkefell believed that regard was returned by Anne. In that case, he would attempt to win her over, as much as he could without compromising his ultimate goal, Anne's complete capitulation to him.

"Gentlemen and ladies cannot be friends, my lord," she said, watching his eyes, "Unless one of them be incapable of the softer feelings that exist between a man and a woman. I know Anne to be tender of heart, so are you . . . incapable?"

He gazed at her steadily, divided as to whether he ought to laugh or take offense. But he caught a gleam in her faded blue eyes, and finally saw beneath the charade of an inoffensive busybody to the steely businesswoman beneath. It was a side of her he had not expected until that moment. Perhaps she could be his ally. "Miss Broomhall," he said, leaning forward, "I am neither incapable, nor unwilling." He did not speak further.

She sighed, eyeing him. "Well enough, for now. But we'll speak again, Lord Darkefell."

He rose as he heard the study door open and Anne's voice in the hall. She entered the sitting room with the vicar, Mr. Barkley, whom Darkefell had met when he arrived. He bowed to the vicar. Miss Broomhall guided the reverend out, talking the whole way, but glanced back once at Darkefell and Anne. She smiled and nodded.

Anne looked troubled. Darkefell took her hand and pulled her into the dark hallway near the landing, and into his arms, anxious to soothe her pain. He would never forget the look on her face that afternoon when he came down the cut to find her, horrified, by St. James's body. But the expression that had hit him squarely in the chest was the gratitude in her eyes, the appeal. It was as if she had lit up from within at the sight of him, and had run directly into his arms. She had spoken with such a tone of gratitude simply for his presence. That was a start in his quest for her tender heart.

He held her close and she nestled there, against his chest. He closed his eyes, aware of every point of contact between their bodies, from his cheek against her hair, his arms wound tightly around her body, her hips close to his, her long limbs. Of all the women in England, why did he have to care so deeply for this one, the most infuriatingly self-sufficient lady he had ever met? But he knew the answer. It was *because* of her independence of character that he had come to admire, and then to love her. There was no one in England like his Lady Anne.

But finally she moved away from him. "I have to go back to Pam, Darkefell. She's alone in the study."

He gazed down at her shadowed face, cradling her cheek in his palm, passing one thumb over her full lips. "How are *you*, Anne? I would give anything in the world for you not to have seen St. James dead like that. Are you all right?"

"He was a friend, and I cared for him. This is awful . . . simply terrible!" Her voice was clogged with unshed tears. She shook her head, shrugging off the emotion. She stared up into his eyes, her gaze searching. "Why won't you tell me what he said that made you attack him? It doesn't matter now; he's dead!"

"It matters even more, now, sweet Anne," he said gently, pushing back some stray hairs and tucking them behind her ear. "I would never taint your memory of the fellow, and he is not here to explain himself."

The door on the landing to the study moved. Darkefell swiftly bent his head and kissed her full on the lips, then released her, as Pamela St. James came out of the study, wiping her eyes, and descended the three steps to the hall.

"Miss St. James," he said, taking her hand in his. "I am so sorry for your sadness. Though I didn't know him well enough to judge, I'm sure St. James was a good and loving brother. The day dwindles. I must go now, but may I call on you ladies tomorrow?"

Anne cast a swift glance at Pamela, and said, "We will be out for part of the day."

"We'll stop in St. Wyllow on our way back here from our . . . our destination," Pamela said, her cheeks reddening. "Marcus's regimental funeral will be the day after tomorrow." She caught her breath and stifled a sob, making an odd sound somewhere between a whimper and a sigh. "I cannot attend. I just can't!" she cried, a hysterical edge to her voice.

Anne soothed her with a hushed word and the touch of her hand on her arm, then turned to him. "Darkefell, we cannot attend the funeral. Pamela is just not strong enough, and there will be so many people! Will you go and tell us about it afterward?" Anne said with a swift glance at her friend, who had ducked her head to hide her emotion. "I know you and St. James didn't . . . didn't . . ." She trailed off, not sure how to broach the subject.

He touched her shoulder and said with meaning in his eyes, "I will go to the funeral. My connection with Colonel Withington will give me ample reason, and I'll come to you after and tell you all about it." He bowed. "I must leave, ladies, but will be in St. Wyllow tomorrow afternoon. If you do not find me there, I'm staying at the Barbary Ghost Inn. The innkeeper was equerry to my father many years ago, and I count Quintrell as my friend."

"Until tomorrow," Anne said, her heart thudding.

"Until tomorrow," he agreed, and strode through the sitting room and out.

Anne stood stock-still, trying to understand her feelings. Darkefell took her by surprise every single time he kissed her, and even in the midst of such sorrow, his kiss had buoyed her, lifting her spirit, setting her heart to pounding, filling her with hope. But, hope of what? That was a question for quiet reflection, not this tumultuous longing to be back in his arms, but quiet reflection did not seem to be in her immediate future, not with so much sorrow and suspicion and uncertainty all around them.

"To everything there is a season, and a time to every purpose under the heavens," Anne muttered.

"A time to weep, and a time to laugh," answered Pamela. "I don't think I shall laugh for many a day, Anne."

• • •

Darkefell and Osei returned to the inn, and the marquess, determined to get to the bottom of the night before's debacle, sternly told Johnny Quintrell to meet him out on the back terrace of the inn, which was close enough to overlook the inlet and cut below Cliff House. He paced the flagstone terrace, squinting across the distance toward the house where Anne resided, comforting her distraught friend.

He was used to getting what he wanted by the simple expedient of going after it. Houses, horses, women, political influence . . . they were all generally a simple matter of making the right moves, talking to the right people, using bribery, flattery, a push here, a carefully worded request there. When any other method failed, a command would bring him whatever he wished. But Anne baffled him. He could not just *make* her marry him. A command was out of the question in this case.

He stared across the cut, the vista of open sky and wild gray sea seeming forbidding and lonely. Was that all it was to him, baffled fury at being repulsed? But no, he was no child, to want what was denied him simply *because* it was denied to him.

Women had always seemed, to him, simple creatures. If you gave them what they wanted in the way of security or financial reward, then they acquiesced to a man's wishes. Men were trickier to bargain with because there was often something deeper that drove them: pride, anger, honor.

But from the beginning it had been apparent to him that Anne was different. Though he did not consider himself to be conceited, he knew most other women would have been ordering a trousseau given half the attention he had lavished on Anne. He had evaded the marriage snares laid for him in the past; many matchmaking mothers and simpering maidens in their first or second or third Season had gone to great lengths to secure him as a most eligible husband.

So why did Anne not want him? She feared marriage as a rabbit feared a trap, as the end of any kind of life. He was beginning to worry that what she truly wanted—it seemed to be some intangible freedom that was not even possible for a lady—he could not promise. And yet, the more he saw her, the more he wanted her. How could he win her if he had nothing to offer that she wanted? He stared out to sea, the gray sky heavy, the ocean churning, white froth on wave tops giving no indication of the muck and filth underneath, dragged up from the seabed. It was a mystery that must be solved if he was to win Anne and find peace.

A subtle noise behind him alerted him to Johnny Quintrell's presence and he turned, examining the fellow. He was stout and fleshy, like his father, a younger version of the man, in fact. Darkefell set aside his uneasy reflections about Anne, and concentrated instead on what he could do that moment, which was solve the problems troubling Joseph Quintrell and perhaps even Pamela St. James's torment, the question of who killed her brother.

"Johnny, I need some information," Darkefell said, eyeing the fellow.

The young man stayed sullenly silent, neither agreeing nor disagreeing.

"Last night went very badly for the smugglers. And yet, from what

I observed, a great deal of goods were being landed. Someone must have felt secure that they would be unobserved last night. Is that a fair surmise?"

Johnny nodded.

"And yet the excise agents were there in full force, which means that either they were given information that a secret landing had been arranged or . . ." He thought for a moment. "Or whomever was in charge thought they had secured the excise officer's agreement to turn a blind eye, and they were betrayed. Is that how it was?"

Johnny Quintrell looked confused for a moment, and then shook his head slowly. "I don't know, milord."

The boy was just another body to carry barrels and crates up the beach, and so merely did as he was told. "But you must know who is behind the smuggling, who directs things, for someone must tell you when a landing is planned."

"Aye, milord." He hesitated, then, fear in his eyes, said, "If I tell you, will he know?"

"The one who directs the operation? Will he know you have informed against him? Certainly not. Nothing will point to you, Johnny, I'll lay my life on that."

He appeared relieved and slumped down on a wooden bench, passing one hand over his grubby face, fair beard stubble adorning his jutting chin. He scruffed the bristle. "I've told you Captain Micklethwaite is one of 'em, sir, but there's another, one who only shows up the night of the landing and directs everything. Must be th' captain's partner. We calls him Lord Brag, for 'is manner, you know. He always says he'll make us rich as lords."

"But you only ever see him the nights of the landings?"

"Aye. And no one knows who he is, 'cause he wears a mask. Lads think 'e's some high muckety-muck."

Immediately Darkefell's mind went to suspicions that it had been St. James. Was he Lord Brag, then? And were he and Micklethwaite partners in the smuggling business?

"When will you hear next?"

"I 'spect t'will be today, milord."

"What have you heard of those who were killed? Did you hear anything about Captain St. James, the man whose body was found on the beach below Cliff House this morning?"

Johnny appeared frightened and shook his head, but then reluctantly said, "That new colonel was in here just a half hour ago, blazing mad and ballyraggin' at Mr. Puddicombe; he said as how the Puddicombe had not done his job from the start, or Captain St. James wouldn't be dead now."

"But you don't know how it happened?"

"Last I saw anything down there was when you dragged me away from t'trouble, milord. And thankful I am," he said, his expression gloomy, "for me best mate was kilt last night. T'would've been me, too, if it hadn't bin for you."

"I'm sorry for your friend, Johnny, but I'm glad you're alive," he said, clapping the younger man on the shoulder. "For your father's sake. And now you see why you must get out of this business. It's dangerous."

"Aye, but I was just tryin' to make a bit extra. I've got a sweetheart, see, and we wants to marry, but her pa won't let 'er. I'm hopin' fer enough to take her away an' get married. She's able to wed without her pa's permission in a week."

"But you won't be able to marry at all if you're dead, Johnny. Have you told your father this, about having a young lady?"

Johnny shook his head. "Didn't want to worry 'im. He's been that cut up since Ma died. No time fer my nonsense."

Darkefell paced the terrace, then said, "Let's extricate you from this mess, find out who killed Captain St. James, and then we'll figure something out for you and your young lady. Now, were others killed, besides your friend?"

"Two more. The excise men took 'em away. Me poor mate's mum won't even have his body to bury, 'cause the prevention men say he's a thief and no-good smuggler, and he's to be made a lesson of." The fellow's face was white, but his mouth was set in an angry line. "Can't even let a poor widow have her son's body to bury when she's torn up and bedoled. Ain't right. That Puddicombe is a proper arse."

Darkefell thought for a moment. If that was true, then St. James's body would have been taken away, if he had died with the other smugglers. He *must* have been killed after the melee, then, but how? And by whom? He would find out for Miss St. James's sake. The tiny voice of conscience whispered that he was set on uncovering the

124

murderer because he still felt a twinge of guilt. He had overreacted, perhaps in bashing St. James so brutally, for there was an ample measure of jealousy in his fury over the man's words. But what was worse, he still couldn't regret his actions, nor would he take them back, given the chance. He'd pound St. James again in an instant, for saying what he did about Anne.

He clapped Johnny on the shoulder. "We'll figure it out, lad, I promise."

Twelve

The evening and night were long and grim, and Anne slept but little. Every time she drifted into slumber, a nightmare of poor Marcus's dead face rose in her bewildered mind, and she awoke crying out. Several times she crept down the hall to huddle in the dark outside of Pamela's door, and heard her friend weeping within. She would then tiptoe down the hall to Marcus's room, where local women, expert in such things, had prepared his body and sat with him. Though Anne did not believe he was there with his corporeal remains—she felt that his soul was long gone to wherever souls went—still, she was relieved he was not alone. She had already guaranteed the local undertaker that she would pay for everything concerning St. James's funeral.

She lingered outside his room for a moment, then tried to return to her own bed, only to be beset by horrors and trembling. Though never overly religious, she even spent part of the night praying. Out of sheer desperation she finally wound the blankets tightly around her, imagining them as Darkefell's arms, and drifted into an uneasy sleep.

Strength returned to her the next morning, but her imaginary night in the marquess's arms left her bemused, for what did it say about her, that she had resorted to such feminine weakness as to imagine his embrace as an aid to sleep? She blushed whenever she thought of it, and it left her faintly disturbed and oddly yearning for him: his voice, his touch, his kiss.

However, that was the subject for another day's reflection. She spent part of the morning doing such tasks as needed to be done, as much as could be taken from Pamela to allow her some serenity, then spent an hour at Marcus's side, thinking and praying. She would liberally reward the women who had looked after him, because he now looked serene and sleeping, a miracle after what his poor body had been through. He had been a good, if imperfect, man, and would be sorely missed, especially by Pamela.

But it was finally time to prepare for the mysterious journey Pamela was set on, and Anne sat patiently petting Irusan, while Mary styled her stubborn hair. Her dark tresses, though silken in texture most of the time, only required the addition of briny breezes to transform into a sea creature of mythological proportions. Mary

126

entered a pitched battle armed with comb and pins, and with ferocious determination, she inevitably emerged triumphant, having subdued the beast.

Anne's hair resembled mortal locks once more. "What slaves we ladies are to fashion," she said, turning her head and gazing at herself in the mirror, "when even a plain woman will take so much trouble over her appearance. I'll never be a handsome woman, but you make me tolerable."

"Handsome is that handsome does," Mary said, finally able to speak now that she was freed of the pins she held in her mouth while styling her mistress's hair. She pushed the last one into place and stood back, giving a nod of satisfaction. She retrieved a refurbished hat, adorned now with dark mourning ribbon to match Anne's dark gown.

"You've been reading *The Vicar of Wakefield*," Anne replied, smiling into the mirror at her maid.

Mary admitted it, her expression dour. "Aye. I've had too much time here to do as I will. I'm enjoying novels more than I ought. It's a shame, when the Good Book has been my meat for so many years, to admit I enjoy made-up tales."

Gently, Anne took her maid's hand and squeezed. "I know you must be dull with such an excess of free time."

"If I could have my way, I'd not be bored, for I'd clean this wretched house from top to bottom, but I canna put a finger on aught without that miserable Mrs. Quintrell takin' offense."

"My mother and grandmother would be horrified if they saw the squalor of Cliff House," Anne said, glancing around her room. She pushed her cat from her lap and he hopped up to her bed. "But you keep *this* room spotless, and I thank you for it." She turned in her chair and stared at her maid.

"I'll tell you something, Mary, that will keep your mind turning," she continued, and related her exploration of the basement the day before, and her discovery of Marcus St. James's workshop. She thought back to the local magistrate, Mr. Twynam's comment about Mr. Puddicombe's accusations, or questions, as he had amended. He had said it was nothing to concern herself with, but that he would need to clear things up with Miss St. James. Though to her knowledge, he had done no such thing.

Perhaps Puddicombe had accused Pamela or Marcus of smuggling. Would he do so, though, unless he had proof? She shared all of that with Mary, but then it was time for her to go, for Sanderson, driving Anne's carriage, was waiting at the door. Before leaving, Anne had to convince Lolly that she and Pamela would be sufficient chaperonage for each other, and that there was very little chance of their meeting Lord Darkefell or any other man that day. She was merely taking Pamela for a ride into the countryside, she told her companion. As far as she knew, that was the truth, because Pamela, looking like a wraith, would say no more than that she had a visit she had to make.

She and Pamela got into the carriage and Sanderson, at a sedate pace, set off toward their mysterious destination. Was this, then, where Pamela had disappeared to, almost every other day of Anne's residence at Cliff House? She hadn't wanted to pry, and curiosity had warred with courtesy for weeks. Her speculation had become wilder and more outrageous, from a secret lover to anonymous good works, but today she would learn the truth.

As they trundled along country roads, away from the seaside, Anne wondered what, or whom, were they headed toward? Was there, in Pamela's family, an ancient parent, or a mad aunt tucked away in keeping? If so, she would not be the first to shoulder the burden of a seldom-seen family member who was not fit for society. Anne gazed out the window as she considered her own complex family situation.

Though she rarely spoke of him, she did have a sibling, a brother, poor Jamey, who lived with a family in the country not far from Harecross Hall. He had first been sent away many years before because Anne's mother couldn't bear to look at him, feeling he was a reproach to her, a constant reminder of her failure to provide a proper heir to the earldom. Also, he was sometimes unruly, and her father's indulgence did nothing but make him harder to handle, the bigger he got.

But now, after so many years, he had calmed and lived a serene life. He had his hobbies and his activities, his daily routine, his collections and his animals. His serving staff was well paid and kept him healthy and happy. He was capable of little more.

As they rattled hither and yon, down valleys and up hills, across the countryside, Pamela having given Sanderson directions as they mounted, both women were silent, lost in their own thoughts. Perhaps too little sleep left her vulnerable, but Anne was melancholy as she thought of her brother. Many years before *she* had been the dependent, and her big brother was her protector from the bullying of a gang of vagabond gypsy children who taunted her for her timidity and small stature. Dear Jamey had struck the biggest boy, and sent them all running, then had carried her home on his back.

She'd never forget him coming to her rescue, her big, brave brother, but all he got for it at home was punishment. Of course, they had only been so far from Harecross Hall because of his wandering ways, but she had looked up to him then, and loved him still. Farfield Farm would be among her first visits when she returned home, to Kent.

"What is there between you and Lord Darkefell?" Pamela said suddenly.

"I beg your pardon?" Anne asked, startled out of her reverie.

"Anne, you *know* what I mean. Please, just talk to me about something," she said, her words jumbled and hurried, "for I cannot stop thinking of Marcus, the last time I saw him, as he hauled me to safety and then went back . . . back to the beach." Her voice broke and she stared out the window at the countryside. She swiped a tear out of her eye and cleared her throat. "Just talk to me of anything . . . your dreams, your hopes, for I have so few of my own right now."

Anne searched her mind for something to take her friend away from her troubles, but maybe her own troubles, as mild as they were compared to Pamela's, would do. "I don't know what to do about Darkefell. He's followed me all the way here even after I rejected his proposal. What kind of man would do that after having been snubbed most firmly?"

"A man in love?" Pam said with a ghost of a smile in the dim interior of the enclosed carriage. "Perhaps he loves you, my dear."

"But how? Why? I've been so rude to him."

"That must be a novelty to the man. I cannot imagine any other woman has ever been rude to him. He is utterly gorgeous, as you must know if you have eyes, and charming. Rich. Titled. I'd marry him myself if I had half the chance, but he has eyes for no one but you."

"What? You would marry him?"

"Good heavens," Pam said, staring at Anne. "Of course I would. I have flung my bonnet at him many times, my dear, but he fails to notice anyone but you."

A thrill ran down her back, and Anne had to admit—to herself only—that the power of that thought excited her, that he loved her so devotedly. But God forfend that she become one of those ladies who exerted power over a man just because she could! Some women, denied any kind of authority in the world at large, satisfied their yearning for command by becoming household tyrants, petty despots, with a devoted husband their first subject.

Not that she thought Darkefell would ever become one of those henpecked men, a slave to his wife's dictatorship. He was not the kind to be a willing servant to feminine whimsy. "It's such a close bond, Pam," she reflected, staring down at her gloves. "Marriage would mean he would own me, body and soul."

"Stop being a dramatist, Anne. The man is besotted with you—"

"Even if that's true," Anne said, interrupting her, looking up and staring at her friend, "that besottedness could end in a fortnight, but I'd be tied to him forever. What then?"

"Then you would be rich and titled and comfortable for the rest of your life." Pamela's voice was clogged by unshed tears, the tone dark with animosity. She laid her forehead against the glass carriage window. "Is that not enough for you?"

Anne stared at her friend's pale face in profile; her expression was icy and bitter. There was so much she didn't know about Pamela, and the recent revelations had pointed that up brilliantly. "Pam, I'm sorry for your financial difficulties, but having money does not solve all of your problems, it only leaves others to plague you."

Her friend shook her head and stared at Anne, her expression twisted with anguish. "How could I expect you to understand? You have a bullying mother who forces you into an engagement you do not want, and poof, your fiancé dies. Poor Reginald, not good enough for you, I'm sure. You yearn for independence, and poof, your grandmother expires, leaving you a fortune, of which you are mistress because of the indulgence of your generous father. You'll *never* understand my life."

Gently, refusing to take offense, Anne said, "I won't discuss this with you right now, my dear, not while you're suffering such bereavement. I haven't forgotten that this is not your first sadness."

Tears welled in Pamela's eyes and trickled down her face. "I'm sorry for being rude. I'm just so tired! And we lost two good fellows in that fight." She mopped her face with a dark-edged handkerchief.

"Oh, Pam, it is such a dangerous game you play!" Anne said, thinking of the lives lost, and the families devastated.

"But we all know the rules, Anne," she said, a harder edge in her voice. "There is not a man there on either side who does not know the score." But she sat up straight as the carriage pulled to a halt and gazed out, eagerly. Her tone lighter, brighter, she cried, "I think we're here!"

They had pulled up to a thatched cottage, a neat but humble abode, and Sanderson opened the door for them and handed them down. Anne followed Pamela, who seemed in a hurry to enter. Her first view of the cottage made her think perhaps her surmise was correct; a mad aunt or crippled parent for whom Pam was responsible now, with Marcus gone? The cottage door opened and a very plump woman holding an armful of what looked like laundry walked out the door and waited.

Pamela moved toward the woman, who set down the bundle. It proved to be a baby, or rather a child, for the little one took a couple of steps before plunking down on the flagged walk.

"Oh!" cried Pam. "He's walking so much better, just since the other day! Edward, my little darling child!" The infant held up his arms with an excited wail of recognition. Pam lifted him up into her arms and turned toward Anne; finally a smile wreathed her gaunt face. "Anne, this is my Edward, my son. Eddie, can you say Anne?"

"Amamamam," the little boy cried, waving one pudgy fist in the air.

"Clever boy!" Pam said and hugged the child to her, kissing his forehead as tears streamed down her cheeks. She met Anne's steady gaze. "This is why I do what I do. I need to create a life for my little boy, my poor fatherless babe."

Anne gaped, unable to think of a single thing to say, clever or not.

They settled inside, in a tiny snug sitting room, Anne, Pamela and

Edward, while Edward's wet nurse, Mrs. Gorse, retrieved her own baby, Fanny, and set her on the floor beside the little boy. Pamela, in hushed tones, explained to the wet nurse about Marcus's death. The woman sympathized, then moved off to make tea. She brought a tray, asking if they were all right for a time, as she had baking and laundering to do.

"I'll look after Edward, Mrs. Gorse, and I'm sure my friend can take care of Fanny for a while, can't you, Anne?" Pamela asked, with a mischievous grin.

Anne recoiled from the jammy hands of the little girl, a blond-haired charmer with dimples and pudgy fists. "I . . . I suppose—"

"Good then, I'll be back in a tic, ma'am," Mrs. Gorse said to Pam, then disappeared, shouting to her maid-of-all-work to hurry along with the wash.

"Talk to me, Pam," Anne said, grabbing a cloth from a neat pile of clean laundry, spitting on it, and wiping the child's grubby hands before the baby could soil the fine fabric of her dress.

"Goodness, you do that very well," Pamela said, watching her clean the child up and tidy the bows on her dress. "Almost as if you're ready to be a mother." Then she sobered, with a doleful sigh. "You knew I was engaged."

"Yes, I remember. I was so happy for you, and so sad when you wrote about Bernard's death." She set the little girl, who appeared to be several months older than Edward, down to roam the room. "Did you marry without telling anyone, then?"

"No, Anne," Pam said, her cheeks pinkening. "If that was the case, as a respectable widow, Edward would be living with me. No, Bernard and I . . . we . . . we anticipated our vows."

Anne felt her own cheeks heat as she thought of Darkefell's impassioned kisses and her own temptation to go further, to ask for more, to discover what lay beyond a kiss. She could not think of condemning Pamela, not if she had felt the same way about her Bernard. It was simple to say one should control one's baser urges, but perhaps without the excessively meddlesome chaperonage she always had, she would have fallen into such trouble. A man as intoxicating as Darkefell, plus time alone, may well have added up to trouble. "And then he died," Anne murmured softly, imagining her friend's horror when she discovered the trouble she was in.

Pamela nodded, her eyes swimming in tears. "I was already two months along, and we were going to be married within days. When Bernard died, I . . . I lost my mind for a while. I moved to this remote cottage, with Marcus's help, had Edward, found Mrs. Gorse, then . . . I . . . I floundered, Anne. I felt like I was drowning in sorrow. It was then, in the depths of my sorrow and illness, that Marcus came to me; I think he was worried that I would destroy myself, if not purposely, then through neglect. He sent me to you, *made* me go to Harecross Hall, for my own good, he said. And for Edward."

Anne's heart ached for all she hadn't known. She reached over and touched Pamela's slender hand. "You should have told me the truth! We could have had Edward and Mrs. Gorse with us."

"No, that was impossible. Mrs. Gorse was already comfortable here, in this cottage. She was a widow before her baby was born, and she cared for Edward so well, I can never thank her adequately. It's a miracle that Edward still knows I am his mother, she's been so good to him."

"But you should have *told* me," Anne insisted. "We could have talked, I would have known more how to help." Fanny toddled up to Anne again and put up her arms. "What does she want?" Anne asked, staring down into the little girl's huge, round blue eyes.

"She wants you to pick her up," Pam said gently, cradling Edward in her arms. The little boy played with her necklace and contentedly patted her cheek.

Anne lifted the child to sit on her lap, and Fanny, in some mysterious baby way, taught Edward to play pat-a-cake. "So this is where you disappeared to so often," Anne said, of the many times in the last weeks when Pam would be gone all day. She glanced around at the tidy cottage, small, humble, but neat and clean. "And this is what you need money for."

Pam nodded. "I've almost got enough. Edward will be weaned soon, and needs a home, and eventually require schooling. I could have him stay with people until he's old enough to go to school, but I'll not lose him like that!" she said, her voice trembling. "He's all I've got. I'm going to go away with him, maybe to Canada. Somewhere where I will not have to explain my life to people, somewhere where nobody knows us, and I can be a widow. Now that Marcus is gone, I have no reason to stay in England, no family at all."

"Does that mean you intend to go on with the smuggling trade?" Anne asked, horrified.

Pamela nodded. "Just one more successful run, and I'll have enough. Just one more!"

Her tone sounded almost pleading, and Anne wondered what she was being asked to do . . . turn a blind eye, certainly, but was there more?

"For Edward," Pam said, caressing her boy's silken hair, brushing it off his high forehead and kissing it once. "I'll not let my son do without."

"If you're unsuccessful, Edward may have to do without his mother!" Anne stated, her tone acid. It was one thing for Pam to risk her own life, but knowing she had a dependent, a child who would be left in a foundling home if she died . . . it seemed selfish. "What if you're caught? You could be hanged, or transported. Pam, really!"

"I have to risk it," she said and hugged her boy close. "I *have* to."

Troubled, Anne watched them together, and at long last decided she could not judge Pam harshly. Her own life was so easy, she had no right to take her friend to task for making hard decisions and difficult choices.

A few hours later, after having a midday meal with Edward, they had to leave. Anne was moved to tears by how fiercely the little boy clung to his mother, tears coursing down his chubby face when she said good-bye. But they had to go back to St. Wyllow, and then to Cliff House.

"What I don't understand," Pamela said idly, as they traveled back the way they had come, "is why Puddicombe raided us that night. He was to let us unload our goods in peace that night."

"Tell me about your arrangement with the man. I cannot imagine what kind of scalawag would take a bribe to turn a blind eye to illegal activity!"

Pamela quickly concealed a smile. "You are such an innocent, my dear Anne, and such an idealist. All men in office are corrupt, one just needs to find what they want." Her smile turned bitter. "We thought Puddicombe was satisfied with money, but lately . . ." She turned her face away to the window.

"Lately what? What else did he want, Pam?"

"That foul creature wanted me! *Me!* He thought I'd become

his . . . his mistress. After all, I'm a fallen woman because I don't live with the protection of a chaperone."

"I'm so sorry, my dear!" Anne said. "I've often wondered why, for my consequence and protection as a delicate lady, the presence of my darling, daft, dotty Lolly is considered necessary when Mary, my very own Scottish wyvern, who would tear the throat from anyone who threatened me with dishonor, is not thought sufficient. An older lady, spinster in her own right, is more fit to protect me when my fiercely loyal papist maid supposedly cannot?"

"Of course, it has nothing to do with the real situation, it's all how things *look*," Pam said bitterly. "Marcus would have killed anyone who did that to me. He would have . . ." She trailed off, her face pallid, all the color she had gained from seeing her son drained away.

"What is it, Pam?"

"Do you think . . . ? No. No, it's not possible."

"Are you asking if I think Puddicombe could have killed Marcus? That perhaps they clashed over you?"

Pam nodded.

Anne thought about it, staring out the window at the gloomy, overcast sky. "Did you tell Marcus what the man was doing, trying to force you into an affair?"

"No! I would never tell Marcus that, for he would certainly have done Puddicombe some damage."

"Then that's one thing we ought to investigate. We need to find out how much Marcus truly knew of Puddicombe's treatment of you. It could explain why your brother went back down to the beach that night."

Pam, with tears standing in her eyes, reached out for Anne's hand and said, "Will you help me find out who killed poor Marcus?"

"If it is possible to find out, I will," Anne said, patting her hand and releasing it. "But I think we ought to bring Darkefell into this, Pam, for he's resourceful and intelligent, and —"

"No. Oh, no!" Pam gasped. "He and Marcus didn't get along, and I couldn't bear if the marquess knew about . . . about everything. Please, don't tell him about my smuggling, and Edward and . . . and everything."

"But Pam —"

"No! *Please*, Anne, don't," she said, tears rolling down her cheeks. "Let's figure this out on our own."

"All right," Anne agreed, reluctantly.

St. Wyllow was quiet, except for an unusual number of red-coated army officers. Anne and Pam got down from the carriage and Sanderson took the horses to be fed and lodged, for Anne said she and Pam could walk back to Cliff House. She did not want her carriage standing outside of the Barbary Ghost Inn if they needed to stop there to speak with Darkefell. She had promised him they would, but now she wasn't sure what to do, with Pam's injunction on telling him anything.

They strolled about St. Wyllow, while Anne thought things through. There were a few questions she needed to ask, she realized. "Pam," she said, glancing sideways, "did St. James have a . . . a lover?"

Pam smiled. "I think so. He was very mysterious about it, but there was a lady in town he would visit."

Anne thought back to market day, and the look exchanged between St. James and the lady she later learned was Miss Julia Lovell's chaperone. It seemed a complicated affair, for the young man, Netherton, had apparently attacked St. James at the ball, too, though she hadn't seen it happen. She stopped walking, and Pam looked back at her, a question in her eyes.

"What is it?"

Anne told her what she was thinking, and Pam agreed it was a promising lead that they could follow up. In the complicated triangle that was St. James, Julia Lovell and John Netherton on one hand, and St. James, Julia Lovell and Julia's chaperone on the other, there was a situation rife with potential for violence, as that Netherton had already shown toward St. James.

Loud voices broke into their conversation, and Anne glanced around. "It's coming from the livery stable," she said. "Whatever is going on?"

The quarrel, for such it proved to be, spilled out from an alleyway beyond the livery to the open green, and Anne, horrified, could see Darkefell at the center of it. Three red-coated officers followed as he stalked away from them.

"C'mon, you coward," one of the red-coated officers, a fleshy, red-face fellow, cried. "You could attack St. James, why not take us on? We won't gang up on ye, just one at a time."

"I will not fight a man with whom I have no quarrel!" Darkefell said, striding across the green.

Anne hurried toward the confrontation, as Darkefell turned to face his tormentors. "Leave him alone," she cried. "He's done nothing to you!"

A tall lanky officer laughed out loud. "He's got a petticoat defender!"

Darkefell's face turned brick red and his hands balled into fists. He glared over at Anne. "My lady, retreat, if you will."

Pamela had followed Anne, and she said, aloud, "Gentlemen, I'm ashamed to see you thus! St. James would not countenance you taking the law into your hands."

"We beg your pardon, Miss St. James," the portly officer said. "But we have reason to believe this fellow murdered your brother," he continued, pointing at Darkefell. "You would not wish us to let him go, would you?"

"I would have you observe the rule of law, please," she said, her tone crisp.

"Good enough," the lanky fellow said in an insinuating tone. "We'll take 'im to the colonel."

"Can't do that, boys," another man sneered, "for our new colonel is in this fellow's pocket, simply because he's a 'milord.'"

"This behavior is unbecoming an officer," Anne said.

Darkefell rolled his eyes. "Fellows," he said, admirably calm. "I did not kill St. James. To make such an accusation is to leave yourself open to the law. But I will not go to law; if you insist, I will gladly fight each one of you, anywhere you wish, but not in front of the ladies!"

"Well and good," the lanky one said. "We'll name the time and place, then, my lord; tomorrow, after the funeral, in St. Ives. Now, excuse us, ladies," he said, his gaze swiveling to the sight of a superior officer strolling the green with a lady on his arm, "we really must be going."

Thirteen

"You both should have stayed out of it," Darkefell muttered to Anne, watching as the red-coated officers strode away, up a lane toward the livery stable. "I was perfectly capable of handling those red-coated simpletons."

His delicate manliness was injured, Anne thought, dismissing his irritation with a shake of her head as Pamela drifted ahead of them, pausing to speak with the vicar's wife, who was guiding a couple of well-dressed, mannerly children toward the church.

The officers' invitation to fight was troubling, but not surprising, Anne figured. She knew how, in a closed society like the military, gossip became fact, fact became insult, and insult became a call to action. Those men probably didn't even know St. James, and Anne told Darkefell so. "I certainly did not recognize any one of them as St. James's particular friends."

"I know that," the marquess said, his tone annoyed, "but I will fight each one anyway."

Anne huffed, following Pamela. "Men! You are incomprehensible creatures, and yet you insist that you are simple to understand."

When the three met on the high street near the millinery shop, Darkefell offered to walk them back to Cliff House, but Anne was not ready to quit the village yet, so she instead suggested tea at the only suitable place for a lady in the village, the coffee room of the post-house inn. He agreed, though he appeared reluctant, to Anne.

When they were seated at a table and served, while townsfolk watched them and whispered, he said, "I went to church this morning, then visited the vicar after."

Pamela paled. Perhaps fearing that his conversation was in reference to her brother's funeral, and unable to face the awful finality, she turned away to the window and stayed silent.

"Miss St. James," he said gently, "I have to ask this: Did you know that your brother had seen Vicar Barkley about posting the banns for himself and Miss Julia Lovell?"

She turned a stricken face to him and cried, "No! He has never said . . . I mean, I knew he was *considering* offering, but . . . no, I didn't know he had seen Mr. Barkley about it."

"He hadn't actually requested the banns, but was going to ask

Miss Lovell's father for her hand within days, the vicar understood. It was all but settled."

"Why wouldn't he have told me?"

"Did you disapprove the match?" Anne asked.

Pam sighed and absently played with the lace on the edge of her sleeve. "I have nothing against the girl, but I felt Marcus was rushing things. And for perhaps the wrong reasons."

Anne understood her; she thought Marcus was considering wedlock to provide security for his sister. With access to the girl's dowry, he could have supported Pam and her illegitimate son, without her having to leave England. But there was a rival for Julia's hand, and Marcus knew it. How did the girl feel? Anne wondered. Which of her beaux did she prefer, Netherton or St. James? Or did she even have a choice? She glanced at Darkefell. "Do you think young Mr. Netherton is someone we ought to be looking at, in our search for Marcus's murderer?"

"I do. He is passionate about Miss Lovell, and murder is a passionate crime."

Anne shivered. He didn't seem to see that the motive he was ascribing to John Netherton could just as easily be attributed to him. She watched him for a moment, his face in three-quarter profile, light where it was turned toward the dull gleam of shrouded sun through the window, and shadow where the light did not fall.

They had already spent many more hours together than she had ever spent with her late fiancé, Reginald Moore, and yet she had so many questions about the marquess. He'd followed her all the way from Yorkshire and gotten in a violent fight with St. James. But would he kill the man in the middle of the night? She thought, given what she knew of Darkefell's character, if he had fought Marcus and killed him, he would have carried the body up to Cliff House and explained himself like a man, rather than leaving the body to be washed about on the tide for them to find later.

But would the magistrate understand that about Darkefell? If the marquess continued to refuse to explain what he and St. James fought about, would he be in danger of arrest? She watched him, aware of a desire to reach out and touch his cheek, the dark outline of his beard showing despite exquisite barbering. She wished she could run her fingers along his jaw, touch the pulse at his temple, kiss the lips that were pressed together as he thought. He had begun to weave a dangerous spell over her, she mused, one of fascination and obsession. She thought about him far too much now. She turned her gaze away, to find that Pamela was watching her with a slight smile on her weary face.

"I think I'll pay a visit to young Mr. Netherton," Darkefell said. "Though I doubt I will tell him my real motive."

"Pam and I could visit Miss Lovell," Anne said, tapping her gloved fingers on the table. "If she had a definite understanding with Mr. Netherton, then it is unlikely he would have considered St. James a serious rival. Perhaps they cleared things up after his attack on Marcus the night of the assembly."

"That *is* one thing you could do that I could not," Darkefell agreed. "Captain St. James's prior connection with Miss Lovell would be all the explanation you need."

Anne rose, and Pam, too, stood. "But I suppose, right now we ought to return to Cliff House," Anne said, thinking that Pam was exhausted and near the end of her tether. She didn't know what else to say to the marquess. Anne was increasingly uneasy with the amount of information she had to keep from him. Without Pam's permission she couldn't tell him about St. James being the ghost, Pam's involvement in the smuggling, her connection to Micklethwaite or even Puddicombe's threats.

"May I speak to you alone, for a moment, my lady?" Darkefell said, his gaze fixed on her eyes.

Trembling a little, she said yes, and they walked out of the inn coffee room toward a tree on the village green, as Pam sat on a bench outside the inn and waited.

Darkefell, brushing against Anne as they walked, said, "I would kiss you, right here and right now, if I could."

Her heart thumping, her breath catching in her throat, Anne said, "You shouldn't say things like that, Tony."

He stopped and stared down at her. The breeze lifted locks of his dark hair from his forehead and he swept them aside. "Why not? Why should I hold back the truth?"

"Do you have anything to say other than . . . other than that you want to kiss me?" She pulled at her gloves and stared off into the distance, toward the church.

He frowned. She wasn't meeting his eyes, and her frankness was one of the things he loved most about her. What wasn't she telling him? "I'm going to ask some questions around the village. Is there anything you're keeping from me, Anne?"

"Why do you ask?"

He grabbed her shoulders and ducked to catch her gaze under the brim of her hat. "Tell me! Was St. James mixed up in this smuggling business?"

"Why?" she blurted out, meeting his gaze. "Have you heard anything?"

"No," he said reluctantly. "But it's a reasonable surmise. Why else would he be on the beach in the middle of the night? He must have been killed down there. I've heard of this Lord Brag who is the masked leader of the St. Wyllow Whips; I've been wondering if St. James was Lord Brag. Perhaps he was in partnership with the boat captain, Micklethwaite." When she didn't reply, he said, "Anne, this is no time to keep things from me. I thought we were working together on this?"

She didn't say anything for a long moment. Then she turned her gaze up to him, but it was shuttered, the clear honesty usually present in her gray eyes clouded with evasion. "Tony, I am bound by promises I have made. I will tell you all I can, when I can, but I cannot promise complete candor."

A cold chill crept into his bones. "Don't do anything foolish," he pleaded.

"I have to go," she said, avoiding his eyes again. "Pam is so tired. You're going to come to us tomorrow, after the funeral, aren't you?"

He assented and watched her go, walking arm in arm with Pamela St. James. What was she keeping from him, and why? St. James *must* have been tangled up in the smuggling business.

A few minutes and a few questions later he had found his destination, and entered a barrister's office on a narrow, sloped back street in St. Wyllow. There, laboring on a stool by the pool of weak daylight streaming in the window, was young John Netherton. Darkefell cleared his throat and the fellow looked up, startled, throwing a blotch of black ink over the document he was copying.

He slipped from his stool, bowed, and said, "What can I help you with, my lord?" as he tidied the blotched document, crumpling it and mopping up the ink.

"Is your master in?"

"No, my lord," the young fellow said. "He's absent today, on business in St. Ives."

"Good. It's you I wish to talk with. Let's get out of the dreadful stuffy room and walk."

Netherton finished cleaning the mess and locked up the office, then the two men scaled the narrow, steep street to the village green. Darkefell wondered how best to bring up the subject of Julia Lovell and Marcus St. James, but he needn't have worried about that. Netherton began the conversation.

"I heard you bested Captain St. James, the night of the assembly. I would have shook your hand if I'd seen that, sir. That man needed taking down a peg or two."

Darkefell glanced sideways. "You do know he is dead, murdered, and in a cowardly, brutal fashion."

Netherton nodded, his open countenance showing no remorse for his previous comment. "Doesn't change the fact that he was a slimy eel, my lord. Those officers, they think they can take anything they want, come into St. Wyllow, drinking, flirting," he said, his voice trembling. In a lowered tone, he added, "Turn a young girl's head with their ways, they do, splashing money about, making promises."

"You're not sorry he's dead."

"I'm not," he said, vehement, his jaw set and chin thrust forward. "He would have been an awful husband to my Julia, an' I heard he was going to ask her pa for her hand. Old Lovell would sell his soul to the devil to climb up in society beyond his family worth, and the captain bragged about his connections, used a lot of big names, Lady Anne Addison among 'em. Not for Julia's sake, though, does her pa want to move ahead," he ranted. "No, it's for his own arse-kissing sake, beggin' your pardon, my lord, for the profanity. He thinks if he can just get in the right circles, he can get himself a knighthood."

Darkefell reflected that he had felt much the same sentiment, that he was not completely sorry St. James was dead, because the captain's death eliminated a rival for Anne's hand. Though the sentiment was beneath him, he still felt a fellowship with the younger fellow. "He was courting Lady Anne, too, you know."

"And makin' love to old Lady Foakes."

"Who?"

Netherton plunked down on a bench in the middle of the green, and put his face in his hands. "St. James was having an affair with Lady Foakes, Julia's chaperone, the one who was supposed to be getting Julia married to someone uppercrust," he said, his voice muffled. He scrubbed his face and looked up. "I'm not good enough for Julia, Lady Foakes figures. Prob'ly right on that score," he said, gloomy. "St. James began to make those sheep eyes at the old bat, and I noticed something odd. Both of 'em—the captain and Lady Foakes—would be gone for a while at the same time. He was giving her what she wanted, and she made sure he was first in line for Julia's hand."

"Did you tell Julia this? That her chaperone and her suitor were having an affair?" Darkefell asked, not shocked, but wondering how it all jibed together.

"How could I? She was confused, my lord," he said, turning his earnest gaze toward Darkefell, his pale blue eyes prominent. "One day, she'd be sure she wanted me, and the next, the captain would come around, sweet talking, telling her stories of places he'd been, things she should see, people he could introduce her to. He'd say she was too good to become a drab housewife—and she is that, sir—and she'd doubt me. I couldn't hurt her by telling her the truth about Captain St. James."

"You're a better man than I, Netherton. I would have used any shred of displeasing information I had to crush St. James's reputation if I thought it would do one single jot of good in the eyes of a lady for whom I care."

"Instead, you beat him good and proper," Netherton said, gazing at him with slavish worship.

Darkefell shifted uneasily. "I'm not proud of that, though I wouldn't take it back. If I had it to do over again, I would have made it a fair fight first, though, told him I was coming for him."

"You can't fight fair with that sort, my lord."

Was that true? In a game where the stakes were high, as high as love and life, was fighting fair for dolts? Darkefell examined the fellow, who had the pale, sallow look of someone who worked too hard indoors, and said gently, "And so now, will Miss Lovell marry you?"

"I don't know. It'll be years before I can marry. But at least she won't marry St. James."

With a social climbing father and a chaperone who wanted her to marry above her station, she would likely marry someone else, though. "Is Miss Lovell's father wealthy?"

Netherton nodded.

"And does he have a son to take over the brewing business?"

"No. Julia is his only child and he's a widower."

"Do you love the law, as a profession?"

Netherton shrugged.

"I would advise you, Mr. Netherton, to do this," he said, then explained a course of action that might be the fellow's only chance at marriage to Julia Lovell in the next ten years.

"Do you think that will work, sir?" the fellow said, a rush of color coming into his cheeks.

"Two things will doom it to failure," Darkefell said. "If your Julia does not love you, there is no hope at all, or if you cannot follow through with what I have suggested, you will fail. But go, do your best. It is taking a chance, but why should you not? You're young and in love."

Netherton stood and turned to him, his pale eyes shining with hope. "I'll go this minute." He grasped Darkefell's hand and wrung it. "Thank you, my lord!" he croaked, and took off, racing across the green, his step light, when just a half hour before it had been heavy with hopelessness.

"That was very good advice, young man."

Darkefell turned to see the elderly blind man who had been speaking to Anne a few days before. He stood a ways away, one hand out, steadying himself on the village green's pump. The marquess stood and said. "Your bench, sir."

The old fellow walked with simple confidence to the bench and sat, both hands cradled over the knob of his hand-carved cane. "Abraham Goldsmith is my name, sir, and you are a marquess, so I've been told. Your fame spreads. That was very good advice you gave to the young fellow. I hope he succeeds. Young love should always succeed."

Interested, Darkefell sat and examined the old man, saying, "Young love often turns into middle-aged anger, and then old cynicism, does it not?"

"If you believe that, my lord, excuse an old man saying this, but you have no right to be trying to marry Lady Anne."

Darkefell grinned. Village gossip; his pursuit of Anne was likely a topic for many a tea table conversation. Let them talk; it mattered not one whit to him. "You think you know her that well?"

"I hear the smile in your voice, my lord, but having talked to her for a half hour, I know her well enough to know that she will never be one of those cynics you talk about." He paused. "I think *you* know that, too, for it is one of the things that makes you want to marry her."

"You don't think I want her for her dowry? It is considerable, you know. Lady Anne is a very wealthy woman."

"I am no fool, just because I'm blind. If you wanted a fat purse, you could pluck any girl from that sad marriage market in London."

"Excuse me saying this, sir, but for you to disparage the Season . . . do your people not arrange marriages, much as we do?"

"Yes, with probably the same mixture of outcomes, both good and bad."

They sat in silence for a while. The old man's words had raised within him again the same question that plagued him over and over: Why did he so badly want to marry Anne? Was it simply true love, a sentiment he had never particularly believed in, in his life, viewed so seldom it was the merest chimera, wavering on the horizon, but never close enough to experience.

Though she had all the allurements he had been taught to consider — impeccable lineage, good dowry, excellent health — a hundred girls would have satisfied the requirements and been more malleable and easy to manage. In truth, he had not looked forward to marriage because his resolute sense of fairness would not allow him to do as many men of his acquaintance did, get the wife with child and leave her in the country for duty, while keeping a mistress in town for pleasure. The idea of being leg-locked for life with a copy of his sister-in-law Lydia, a girl who would vacantly stare at him if he sharpened his wit on her, a young lady who did not know the difference between a spinet and Spinoza, filled him with a sense of uneasy desperation. Certainly there were girls with minds ready enough to be taught, but did he want to become some husbandly schoolmaster, trying to cram enough knowledge and thinking into a young lady's brain so she could be sufficiently sharp and able to hold a conversation outside of the marital bed?

But Anne! From the first moment he met her, he had a burgeoning hope that life—*his* life—need not be a solitary journey. He had never been attracted to any woman in quite the way he was to Anne. Plain, outspoken, unmanageable, independent, smart and contrary: she was all that and more. He would never be able to ride roughshod over her, and that excited him. She would challenge him at every turn. He'd always been sure a wife would either bore him within a half year, drive him wild with impatience, or make him despise himself *and* her because of her inability to stand up to him. Not one of those things worried him in the slightest about Anne.

And he thought he might love her, for she inspired a tender protectiveness he had never felt toward any woman. Though he was just as likely to experience a desperate exasperation over her inability to stay out of trouble, but that was a small price to pay for such joy as he found in her presence.

How could he convince her to marry him? What if she was the only woman in England with whom he could find happiness, and she adamantly refused his offer? It was unthinkable. Even worse, what if she married someone else? All hope of winning her would then be dead. He found himself rambling about it all to Abraham Goldsmith, who admirably listened without comment.

"She's damnably independent," Darkefell finally grumbled. "Why can't she be a little more . . . well . . ." He trailed off and sighed.

"A little more *less* herself?"

"Ridiculous, of course. I take your point." Darkefell sighed and stuck his booted feet out in front of him.

"I will not belabor it, my lord," the man said. "You will have to keep doing what you are doing. If you cannot capture her by being yourself, then you will never catch her by being anything else."

Darkefell stood and stretched. A carriage drove up to the post-house inn and the magistrate, Mr. Twynam, got down. The moment he caught sight of Darkefell, he beckoned him, so the marquess politely took his leave of Abraham Goldsmith and strolled across the green.

"Just the gentleman I came here looking for," Twynam said. "I have been out to the regimental quarters near St. Ives, my lord, and they've made some serious charges."

"Who exactly are 'they,' Mr. Twynam?"

"Some of the officers who witnessed your attack on Captain St. James." Twynam examined Darkefell's face. "They claim that the attack was unprovoked, that you flung yourself at St. James when he was not ready, shouting that you'd kill him. What say you to that?"

Darkefell was taken aback. "I would say that you have two choices: either I did what they claim, or I had provocation enough."

"If I am to believe the latter, sir, it would be best for me to know what was said, so I can not only judge the gravity of such an affront to the lady, but also combat the military officers' claims that there was no insult from St. James."

Darkefell sighed and looked off, down the long high street of St. Wyllow to the ocean. It was turbulent, dark gray with white caps, mirroring the gray sky and white clouds scudding across the expanse. "Mr. Twynam," he said with deliberation, meeting that man's gaze, "I will never divulge to another soul what was said about Lady Anne. I don't think it's necessary, since there were a half dozen men there who heard it. Let one of them repeat what St. James said, for I never will."

"My lord, I have learned that you followed Lady Anne here from your home in Yorkshire. I believe you wish to marry her, and that leads me to wonder if, as she was often in the company of Captain St. James, and the two had a friendship of long standing, he may have had similar aspirations to her hand. Perhaps you felt it necessary to rid yourself of a serious rival? I would suggest you do yourself the favor of telling me what was said that caused you to react so very violently."

"No."

"Why not? It cannot harm the lady, my lord, for I will swear to you it will not be repeated by me."

"I don't think it necessary that you know exactly what was said. It is sufficient to say that among men, sir, comments about ladies are often blunt, rude and sometimes crude. But I expect that if you overheard something that disparaged a lady with whom you were connected — your wife, or a daughter — you would launch yourself at the man who said it and beat him to a pulp. St. James is fortunate that I did nothing more than bloody his nose and give him a black eye and swollen lip."

Twynam took in a long breath and patted his paunch, his expression thoughtful. "You do realize, though, my lord, that I must then count you among those I suspect of murdering Captain St. James."

"I understand, but I did not do it."

"Can you tell me unequivocally where you were the night he was killed and do you have some proof?"

Darkefell smiled. That would hardly help. Telling the magistrate that he was down on the beach rescuing Johnny Quintrell from the excise officers' raid would not do. "I was out, walking," he said, which was strictly the truth, but he followed it with a bold-faced lie. "I met no one, and no one talked to me."

Fourteen

Though she had intended to walk back to Cliff House with Pam, her friend was exhausted and overwrought, so Anne summoned Sanderson from the livery stable and had him take Pam home. The day had already been long and difficult, but Anne had new ideas, and was going to pursue her own line of investigation without interference.

After asking the post-house owner a few questions, Anne approached a large house on the outskirts of St. Wyllow and took a visiting card out of her pocket. She strode up to the door and tapped. For her own consequence and reputation it would have been better to have a footman, tiger or even her driver, Sanderson, but she didn't have time for formalities. A woman in her position was allowed some eccentricities away from the strict social correctness of London or Bath, and few would turn away Lady Anne Addison. She was too valuable a connection to make.

A butler opened the door, but she had a sense that he had only hastily donned his wig and jacket. He was quite possibly a groom or held some other position in the household at other times. He took her card after an appropriate greeting, and stammered an invitation to enter and wait.

In short order she was shown to a small sitting room on the first floor and joined by two women, Miss Julia Lovell and Lady Foakes, the wife of Baron Foakes of nearby St. Agnes, Anne learned, as the woman made sure to give her title and lineage. They established, in conversation, that Lady Foakes was Mr. Lovell's sister and Miss Lovell's chaperone, accompanying her to every soiree, ball, assembly, fete, breakfast and soon—plans made just since Captain St. James's death—to Bath for the summer. As the conversational flow faded, Anne had to swiftly decide how to proceed.

But Miss Lovell took the initiative and introduced a topic. She leaned forward and said, her voice soft and breaking, "I would so like to extend my sympathies to Miss St. James. I was . . . I was very sad to hear of the captain's death . . . uh, passing."

Anne's gaze flicked back and forth between the two women, and she noticed Lady Foakes's eyes misting.

"He will truly be missed," the lady added to her young charge's expression of condolence.

"Indeed he will. I have known Captain St. James for many years, and will miss his joy of life, his sense of humor, a hundred things!" She felt the pain well up in her, for the specificity of what she would miss about St. James had not occurred to her until that moment.

Lady Foakes choked back a sob. With a hurried "excuse me, please," she rose from the settee and rushed from the room.

That was exactly what Anne had wanted, a moment alone with Miss Lovell. She mastered her own emotion, and swiftly said, "Miss Lovell, I did wish a private audience with you."

The young girl started, and sent a glance toward the door where Lady Foakes had disappeared. Hesitantly she said, "Why, my lady? We have never met."

"No, but I know you as a friend of Marcus's."

The girl stayed silent, but blushed, from her neck up to her cheeks. In London society such an unconscious display of emotion would be condemned, but Anne blessed her involuntary reaction, for it told her much. Gently, Anne said, "I understand that in his way, St. James was courting you, and that marriage had been spoken of."

"By my father and Lady Foakes, yes."

"But not by you?"

"I . . . I did not think it would come about."

"Why?"

The girl cast another glance toward the green and gold door. Then she fastened her gaze on Anne and leaned forward, whispering, "My chaperone and Captain St. James were . . . that is . . ." She trailed off and shook her head, unable to say the words. Her color heightened.

"They were entangled?"

She nodded. "My aunt . . . that is, Lady Foakes thinks I am silly and dim, but I'm not. I knew when they would slip off together. I think . . . thought it was disgusting." She primmed her mouth into a thin line and straightened her back.

"And that was reason enough for you to think the proposal would not happen?"

The girl hesitated yet again, but then finally she said, "Nooo, I suppose it was not that I didn't think he would ask me to marry him, though I was trying to discourage it," she said, her speech becoming a little confused as she tangled herself up in words. "What I meant to say is, he may have asked, but I would not wish to marry a man who would . . ." She broke off and shook her head again.

Despite the girl's reticence, Anne understood her. "Let me get this right: If Captain St. James had proposed, you would have refused him?"

With an expression of some relief, Julia Lovell said, "Yes."

"My understanding is that there is another gentleman you prefer."

The girl was silent, casting another glance to the door.

"Miss Lovell, I will be frank with you. I have heard that you and Mr. John Netherton have an understanding of a sort."

Miss Lovell nodded, blushing.

"So," Anne said, moving about on her uncomfortable straight-backed chair, "is the setback prohibiting marriage that he may not be financially able to wed for some time?"

Again, Julia Lovell nodded.

"Did Mr. Netherton know you would have refused Captain St. James?"

"I told him so, but he was still angry at the captain's seeming to think he could just ask, and I'd fall into his lap." The girl smiled, a sly, self-satisfied little smirk. "John is exceedingly jealous of my regard!"

And Miss Julia Lovell enjoyed the power that jealousy gave her, Anne thought, the power to torment an infatuated young man. It was not a pretty picture, the girl's smirk, however, for most of her life Julia would be dominated by others, with little choice beyond what gown she would wear, or what party she would attend. At this moment in her life, choice over whom she would marry was the most control she would ever wield.

Anne sympathized with her predicament enough that she could not condemn her petty, but transitory, tyranny. "I can't tell you what to do. I don't know if your young man will be able to marry any time soon, and I don't even know if it is right for you to wait for him. But I do know this," she said forcefully. "Do *anything* rather than marry where you have a strong disinclination. This is *your* life,

Miss Lovell, the only one you will have before heaven, and you have a right to decide how you will lead it."

Julia sighed and nodded. "I wish I could convince my father to let me follow my heart," she said in sentimental tones. She moved a ring around on her finger. "But I should not like to be an old maid."

"Better an old maid than a miserable wife. Hold out, my dear, hold out. Don't let anyone bully you. I am fortunate not to be trapped in a marriage that would have been a torment to me, but my current good fortune was at the expense of a tragedy that I must regret. My fiancé died before we were to wed, or I would be an unhappily married woman right now. Do *anything* rather than be forced into that sorry state."

Anne was about to leave, but Lady Foakes came back that moment, in command of herself once again and explaining her tears by saying she had gotten a mote in her eye. She had ordered tea while out of the room, so Anne remained and they spoke desultorily of the neighborhood.

The name Puddicombe came up in conversation, and Anne remembered taking one of the officers to task at the regimental assembly for his insulting manner concerning Miss Harriet Puddicombe. It appeared that Julia and Harriet were friends.

"I feel so sorry for Harriet," Julia said, putting down her cup with a clatter. "With a father like that! He's brutish and cruel. He reminds her all the time that he spent a lot of money on a Season for her, in London, and yet she did not come home betrothed."

"He expected perhaps an earl?" Anne said. Both of the other women looked a little shocked at Anne's blunt remark, so she continued, "I've seen Harriet Puddicombe. She seems a very pretty girl, but most men will look for more than a pretty face and small dowry. Her father would be better off letting her go to Bath, where she can mingle and get to know a variety of young men."

Julia and Lady Foakes exchanged glances.

"He wants to send her to Bath with me," Julia said stiffly, "now that it is being talked of. But she doesn't want to go. There is someone in St. Wyllow that she plans to marry."

"Does her father not approve?" Anne asked.

"He doesn't know, but if he did, he would never approve. But Harriet will turn twenty-one in a few days, and then she and Johnny

Quintrell can be married any time they like, without her father's permission."

"Johnny Quintrell?"

"Yes, the son of Mr. Joseph Quintrell, who owns the Barbary Ghost Inn. Mr. Puddicombe would think Johnny beneath his daughter, but Harriet longs to marry him. They are desperately in love."

After a few more minutes of conversation, Anne said good-bye to the ladies and strolled into the heart of St. Wyllow, contemplating what she had learned. She wasn't sure if John Netherton's extreme jealousy toward Marcus, balanced by Miss Lovell's apparent determination not to marry Marcus even if he asked, helped or hurt the case against John Netherton as murderer, but she also wasn't sure she wanted to make that case. It was more important to her that Darkefell was *not* considered a suspect than it was to provide Mr. Twynam with alternatives.

Julia Lovell's dilemma had caught her attention. Anne had been bullied into accepting the first proposal of marriage she ever received at the tender age of eighteen, and ever since, she had a horror of girls being forced to make such a momentous decision just to satisfy a father or mother's ambition. Her own fortunate escape from what would have become a wretched marriage had been purchased by her fiancé's death at the siege of Yorktown in the war with the colonies; it was certainly not a cheerful release, though she was nonetheless grateful to providence. She hoped that she would have had the fortitude to jilt Reginald before they married, but she very much feared that the girl she was at eighteen would not have had the courage to face the condemnation of society, nor the wrath of her mother.

A familiar face caught her attention, and she cried, "Mr. Goldsmith!" as she crossed the green and sat on a bench beside him. "It looks like it is going to rain. Do you wish company on your walk home?"

"I'll not leave the green yet, my lady. You sound — pardon me for saying it — a little tired."

"I am," she said, sitting back against the bench and closing her eyes for one long moment. But the image of poor St. James dead recurred.

"I was sorry to hear about your friend, Miss St. James's brother, dying so tragically. That poor young woman, left with no one. I have heard she was devastated when her betrothed was killed, and in such a similar way!"

"I beg your pardon?" Anne perked up. "A similar way?" For the first time, she realized she did not know how Pamela's fiancé had died.

"He was a local fellow, I've heard tell. Involved in smuggling, and got in too deep, it's said. Those smugglers, they're a dangerous lot, treacherous and deadly if crossed."

Her stomach clenched. "There are, I understand, different gangs of smugglers," she said cautiously. "Do you know, was he involved with one particular group?"

"A local sea captain is in the trade, I've heard; him and the young lady's gentleman were partners."

"Would that be Captain Micklethwaite?" Anne's mind was reeling at the new information; what did it mean that Pam's fiancé had died in the same way as Marcus? And why had she never said it?

"Yes, Micklethwaite's the name," Mr. Goldsmith said. "But you did not hear that from me, my lady. Surprising how much people say in front of an old blind man because they somehow think he is deaf as well as sightless." He chuckled.

But Anne did not laugh, for her mind was still whirling with speculation. "But how exactly did he die? You said it was similar to Marcus St. James's death?"

"All I have heard is that the poor fellow's body was found after a night's raid by the excise men, on a beach below a cliff. He took a bullet to the heart, I understand. But some whisper that his partner, Captain Micklethwaite, wanted him dead because he bragged too much and too often about how much money he was making from the trade."

"That would certainly make him a liability." She had been considering Puddicombe as the possible villain, but perhaps she had been looking in the wrong direction. But even if the smuggling sea captain had killed Pam's fiancé, Bernard, why would Micklethwaite have wanted St. James dead? Marcus was closemouthed, and never breathed a word of the smuggling to anyone. "Have you told any of this to Magistrate Twynam?"

"Begging your pardon, my lady, but an old blind Jew telling that gentleman anything? P'raps he is a good magistrate, but high in the instep and a hard man. He'd be more likely to spit at me than talk to me."

Anne bowed her head. Some believed Jews to be liars, others despised them as murderers of Christ. If the magistrate believed either of those things, he would dismiss out of hand any information from Abraham Goldsmith. "Why are you telling *me* this?"

Abraham Goldsmith stilled. He tapped his walking stick on the ground and said, "There is a rot in this town, people dying who should not die, young men, fathers, providers. I would see it stopped, but a man like me . . . I must be careful not to bring down anger on my cousin, who has enough difficulty making her living as it is, a Jewess in a small Cornish town, depending upon people's custom as a seamstress, but *you* . . . I knew from the moment we spoke that you had the light in your heart, the brightness that guides a will to do right. *And ye shall know the truth, and the truth shall make you free.*"

She stared at him. "That's from the New Testament!"

"It is." He grinned, his gnarled hands caressing the top knob of his stick. "In Kent, a very kind — if misguided — Christian lady thought that if I heard 'the Word,' I would convert. She talked about someday forming a society for that purpose, the conversion of Jews to Christianity. How could I take offense? It was kindly meant. She was very sincere, and I am not one to turn away kindness, in whatever form I find it."

Anne bit her lip, then realized she did not have to restrain herself. She chuckled, and it felt good, after so much pain. "Thank you," she said. "Thank you, Abraham Goldsmith, for making me smile in the midst of so much woe." She put one hand over his, over the head of the stick. His joints were knotted with arthritis, and she wondered how much pain it caused him to carve as he did? "Now, do you know anything else you think you should tell me?"

"Yes," he said with a sly smile. "Did you know, some of those boys who are hired by Mr. Puddicombe, the prevention man, they swear that some of the explosions that accompany the awful Barbary Ghost appearances come from *behind* them?"

"Behind them? How could that happen?"

"I would say that not all of them are from the same source."

Anne pondered. Puddicombe, who was supposed to be paid off for ignoring the St. Wyllow Whips' smuggling, while arresting others who used the sandy stretch beneath the town or along the nearby shore to land smuggled goods, was pushing Pamela for more; more money and more of herself. Had he decided to get rid of Marcus, who could have been a danger to him? Was he also trying to confuse the raids by setting some of the explosions himself? It would certainly make it easier to explain his decisions to retreat to the higher in command to whom he answered.

The drizzle became more pronounced, and Abraham Goldsmith rose. "I think it is a little wet, my lady, even for me."

"May I walk you home?" she asked.

He shook his head. "If you have been asking questions about smuggling, you will have enough trouble in this town without being seen as a friend to me and mine. Some would damn you as a heretic, even for that kindness."

"Mr. Goldsmith, first, I have been very circumspect in my questions. No hint of smuggling has passed my lips. And second, this is not *my* home and never will be, nor am I in the slightest bit worried about what people will say about me. I recognize the value of my good reputation, but as the years pass, I become more secure in my own judgment, and less likely to let anyone stop me from doing what I think right, and what I think proper, and what I think pleasant. My father says one should never miss any opportunity to combine kindness with friendship. Let me meet your cousin, and see the walking sticks you carve, sir."

"Your father sounds like a remarkable man, my lady."

"He is," Anne said. "He's wonderful."

"Lord Darkefell, too, is an unusual man," the fellow said, as they walked.

"You've met him?" Anne said sharply, wondering at the abrupt change of topic. She had her arm through the elderly fellow's, but their progress was slow across the slick grass.

"Yes, my lady, I've met him. A fine fellow. I did not expect him to speak with me, but he did."

She smiled. "He's one of a kind, sir." She sighed. One of a kind. If she believed that, then perhaps marriage with him would be completely different from any marriage she had ever seen. What would that one-of-a-kind marriage be like?

• • •

Darkefell had cornered Johnny Quintrell again and asked questions he had never thought to ask before. The Lord Brag Johnny spoke of was a recent incarnation of a smuggling leader, as recent as a year or so ago. The marquess also established, from Johnny, that Captain Micklethwaite lived some distance down the coast, having moved there from a house much closer to St. Wyllow, a house that he still owned.

That abode was Cliff House.

As a misty rain began and all sensible people retreated indoors, Darkefell and Osei went to examine the beach below Cliff House and the cut that divided it from the headland. Though the tide was at low ebb, waves pounded the beach, leaving only a sliver of land to traverse. Darkefell showed Osei where the crevice was in which he and Anne had found the ghost costume.

"But I have heard tell, my lord," Osei said, talking loudly over the thunder of waves as he took off his rain-spattered spectacles and wiped them with a cloth, "that the coastal cliffs are riddled with caves, and these have been used with good effect by smugglers. Could there be another cave along here, a deeper one, someplace where supplies are kept, or the smuggled goods stored?"

The rain pelted down harder, but Darkefell was in a perfect rage to do his utmost to keep Anne from harm at the hands of the smugglers, the excise man, or whomever else threatened her. He would not trust her to keep herself safe. She seemed intent on proving that a woman could do anything a man could do, and while he was sure that was not so — and he truly hoped someday to be able to show her the things *he* could do that a woman couldn't — he would not say that, for to counter her was to enrage her. While not afraid of her fury, angering her needlessly was counterproductive to his ultimate goal, her consent to marry him. He hoped he was wise enough not to cut off his nose to spite his face.

He scanned the cliff side below Cliff House, striding along the hard-packed sand with Osei following. Waves lashed the shore, and he had to skip closer to the cliff to avoid them on occasion. "There," he pointed, indicating a dark hole in the cliff partly concealed by a rock that jutted out. He scrambled up over the slippery, wet rocks, and Osei followed.

It was a natural cave that first expanded, beyond a narrow cleft, then tapered as it went deep into the rock. The sound of the waves echoed weirdly in the natural cavern, sounding almost like an opera house audience's applause at times. The light dwindled as he clambered back, but at a certain point, as the cave narrowed, he could see that the walls smoothed and began to show the effects of man, in tool marks and chipping, the flatness of the walls, and the increasing evenness of the floor. "This is the smugglers' work, mark my word," Darkefell said, stopping to catch his breath.

"But *which* smugglers, sir?"

"Good question. This tunnel could be a hundred years old and I would not know it, nor does that matter. I don't know where it ends, but it would be interesting if it was near Cliff House." He sighed in frustration. "We didn't bring a lantern, and it grows dark in this depth."

"But ahead, sir," Osei said, squinting into the distance. "I think I can see an end."

Darkefell moved forward, feeling along the wall as he went. Not twenty feet along he came to an end, with the unexpected finish of a planked doorway. Locked. Securely. From the other side. He put his hand against the door. "I wonder what is on the other side of this door?" He looked over at Osei in the gloom. "I think a lantern and some bolt cutters will tell us, eh?"

The other man's dark face split in a smile. "Indeed, sir."

"Later," Darkefell said. "For now, let us go back to the inn. A storm is approaching, unless I'm mistaken."

Fifteen

Anne waited at Mrs. Rebecca Miller and Abraham Goldsmith's home until the rain let up. It was the most relaxed she had felt since coming to Cornwall. In their small home, with the good smells of bread baking, a soup pot bubbling over the fire and Rebecca, a slim, dark-haired woman, sewing by the dim, filtered light of the window, Anne talked with Abraham. He was a fount of knowledge of Hebraic history and lore, one of her father's interests, so it was more like being home than anywhere she had been in recent weeks. She then admired his canes; he had carved cane heads in the shape of foxes and horses, and had taken much of his inspiration from remembered views of the natural world, from when he had his sight.

He had already begun carving the walking stick for Anne's father from a lovely piece of alder, and she was able to suggest some other ideas for the carving of Irusan's shaggy head, taking Abraham's gnarled hand and illustrating what she meant by moving his fingers over the carving. She promised to go to a jeweler in St. Ives for the emerald chips to place in the eye cavities.

Finally the rain let up just enough for Anne to leave, so, weary from a long day, damp and achy, she walked to the livery stable and Sanderson hitched the horses to the carriage yet again and took her back to Cliff House.

The tension bubbled up within her as she dismounted the carriage, sent Sanderson back to St. Wyllow, and entered the house. Lolly was upstairs in Anne's sitting room teaching Robbie his letters and numbers, for the boy's education was woefully inadequate. Mary sat and repaired damage to Anne's extensive wardrobe. Pamela, as far as anyone knew, was still sleeping.

Anne, unneeded upstairs, descended. She had a lot of thinking to do, for she was deeply troubled by what she had most recently learned, that Pamela's fiancé was likely murdered, and her own conjecture that it was by the same man who killed Marcus, either Puddicombe or Micklethwaite. She glanced out a window and saw that the rain had stopped, and she badly needed some solitude to think. Mrs. Quintrell, her daughter Lynn and even Alice were making far more noise than any properly trained servant should.

Their slackness and ineptitude would not be borne for one

moment in a well-regulated household, however, this household was anything but well regulated. While at first the unruly nature of the household had not bothered Anne in the least, and she had found much entertainment in the squabbles perpetuated by the irascible Mrs. Quintrell (the woman quarreled with the coal man, the butcher and the rag and bone man, among others), she was beginning to be irritated by the Quintrells' slovenly habits and poor attitude toward their tasks. Servitude was a skill, Anne believed, giving dignity to a servant when they performed the function with ability and a keen eye to perfection. But it was not her household, and not her business to discipline the staff.

Anne escaped through the side door and slipped around to the back terrace hoping for silence, the roar of the ocean and the howl of the wind the only sounds she wished to hear. But as she strolled out to the flagged terrace, she heard voices, and when she turned a corner, saw that Pamela and Captain Micklethwaite were at the edge of the flagstone terrace in deep conversation. Anne's friend looked poorly, her complexion sallow, her cheeks hollow, and the dark circles under her eyes had become pouches.

Pamela noticed her, and called out, "Anne!" and held out one hand.

Anne approached, and her friend took her hand and tucked it into the crook of her arm, as if she felt the need for solace and support. But her conversation with the captain was apparently amicable. He, a ruddy-faced sailor with a pipe in his hand, eyed Anne, but did not speak.

"Captain Micklethwaite, my friend knows everything," Pam said, then added hastily, as the gentleman showed signs of alarm, "but not from me! She guessed much and heard more, and knows all, now. But she would never do a thing to harm me, and I trust her." Pam turned to Anne. "The captain was just telling me that he has arranged one more large landing. He knows I wish to get out of this difficult business, and has agreed to help me retire from the trade. Lord Brag will have one last hurrah." The ghost of a smile flicked across her face.

"When?" Anne asked, examining the man, wondering if this fellow had killed both Pam's fiancé and her brother. If she had suspected that, surely she would not be doing business with him, but for all her worldliness, Pam was sometimes too impetuous and trusting. There was more than one kind of naiveté in the world.

"Not sure what night," he said.

"We must not trust Puddicombe now, the captain agrees. He has proved to be treacherous. In the past we would have informed him of our plans so that he could ignore our landings, or on occasion appear to try to catch us, only to be turned back by Marcus's explosive apparition." Her voice caught when she said her brother's name.

Anne watched for any sign of consciousness on the captain's part, but he was solemn and unmoved. And yet . . . there was something about him that nagged at her, something she felt rather than saw.

"But I'm not using me own boats, Miss St. James." He glanced at Anne, but continued. "I've told all an' sundry that me two boats is busy with a couple o' lawful runs to Ireland and up north, an' I've hired a boat from a fellow in Bristol, one 'oo understand the business and can keep his mouth shut. The goods is coming from the low countries, due here in these waters 'bout now. Me friend's boat is coming down tomorrow, an' we'll then figure tides and time, an' unload." He clamped his pipe between his teeth and rubbed his hands together.

A few more words were exchanged, then Micklethwaite left.

"Are you sure this is wise, Pam?" Anne said, watching him disappear around the corner of the house. "Men have died. It is a lethal and terrible business you are in."

"But it is the only way I can earn enough for Edward and I to live in a decent manner. I will not let my boy starve, nor suffer and want in his life!"

"Look," Anne said, turning to her friend and clutching her shoulders in her hands, "I know how you feel about making your own way, but I would gladly give you enough money, whatever you would make from this landing, to quit now!"

Pam stiffened. "If you do not wish to help, then say so now, Anne, but do not suggest giving me charity another time." Her pale face was set in a grim expression, and she folded her arms over her chest.

Stymied, Anne gritted her teeth, not sure how to proceed, but knowing that to press harder was to offend Pam deeply. For two close siblings, Pam and Marcus could not have different characters. Though Anne admired Pam's independence, she would have preferred a touch of the cynical greed that characterized Marcus in his worst moments. She sighed, and capitulated. "You *know* I'll help, Pam."

Pamela, tears in her eyes, smiled through them. "This is to bring me a lot of money, Anne, more than you could possibly give me anyway, even if I were so cowardly and mercenary as to take your excessively kind offer. I know the risks and I'm willing to take them. It is a lot of goods, so much that Micklethwaite suggested, and I agreed, we must use the cave passage."

"The *cave* passage? What do you mean?"

"Just you wait until after dinner, and I'll show you!"

The Quintrells finally departed and dinner — overcooked mutton, *again*, accompanied by delicious biscuits baked by Lolly — was consumed. Anne waited impatiently until her companion nodded over her stitching in the parlor. The older lady finally excused herself and went up to bed.

Pam and Anne lit lanterns, and Pam led the way downstairs to the cold cellar.

"I've been down here, Pam," Anne said, her voice echoing in the stone cellar. "I found Marcus's workshop. He has a complete store of gunpowder and fireworks chemicals."

"You know what he was like," Pam said, her voice trembling. "He could never resist a magician's trick, or a sorcerer's chemistry. Playing at the Barbary Ghost and having a reason to make smoke bombs and fireworks was a joy for him."

"I certainly didn't find any tunnel while I explored."

"Just wait!"

They threaded through the warren of small rooms to what Anne thought must be the very end of the cellar, the last room she had discovered. A dusty old carpet hung against the back wall. Pam pulled it back to reveal a locked door.

She toyed with the padlock and talked nonstop, her nerves clearly stretched almost to breaking. "The authorities are very much up in arms right now. Last month a smuggler's shallop, the *Happy-Go-Lucky*, fired on a revenue lugger off the south shore of Cornwall, at Mount's Bay. The fools!" she cried, clattering the lock, the sound echoing through the confined space. "Firing on the prevention men only made them a target! Most of the crew were taken into custody, to Pendennis Castle, but escaped."

"Escaped?"

Pam smiled, the expression fleeting across her lips like a shadow. "Oh, I don't think that is any coincidence, my dear Anne, that so many were able to escape from such a fortress. I've told you, bribery infects the highest offices of this land, and the revenue service is especially polluted. At every point in our country where money is collected, the men doing the collecting watch the gold pass through their hands and they become avaricious. Thank goodness, for my sake!" she said, with another brief smile at her friend. "I cannot imagine the escape from Pendennis was effected without some help from men in positions of trust. Cross their palms with silver or gold and you can get anything."

Anne was silent, wondering what this had to do with anything.

Pam set her lantern aside on a pile of wooden crates, took a key off her chatelaine and put it to the lock. "Anyway, it is my feeling that until they get those scoundrels—the escaped *Happy-Go-Lucky* crew—the revenue service will not commit a cutter or any sea support to *this* coast. This last landing should be safe from seafaring intervention. Then I'll be out of it. We've been too busy here, and I feel certain that the excise office will investigate Puddicombe's failings soon. Micklethwaite can do whatever he wants, find another partner or retire."

She grunted, having trouble with the lock. "The authorities *must* suspect Puddicombe, for he is clumsy in his machinations," she continued, bending down and peering at the lock more closely. She then fitted the key straight in and turned it. "I think they will replace him soon, and they'll move in some sea support to try to clean up this area. I will be long gone, my lease given up and moved, with Edward, to somewhere safe and snug, across the ocean to Canada!"

"Pam, your fiancé . . . how did he die?"

She turned, her breath caught in her throat. "An excise man's bullet. I was living in rooms in St. Ives at the time and was not here, of course. Anne, it was terrible! Micklethwaite himself carried his body up to this house, he told me, but it was too late."

Victoria Hamilton

Cold with foreboding, Anne said, "Are you sure it was a revenue bullet, and not one of Micklethwaite's?"

"He'd have no cause, Anne!" Pam said, pulling the heavy padlock off the latch and setting it down on the stone floor. The flickering light of the lantern showed her expression, a willful one of defiance. "It was an accident, pure and simple. It had to be! Puddicombe's men were having to make a show of their work. They caught some other smugglers the next night. Poor Bernard; he was just in the wrong spot."

Anne held her tongue, unconvinced, as she followed Pam down the tunnel, stepping carefully as the tunnel narrowed. She shivered, but followed her friend until they came to another padlocked door.

Pam took another key off her chatelaine and fit it to the lock of that door. When she opened it, the sudden rush of cold salty air set Anne back on her heels, and the increase in sound, a weird echoing of the crashing waves, made her clap her free hand over one ear. Pam laughed. "This is how it will be done!"

Anne held up her lantern and followed her friend down the tunnel, which widened into a cavern.

"We'll not go all the way tonight; I can feel that the wind is up, and the tide, too. The water at high tide doesn't quite reach this cavern, but if waves wash in, it doesn't affect goods stored in the tunnel, as long as we bring them far enough along. If you felt it as we walked, the tunnel descends toward the sea, slightly."

"I noticed. Is the whole tunnel man-made?" Anne asked, putting out her free hand to touch the rough wall, holding up her lantern and gazing around.

"Not all, just from the cellar of Cliff House to that door we just passed. This part to the beach is natural cave and passage, a deep fissure in the rock that was lengthened by some long-ago smuggler into a tunnel to Cliff House. We land the goods on the beach below—this cavern comes out on the rock face down about fifty yards from the crevice Marcus used for his Barbary Ghost trick—then the goods will be moved along this tunnel until we get them to the other side of the door. We lock it securely, and the goods are safe. The next few nights, we move the goods out, through the house."

"What about Mrs. Quintrell and Lynn . . . and Alice?"

"No one in Cornwall notices things they should not. It is the way here."

"Risky, Pam, very risky. Too many eyes and ears."

"This is how we effected the smuggling until you came to stay with us," Pam said, defiance in her voice.

"And spoiled your plan." Anne was stricken by a sudden thought. "If I had not come to stay with you suddenly, and without warning, St. James would not have died! He wouldn't have been on the beach and would not have met his awful fate."

"Anne, it was *not* your doing, for I believe it would have happened just the same, no matter what," Pam replied, a catch in her voice. She took Anne's arm and squeezed it to her. "God had his hand in this. Edward and I will leave England now, with no ties to bind me. I'll take him to Canada, and there he can become anything he wishes. I have been suffocated in this societal prison, without my baby! But I don't know if I could ever have left England if Marcus had lived."

"Pam, Marcus said he helped you because your penury was his fault, and he had to make up for it. What did he mean?"

She sighed. "I suppose it doesn't hurt to speak of it now. St. James speculated with our family money, the bit that we had, and lost almost all of it."

They retreated back the way they had come, and Pam locked the tunnel door. They went back to the cellar and Pam locked that door too, pulling the dusty carpet down over the door, concealing it completely. She moved her lantern, setting it up on a high shelf that held preserved jars of fruit and vegetables. She then put both hands on Anne's shoulders. "I need your help for this," she said, a great seriousness on her ghostly pale face.

"For what?"

"I should not ask, but you said you wanted to help. The night we do this, will you come down from this end and unlock the door and direct the dispersal of the goods in the tunnel, while I am outside on the beach, directing the landing?"

Anne's stomach convulsed, and she hesitated. It was wrong, she thought, to go against the government, but more than that, it was dangerous. Not even her father's position could get her out of trouble if she was caught, and she would bring untold shame to her family.

"I have no one else to turn to now that Marcus is gone." Pam's eyes welled with tears. "And no one else I trust, as I trust you."

"I'll do it," Anne said, putting aside her doubts and surrendering to an overwhelming need to help her friend.

Pam, weeping, handed her the padlock keys. "Thank you, thank you," she said, throwing her arms around her friend and hugging her close.

Later, Anne sat at the window in her room, frayed nerves not allowing her to sleep. Irusan stretched out on her lap, flexing his claws and hooking them into her skirt fabric over and over. Mary had come in and gone out several times, tidying, cleaning, arranging, but finally she crept in and sat down on the edge of Anne's bed, saying, "Milady, you'll no deceive me. Something is wrong."

"There are a lot of things wrong." She trusted Mary utterly, and told her what she was planning to do to help Pamela.

As could have been expected, her maid protested vociferously. "That's madness! I'll no stand by and let you cast your lot in with thieves an' cutthroats!"

"Shush!" Anne said, casting a worried glance at the door. "I've not given Lolly enough wine tonight that she's sleeping soundly. I'm saving that for when I need her to be somnolent."

"At least let me help, milady!" Mary said, her voice clogged with emotion.

"This time, you must *not* help me," Anne said, using a tone she seldom took with her maid. "I'll lock you in, if need be. Mary, you have a son. If we were caught, I wouldn't be able to protect you. You're a servant and a Catholic; how do you think you would be treated? When do you think you would next see your son?" she scolded. "I'd never forgive myself if you and Robbie were parted."

Mary hung her head, but did not protest again. Finally, after a few minutes' silence, she raised her face. "Then at least tell Lord Darkefell. Let *him* help you," she pleaded. "He'd do anything for you, milady."

Anne sighed, wondering if that was true. Would he do something so dishonest, so unlawful? Would he put himself at so much risk? It didn't matter, she would never let him, for he, too, had people depending upon him. If he died, his brother John would take over the title, and John had no head for all of the business required of a marquess. Innocent lives would suffer.

But more pragmatically, she had another reason for leaving him out. "I promised Pam I wouldn't tell him. Help me out of my dress and then go to bed, Mary. And sleep. The landing won't happen right away, you know. Anything may occur before that. Never borrow trouble, my nanny used to say."

"Wise woman," she said, Scottish gloom tainting her tone with foreboding. "But we're not borrowing trouble," she continued, her eyes wide, as she undid Anne's gown and unlaced her stays. "We're seeking it out, hunting it down, and demanding that it descend upon us."

Anne laughed. "Now that sounds like my Mary," she said, picking Irusan up, gently, and putting him on her bed. She gave her maid a gentle shove toward the small dressing room she and Robbie were using as a bedchamber. "Go to bed. Sleep."

Mary carried her clothes but turned and gave her mistress one long, hard look before closing the door behind her.

Sixteen

The next day dawned stormy and miserable, but Pamela left early to visit Edward, taking advantage of Anne's offer of Sanderson and her carriage. She was going to tell Mrs. Gorse that within weeks she would be taking her son to their new life together. Lolly was again teaching Robbie, for it seemed that they were at an especially difficult part of his lessons, English grammar, and Mary, anxious for her boy to move ahead in life, wished him to have the benefit of such a patient teacher as Anne's companion. Beneath Lolly's fluffy exterior beat the heart of a tyrannical governess.

Anne, restless after a sleepless night and conscious that this morning was St. James's funeral, tried to read, though she could not attend to the book's lines, nor remember what she read, then ate a solitary luncheon. Lolly was still wholly occupied with Robbie's lessons, much to the child's vocal dismay.

After the midday meal, Anne paced the terrace for a while, but the weather drove her indoors after half an hour. The day dragged on in dreary monotony, and finally she knew she needed to do something or she'd go mad from boredom. Donning a cloak, she waited until Mrs. Quintrell was occupied and slipped down to the cellar with a lit lantern. Keys in hand, she stole through the cellar to the tunnel door, pulled the heavy rug aside, coughing a little at the dust, and unlocked the padlock. She pulled the door open as quietly as she could, slid into the tunnel, and pulled the door closed behind her, hoping if Mrs. Quintrell did come down to the cellar for something, she wouldn't come so far.

She held the lantern up. The tunnel was scary even in the daytime, but if she was going to help Pamela with one last smuggling run, then she was going to do it right. She wanted to know where and how this tunnel erupted into the cliff face, but it was certainly quicker and more sheltered to approach it from the tunnel side than it would be to go all the way around by the beach.

The tunnel was longer than it had seemed the evening before; light from her lantern shimmered, illuminating only about ten feet ahead. She walked carefully, keeping an eye out for creatures, warm or cold-blooded. As she crept down the tunnel, she was plagued by fretful thoughts.

What did she want to do with her life? Was she destined to become simply a wife and mother, another in a long line of maternal vessels dedicated to continuing a noble lineage? She wanted more for herself, but what?

Though she felt strongly about the ills that plagued their society and the measures she believed were necessary to produce a more just world for them all—Catholic emancipation, the abolition of slavery, improved legal rights for abandoned or mistreated women—she did not feel called to help the many who were already fighting for change. Everything she had to say had already been said by more eloquent men and women. She attended church, but was not especially religious, so "good works" through the church did not appeal. She provided money for a few projects, including a dame school near Harecross Hall and a refuge for women whose husbands had abandoned them or perished, but when she went to them to help, she only managed to interrupt the hardy women she had hired to do the actual organizing and labor. She left the schemes in their capable hands and provided advice and money. If the first went unheeded, at least she knew the second was always useful.

She read widely, and not just male writers, finding obscure works by Mary Astell and the even more obscure works of Aphra Behn interesting in the light they shone on feminine abilities, but she was no writer herself. Letters were necessary on occasion, but she had not the gift of talking infinitely on unwise things, as many women did, or deeply on one thing, as some women did. Was she no more than a butterfly, then, flitting through life, touching on flowers, sipping nectar, to leave no lasting impression once she was done and gone to whatever lay beyond the veil? Should she just marry Darkefell, enjoy his lavish attentions, and when those faded—as inevitably they must—content herself with children and the limited sphere afforded her as a female?

She put out one hand and touched the rock wall of the tunnel, trailing her fingers along it as she walked, like the gray ghost of the sad woman who was said to haunt Harecross Hall. The spirit, a lady from the time of Queen Elizabeth whose lover pushed her down some stairs and broke her neck, after breaking her heart with another woman, walked the halls on the anniversary of her murder, people claimed. She had never seen it, but then, she didn't believe in ghosts.

Her thoughts returned to marriage and the marquess. The idea of marriage to such a man, one for whom she felt some irritated affection, and much heated desire, was fascinating. And yet, Darkefell would surely not be faithful in marriage, not after the first rush of affection and glow of sexual attraction had faded, as it must, with time. And it would break her heart into a thousand bleeding pieces if he wed her, bedded her, and then went off and found pleasure with another woman.

She stopped, hand out against the chill stone. Why would it hurt so badly if he abandoned her?

There was only one answer. Her heart pounded. Damn her stupidity! Despite her intentions, despite leaving Yorkshire like a coward, despite every attempt to remain cool and detached, she had fallen in love with the man. It was more than the faint "irritated affection" she had just called it; it was love, adoration, a veritable flood of emotional attachment.

She took in a deep, trembling breath, her first as a woman in love. And yes, acknowledging it had changed her subtly. Some questions in her heart were answered so swiftly as the time between one breath and another. Would she ever fall in love? she had wondered. Yes, completely and fully, for Darkefell filled her mind with amorous thoughts and her body with amorous longings, but beyond that, his mind, intelligent without being scholarly, satisfied her in ways no intellectual ever could.

There was a precipice between like and love. She had not seen it, and fell before she could stop herself. She loved him.

She approached the tunnel door ahead, beyond which lay the cavern and ocean, as if she were an automaton. She had the key in her hand, and saw the lock, put the lantern down on the floor of the tunnel, her mind turning, her head spinning with new thoughts, new wonderment. She was in love. Had she ever felt thus before, the gladness at seeing him, the need to hear him say her name, the rush of pleasure when he did?

Never. Never with any man in her life. He was the one.

The roar of the ocean beyond the door filled her ears, and she fit the key into the lock, turning it, the heavy padlock snapping open and falling from the hasp. She swung the door open and picked up the lantern. When it shone down the tunnel, she did not expect to see Lord Darkefell.

"Tony!" she gasped.

He grinned and held up his lantern, too. In his other hand he had a crowbar. "Well, hello. This is an unexpected pleasure, my dear lady."

Anne saw Osei come up behind Darkefell, and tried to assemble her face into an expression more suitable, but she still gawped and babbled.

The marquess gazed at her steadily for a long moment, then turned to his secretary and said, his tone casual, "Osei, be a good fellow and leave us alone? Take the crowbar away, since I will have no use of it."

The secretary bit his lip, smiled, met Anne's gaze over Darkefell's shoulder and shrugged. "Very good, my lord. Shall I assume that I am to go back to the inn?"

"Yes. Do just go away."

Anne, with the new discovery of her feelings raw in her heart and her mind, stammered to the marquess, "Where did you come from? Why?" Her heart felt like it was going to burst from her chest, and it left her feeling queasy and faint. "Mr. Boatin," she called out to him, beyond Darkefell. Her voice rattled with desperation. "You don't have to leave."

"But I do, my lady." The secretary bowed, picked up the crowbar, and turned to go, then turned back. "My lord, shall I order your supper at the inn?"

"Just go away," Darkefell growled, staring into Anne's eyes.

She looked away from his searching stare. Once they were alone, with the roar of the ocean in her ears and her lantern flickering, she met his gaze and said uncertainly, "I should go back."

"No, you've come this far—come all the way."

Her heart pounded. Their words, the dual meaning threading through them, left her feeling sick and light-headed. But she let him walk her the rest of the way down the tunnel until it opened into the natural cave and she could see, through the cleft opening, to the gray sky and tossing ocean beyond. A single seagull sailed the briny blast of wind, wheeling and arcing in the sky, a dark, elegant V against the slate-tinted clouds.

Darkefell took off his coat and laid it on a rocky outcropping near the cavern mouth, but far enough back that they didn't get sprayed by the waves or blown on by the wind. "Sit, you don't look well," he said, yanking off his neckcloth and tossing it aside, as if the constriction was annoying to him.

"Thank you very much," she said, her tone as tart as she could manage, while her gaze wandered to the narrow V of skin revealed by his shirt. A curl of dark chest hair peeked from the gap in the snowy white linen.

He cast her a quizzical glance as she settled herself on his jacket.

Something had changed between them, but he couldn't figure out what. He stood for a moment, undecided, then walked to gaze down the tunnel. "May I assume that this tunnel comes up somewhere in Cliff House?" he asked, then looked back at her.

"Yes, in the cellar. And what were you doing with a crowbar, my lord?"

He sighed. Back to "my lord." He like it when she called him Tony, the intimate sound of his name on her tongue making him flush with desire. "What do you think? I found this tunnel, but the locked door made it impossible to investigate further, so I came back today to see where it led. I suspected Cliff House. Did you know that Captain Micklethwaite, well-known smuggler, owns Cliff House?"

She nodded.

"Now I asked myself, why would he rent this house to anyone when he could have access to this lovely isolated little beach, and the tunnel that would allow night landings of smuggled goods? If it was leased to someone who was a partner to him in the business, then it made sense. But a young lady?" He paced, working through the thoughts even as he presented them to Anne. "Ah, but Miss Pamela St. James is an unusual young lady, living virtually alone and unprotected, with just her brother as a nominal chaperon. Perhaps, then, it is she who is Lord Brag, and not her brother, as I was thinking?"

He turned and looked down at her. Though her expression was not as open as it had been, he thought he detected the truth. He crouched down by her. "That's it, isn't it? Pamela is involved, and deeply."

"I cannot confirm or deny, Darkefell. Pam is my friend, a *good* friend . . . she has complications—"

"A fiancé who died, perhaps in the same business she is involved in. You're worrying me, Anne."

"Not deliberately, I assure you," she said, her voice calm, her manner increasingly self-assured.

He thought about it a moment. "Why were you coming down here through the tunnel?" he asked, looking directly into her eyes. "This is it, isn't it? You're going to help her with a smuggling run." He grasped her hand and held it between his. "Don't do it, Anne," he urged, kneeling before her, her hand clutched to his chest. "Think of your life, your reputation! Don't assume your father's title would protect you."

She sighed and bowed her head.

"Anne, this is a dangerous business! Look what happened to Captain St. James." He released her hand and, without prompting, told her the details of St. James's funeral that morning. It was, of course, a solemn affair, with a dirge composed for the occasion played by the military band as St. James's coffin rested on the lich-stone at the cemetery, waiting for the regiment's vicar to read the service for the dead. Colonel Withington, poetical by nature, had written an elegy and read it. Anne wept for Captain Marcus St. James, happy that in the end his companions, those men of the Light Dragoons, had been his final friends.

"And the men who wished to fight you?" she asked, looking up into his eyes.

"We did not come to blows," he said gently. "We all were suitably impressed by the solemnity of the occasion, I hope, and ended by shaking hands. I am under no illusions; if we should meet another time on the streets of St. Ives, I think it will be a very different matter, but for now, there is peace."

"*Mors ultima linea rerum est,*" she said, her voice echoing strangely against the cavern walls. She continued, "Even, it appears, animosity."

"'Death is everything's final limit.' Quoting Horace, Anne? Why would I be surprised?" He smiled, faintly. "But do you not believe that something goes on beyond death?"

She shook her head, tears shining in her eyes, glinting in the lamplight. "I don't know, Tony; I just don't know. I know so little, I sometimes think."

Anxious to distract her from the sad topic of her friend's funeral, he said, "Tell me about it all. Tell me about what you have learned about the smuggling operation."

He had guessed all of the important parts, so she told him the rest, how Pam's fiancé had died, and after a break to recover, how Pam had taken over the smuggling partnership and become Lord Brag. She explained how St. James was the Barbary Ghost, with explosions rigged and fireworks. She even told him her own worries, that Micklethwaite was responsible for Marcus's death.

He perched on a rocky ledge a ways away from her and watched her expressions as she told him all. "How did you meet St. James and his sister?"

"I met them in my come-out Season, in London. Though I was already engaged, I remained there with my parents, for my mother adored the London Season and would never leave until there was no one left in town worth visiting. St. James was just about to buy his commission, and Pam was in London with her aunt." She hugged her knees, her gaze unfocussed. "I found her a delightful change from the other girls who were as green as I, but twice as idiotic. If I had met her before I engaged myself to Reginald, the engagement might never have happened, for she was independent in a way I admired, and wished to emulate."

"What do you mean, you would not have become engaged to Reginald?" He stared into her eyes; they were misty with remembrance, the gray like the ocean on a turbulent day.

"I never loved him," she said simply, "I was bullied into accepting him and regretted it almost immediately, but did not have the courage to jilt him."

He took in a deep breath; so, he did not have to fight a dead love for her regard. What was holding her back, then, from accepting his proposal? Simply her need for independence, the trait she most admired in Miss St. James? "Did you . . . fall in love with Captain St. James?" The pause had been occasioned by a sudden fear of the answer, but he forced himself to finish the question.

"Oh, Lord, no," Anne said, meeting his gaze and smiling, sadly. "Marcus was always . . . well, he gave me confidence. He flirted with me, and introduced me to other young men who flirted with me. He was good for my sense of worth, my battered pride and dignity. I had been humiliated into thinking that what I had to offer was not enough, that somehow my humble appearance was more damaging than my intelligence could ever compensate for. Together with Pam, they made wonderful friends to me."

"But you never considered marrying him?"

Her expression veiled. "Perhaps I did. He asked me often enough. I thought he would be an undemanding husband, since he wanted nothing more from me than my purse."

He felt a fury well up in him, and yet a gladness twinned it. He knelt in front of her again and grabbed her hands, clutching them both to his chest. "Then I thank God he died!" he growled, his tone filled with suppressed ferocity. "You deserve more than an undemanding husband, Anne. You deserve a husband who *will* demand of you . . . all the love in your heart, and the sweet satisfaction of your body and all the commitment of which a woman of your ilk is capable."

Her breath caught. "Tony!" she cried, staring up at him.

He knew an advantage when he had it. With fumbling fingers he undid her cloak and let it fall away. The roar of the ocean beyond the cave mouth filled his ears, but he felt it all slip away as he stared into her gray eyes. Gray should be cold, but her gaze was warm, welcoming, like mist over heather. He touched her cheek, cupping the soft contour in his hand. "Anne, I've tried to command you, I've shouted and bullied. You've stood steadfast like no other woman. I shouldn't admit it, but I admire your self-reliance. It is beautiful, womanly. But . . ." He broke off.

Her gaze never left his as he trailed his fingers over her neck, down the silky skin of her bosom.

Anne wondered if he could feel her heart pound. The warmth in his brown eyes, the sense she had of him pulling her toward him just with the depth of his gaze . . . she was lost in feeling, her recent self-discovery making her raw with a desire to have him touch her. Had he sensed that, and was that why he had taken her bonnet off and now trailed his thick fingers over her skin? He left a path of fire, and she sighed, trembling and closing her eyes.

His arms enfolded her and he laid her back on his coat and her cloak. Her hands went up to his shoulders to keep her steady, because she felt everything whirling around her. But the sensations didn't diminish as his bulky shoulder muscles flexed under her fingers and his lips touched hers, delicately at first, then with increasing pressure and heat.

She should be uncomfortable on the rock floor of the tunnel, but he protected her with his arms about her, cradling her as he kissed first her lips, then her cheek and chin and . . . oh! He pulled at her fichu with his teeth and removed it, then down her throat he kissed, trailing to the pulse at the base and licking, his tongue warm and wet. His breath was hot and shivers ran down her spine as he kissed, lower and lower; now his lips pressed to the soft skin of her bosom. She arched in his arms, her body shivering to life, sending trills of feeling down her back, over her arms, up her legs, all coming to a heated point within her cradle of desire.

"Kiss me," he commanded and claimed her lips.

She obeyed. But such a kiss! Impudently, his tongue sought shelter in her mouth and thrust, reminding her of that sexual dance unknown to her except in thought and vivid conjecture. Her skin warmed as if licked by flame, as he moved to lay upon her.

He pushed against her. "Does this frighten you?" he asked, thrusting, the evidence of his need hard against her.

Sighing against his neck, she whispered, "What, the thought of that unnatural invasion? Or rather, the thought of that very *natural* invasion?"

"Yes." He kissed her neck and moaned, pressing against her.

"No," she murmured, lost in ardor, "for rather than the natural abhorrence I am supposed to feel as my maidenly modesty is threatened, I feel a . . . reluctant curiosity."

"Reluctant?" He chuckled and kissed her again, deeply, and more minutes were lost in a whirling fog of sensual enchantment. "You do not *feel* reluctant, my lady, and we could ease that curiosity forever, here and now."

She opened her eyes to look up at his face above her in the dim light of the cavern. His eyes, dark pupils dilated, had a drugged sensual look, the eyelids drooping, his lips with their mingled moisture still clinging, his cheeks suffused with wanton color, just as her own were, no doubt.

"I am not a child, sir, who cannot wait to have my curiosity sated," she said tartly, seeing ahead the yawning chasm of mindlessness, and fearing the plunge. "I will wait to a more appropriate time and place for those answers."

He kissed her again, harder, with an urgent yearning that called out to her. He tugged her bodice lower, and kissed the swell of her bosom. She found that she was whispering his name aloud, and it echoed back to her repeatedly, like the sound of the waves. She could feel his heart pounding, but he suddenly stopped, his body arching away from her.

"If we do not stop now," he growled, his voice hoarse, "then I shall either disgrace myself or be in some pain."

"What do you mean?" Her education had left her with some lapses, then?

"Don't make me explain."

"Please," she whispered, reaching up and cradling his face in her hands. "Please, tell me. It appears that I know so little about some things."

He moved off of her and pulled her to him. She faced away from him, and his arms bound her close to his body, his lips to her ear. The sensation of his breath made her eyes roll back in her head, but she concentrated, listening to his explanation. Faltering at first, he explained that to continue to kiss and touch would arouse him more, while he made every attempt mental and physical to keep from releasing, and that circumstance, were he successful in keeping from spilling his seed, would eventually bring him some pain.

"Oh. We shouldn't kiss. But . . . we can talk?" she whispered.

"Yes," he said. He hugged her close and kissed her ear. "Yes, we can talk."

She was embarrassed by his frank explanation and shocked by the mechanics of his body, but less than she thought she would be, given what she herself was feeling toward him. He held her so close, she could feel the evidence of his arousal; it was enticing—that swollen lump butted against her bottom, clearly defined even through thick layers of clothes, and she longed to push back against it. Arousal, he had called his feeling, and so hers must be termed. Arousal, *sensual* arousal. She could now give a name to what she had occasionally felt.

Her heart pounded. It was all a muddle, a jumble of confused feeling and sensation, and would require the coolness of solitary reflection to sort out. The lantern had flickered and gone out, so the cave was dim, and the only sound was the roar of the waves and wind outside the cave drowning out every other noise.

For a few minutes she just lay still, feeling the steady, reassuring thump of his heart against her back. But then she rolled over in his arms and looked up at him, examining the perfect planes of his face in the shadowy dimness, high cheekbones, jutting jaw, and the dark, thick brows that hovered over his gorgeous eyes. "You are a very handsome man," she said, her breath catching in her throat, as she trailed one finger over his jaw.

He stared down at her. Would he lie and tell her she was beautiful?

"Anne," he said, and kissed her lips, gently now. "I think you've spent your whole life with an excess of consciousness about beauty, or the lack of it. What does your mirror tell you about yourself?" he mused. "Do you see your eyes, gray like mist on the moors, and yet so warm, so inviting? Do you notice your beautiful lips, plump and pink and wanton? They make me ache with desire, and I can never see them without wanting to kiss them." He did so, again and again.

She relaxed, closing her eyes and enjoying the kissing. He was not going to pretend she was a beauty, then, as other lying men had done, in anxiety to attach her for the benefit of her wealth. And yet he had praised her looks in ways that she knew could be true. When he finally stopped kissing her, she opened her eyes and gazed up at him. "Why did you shout that awful proposal the night Grover almost killed me?"

He smiled, ruefully, and the corners of his eyes crinkled. She traced the crinkles with her fingers, then laid her palm against his cheek. His face was warm, and the skin hear his hairline was damp with perspiration, even though the cave was chilly.

"I knew, in that moment, that to lose you, either to death or distance, would hurt damnably," he murmured, gazing into her eyes. "My only thought was, I must have you and keep you safe."

"Why?"

"Haven't you figured that out yet? Anne," he whispered, and cradled her face in his big hands. He searched her eyes and said, "I never thought to say this in my whole life to a woman. I never expected to *feel* so much, to *want* so much, to *need* one woman so *damn* much. I *love* you, Anne, completely, down to the depths of my soul."

Seventeen

The confession was made. He had wondered how he would say it, when he would say it. If he *should* say it. But it was done.

She didn't reply, and a coldness permeated him.

He wound his arms back around her and squeezed her tight. "So, no more nonsense about helping Pamela with her smuggling. I know you intend to, Anne, I can tell, even though you have not confirmed or denied it." He kept talking, afraid now that she would gently tell him she didn't love him. "But you must not do any such thing."

"I must do what I wish," she said, beginning to squirm. "Who would I be if I acquiesced to your command in this case, when it concerns a friend so dear, one who has lost almost everything?"

His stomach clenched. Trying to keep his tone casual, he said, "When do you intend this? Is it already planned, or will you learn more? Have you already agreed?" The sharp edge of his words knifed through the echoed susurration of waves that filled the damp cavern. He hadn't succeeded at keeping his tone relaxed.

She stilled in his arms, then pulled away from him and sat up. Through the dim half-light of the cave, she stared at him, her gray eyes wide. "Questions. We always come back to that, don't we, Tony? I'll tell you no more, for I won't have you do something drastic."

"Drastic? What do you mean?" He sat up. "Drastic? Like stopping you from making what could be a fatal mistake?"

"You must have some faith that I can take care of myself." She rose and dusted herself off. "I've lost all sense of time. How long have we been down here?"

"I'll not let you change the subject, Anne." He scrambled to his feet and took her shoulders in his hands. "Look at me!" he commanded, shaking her and staring into her eyes, ducking slightly to confront her downcast gaze. "You must do nothing dangerous. If Pamela is going to risk her life, let her. This is not your fight."

"I am my own woman, Tony."

She put her arms around his chest and hugged him. The smothering fear of losing her overwhelmed him and he clutched her to him, hugging her close. He must tread carefully. She was like quicksilver; the tighter he tried to hold her, the more rapidly she eluded his grasp, slipping away from him to re-form, whole and alone, separate. He knew damn well the only way to handle her was gingerly, and yet his anxiety for her well-being made him hasty. "Be reasonable, my dear one," he said softly. "This is not your fight, nor are you responsible for helping Pamela St. James with whatever scatterbrained problem she has gotten herself into."

Anne stiffened.

At least she was listening, he thought. He must press on, regardless of the consequences. She *must* listen to him. "Her irresponsibility must not taint your life with its stain. I would be remiss if I did not point out to you that she is already dangerously close to being considered a fallen woman. While her brother was alive, she was protected by his nominal residence in this house, but—"

She jerked from his arms and backed away, eyes blazing with anger. "Enough!" she said, her voice echoing in the cave mouth. "Enough, Tony." She gathered her cloak and swirled it around her shoulders, fixing the clasp at her throat. "I must do as I see fit."

Anger made him impatient. "I will not let you endanger yourself, nor will I allow that young woman, with her foolishness, to damage your reputation." He grabbed her arm, desperate to make her promise not to join Pamela St. James in her enterprise. "Listen to me, Anne! I will take you away from here, to Bath. Let me take care of this, and I promise you, I'll make sure Miss St. James stays safe."

She stared at him, her eyes wild with fury. Baffled, he backed away from her. What had he said?

"You will *never* understand," she cried.

"Understand what?"

"That I wish to do these things for myself."

"Why should you?" he asked, perplexed. "I told you, I'll take care of it all. Isn't that what's important here? That Miss St. James is safe, successful, and that you are safe, too?"

"Oooh!" She swiped at her hat on a nearby rock, missed it, and made another grab, successfully grasping it and clamping it on her head, ruining its shape in her agitation. She stopped and fought to regain her temper. She turned to him, and there was a frightening sadness in her eyes. "You just don't understand, and I thought you might. You say you love me. How can you love me when you don't even understand me?"

180

"Then tell me!" he said, holding out one hand to her.

"No. We've come too far for that. If you can say you love me when you don't even know me, then that's it."

He felt a cold fear clutch his belly, but it was warmed by the flame of his anger. "Don't say anything you'll regret, Anne."

"Don't threaten me," she said, her chin jutting pugnaciously. "Don't you *dare* threaten me. If my friendship with Pam displeases you, if you can with a sober expression claim Pam is close to being a fallen woman because her brother has died, if you are *offended* by my remaining in this house, then I would advise you to take yourself away from here and return to Yorkshire. Go. Run. Consider yourself fortunate that I don't hold you to your ridiculous proposal."

"Anne, I'm warning you," he said, the flame leaping into a searing fire of baffled fury. "Don't threaten *me*, and if you think I'm going anywhere, then you have mistaken me. For I *will* save you from yourself. Women's tempers were not meant for action. I will protect you from your own inexperience in matters such as this. You cannot conceive of how this could harm you, but I won't let it."

"Oooh!" She balled her hands into fists and shook them in the air. "Oh, to be told I'm incapable of rational thought, that I don't understand life, by one prime example of the miscreant sex I have fought my whole life: men! Men, who insist on keeping me packed in cotton wool so I will not hurt myself."

She glared at him, but then continued, saying, "Do you think that for my twenty-four years I have read only ladies' magazines, the ones that tell me I am poorly formed for decision making? That claim I'm impetuous and a danger to myself, therefore I am given in subjugation to some man?" She turned and strode back down the tunnel.

But she paused, turned back, and said, her voice calm, if her expression was tight-lipped, "I know your education has taught you that women are to be guarded, for their virtue rests on the fragile knife edge between their physical strength and their moral understanding, both so much less than a man's as to give their guardians justification for interfering in their life at every turn." She shook her head. "But I thought you were capable of independent thought, that you had begun to take me at my word, and to trust that there was some measure of intelligence in my brain. Go find a woman who wants your interference. *Go*, damn you. Find a lady who will wish to be protected and coddled and cosseted and kept from any kind of life! That is not me!"

And she was gone.

• • •

Darkefell had grabbed his jacket and neckcloth and stomped away from the argument with Anne, sure that he must go home to Yorkshire or go mad. When he pulled his jacket on, he discovered her lace fichu was jammed down one sleeve, and he stopped, riveted. He lifted it to his nose and inhaled Anne's essence. Love was madness, and if he was going mad, then he would go all the way. He stuffed the wispy triangle in his pocket.

A long walk and a few hours' reflection brought him back to rational thought. He would never leave Cornwall while Anne was in danger, and if she intended to help Pamela St. James in the smuggling, then she was certainly in danger. Whether she liked it or not, he was going to intervene. When he got back to the Barbary Ghost Inn, he summoned Johnny Quintrell and had a long talk.

The next morning, while an increasingly ferocious wind whipped down St. Wyllow's sloping street, Darkefell, Johnny, and Osei paid a visit to an ostentatious house far too large for the owner's apparent income; it was the abode of Mr. Francis Puddicombe.

"Will you let us in, Harriet?" Johnny asked the pretty girl.

Her face pale, and tear trails down her cheeks, she at first shook her head, gazing in wide-eyed terror at Darkefell and Osei. But Johnny whispered some words in her ear, she blushed and finally nodded. Puddicombe was absent on business, his daughter said, and that was exactly as the men had planned it should be. They entered the grandiose abode and were led to a sitting room on the second floor, decorated lavishly in execrable fashion, oriental paper and silks, dark wood furnishings and heavy draperies.

"Miss Puddicombe," Darkefell said, trying to get comfortable on the lumpy, ill-made sofa, "please, do not be alarmed by our incursion into your home. We wish you no harm, as Johnny can attest."

She still had not met his eyes, but Darkefell was accustomed to that, for his elevated station commanded abashment in some, fear in others.

"He's our friend, Hattie," Johnny said, taking her small, soft hands in his. He sat beside her, his knees touching hers, his broad, plain face clearly showing his adoration of the pretty girl. He squeezed her hands, and said, "Tell them, Hattie; tell the gentlemen what you've told me."

With his gentle encouragement, Harriet Puddicombe tremblingly admitted that she had overheard her father on many occasions speak with men about night landings. She hesitated, though, in connecting her father to more in the way of criminal activities.

Osei finally spoke up. "Miss Puddicombe," he said, "these are dangerous men your father is dealing with. Are you not concerned that he will meet his end at their hands if he is unwise enough as to trust them? Is it not your duty as a daughter to preserve his life if you can, be it even through what may seem betrayal of your daughterly duty?"

She hesitated, but then, her lower lip trembling, asked, "But if he is discovered to have taken part in the smugglers' trade, will his life not be forfeit on the gallows?"

"Punishment for such an infidelity to his public office would not be death, miss," Osei replied. "He may be incarcerated for a time, and be levied a fine, but it seems to me that would depend upon the decision rendered by the local magistrate, Mr. Twynam. If his case were pled by so illustrious a personage as my lord, the Marquess of Darkefell, I think that his verdict will rather err on the side of mercy."

"Would you take his part, sir, if it should appear that Mr. Twynam will be harsh?" she said, turning her gaze to Darkefell.

The marquess shifted, uncomfortably, but knew he must tell the truth. "It depends upon what your father may have done. If his sole participation in this scheme is as a smuggler, then I can promise you my support. My concern is mostly with finding the perpetrator of Captain St. James's murder, and keeping others involved in the smuggling, including your young man, here, safe from harm."

She sighed, looking relieved, but Darkefell was not done.

"However," he said, his tone serious, "if your father has done more, if his deeds include such a foul one as murder, then I cannot, nor would I ever, help him escape his just reward." He watched her face, the tears clouding her blue eyes, the trembling lip, the nose clogged and dripping as she applied a handkerchief delicately.

Johnny spoke up then. "Harriet, your pa hurt you bad. How many times 'ave I seen the bruises on your arms with me own eyes?" He paused, but then, his expression set with resolve, went on: "Hattie, my girl, do you not want t'marry me? Me da has promised his help, an' you know 'e's a man o' his word. We can be married right off, and be happy. You deserve that, after the life you've been pushed into."

She met his look and capitulated. Sobbing, she said, "Do what you must, gentlemen. Johnny is right; my father can be cruel, and I can no longer live like this. I want to m-marry Johnny! If . . . if my father had any part in the death of poor Captain St. James, then . . . then . . ." She broke off, weeping, and collapsed against her fiancé's shoulder.

That was all the encouragement and permission Darkefell needed. He and Osei left Harriet and Johnny to plan her escape, while they searched the house from top — the excise man's office — to the bottom, the locked cellar. What they found was well worth the risk, and Darkefell, amused at his part in this escapade, now knew he would proceed with his own plans for the final smuggling run. He would not allow Anne to be hurt, nor would he let her stand alone with her friend. If reputations were to be damaged, his would suffer along with hers.

That evening, Darkefell sat in his room at the Barbary Ghost Inn writing a letter to his land agent concerning his still-pending purchase of Hiram Grover's estate. Since the man's body had not yet been recovered, the sale was stalled, the manor servants on half pay, and the ongoing costs of feeding the remaining livestock and caring for the house and attached acres fell on Theophilus Grover. As a vicar, the young man, newly married, was not deep-pocketed enough to pay.

Darkefell authorized Mr. Posthumous Jones, his agent, to pay all associated costs until such a time as Grover could be declared dead, or was discovered. It would not benefit the estate to let it fall into ruin, nor would he allow livestock to starve, nor should the human serving staff who still cared for the house, grounds and stables suffer. The estate was intended to be a gift to his brother, John, and Lydia. She had been complaining for some time about living with their mother, the indubitably strong-willed dowager marchioness, and this would at least remove them a quarter mile. But none of it could be solved until the legal tangle of Hiram Grover's death or disappearance was settled.

Osei was busying himself with the multiple duties he had assumed as factotum while they traveled: secretary, valet, oddsbody, and coconspirator. He readily answered the hesitant tap at the door, and opened it to Johnny, who stood in the narrow hallways shifting back and forth on his feet, appearing uneasy. Darkefell observed him from the desk by the window. The dark circles under his eyes and his pallid complexion did not seem natural in such a hardy young man.

"You don't look at all well, Johnny," Darkefell said, folding his letter and setting it aside. "What is going on?"

"Beggin' yer pardon, milord, Mr. Boatin," he said, leaning against the doorjamb, but looking over his shoulder down the dim hall. He leaned into the room and whispered, "Micklethwaite 'as called a meetin' fer tonight. I suspect we'll get our marchin' orders, as to the big landing. 'E's on 'is way now, to th' pub down't th' dock."

"Pub?" Darkefell asked.

"Aye, the Dirty Dog. Only seamen goes there, milord."

"And so shall we," Darkefell said.

Johnny looked at him askance, dressed as he was in a richly patterned banyan of purple and red, and a tasseled cap.

"Not dressed in this," Darkefell said with a grin. He shrugged it off and tossed it aside, to show himself dressed in just his smallclothes. "Nor can Mr. Boatin show his face without being recognized, for I have seen no one else of his particular dusky complexion here. No, we must find someplace to conceal ourselves at this 'Dirty Dog.'"

Johnny thought for a long moment, then snapped his fingers. "I knows where y'both can hide."

Thus it was that an hour later, dressed in disreputable clothing donated by Johnny, articles raggedy enough they had been consigned to a rag bag, Darkefell and Osei huddled in the darkest corner of the low cellar under the Dirty Dog, a pub that lived up to its name in filth and smell. And probably in being flea-infested, for Darkefell had an uneasy sensation that he would be covered in bites by the time he crawled from his hiding place.

The things to which he would subject himself, and all for the love of a woman, he reflected in the dark silence. How many times had he made sport of love poems detailing male heroics to win the love of a woman? And yet he had willingly crept under a filthy cellar with the stench of fresh urine and decaying fish all around him, and all hoping to aid Anne.

Above was a small private room at the back of the Dirty Dog. Through the crevices in the floorboards a little light leaked, and as Darkefell's eyes grew accustomed, he could at least see his surroundings as a collection of shadows. Soon he heard the tramp of booted feet, the obscured murmurs of several men, and many rumbling belches and the unmistakable sound of spitting.

"How far will a man descend, Osei, to win fair maid?" he murmured, bemused.

"He will descend at least to the cellar, sir," the secretary swiftly, though softly, replied. "Do you intend, then, to relate to Lady Anne all about this particular adventure, including the eruptions from above, as evidence of your devotion?"

Darkefell stifled a laugh as a flatulent explosion from someone above reverberated through the tight space. "What do those men eat, I wonder, to produce such odious noises? And how do their ladies put up with them?"

But he became serious as the strident voice of command, belonging to none other than Captain Samuel Micklethwaite—a little muffled, but still heard easily enough, and clearly the ship captain's hearty tone and accent—called them all to order, or, in other words, told them to "shut their gobs and listen."

As soon as the weather broke, the lads and Lord Brag would be landing a great haul on the beach below Cliff House, Darkefell translated from Micklethwaite's rough accent. All hands would be needed, and there would be no fear from the excise officer, the captain confidently stated, for silver had crossed palms.

At length, after a great deal more drinking and shouting, the sound died and Darkefell, his legs cramped from the tight quarters, crept along the passage and through a cellar door into the black night, followed closely by Osei. Darkefell breathed in deeply the relatively clean scent of seaside air. The odors of the dock were as nothing compared to urine and rotting fish.

"Milord," a voice whispered. It was Johnny.

"I told you not to say that word as long as we were at this place," Darkefell warned the lad, keeping his tone low and trying to see through the murky dark and shadows of the back alley. They quickly discussed their plans as they walked back to the Barbary Ghost Inn, and the marquess and his secretary then returned to their rooms.

It was the middle of the night, but Osei lit a lamp so they could shed their rags and wash the filth of the Dirty Dog from their skin. Darkefell saw, as the light leapt, casting weird shadows up the walls, that his secretary was shuddering as if chilled.

"What is it, man? You look as if you'd seen the proverbial ghost?"

Osei shook his head, but after a moment, he sank to his knees on the floor, still shuddering and retching. He covered his face with both hands.

"What is it?" Darkefell asked, kneeling by him. "Osei, speak to me!"

"That place, that hole under the Dirty Dog . . . I held it off as long as I could, sir, but coming from it . . ." He shook his head. "It was so like the hold of that slave ship, the smell, the darkness, the sounds of feet stomping on wood above. I am sorry, sir, but it took me by surprise. I must gather myself." He shrugged off his employer's hands and stood, shaking himself. He turned to the marquess. "I beg your pardon, my lord," he said, his spectacle glinting in the lamplight. "I did not mean to make a spectacle of myself."

Darkefell stared at the younger man, examining a face that mapped the horrors he had endured at the hands of slavers. "Only you would call a momentary lapse in private 'making a spectacle of yourself.' Think nothing more of it."

Osei's reaction left Darkefell in a serious mood, and he once again wondered what he could do for the fellow that he had not already done. It was then that he remembered Osei's occasional remarks about his sister, who had been taken into slavery at the same time as he, but who had disappeared into the hold of another slave ship. Could anything be done to reunite the siblings? He wondered. He must write another letter in the morning. Until he received an answer, he would say nothing to his secretary.

• • •

For two long days, a wild storm raged, scouring the beach.

Darkefell knew the smugglers' goods could not be landed in such weather, and had heard as much from Micklethwaite. He spent the intervening time to good end. He did not yet know, perhaps, who had murdered St. James, but he did know too much to be easy.

Never intimate with smugglers, the marquess learned much from Johnny. A smuggler's cutter or lugger would weigh anchor some ways from the beach, as near as they could safely go, and then rowboats would be employed to ferry the goods to the beach. There, as he had observed when he had saved Johnny from harm, local men with carts would gather, and stout fellows would carry the goods from the rowboats to the carts, and thence inland. Or, as was going to happen this time, the goods would be carried directly into the tunnel below Cliff House, to be distributed on subsequent nights.

Finally the storm blew itself out and Thursday—it was already late in May—dawned sunny and calm. The landing would take place that night, Darkefell knew, as they had not too many nights of low tide left. One thing worried him: Micklethwaite had hired a boat to do this run rather than using his own. He had reassured his men that it was solely because the officials were looking at his operation too closely, so he had arranged to have both his boats tied up with legitimate runs. No one, he explained, would be expecting the St. Wyllow Whips to be out, if they believed him to be a part of that gang. It made sense, but Darkefell was worried.

He had tried to visit Anne, but she wouldn't see him. He still didn't understand what he had said or done that was so wrong. She was being foolish and taking unnecessary risks. Why wouldn't she let him take care of things? If Miss St. James's finances and safety were all that truly mattered, wouldn't the affair be safer in his hands? As a man, he was used to action and accomplished in planning, much more so than a couple of young ladies. The contradiction in her behavior baffled him as he tried to make sense of it.

Thursday afternoon, with Osei for company, he walked the short distance from the Barbary Ghost Inn to the side of the cut opposite the bluff beyond Cliff House, to observe and think about the landing he assumed was going to happen that night. He had a spyglass, and lay on the cliff examining the shore below where he thought the tunnel came out.

"Right there," he said, and handed the glass to Osei, explaining to him how to find what they were looking for. Osei spotted it with no trouble, and trained the glass along the beach. Darkefell rolled over on his back and stared up at the sky, watching puffed white clouds scud across the blue. "How am I going wrong, Osei? What offended Anne so much about me wanting to protect her? I fear for her life in such an enterprise as this. Smuggling! What kind of man would I be if I did nothing and let her do what she would?"

"I was not there, sir, and did not hear how you phrased the things you said."

"But I've told you *exactly*."

"Pardon me, sir," Osei said, taking the spyglass away from his eye and glancing over to his employer. "But you told me what you said, not how you said it."

"Surely that's the same thing?"

"Not at all. I have observed that when we relate what we have said to another, we summarize, not using the exact words. Nor are we able to duplicate the tone, the facial expressions, the exact phraseology utilized."

"How like a woman to care about that," Darkefell said.

Osei did not respond.

Darkefell rolled over onto his side and watched his secretary lift the spyglass again and gaze down the beach. His secretary's thin, dark face was set in an expression he knew well now, after five years of having him in his employ. Osei had his own opinions, but had not expressed them all. "Do you not think that unreasonable," Darkefell pressed, "to care so much how a thing is phrased?"

Still Osei said nothing.

Darkefell sighed in exasperation and swept his unruly hair off his forehead. "I give you permission to speak freely, Osei. I think you understand the lady well, perhaps better than I do, and I'm asking your opinion."

"Words are significant. They hold weight and meaning, each one, individually," Osei said slowly. "But tone is of import, too. How you are told to do something is *very* important, for beyond the words lie many implications. The tone in which words are delivered can say 'you are a fool, so I must treat you like one,' or 'I trust your shrewdness in this matter.' I suppose, having been in a subordinate position for some years now, sir, I know what it feels like to have my intelligence slighted—"

"When have I ever slighted your cleverness?"

"I did not say *you* did so, sir."

"I beg your pardon for interrupting," Darkefell said. "I'm impatient, aren't I? I jump in too quickly, before hearing people out." And he accused Anne of impetuosity? "Who, then, would dare slight your intelligence?"

"At first, when you hired me as your secretary, Mr. Jones," Osei said, referring to Darkefell's land steward, Mr. Posthumous Jones, "did not make it simple. He questioned everything I said, and disbelieved every order I gave. Do you not remember how often he came to you for clarification, when I had said exactly what you told me to say? You would reaffirm it, but it was three years before he began to believe me. You even asked me once if I relayed your messages to Mr. Jones and others completely."

"Why didn't you complain to me? I would have *made* him pay attention to you."

"Sir, that would just have proved Mr. Jones's point, that I was not able to make decisions for myself, nor solve problems on my own. I persevered."

"And now?"

"We are beginning to have a good understanding, Mr. Jones and I. I think I have won his respect, finally, and it is worth having, for he is a good man underneath it all."

"You must have been relieved when I sent him to London on business a couple of months ago," Darkefell said wryly.

"It does make my job simpler, not to be questioned at every turn."

"But how does that equate with my desire to protect Anne from harm?"

Osei sighed, and framed his answer carefully, frowning into the distance. Darkefell watched his thin, dark, intelligent face. He began to see how Osei had struggled, and yet had kept the struggle to himself, preferring to make his own way and fight his own battles.

"Lady Anne has lived her whole life — not just the few years that I have endured — within a society that expects her to be someone she is not. From what I have observed of your English society, ladies are thought to be impetuous, and so are not trusted to make decisions affecting their own lives."

"She *is* impetuous," Darkefell said.

"So are you, sir, but your impetuosity, even when it results in a bad end, is called risk-taking, daring, boldness. When you speak up, you are called courageous and manly. When she speaks up, she is called unwomanly, unattractive, silly, ill-judged. Shrill. Irritating. If she wishes to make her own decisions and choose how she wishes to live, it is thought to be wrong-headed and dangerous. I ask you, why is it dangerous to allow a woman to make her own decisions about life?"

"I am beginning to think men don't allow women the freedom to choose for themselves how they live, because we fear they will decide they don't wish or need us as husbands." Darkefell frowned off into the distance. "Listen to me: 'allow women the freedom.' I wonder how much there is in life that I don't understand."

Osei smiled and didn't comment.

"Will Anne ever accept my proposal?" He thought of her life, as a being of intelligence, courage, and wisdom, and yet she could not work, nor order her own life, nor command her own money. She could not purchase land. She could not choose a representative in government. On marriage she would lose even the right to speak for herself in court. Frustration must attend such limitations on action, when the woman was as accomplished and intelligent as Anne.

He had been taught his whole life that women did not wish such things as to be in charge of their own destiny, that it was too great a burden for frail shoulders to bear. But that wasn't true, clearly. "I've offended Anne terribly, Osei. I see that I should have offered to help, not told her I would send her away and do it all *for* her. But I cannot and will not allow her to fall into danger because I did not frame my offer of help in such a way as to be acceptable to her. I must risk that she will turn me away forever, while I do what I will to keep her safe."

Osei nodded. "I know."

"And it has nothing to do with distrusting her judgment as a woman. But I cannot sit on my hands while I fear for her life."

"I know."

"So the plan goes on," Darkefell said. He stared down at the beach. "I pray it goes well." He stuck his hand in his pocket and fingered Anne's lace fichu. "Tonight will tell the tale."

Eighteen

"I'm worried, Mary," Anne said, pacing in her room. Irusan sat on her bed and watched her, his green eyes fixed on her face. "Something is not right about this whole mess, and yet I cannot make Pamela listen to me."

"Aye, that's what I fear. She's trusting folks you have no reason to trust. But you must not risk your own life, milady, trying to save hers!"

"I know, I know. Darkefell tried to make that same point two days ago," Anne said, and did not need to elaborate because she had told Mary about meeting him in the tunnel, though she didn't confess *all* that had occurred between them. "Was I wrong, Mary?" She stopped in front of her maid. "Should I, for *Pam's* sake, have let Darkefell take over?"

Mary didn't answer, and just watched her mistress as she tried to repair the damage to another of Anne's hats. It was late afternoon, and the storms of the last two days had finally calmed. Pam had received word that the run was going to be that very night, just a few hours hence.

"If my only thought is for Pam's safety, and I do know Darkefell to be competent and as good as his word, should I have let him take over?" Anne pondered that question, drifting over to the window and staring out without seeing. Pride must not get in the way of helping Pam to the utmost of her and anyone else's ability. If Darkefell was the most capable of helping her in this final foray into the criminal world, then he should have been allowed to take over. But she shook her head.

"No," she said, turning away from the window. "He doesn't care for Pam as I do. He would do what he could, but I will do more. I owe so much to her, more than anyone will ever know. If he had only offered to help me, rather than demand I leave, I may have accepted his assistance, for he's a good ally. But he would have bundled me off, and I cannot just go away and hope for the best. What kind of friend would I be?"

"You're not a foolish woman, milady," Mary said, frowning as she tried to prop up a broken feather. But there was no hope for the plume, so she removed it and tossed it aside. Irusan, in a rare display of feline fancy, leaped upon it, chewing it and tossing it around on the bare wood floor.

"I wish Darkefell fully believed that. I'm afraid I was very rude to him, but he will not accept that I am no fool. He *claims* to think me intelligent, but then goes on to command me in the same tones as any other man."

"He *is* just a man, milady," Mary said, poorly trying to hide a smile.

Anne picked up the feather and tossed it in the air, letting her cat race after it, dashing across the polished wood. She laughed at the injured look on his face as he slid into a wall. He stalked away and sat in an inelegant pose to wash his bottom, one leg stuck up in the air. His nonchalance was feigned, Anne knew, because he despised being laughed at. He demanded respect, and so did she.

Anne couldn't stop thinking about Darkefell's confession, his claim that he loved her. It had deeply touched her and she had been about to confess her own feelings, before he commanded her to stay out of Pamela's troubled life. She stiffened her backbone, putting thoughts of Darkefell away.

"All right," she continued, "back to the smuggling run tonight. I'm fortunate that I have set my own course of study over the years. For a while, I was interested in chemistry, and learned the rudiments of some chemical compositions. I've been working on something for the last couple of days." She slewed a glance toward her maid. Though they were very much mistress and maidservant and very different in a multitude of ways, Anne would have been a fool not to listen to and consult with a woman of so much strength and integrity. It didn't change the fact that her final decision was always her own.

Mary eyed her fearfully. "Why do I no' like the poor direction this is taking?" she said, her *r*'s rolling with agitation.

Anne sat on her bed and Irusan leaped up onto her lap. She ruffled his thick mane of fur. "I said I would not allow you to help tonight, but I think I may need you," she confessed. When she explained what she required, Mary reared back in amazement.

"Milady, I could never do that!"

"I don't even know if you'll need to, but I can't think of any other way. I can't be in two places at once, and there's no one I trust as I trust you," she said, echoing Pam's words to her. "Please, Mary, I've asked you only to do the part I think you can handle without danger to yourself. Once you've done your part, I want you to scurry back here, to Cliff House, and safely into bed."

"You don't think I'm worrit about my own safety, do ya?" the maid said, anger flaring in her mild eyes. "I'd go to the ends of the airth for you. But I just don't know if I can do it."

Anne reached out and put one hand on her maid's wiry arm. "I have faith in you, Mary. I have faith in your intelligence and ability."

"All right," Mary said, covering Anne's long-fingered, strong hand with her own. "I'll do't, milady." She crossed herself.

"Anne, dear?" Lolly called out, tapping on her door.

"Yes, Lolly . . . come in," Anne called, squeezing Mary's arm and releasing it. For the next half hour she listened to Lolly's litany of complaints about Mrs. Quintrell, and soothed the companion's hurt feelings, all the while planning in her head that evening's work. She had a lot to do before then, and some of it required that no one observe her. Not even Pamela.

• • •

It was late, and down at the ocean the tide was turning, pulling back from the shore, each wave just a fraction of an inch lower on the sandy beach than the one that preceded it.

Inside Cliff House, Lolly, having imbibed a goodly amount of excellent fortified wine, was snoring, and Robbie was sound asleep, weary from another day of letters and numbers. Mary paced the wood floor, alone in Anne's chamber for fear of waking her child. But Anne and Pamela were in Pamela's bedchamber, almost ready to go, Anne having substituted for her friend's maid, Alice, who was busy on some vital task devised by her mistress.

Anne had helped in every detail of Pam's elaborate costume, but still was amazed by the transformation. She gaped at Pam, now dressed in the best of her brother's clothes, a brocade jacket, plumed hat, tight breeches, but her own boots, custom fit from a cobbler in St. Ives, she said.

"I had to give some explanation why I needed a pair of boots," she said, glancing into her mirror and catching Anne's eye. "So I said it was for a costume party in London." She turned around, slowly, and held out her hands. "This is it, the last time Lord Brag will command his smuggling gang."

Anne's stomach clenched. She put one hand flat over her belly and said, "Then let's make it a good one." She paused, but decided one more time to warn her friend about the men upon whom she relied. "Pam, do you really trust all your men, Micklethwaite, especially?"

"I do," she said blithely, turning to examine herself in the mirror again. She donned her black cloth mask and smiled. "I have too much information on the good captain to think he would do otherwise than keep his word to me. What possible reason could he have to cross me? We both profit in this enterprise."

"There are other things than profit, my dear, unfathomable reasons for betrayal."

Pam whirled and took her friend's two hands in her own. With a teary smile, she cried, "Anne, stop worrying. We have an enormous shipment tonight; at least twenty thousand pounds or more in goods is coming ashore, and my share will amount to at least four or five thousand pounds. Everything will go well, and with my share I'll be able to leave St. Wyllow. Edward and I will live upon it for thirty years in Canada!"

"I'll never see you again," Anne said, tears welling in her own eyes.

"You don't know that! I may come back, or you may visit."

Anne pulled her into a hug, then set her away. "It's time."

"Your part is simple, Anne," Pam reminded her. "All you have to do is open the tunnel door, direct my boys, then, once the goods are unloaded, lock it up for me again."

Anne smiled. "Don't worry about me, Pam, just keep your mind on your task and be careful." On her way to the tunnel, she had a slight detour planned, into Marcus's workshop.

• • •

"If I was the smuggler," Darkefell whispered to Osei, "I would take advantage of the high tide to row a boat right up to the tunnel cave and unload. You'd need fewer men that way."

"You would make an accomplished criminal, begging your pardon, sir," Osei murmured, a smile in his voice.

They crept through the dark along the wet beach, not daring to carry a lantern, and so depending on the faint differentiation in light and shadow from the cliff and water. "I have a bad feeling about this," Darkefell murmured. They both wore dark clothes, and Darkefell had smudged his face with lampblack, trying to conceal any gleam of his pale skin, but he was perspiring and the ocean mist was clinging to his cheeks and forehead. He had the awful feeling the lampblack was streaking, but he dared not mop his face, for fear of wiping the soot off completely.

Both men stopped and listened, as they had done often while approaching the site for the smugglers' landing. The ocean had calmed, and the receding tide tossed playful waves on the shore. The sound was the merest whisper and nothing more. But this time when they paused, Darkefell heard another sound; the plash of oars in water echoed faintly against the rocky cliff side. He looked out over the ocean and saw a light winking, a signal to those onshore, no doubt.

His was a difficult position this night. His intent was to be an observer. If things went well and there was no danger, he would not interfere. Anne, he was certain, would not get herself involved in an ongoing smuggling affair, so his assumption was that Pamela St. James was doing one last run. Perhaps it had already been arranged before Marcus's death, or perhaps she needed the money.

Her brother's death would have left her in a difficult position, for his commission was surrendered to the crown upon his death, its entire value gone in an instant, and she may have had his affairs to put in order. If he had died insolvent, all his debts would descend upon her as his only surviving relative. Darkefell had done his utmost to keep from judging her, though his anger burned brightly at Pamela's involving his Anne in such an illicit and dangerous affair.

Not that anyone could keep Anne out of it, if she had made up her mind.

But if things went badly, he and Osei were both armed. He had tried to keep his secretary from coming with him, but the fellow was fond of Anne too, and insisted on sharing the danger with his employer. Osei, as mild as he seemed, was a good fellow in a tight spot, wiry and athletic beyond a slight limp he worked hard to mask, the remnant of an injury sustained when he was thrown from a slave ship six years before.

As a young prince, in Africa, Osei had been trained in warcraft, and though tribal warfare and smuggling were vastly different events, the characteristics needed, those of steady nerves and decisive action, transferred perfectly from one activity to the other. If Anne was in peril, Darkefell was going to whisk her away, hand her over to Osei, and then make sure Pamela St. James escaped harm.

Both men hunkered down close to the cliff in the shadow of a jutting rock outcropping that sprung from the beach. The plash of oars got louder. A group of fellows — Johnny Quintrell was among them, but if things got dangerous he was dedicated to assisting Darkefell and Osei — silently emerged from the shadows near the tunnel entrance. The figure in front, illuminated by a lantern on a rock outcropping, was garbed in dashing array and waving a cutlass with debonair abandon.

"Now, men," the smuggler said, cultured voice strong, "Unload the goods swiftly, carry them to the base of the cliff and hand them up to the fellows above. Ropes are only for the heaviest crates. Work quickly, be diligent, and there will be an extra reward for you all!"

"That must be Lord Brag," Darkefell murmured. "If I'm right, it is Miss St. James in her brother's clothes."

"The figure is slight enough to be the lady," Osei agreed.

The carriers got to work by lantern light. Another rowboat slid ashore, piled with more goods. It was going smoothly. Darkefell wondered if he had been vigilant for naught. Had he worried about Anne, only to find she did not need him? The rowboats returned to the water, as another came in to shore. It was a large shipment, and Darkefell thought the tunnel must be stuffed with goods by now. They could not move all of that out of the tunnel in one night, certainly, and would need several nights of cover to do so.

He heard rustling behind him and turned, still hunched down between the rock outcropping and the cliff face. He stiffened. Movement. He dug his elbow in Osei's ribs and his secretary turned, too, and drew in his breath quickly, quietly.

This new band of men creeping toward the smugglers was either a rival smuggling gang or the excise officers. Darkefell had cast about for information among locals who were willing to talk and found out that rival gangs often raided each other's stashes. All-out war was not uncommon. The St. Wyllow Whips gang had been fortunate so far, but Darkefell knew that was because they had Puddicombe, the excise officer, in their pocket, his silence bought with exorbitant bribes. But who was this, and why were they sneaking up on the smugglers?

He indicated to Osei to follow him, tugging on his wrist, and the two men slipped along the cliff face, keeping pace with the stealthy movements of the band of men creeping toward the landing site. One of the smugglers shouted out suddenly, and the lot of them looked up from their tasks.

The group of men approaching suddenly rose and began to run down the beach toward the smugglers, but their progress was cut short, very suddenly, and very violently. Above, something swung out from the cliff and a loud *pop* echoed, while an explosion of sparks showered down. Then an explosion among the raiding party scattered them. Voices cried out, one calling, "Mr. Puddicombe, what're we ta do?"

Some of the smugglers, meanwhile, hastened to push the rowboats back out to sea, while others, faintly visible by the light of lanterns, dispersed.

Darkefell looked above; lit by a flare, a gruesome specter hovered off the edge of the cliff, a ragged piratical form. A hideous moaning wailed, echoing down in the cut and around them. Something dropped a few feet from his hiding place and exploded in a shower of sparks, and the group of men huddling together, some of them crying out to each other questions about what was going on, leaped and yelled at the explosion. Smoke drifted around, and confusion reigned. Who belonged to what group? Who could tell?

The specter above burst into flames, accompanied by shrieks and howls so frightening some of the men just beyond cried out and retreated. More huddled together, but when ragged bits of flaming cloth fell in a shower of red sparks, and embers landed on the wet beach, sizzling and popping, they scattered. The stench of gunpowder and kerosene filled the air, and more explosions blasted the sand around them.

Under cover of the yells and percussion of explosions, Darkefell said to Osei, "Let's go to the tunnel."

They ran, while other explosions rocketed around them. His mind tumbling, he wondered what was going on. What was that specter? The infamous Barbary Ghost? If so, who was wielding it? And where were the explosions coming from?

He would find out once he got to the tunnel and found Johnny Quintrell.

• • •

"Damn them, *damn* them!" Pamela cried, her back to the tunnel wall. She pulled off her black mask, sweat gleaming on her face in the dim lantern light. "Who double-crossed me?"

"I would bet on Micklethwaite," Anne said, out of breath. The grenades and smoke bombs she created from Marcus's provisions were almost gone, but fireworks exploded above, and the effigy was still aflame, thanks to Mary's timely effort. This was the Barbary Ghost's revenge, reprisal for the tragic wrong that had been done to poor Marcus St. James. Anne could only hope that the rest of Pamela's helpers had scattered, and that they could get all of the goods down the tunnel and behind the locked door before whomever was on the beach figured out they were out of explosives.

"Micklethwaite? Why?"

"Later," Anne said, lifting a crate and lugging it down the tunnel. She was only supposed to open the tunnel door, but she had always intended to do much more. Pamela was too trusting. Anne had suspected from the start that there was betrayal afoot. As she returned to her friend, she continued, "Right now, let's just get this task finished."

There were only a couple of the most trusted of the young men left to help them, and Anne shouted to them to move the last of the ankers of gin and crates of goods down the tunnel just beyond the plank door. If she and Pam could manage that, and send the young fellows up through the house and out—she prayed to God that Cliff House was not surrounded by prevention men—then they may yet escape harm or charges. Mary had done her part above on the cliff, swinging the effigy of the Barbary Ghost out, setting the fireworks and flares alight, and letting the stuffed pirate blaze, dropping bits of stinking, flaming cloth all over the raiders, whomever they were. Her banshee wail had been a bit of inspired theatrics Anne silently blessed her for.

Speed was vital right that moment. Anne firmly believed their assailants were locals hired by the excise man, Puddicombe, in a plot to blame all of the latest events on Pamela and Marcus. But she still thought it was possible that Micklethwaite was somehow involved, too.

She heard yells and confusion beyond the mouth of the cave. Good! She hoped they were running about in the dark in confusion. Of all things, Pam and her gang needed a few more minutes to get the goods in and lock the door, then delay any search of Cliff House until the goods could be moved inland.

Tubs, kegs, crates, oilcloth bundles: all were shifted swiftly, though they only had two of the most trusted fellows helping. Two? Why, Anne wondered, did there seem to be double that? Her stomach dropped. Could a couple of the prevention men have joined Pamela's crew, thinking to get in and get evidence that way?

She uncapped her light directly in the face of one of their helpers. "Mr. Boatin!" she gasped.

He put one finger over his lips. "Hush, my lady! Hush. We are here to help only."

"We?"

He pushed her hand, swinging the lantern around to shine on Darkefell's soot-smudged, streaky face. A bubble of laughter welled up in her and burst out.

"You look like a Welsh miner!" she whispered, giggling.

"Watch your tongue," he growled. "Or I'll smudge your face too!" He grabbed her arm, pulled her close and kissed her, full on the lips. "There, now you're thoroughly besmirched. Let's keep moving!"

Nineteen

Seeing Anne safe, knowing she was working just yards away from him, lightened Darkefell's temper, especially seeing her laugh at him, and feeling her lips against his. But their night was not done and they had to hurry. The prevention men would not be stopped for long. While he helped shift goods along the tunnel to beyond the plank door, he muttered what he had seen to Anne. In turn, she told him her part of the night's happenings. Her maid, Mary, had performed her part to perfection, hoisting the Barbary Ghost manikin and setting it ablaze. Anne had constructed the manikin from St. James's ghost costume and flour sacks, then stuffed handmade fireworks in the arms; that was the source of some of the crackling and display of light, she told him.

"I also made grenades," Anne further explained, pausing for a moment in her work, panting at the heavy toting. "I lit them from the lantern and threw them. They didn't have a lot of charge. Mostly they were smoke bombs, with some chemicals to make sound and light. The idea was to frighten the invaders, not hurt them."

"You made *grenades*," he said, staring at her in the gleaming light of the lamp.

"I had a lot of extra time in the last two days," she said primly, chin up. Her gaze did not waver from his.

"Time in which you would not see me!" he growled, narrowing his eyes.

"I was angry. I will not be told what to do, nor when, nor how. That part of my life ended the moment Reginald died."

"You felt that his death was a reprieve from a life sentence of certain unhappiness," he mused, and saw from her expression that he had hit on the truth. He saw what he was up against, then; she would not go lightly into marriage this time, for she had felt the full devastation of having made a grave error in agreeing to marry a man she could never love. But he would not dwell on it that moment. He smiled at her, shaking his head. "What kind of education could a young lady possibly have that would teach her in the art of making grenades and fireworks? I'm amazed, Anne. And alarmed."

She chuckled, then resumed her task, carrying a crate from the tunnel entrance and handing it to Osei Boatin, who carried it the rest of the way down the tunnel, past the door. "It was all there in Marcus's little workroom off the cellar. I found the saltpeter, potassium and nitrate, the pottery shells for the grenades, and his extensive notes." Her tone was more sober when she added, "I think I was just finishing what he had planned, that rout of the excise men."

"But did you *know* they would interrupt this landing?"

"I strongly suspected it." She finished setting one crate upon another and straightened. "Darkefell," she whispered, the hiss of her voice echoing in the tunnel. She pulled him aside. "I've been thinking about this for days; I believe that Micklethwaite is double-crossing Pamela. He's going to lay the blame on her for the whole thing. That's why he's not using his own ship for this landing. I've been wondering if he and Puddicombe are in this together. I still don't know why, and I don't know if it is linked with Marcus's murder, but it seems logical to me that those two men are somehow allied."

He nodded in agreement. "Puddicombe is there, leading the raiding party; I heard one of his men call him by name. Your theory is sound, and I have information that supports it. If you had deigned to speak to me in the last two days, I would have been able to tell you. But we must hurry. Let's get this done tonight and figure out what to do about the rest later."

They could hear voices outside the tunnel, and hurriedly worked in silence. Finally, there was nothing left to do, and Darkefell closed the tunnel door and Anne locked it, while Pamela got her boys (as she called the most trusted young men who helped her) out of harm's way by guiding them along the passage and up through her house. Osei, at the marquess's insistence, helped her. Anne and Darkefell remained behind, listening and waiting.

The gang of prevention men finally approached the tunnel door and hammered on it. "Damn them t'hell! If they hadn't tried to blow us up, we'd've got 'em," a gruff voice bellowed.

"Puddicombe, I think," Darkefell whispered in Anne's ear.

"Shall we beat the door doon, sir?" a voice beyond the door cried.

Darkefell reacted quickly. "Set the fuse, laddie," he shouted. "Let 'em beat the door down; they'll get a mighty blast from Lord Brag!"

At the sound of the excise fellows scampering away down the tunnel, shouting in their haste, Anne fell on the tunnel floor laughing, one hand clapped over her mouth. Darkefell pulled her up and to him in one swift motion, and took her lips in a breathless kiss.

"Not now!" Anne whispered, trying to hide her pleasure at his impulsiveness. She smacked his cheek, then took his hand. "We have to go up through the house."

She thought they would come up through the cellar to calmness, but it was not to be.

Mary, holding a candle, greeted her at the top of the cellar stairs, saying, "Milady, there's people outside the door, an' I don't know what to do! There are . . ." She broke off, looking over Anne's shoulder at Darkefell. "Well, now," she said, her tone tart, "I saw Mr. Boatin, and now Lord Darkefell."

"Who is it outside, Mary?" Anne asked, shaking the dust from her skirts.

"I don't know."

Anne bustled through the kitchen and up to the sitting room near the front door. Through a window, she tried to see, but the cloaked men were impossible to identify in the dark. Horses and men milled around, and Anne desperately wondered, was this the excise men? Would they storm in, search the house and find the tunnel filled with smuggled goods below? She whispered this question to Darkefell.

He moved to the window and tried to see out, but shook his head. He returned to the two women. "Have they come to the door?" he asked Anne's maid.

Mary shook her head.

"They seem to be talking," the marquess said, his brows furrowed. "Conferring on their next move, I'd wager."

From upstairs came a howl of dismay, and outside, the men began to beat on the door and shout to open up. Anne, her hands clapped over her ears to shut out the sudden din, cried out, "What's going on?"

Thudding in the stairwell informed them they were to be joined momentarily. Lolly, gray hair sticking out in spikes from under a lace bed cap and round face slathered with lanolin cream, stumbled over to Anne, crying, "Men! I heard a noise, and then a young man came into my room. Oh, help!" She stared at Anne in dismay. "Why is your face smudged with black, Anne, dear? What is going on in this madhouse?" She then whirled. "Lord Darkefell!" she squawked, thrusting Anne in front of her. "What are you doing here? And your face, my lord . . . lampblack . . . oh, my! *Shocking*."

"Lolly, shush! We have to figure out what's going on."

A high-pitched inhuman wail echoed down the stairs and Anne could hear Pam shriek, "Irusan, no!"

"Oh, heavens," Anne said, picking up her skirts and racing up the stairs. What she saw was her cat confronting a young fellow in the dim upstairs hallway. He stood still, his hands up in a defensive gesture, and Pamela appeared halfway between hysterical laughter and tears at the scene.

"I told Johnny that Irusan wouldn't hurt him," Pam said, "so the boy leaned down to pet him, but Irusan took offense."

"Irusan, behave yourself," Anne said sternly, then turned to her friend. "Pam, where has the other one of your fellows gone?"

"Out a window. I'm afraid he frightened poor Lolly by stomping through her bedchamber, but that's the swiftest route to the roof near an overhanging tree, and thus away. Johnny, here, stayed behind to help. I tried to make him go, but he insisted on staying, as did Mr. Boatin!"

Osei, his dark eyes sparkling with excitement, joined them. He stared at Anne's face but said nothing as she grabbed a doily from a table in the hall and began to scrub her lips and chin before anyone else decided to point out that the lampblack from Darkefell's face had somehow, miraculously, transferred to surround her mouth.

Darkefell ascended the stairs, likewise busy with a wet cloth, rubbing the lampblack from his face, and said, "Johnny, did you have a look out?"

"Yes, milord," the young fellow said. "I peered down from the second-floor window. The men outside are not together, I reckon. Puddicombe is out there, but so's Mr. Twynam; I descry the magistrate from his girth and seat upon t'horse."

Anne stared at Darkefell, the cloth forgotten in her hand. "You know this fellow?" she asked the marquess, waving her hand at Johnny.

"Yes, he's the son of my friend, Joseph Quintrell. I told you about Joseph, Anne; he's the owner of the Barbary Ghost Inn."

Anne, her mind spinning, saw that Darkefell had been keeping an eye on things using the boy as a spy. But she had no time to think it through, whether to be pleased or offended. The clamor downstairs was intensifying, and she couldn't leave Lolly to manage alone.

"Let me handle this," Pam said. She was now in her nightgown, no trace of her Lord Brag outfit in evidence. She said, "Anne, make yourself respectable," and sailed downstairs.

Darkefell turned to Johnny and said, "Stay up here, lad, out of sight. Are you ready to do what I asked? With Twynam here it may be necessary."

"Aye, sir."

"Osei, help him, will you? There's a good fellow," he said, clapping his secretary on the shoulder.

Anne and Darkefell descended, consulting each other about the lampblack removal, both finally clean of the black smudges. Darkefell wiped one last spot from her mouth and stole a kiss. Anne, her cheeks burning, didn't reprimand him.

Lolly, clutching her voluminous wrap around her plump form, was bent over, shouting through a crack in the front door. "Whomever you are, go away. This is a respectable house and we are respectable ladies. Go away!"

"Madam," came a baritone voice through the door. "This is Magistrate Twynam. We've met before. Let me in! I merely wish to confer with Miss St. James."

"Then come back at a decent hour!" Lolly said, straightening and crossing her arms over her chest.

Anne gently pushed past her companion and stepped toward the door. "Mr. Twynam, this is Lady Anne Addison."

"Yes, my lady," he said, his stentorian voice carrying easily through the oak door.

"This is highly unusual behavior, to come here at night. Do you have news about the murderer of poor Marcus?" She glanced over at Darkefell and raised her eyebrows.

"My lady, if you will let me in to speak to you and Miss St. James, I will tell you why I am here."

"Why can't you do that through the door? Some of us are in our night attire, sir! This is highly irregular behavior."

There was silence.

"Who is with you, sir?" Anne demanded. "I hear other voices."

She could almost hear the man think. There was still silence.

"My lady," he finally said, "I will not lie to you. Mr. Puddicombe, the local excise officer, is with me, though we did not come together. He has made some serious accusations."

"You've said that before, then never explained yourself. Give me five minutes, Mr. Twynam, to make myself decent," Anne said.

"What are you doing?" Pam whispered, pulling her away from the door.

"We have to let him in," Anne murmured, catching Darkefell's eye, "or he will jump to conclusions, if he hasn't already. Pam, you *must* make an appearance and seem innocent of anything and everything. You've done some theatrics; outraged innocence must be your character."

"Anne's right, Miss St. James," Darkefell whispered.

Lolly, her eyes wide, had stood back when she saw Darkefell there, but she grabbed his arm and said, "Young man . . . I beg your pardon, *my lord*, you must not be seen when those men come in here. It would be the death of Anne's reputation."

He smiled down at her and patted her hand. "Don't worry, Miss Broomhall, I won't be anywhere in sight."

Lolly turned to Anne and said sternly, her blue eyes narrowed, "I don't know what is going on in this house, but it stops tonight. You cannot behave this way, Anne. Consider your poor father, if you will not think of your mother."

"I know, I know." Anne regarded her fondly, but with some exasperation. "I imagined you would still be asleep. Was the wine not enough to keep you snoring?"

Lolly ignored that remark, sniffing and turning her face away.

Anne waited until Darkefell had slipped down the back hall and Pam was ready, then she unbolted the door. Magistrate Twynam strode in, bowed, and glanced around. Puddicombe followed, twisting his hands over each other again and again. He peered over Twynam's massive shoulder, his gaze darting everywhere, and stood on tiptoe to stare at Pamela.

Holding one hand out flat behind her in a gesture intended to keep Pam from talking, Anne waited, assuming a look of defiant expectation. One thing she had learned from dealing with village busybodies, talking to them gave them ammunition. After becoming weary of repeated questioning as to when she planned to marry, she had practiced a frigid hauteur that froze the busiest bodies to the marrow. She did not expect the technique to work with a man like Twynam, but it was worth an attempt.

The man moved ponderously forward, and let Mr. Puddicombe past him, into the cramped sitting room. Neither Anne nor Pamela asked them to sit.

"Did you not hear what was occurring on the beach below your home this night, Miss St. James?" Twynam finally said, after a few moments of silence.

Pamela looked from one man to the other, an expression of puzzlement on her face. "I do not know to what you refer, sir."

"She's lying," Puddicombe burst out, moving forward and shaking his finger in her face. "She's lying to you, sir. She is not only aware o' what's goin' on, she's taking part in it! She's one o' them dastard smugglers."

Pam played her part to perfection. "Mr. Puddicombe!" she cried, rearing back. "*Smuggling?* What lady would ever do such a thing?"

"Really, Mr. Twynam," Anne said dismissively. "You're here because of *him*? I thought you had some news of St. James's killer. Is that not what you're doing, searching for a murderer?"

He nodded, but his gaze stayed on her face. Anne met his eyes. Years of being on display at public events stood her in good stead. She gazed at him steadily, examining him in the weak lamplight. "I'm waiting for an answer, sir," she finally said. "Are you not concerned with who killed Captain Marcus St. James?"

"Don't let that 'un push you 'round, sir," Puddicombe said, sweat beading on his forehead as he shook his finger in Anne's direction.

Twynam turned, slowly, and stared at the excise officer. "Puddicombe, I would advise you to keep your mouth shut. And never speak to a lady in such a way, not in my presence."

Puddicombe harrumphed, but was silent.

"My lady, Miss St. James, Miss Broomhall," he said, bowing to Lolly, "I must confess I do not know why I'm here tonight. I received a message an hour ago telling me that Miss St. James had need of me, and wished to tell me something of great import."

"I sent no such message!" Pam declared, genuine puzzlement on her face.

"And you say something was occurring on the beach below Cliff House property?" Anne asked.

"Yes, according to Mr. Puddicombe. Explosions, rowboats, men, torches, a flaming manikin. Such goings-on, it beggars belief that you heard nothing."

"Good heavens!" Anne cried.

"That is utter nonsense," Lolly added, but then she gave Anne a long hard look.

Anne, to distract the magistrate from Lolly's accusatory gaze, said, "Sir, the walls of this house are three feet thick, and we are protected from the beach below by a cliff and bluff, so if anything did happen outside, I'm not surprised we heard nothing. But I am shocked that you are even listening to this . . . this gentleman." She sent a contemptuous look toward Puddicombe, who appeared more choleric by the second, his face gleaming crimson in the yellow lamplight.

"In fact," she said slowly, injecting her tone with dawning suspicion, "I think he is highly suspect himself. Have you not wondered why he never seems to catch the one band of smugglers, the St. Wyllow Whips as even I, an outsider, have heard them called?" She hesitated, but surged on, wishing to confuse matters even more. "Why, I should not be surprised if he is one of that gang. His position would make it a simple enough matter."

Apoplectic with fury, Puddicombe jumped up and down, shouting incoherent curses.

Pounding on the door added to the din, and Anne hopped over to it and flung it open, to find Darkefell and Osei there. He seemed terribly out of breath and his color was high, but he had a slight smile on his lips and he winked at her.

"Lord Darkefell!" she exclaimed, standing back to let him enter. "What are you doing out this night?"

He elbowed past Anne. "Mr. Twynam, arrest that man," he said, pointing to Puddicombe. "For he is in league with the real smuggler, Micklethwaite, who even now is sailing away on a boat he hired to fool you, and anyone else who looked too closely at his smuggling empire. I have proof."

Twenty

"You say you have proof of this, my lord?" Twynam asked.

As Puddicombe, becoming more frenzied, protested the charge and leveled various wild accusations and Lolly cried out about the noise and hid from Puddicombe behind the enormous magistrate, Darkefell, speaking loudly to be heard over the hubbub, said, "Yes, Mr. Twynam, I have evidence aplenty. I have been investigating on my own, for I had some suspicions in his direction."

Puddicombe stilled and narrowed his eyes, the folds of flesh wrinkling, dander from his thick eyebrows flaking onto his cheeks. "Here, now, what d'you mean?"

"I mean you and Micklethwaite, Puddicombe. I mean you are a traitor to the vow you made to the crown. And beyond that, you're a bully and a scalawag."

"He don't know nothin', Mr. Twynam, sir. Not a thing."

"How do you know that, Puddicombe? If we went to your house right now and looked in your cellar, do you mean we wouldn't find, oh, unstamped goods? Tobacco, perhaps? Brandy? Lace, bolts of silk?"

Puddicombe paled and his mouth clamped shut. Darkefell noticed Anne staring at him, and he felt a welling of hope that his actions would impress her favorably. She needed to see him as a man she could trust to do the right thing. But he turned his attention back to the task at hand.

Twynam motioned to a couple of his men and had a hurried conference, then sent them on their way. Darkefell repressed a smile, happy that Harriet Puddicombe would not be in the house. She had escaped her brutal father's keeping while he was busy with his night's work, and would already be snugly safe at the Barbary Ghost Inn, in the care of Joseph Quintrell's housekeeper, a redoubtable lady with a ferociously good reputation.

All the effort put forth by himself, Osei, and Johnny Quintrell would now come to fruition. He ruthlessly pushed back his own uneasiness at helping Miss St. James in an illegal activity. It wasn't for her sake he had risked so much; it was all for Anne.

What Twynam's men would find at Puddicombe's house would be enough to satisfy any qualms the magistrate might have about accusing an officer of the crown of such a deed. Besides the smuggled goods, there were, in his library, notes of tide schedules and when goods could be expected. There was even—crowning glory of his investigation—a letter to Puddicombe from Micklethwaite, which Darkefell had left in a particular spot that would allow searchers to discover it easily. It did not spell out the alliance between Puddicombe and Micklethwaite, but implied it, while pointing no finger at Pamela, for it only ever mentioned Lord Brag. That was of prime importance, to leave no stain on Pamela that could result in charges against her. He would never have pointed the magistrate toward Puddicombe if he hadn't been confident there would be no hint of guilt attached to the lady.

"In fact," Darkefell said, leveling a serious gaze at Anne and nodding faintly, "I have evidence that Puddicombe, here, killed Captain St. James."

Twynam bellowed, "What?"

Pamela cried out, "I don't believe it!"

But Puddicombe's shout was even louder, as he was pushed to the brink of apoplexy by the awkward nature of the accusations. "Liar! I didn't do it, Micklethwaite did. I'll not let that bastard pin the blame on me," the man said, pointing at Darkefell. "Never was my idea to kill the cap'n, t'was Micklethwaite said we needed to get rid of 'im 'cause he was threatening if we didn't leave 'is precious sister alone he'd expose me!"

An immediate silence fell. Darkefell and Twynam, with similar grave expressions, took both of Puddicombe's arms.

"Mr. Puddicombe, you are under arrest for conspiring to cheat his majesty out of his due rights, and of failing to perform the office for which you were hired," Twynam said. "And the charges against you will include conspiring to murder Captain Marcus St. James."

"You animal," Pamela cried and flew at him, weeping. Anne grabbed her around the waist and pulled her away. "Let the gentlemen take care of things," she cried. "It's over, Pam." She took her friend in her arms and rocked her. "It's over."

• • •

The rest of the long, sleepless night was taken up in recriminations, accusations, and explanations. In the end Twynam, though he held Puddicombe in his custody, had apparently not decided whether to believe even so august and lofty a man as Anthony, the Marquess of Darkefell. He needed to sort out Puddicombe's claim that it was Micklethwaite who committed the murder of Captain Marcus St. James, and Micklethwaite's likely accusation of Puddicombe.

Who had actually done the killing? It was not clear to anyone.

To that end the magistrate sent his brother-in-law, who owned a fast cutter, out in pursuit of the mysterious boat for hire, while he had some trusted men search Puddicombe's home as well as Micklethwaite's. Within the next few days, Anne prayed that they would have a definitive answer as to who killed Marcus.

When the household was finally left in peace, Anne made sure Pamela was put to bed with a tea of Lolly's creation supposed to guarantee a deep and dreamless sleep. Pam needed that. Lolly and Mary were going to take turns at Pam's bedside. Osei went back to the inn with Johnny Quintrell. Johnny and Harriet were to marry that very day, for Darkefell had obtained a license for them to wed immediately as his gift to the pair; but as simple an affair as it was to be, there were still some things to be done. Joseph was beside himself with joy at his son's marriage, and alternately wept and laughed, making him useless to execute plans of any sort.

"Come for a walk," Darkefell said to Anne, as she returned downstairs from Pam's bedside.

Anne was weary but knew she would be unable to sleep, even if she went to bed. She nodded, retrieved her Kashmir shawl from the sitting room, and they strolled out to the bluff overlooking the ocean. She wrapped the shawl around her and stared out at the stars. Darkefell pulled her close, her back to his chest, and wrapped his arms around her.

"Tony, Pam has a child, a son. His name is Edward," she said as he rocked her back and forth, holding her close. She leaned her head back against his broad chest. The comfort of his strong arms was intoxicating; it invaded her body with warmth and a sense of calm. "She was engaged to be wed, and so she and her fiancé . . ." She broke off. "She found out she was with child, and they were to marry within days, but Bernard died."

"Mhmm," he said.

His bass murmuring vibrated through her from her backbone to her breastbone, leaving her tingling with yearning. She had to keep talking, keep thinking other things. "I don't suppose it excuses it, but that's why she did this, the smuggling. She wants to make a life for them both together."

"It won't be easy for her."

"She's going to Canada, for she has family in Montreal. I'm going to miss her, but I suppose it's the best way for her to make a good life for her child." She turned in his arms and laid her head on his chest, with her lips near the pulse beat at the base of his throat. His black shirt was open, his bare skin entrancingly warm. She nuzzled and his arms tightened around her. She turned her face up to his, knowing his lips would meet hers.

She lost several minutes in mingled comfort, desire, and a fog of delight. His lips, moist and warm, clung to hers. The thought of making love had never left her mind in the last month. When she was with him, as little as she knew of such things, she could *feel* how good it could become with such a man. He was everything a woman could want: commanding yet tender, skilled and yet eager. She wasn't frightened of it, beyond some virginal nervousness. The mystery of lovemaking added enticement rather than fear.

When she became next aware, she noticed the silvering of the sky. "It's almost dawn," she murmured against his skin. She twirled one finger in the hair on his chest, where his shirt was open. The sense of sleek musculature beneath his skin made her wild with a craving to touch and be touched.

"Mhmm," he murmured. His thick fingers tangled in the short strands of her hair on the back of her neck.

They were silent again for several minutes. Pressed close to his body she could feel the stirring of excitement in his body, the pulse of desire. Anne closed her eyes. What was holding her back from marriage to Darkefell? He was intelligent, rich, healthy, generous, relatively good-natured — apart from his occasional black moods and towering rages — and she believed in her heart that he would be a good husband and father.

At least . . . a good husband as far as husbands went, and a good father assuming she wanted children. But children would come, whether she wanted them or not. Ah, and *there* was another wrinkle she hadn't explored in her own unlovely character. Perhaps she didn't want children. She felt no melting sensation at the sight of sticky fingers and the sound of childish coos. She did not long to hold one, nor did she think them enchanting. But Darkefell, as marquess, would need an heir, and sexual contact, in which she was *intensely* interested, resulted almost inevitably in pregnancy, with all the attendant discomfort and fear. She looked back a few weeks to how blithely she had assured Lydia, her dear friend, wed to Darkefell's brother, Lord John, that there was nothing to fear in childbirth. What a fraud she was! Women died every day giving birth, and she desperately feared death.

Perhaps her faith was not strong enough, for she felt no assurance that there was more beyond the bleak darkness of the grave. And yet, if she did not do what she wanted on earth—and making love to this man who held her was an enticing possibility — then what good was her life to her. She shook her head, feeling numb with confusion.

She took a deep, quivering breath. Of course, setting aside the possibility of death in childbirth, once a child was born, she would not need to be concerned; her children would have the standard succession of wet nurse, nursemaid, nanny, governess, and boarding school to raise them. A strong wave of revulsion shuddered through her. If she set aside her own feelings toward offspring and put herself in the children's place, she felt sorry for the babes. She had despised her own nanny, a nursery despot whom Anne suspected had put laudanum in her milk to make her sleep. And boarding school, which Anne had suffered for only a few months before weeping to her father to bring her home, had been a scarring experience. She had learned her lessons, after that, at his knee, and would always be grateful to him for his intelligence and patience.

Rolling over her in waves came a longing to see her father, the dearest man in the world and the center of her universe. He was her guidepost in every conversation she had with herself over morality and common sense. She may dismiss him in her mind occasionally as easy prey to daughterly persuasion, too lax when it came to letting her do exactly what she wanted, but he had raised her to have strong feelings, strong convictions, and a strong backbone. Her mother despised such things, feeling that it behooved every girl of

Anne's stature to grasp as high a mate as she could possibly manage and then let her husband do everything for her after that. What use was learning, logic, deep thought, when those things could not get a young lady a husband?

Darkefell, a marquess, was beyond even her mother and grandmother's ambition for her, which was why they had sent Lolly to Cornwall. In her conversations with Lolly over the last week, it had become clear to Anne that her companion was trying to do justice to the Countess of Harecross and the Viscountess of Everingham's wishes, while being a true friend to Anne. It was an untenable position for the poor woman to be in, and Anne did not blame her for her muddled unhappiness of the last few days.

Darkefell knew that Anne was thinking deeply, but he was torn as to whether he wanted her to do that or not. He leaned down in the silvering dawn, put one finger under her chin, and kissed her lips. "Kiss me again, Anne, my sweet?"

"Mmm." She kissed him, deeply and thoroughly. But then she broke away from his lips, saying, "Tony, you've told me you love me. Why?"

He chuckled. "Because it happens to be true."

"No, Tony, I don't mean why did you tell me, I mean why do you love me?" She pulled away from him and wrapped her arms around herself, standing close to the edge of the bluff.

He watched her, how the gray of her eyes picked up the silver dawn and the color of the ocean. "Honestly? I am a difficult man, Anne. Difficult to love, difficult to get close to; moody, austere, cold. *Difficult*. Women have always told me they couldn't guess what I was thinking, and it made them uneasy, but it never seems to distress you. If I push, you push back. If I'm moody, you don't seem to allow it to have the slightest effect upon you. You are exactly what I need."

It wasn't the right answer. Her eyes grew frosty and her expression perturbed. Did she need hearts and flowers after all? Did she need to be told she was beautiful, and have poetry spouted at her? He opened his mouth to say some untruth, to say anything to bring the warmth back to her gaze, but then he closed it again. She had serious doubts about him, and he didn't blame her, but she must make a decision about him. "What is it, Anne? Why do you doubt me?"

"I don't doubt you at all, I doubt *me*." She turned away from him and stared out to sea. "I don't know if I ever want to get married, Tony. I'm not formed for marriage. I'm as moody as you, maybe more. I can be austere, cold, difficult, too. How would we ever get along?"

"Anne, my dearest one, you're also warm, passionate, intelligent, reasonable. More reasonable than I."

She smiled faintly, glancing back at him. "Is it reasonable for a woman to dread that which comes with marriage? I refer not to the marriage bed," she said, blushing and looking down at the ground. "Nor to the childbirth bed. Though that thought has given me pause for reflection." She met his eyes again. "But I fear that separation which is inevitable; a woman must forsake all that she holds dear, her home, her family, her roots, to pick them up and transplant, like a good potted plant, to the native soil of her husband. And her freedom. She gives up whatever measure of freedom she owns."

"I understand all of that, Anne, but ours will not be a simple marriage of some miller to a maid. With such power and wealth as I have, I may grant whatever leave a wife should want, to travel to Kent, if it is there you wish to go, or Bath." He gazed at her hopefully, but felt a coldness clutch him, as cold as the sea breeze that stiffened, rushing in from the ocean. She looked *more* perturbed, not less.

"Ah, and there is that," she said sadly. "Your language, my lord, reveals you to be a true man of your position. You would 'grant' your wife 'leave.' What kind of freedom is that?"

"I didn't mean it that way, Anne," he said, becoming irritated. "You take every word and dissect it."

"What else do I have but words?" she said, her tone filled with exasperation. "What does any woman have before marriage but *words*?"

He took two strides, grasped her to him and kissed her hard, all of his fury and irritation finding an outlet. "You have *this*!" he said.

She kissed him back with equal fury and they sank to the thick, damp grass on the bluff, finding release in powerful emotion. He felt her soften, passion warming her, and the idea flashed across him: if she lay with him, she would marry him, he knew it to the depth of his core. As outré as she seemed, beneath her external outrageousness was a woman who valued herself, and he felt sure if he could make her see how much he could give her within marriage, she would submit.

He fumbled at her skirt and lifted, it, stroking her leg, finding his way above the stocking to naked flesh. She moaned against his mouth and opened her lips, letting him surge in and thrust into her mouth. He hardened, the thought of making love to her all the aphrodisiac he would ever need. "Anne, I want you," he whispered against her lips. "Please!"

She stilled, and rolled away from him. She struggled to her feet, her face red in the glow of the morning sun that rose beyond the horizon. "I can't, Tony. I just can't! Not out here, not in such a quick and frenzied fashion. I must go . . . I must go and see to my friends." She turned and fled, racing away from him toward the house. He was left alone, to cool the flames of his ardor, dousing them with the coldness of reality.

She had so much self-control. He wished she possessed the qualities some men of learning claimed as women's frailty. If only she *was* impetuous enough to make love to him, trusting enough to marry him, fragile enough to need him. And weak enough to submit to him. He hammered the earth and swore. Damn her independence!

Anne stumbled back to the back door of Cliff House, emotion blurring her vision. Furious and sobbing, she couldn't think of anything but Darkefell. She paused, not wanting to enter the house in such a state, and slumped down on a bench on the terrace. Trying to master her emotions, she swallowed and gulped in several breaths of misty night air.

"Damn you," she muttered, hammering her fist on the bench. Her voice was clogged with tears, and she wasn't sure if she referred to her would-be lover or to herself and her wild tumult of sense and emotion. Darkefell had a way of setting her off-kilter with seductive kisses, taking her to the brink of fleshly submission, only to spoil it all the next moment with some idiotic attempt to impose his will on her.

But she would not be some Niobe, streaming copious tears, though at least Niobe had a good excuse for her weepiness. Anne did not. Being loved by an irritating man did not constitute a reason to cry.

Wiping the dampness from her cheeks, she sighed, rising. "At least this is over," she said aloud, testing her voice, clearing it of unshed tears. "Those dreadful men are stopped. Pamela and her little Edward will live in peace."

Weary to the bone, she started toward the back door, stealthily, intending to slink in and up the stairs. But she was jerked from her lassitude by a callused hand clapped over her mouth and a muscular arm around her body.

"Filty slut," a voice growled in her ear, the feel of hard bristly whiskers and the sour stench of reeking breath overcoming her. "I'll not be beggared by the likes o' you!"

She struggled, but the bulky man was too strong and too angry. It was Micklethwaite! She tried to scream, hoping Darkefell would be near, but the sea captain's hand over her mouth gagged her. She struggled and kicked, but he hauled her away.

"You're a'comin' wit me," he chortled in her ear. "I'll hide ya away and get that markwis to give me money to see you again. He seems to value yer bony arse." He dragged her away from the terrace.

She bit his finger, and when he yelped and pulled his hand away, she shrieked, "Let me go! Help! Hel — "

He clapped his hand back over her mouth, grunting in pain. With his free hand he slammed his fist on her skull and her vision blurred, hot tears from the stinging blow welling in her eyes. Her knees buckled from the pain.

"Shut yer chatterer," he growled and began dragging her away from the house. "If ya had yer way, I'd be caught by the magistrate, but I never was gonna be out there with those slugs I hired fer this job. D'ya think I'm a fool? T'was my job to make sure the slut was caught right an' tight, so's Puddicombe an' me could form a proper gang wiv no breech-clad wimmin involved!"

If there was ever a time when she needed to control her emotion, Anne reeling from pain but furious, knew this was that moment. She slumped, making herself a dead weight, and the captain grunted. She would not be taken by surprise, like the last time she had almost died.

"Stand, damn yer hide! Stand an' walk!"

Micklethwaite was huffing and puffing, his foul breath becoming more labored as she resolutely dug her heels in, making her body harder to carry or drag. To struggle would have invited violence, but resistance through passivity left him baffled, albeit still furious.

It seemed an interminable time, but as she suspected he would, he finally paused and took his grimy paw away from her mouth to wipe the sweat from his brow. She looked up and saw that he had hauled her toward the cliff; swiftly, summoning every ounce of energy and courage, she gave one quick kick backward to his knees with a loud yell. He buckled and she sprinted away from him, but her damnable skirts tangled, and she tripped, seeing, in that moment, Darkefell striding away from her on the bluff on the other side of the cut.

"Darkefell!" she cried, but the breeze whipped the word back at her with blowing sand, in a mockery of the danger she was in.

"Shut yer trap," Micklethwaite grunted, charging after her and grabbing her arm, hauling her to her feet. "Everything went wrong 'cause o' you, girlie, an' you're gonna pay. Wimmin ain't got the right t'interfere wiv men."

But Anne would not be taken so easily now that she was aware. She struggled and they staggered sideways, coming close to the cliff. The tide washed in below, and Anne knew, if she fell into the ocean, she would be pulled under by her skirts and drown. No one would get to her in time.

Twenty-one

Darkefell, fury slashing through him, strode back toward the inn after climbing across the cut and clambering back up to the grassy bluff. He had come to Cornwall sure of his suit, knowing he had all a woman could want and that Anne's ultimate capitulation was a foregone conclusion. But now, he no longer knew how it would all end.

She could not mean to live as a spinster forever. That was madness! No woman he had ever met had wanted such a life, wandering in the nebulous world between unformed girl and respectable wife. Spinsters were those poor souls for whom no mate was available. They were eyed with pity and lived in shame. It was not a choice, but a fate. Superstition and cant tongue doomed them to lead apes in hell after death.

He stopped. It was all true, he thought, but why? The wind tugged at his hair, and he impatiently brushed it back. A noise floated on the breeze, perhaps a seagull's mournful cry.

Why was a woman alone a pitiable thing? Anne was not pitiable; she would *never* be pitiable.

He turned, determined to go back to her and demand she listen to him yet again, but he froze, horrified. At such a distance, to witness Anne, teetering on the brink of oblivion, wrestling with Micklethwaite! The smuggling captain was throttling her and they were on the edge of the cliff. He bolted into action, but even as he began to run, he knew it was too late; he'd never get there in time. Pain ripped through his chest. His own humiliated anger had sent her away from him to danger.

Anne wobbled on the precipice, lights dancing in front of her as the captain squeezed her throat. The moment came, blackness beckoning, the grave yawning as inevitable before her, as close as the cliff edge.

"No!" she screamed, but it came out a gurgling caw. Struggling with her skirts, she raised her right knee and kicked back, connecting with the vulnerable male parts concealed beneath his breeches. The captain, his black eyes wide with surprise and horror, thankfully released her throat and she twisted away from him, teetering on the edge of the cliff. The next events occurred in seconds, but somehow it seemed as if it were all slower, the world whirling at a reduced spin. Micklethwaite's ancient frock coat, shiny from long wear, flew open; he staggered, and shouted as he went down. She wobbled to the edge and saw him, facedown, the tidewater catching him and lashing waves driving him under.

He was dead. This time, unlike with Hiram Grover, there was no uncertainty about the murderer's wretched fate. And once again Anne had cheated death.

Strong hands caught her from behind and pulled her back. Darkefell! She turned in his arms and buried her face in his neck, sobbing with relief. She was alive!

• • •

Two days had passed. Anne stood on the bluff overlooking the ocean, the wind tugging at her bonnet and skirts, clouds scudding overhead. Irusan was hunting rodents or a snake in the long grass.

Poor Marcus, gone forever. One of the young men who had been there on the night of the failed raid, the night Marcus had died, had witnessed what had happened and come forward, finally, when assured he would be safe by Puddicombe's arrest and Mickle-thwaite's death. He had come back to the site of the raid looking for the knife he had been carrying but dropped along the way, and he overheard everything.

Marcus and Puddicombe argued, the lad said, the subject being the officer's sister, Pamela, and threats Puddicombe had made toward her. Marcus threatened to beat Puddicombe to within an inch of his life, and the excise man, with one swift motion, had slashed his throat. The murderer had made an interesting statement as his victim died at his feet, saying aloud that Marcus had gone the way of Bernard, Pamela's fiancé, for both had crossed Puddicombe and both had paid.

The young man had been sore afraid of the excise man, given what he had witnessed, but the arrest had encouraged honesty. It was all out in the open now, Puddicombe's long history of taking enormous bribes to fail to capture the St. Wyllow Whips, and other gangs before them. But someone would always die, the smugglers would disband, to be replaced by another. Harriet, now married to

Johnny Quintrell and living with her husband at the Barbary Ghost Inn, had been a valuable informant. She had not connected all that had gone on, but she had heard much, and could repeat verbatim interesting conversations between Micklethwaite and Puddicombe.

Now that Anne had a breathing space, with Puddicombe jailed for smuggling, fraud, and murder, and Micklethwaite's dead body buried in a pauper's grave in unconsecrated ground, she could think about Marcus. Anne missed his teasing smile, his intelligence, and the knowledge that he was there to look after Pamela, always thinking of his sister, the bond between them solid and permanent.

Now Pam would need to be the caretaker for her little Edward. But with two days' rest, and the worst behind her, she seemed capable of it, ready to move on, not forgetting her brother but remembering him with fondness, not pain. Edward was weaned, and Pamela was planning to book passage to Montreal. Anne's bruised throat was healed. She missed Marcus, and already missed Pam, though she was not yet gone. She sniffed and bowed her head, pummeled by the buffeting wind on the bluff.

"No crying," a voice behind her said. "We got the bastards, and that's what Captain St. James would want."

Darkefell. Anne turned and melted into his arms. "I just miss poor Marcus. But Pam is doing well, better than I thought she would."

"She has a purpose. Her little Edward needs her." He folded her in his arms and they stood for a while, stronger together against the battering winds. "And speaking of needing . . .," he said, holding her away from him and gazing down into her eyes.

She stared up at him and knew what was coming.

"Anne, I've told you I love you," he said gently. "That's forever. I'm a man who is very set in his ways, and once I make a decision I never change my mind. I love you, and I want to marry you."

This was the point at which she should answer, either yay or nay. She stared up at him. A long moment passed. His expression changed, and she knew she had hurt him with her pause.

"If the answer was yes, it would have been swift," he said.

She laid her head against his chest for a moment, listening to his heart thump, then pulled away from him. All she could be was honest, and she didn't know if it would hurt him or not. "I just don't know, Tony. You're asking me to make a decision for the rest of my life. At eighteen that was easy, but for some reason, at twenty-four, it has become so difficult."

"Do you love me?" he urged, his dark eyes full of intensity and passion.

"How can I know? I *think* I do, but . . . how does one know for sure?"

"If you can even ask that question, then you don't love me." He dropped his hands from her arms.

She stared at him for a moment, feeling bereft. "I don't think that's true, you know. I think, for me, even if I do love you—and I feel it, Tony, I do!—I can still be unsure about marriage."

"My God, just take the chance!" he said, grabbing her shoulders in his hands. He shook her slightly. "I'll make you happy, I swear it! I'm sure enough for both of us. Marry me, Anne!"

She tore herself away from him, staggering backward in the thick grass. "Just give me time to breathe! Give me time to think!" She clutched her head in both hands, crushing her bonnet yet again. By the end of her relationship with Tony she would have no decent bonnets left. She took in a deep breath and let it out, slowly, looking up at the tree from which still dangled the charred remains of the Barbary Ghost effigy. "I'm going home, Tony, home to Kent, to Harecross Hall."

"I'll come, too, and meet your father," he stated. "I know he's important to you. I'll meet him, if it will make you more sure."

"No!" she said, holding up one hand. He was willfully misunderstanding her. "No. Please, Tony, just let me go away to think. And promise me that you'll not follow me. Please?"

She stared into his dark eyes, and the pain there had her almost wavering, almost taking back her words. But the trembling fear inside her was real. How could she say yes, feeling as she did? She would be less than honest if she said yes to his proposal, less than honest and less than fair, for if she ultimately decided she could not marry him, how much worse would it be if they were engaged and she had to break it off?

His expression darkened and his sensual mouth thinned to a bitter line. "Do you really think all I have to do in my life is wait for your gracious answer? Is that fair, Anne?"

"No," she shot back, hugging herself. "Not fair to *you*, perhaps. But my task in this life is to be fair to *myself*. By saying yes, I would be giving you what *you* want, but I'm not sure if it's what *I* want. I will not answer; I will be happy, wed or not! Give me time!"

He was silent, staring at her, his mouth drawn down. The ocean breeze lifted his dark hair from his forehead and he impatiently swept it back. "How much time: a day, a week, a month? A *year*?" he shouted. "What do you expect?"

"I know I'm not being fair to you," she cried and turned away. She stared out over the ocean. "And I don't expect you to wait. If you can love someone else, then go to her."

"Don't be absurd!"

"I'm not being absurd." She turned back and stared at him. His dark eyes were wild with suppressed anguish, and she felt her heart squeeze in her chest, constricting, knowing she was causing him pain.

"You're being worse than absurd," he shouted, grabbing her wrist. "You're throwing it all away. You're behaving as though what is between us is unclear."

"But it *is* unclear," she said, pulling her wrist from his grasp. "It just is not as simple for me as it is for you, Tony!" She turned away so he would not see the tears in her eyes. Silence. Staring off over the ocean, she sobbed, her voice thick with unshed tears, "Tony, please! It's all I can do. Let me go home and think. Don't follow me." She turned around to him, but he was walking away, toward Cliff House. And when she got back to the house, he was gone, having said a hasty good-bye to Pamela.

Cold fear clutched her heart. Had she chased him away forever? What else could she expect? She could do no more, nor any less. This was her life and she must direct it as she thought right.

Another two days later, everything was finally settled. Anne had made good on her promise to Abraham Goldsmith to buy gem chips for the eyes of the cat on the head of the exquisite carved walking stick he wrought, and it was done, polished, wrapped in fine fabric to protect it and stowed in Anne's trunk. Anne would always remember her time spent with Abraham and Rebecca as the most peaceful of her visit to Cornwall.

Magistrate Twynam had been back several times to Pam's home, and it was clear that he suspected there was more to the story of the smuggling gang than he was being told. But his frequent reappearance often seemed to have more to do with Lolly's delicious cooking than any further questions, and in the end his questions were mostly, "Miss Broomhall, have you made fresh scones today?" and "Miss Broomhall, would you care to accompany me to the village for tea?"

Anne was bemused by Lolly's hauteur in the face of her weighty admirer's compliments and blandishments. If they had more time to spend at Cliff House, something may even have come of it, for the gentleman was well fixed and a widower, with grown children.

But they had to leave.

Pam's affairs were straightened out, the smuggled goods sold off to her contacts. With Micklethwaite dead and Puddicombe in jail, she had made much more money than anticipated, but she had given a good amount to Harriet and Johnny to begin their marriage properly, and made sure all of her "boys" were amply rewarded for the risks they had taken in the smuggling trade. Mrs. Gorse had been paid for her services, and Edward was now with his mother, for Pamela no longer cared about her reputation in St. Wyllow. In a sense, she had already flown from English shores to a better life in the colonies.

Alice, Pam's little Cornish maid, was going to move with her to Canada, for she had no family, and was fervently loyal to her mistress; Anne was relieved to know Pamela would at least have some companionship, even if it was just a maidservant. Micklethwaite's heir, a distant cousin in Devonshire, had already been to Cliff House and was to move into it the moment Pamela was gone.

Finally, it was time to go. Anne walked the halls of Cliff House, thinking how many things had changed since she had arrived. Darkefell had left Cornwall, and though she had asked for time before giving him a definitive reply to his second proposal, his abrupt departure and his anger left her wondering if he even wished for a positive answer now. If she had chosen differently, she could be going home to Kent an engaged woman. She descended the stairs to the ground floor, pressing one hand against her stomach, which had been roiling for days, since that last scene with the marquess.

What if she had made a dreadful mistake? What if she never saw him again? She hadn't intended to mistreat him, nor was she trying to be coy, but it was her *life* they spoke of, her *whole* life. Everything about it would change the moment she said that one little three-letter word, the very instant she said "yes."

Sanderson waited outside with the carriage once more, just as he had a hundred times before. Lolly, Mary, and Robbie were already in the carriage, but Irusan stalked beside her, down the stairs and out to the front, where Pamela, holding Edward, stood. Pam already had tears in her eyes.

"Pam, darling, don't cry," Anne said. "You and Edward are to come to me in Kent for a long rest before you sail. Summer crossings are plentiful, and you can come to us for a month or more. You know my father will adore seeing you again."

"Your dear father; so kind, so gentle!" Pam said, her voice clogged with unshed tears. "But Anne, I think the break will be easier if I just leave. There is a ship sailing from Penzance in a week. I've already booked passage to Montreal and written to my cousin there to expect me."

Anne felt her heart constrict. "I'm going to miss you so!" she cried, hugging her friend and Edward to her. They stood thus for a long time in the late May sunshine, but as much as it hurt, Anne knew she must go. "Good-bye, dear heart," she said, caressing Pam's pale cheek. "Write to me and tell me all about your voyage, and your new home." She then took Edward's chubby fist in her hand and kissed it, the skin soft under her lips. "And good-bye, little Eddy," she said, pinching his cheek. "You take care of your mama for me. She is precious beyond words."

Anne turned to leave.

Pam said, "Wait!" She set her son down on the doorstep and took Anne's hands in hers, staring into her eyes. "Anne, I must say this. Don't push away a chance at love. You know, Marcus cared for you very much, but sometimes he could be such a dolt. One of his friends told me Darkefell truly was standing up for you that night at the assembly, when he attacked my cloddish brother. Marcus was trying to be witty, but did it crudely. As much as I loved my brother, he would have made you a dreadful husband. The marquess . . . I like him very much, for there is a kindness beneath his hauteur. A man like that does not come along every day."

Anne was silent, not sure how to answer.

"You've wounded him terribly. Such a man does not offer his heart, only to have it dismissed as an unworthy gift."

"I did no such thing, Pam, I merely asked for time to think over his proposal."

"Then think, but I hope it's not too late. He was dreadfully angry the last time I saw him. Think about what you're throwing away." Pam cupped Anne's face with one gentle hand. "Darkefell loves you; I don't need to hear it from him to see it in his eyes, the way he looks at you, the care he takes of you. I had that with Bernard, and even though I lost him, I wouldn't have missed it for anything, the love, the care, the tenderness of a worthy man." Pam hugged Anne again and gave her a little push toward the carriage. "Now go, and think about what I have said."

Tears in her eyes, Anne climbed into the carriage, followed by Irusan, and waved goodbye.

First, they would stop at Bath to drop Lolly off, and thence to Kent. Home beckoned with the warm light of paternal love.

• • •

"Papa!" Anne cried, her skirts rucked up in her fists, racing up the stairs of Harecross Hall, along the gallery and through the library door, followed closely by Irusan, who seemed delighted to be home, too. "Papa!"

And there he was, sitting in a golden pool of light with a stack of books in front of him on the desk, his balding head gleaming, his pouched and rheumy eyes watering, his posture stooped. He straightened, his leather chair creaking with the movement, and the gladness in his eyes was a delight to see. "Annie! My dearest child! You're home."

She raced across the room and threw herself into his open arms, on her knees, as Irusan leaped to the desktop, scattering books and papers and crooning his own happiness to be home. The earl rocked her, holding her close while Irusan butted them both with his massive head and purred. When Anne finally looked up at her father, it was to see tears in his eyes.

"Papa, is everything all right?"

"It is now," he said. "You're home. I've missed you so, my darling girl."

"I've missed you, too. I have so much to tell you! But right now, this is good enough." She hugged him close, breathing in his ineffable smell, of old books and hair pomade, pipe tobacco and port. "Oh, Papa, I have missed you so terribly."

Two weeks later—the middle of June—life had settled into familiar patterns, though there were a few unfamiliar problems to deal with, as well. In Anne's absence a distant cousin with her several children had entrenched herself at Harecross Hall, and it would take some diligence to rid the manor of their pestilential habitation.

But still, life went on. Anne conferred with cook most mornings, and then the housekeeper. She made parish visits for the vicar, who was still unmarried, and therefore had no wife to fill that valuable post of minister to the sick, old, and crippled. She settled arguments among some of the local women, delivered food to the needy, and helped the teachers at her dame school plan for the next year, now that most of the students were busy helping their families with the farmwork.

In other words, she did the tasks her mother, as countess, should have done, but didn't because of her estrangement from the earl. Anne's mother had not visited Harecross in two years, and would not deign to set foot there, even with the incentive of a daughter who had received an extremely eligible offer of marriage from a marquess. A flurry of letters had followed Anne to Kent from Bath, but the countess herself would not come to Harecross Hall.

Walking the wild coastline near the village of Kingsdown on a breezy late spring day, looking out over the channel from the chalk cliff, Anne was beginning to feel that all the exciting events of the past months were receding to that gray area of memories and dreams, even the powerful arms and seductive kisses of Lord Darkefell.

Beloved Tony.

Well . . . no. She was lying to herself, for she would not, *could* not forget his kisses, and the feel of his heart thumping against hers, and the wild sensations that coursed through her when she had let him go too far for modesty, but not far enough for desire. She closed her eyes, the salt dampness of the wind tugging at her bonnet. Every time she stood still, she could feel Darkefell with her, and she wanted him. She ached to see his face, to hear his voice, to feel his arms.

Had she been a desperate fool to feel the need for solitude in which to consider her feelings for him? Wasn't this madness pulsing through her veins proof that she loved him deeply enough for a lifetime commitment? She just wasn't sure anymore what she felt or wanted or needed. It was all a tangled blur, and she was going to make herself wretched if she continued to yearn for him in such a schoolgirlish fashion.

She turned away from the choppy view of the channel and walked inland, along a well-known path from her home of Harecross Hall, past Wroth Farm, and over a hill past a wooded valley hugging the Wroth Hill Stream. She carried a laden basket and had an objective. Her father was terribly worried and in a dilemma. Early in the spring a band of gypsies had politely begged permission to camp in a field quite a distance from the house, promising not to cause any trouble, and to keep the peace. The earl, always interested in language and culture, had agreed, asking only that he be allowed to meet with some of the elders to study their Romany language. He had a theory that if he could trace the roots of their native tongue, it might lead to some surprises about their country of origin. He did not believe they were originally from Egypt, as most claimed, nor from Hungary or Romania, as was also commonly conjectured.

But a few of the local farmers, including the earl's own home farm tenant, complained that the gypsies robbed the henhouses, fished from the stream, and stole. The earl thought that a few of the local ne'er-do-wells were taking advantage of the presence of the gypsies to run wild, but could not prove it. Unhappy, but sure of his duty to those who depended upon him, he had decided the gypsies must go to keep the peace with his villagers.

However, they were being slow to move. Always, it was *"tomorrow . . . we'll go tomorrow."* Their tomorrows were used up, but the earl didn't know how to enforce his command, other than by taking drastic measures. His steward was recommending burning their tents and caravans, but the earl would not hear of it.

Anne was visiting to see if she could ease their way off of Harecross property, and she had some gifts for the children and old folks. Gifts had a way of softening bad feelings. There was one old woman her father found especially intriguing, because she told tales of being related to European royalty, and though he did not think the stories were true, he would have liked more time to get as much information as he could, to try to figure out if it was true or not. That was not to be, but he had sent, by Anne, a very fine broach that she could keep or sell, as she saw fit.

Walking the path she had taken as a child, over hills, across open fields, away from the windy, high-cliffed shoreline that the gypsies disdained, she remembered her childhood run-in with the gypsy boys, who had made fun of her and tore her gown. Her big brother, Jamey, had beaten them and sent them back to their camp chastised and bloody. It was past time that she should visit Jamey. Depending upon his state when she saw him, the visit could be easy and fun, or sad and tiring. But she would make the effort. Spring was usually good for him, as he loved flowers and butterflies, caterpillars and birds.

What was Darkefell doing that very moment? she wondered. Was he somewhere thinking of her, too?

She sniffed. Likely not. He was probably recovering his equanimity and wondering why he had followed a stiff-necked, long-nosed spinster all the way to Cornwall, and thinking what a lucky escape he had had. She didn't want to imagine that, but it could be true.

She put those morose thoughts out of her mind as she approached the gypsy encampment cautiously. Perhaps it was foolhardy, but she had slipped away without any escort. Mary would have come, if she'd known, but Anne had been to the camp before, and didn't feel any sense of menace from these folk.

The site was a straggly group of tents and carts, circled around a central area where a big fire smoldered, and a pot hung over it. Rope lines of clean clothes were strung from tree to tree. At this time of day, Anne knew it was mostly women at the camp, some young but many more older, stirring pots, washing laundry, and looking after the multitude of dark-haired, dark-eyed children. The younger men were gone off to work on local farms, for farmers did take advantage of their strong backs and inexpensive labor, even as they demanded that the gypsies be evicted from the earl's land. The older men would be selling tinker's wares or following their trade, mending pots and sharpening knives in the village of Kingsdown and beyond as far as Ringwould.

She was about to make her presence known, when she saw something that made her stop dead; it was a familiar profile. A man stood talking earnestly to a pretty young gypsy woman who held a baby to her breast. Her heart pounded. The man's dark curling hair reached his broad shoulders, and the prominent nose and full lips were evident even at a distance.

Her heart pounded, her nighttime dreams and daytime yearnings throbbing through her in an instant. She couldn't help herself; she cried out "Tony!" and started forward, dropping her basket in her haste.

The man turned, stared at her in alarm, and took off, running. She picked up her skirts and ran after him. "Tony, wait! Stop!" she cried out. "What are you doing here? Why are you running?"

But he was faster than she, and galloped over a hill and was gone, while she, confined by her skirts and shawl, was fettered. She stopped running and, gasping for breath, leaned against a tree. What was Darkefell doing near her home, when she had told him to stay away? And yet, was it really Tony? It had looked eerily like him, and he had turned at the name called out and looked like he knew her. There was something not quite right. Surely Darkefell was taller? And broader of shoulder? And . . . more handsome?

But it *had* to be him! There could not be two men in England so similar. Furious, she clumped back to the camp, retrieved her basket, dropped it with the gypsy women, who steadfastly refused to even understand her questions about the dark-haired man she had seen, and then stomped off home, slashing through the lengthening grass, her skirts whirling about her.

Darkefell could be anywhere by now, for she doubted he'd go back to the gypsy camp. But why was he there, sneaking around like a bandit? Was he spying on her? It made no sense.

But if she couldn't find him, then she would send a letter to Darkefell Castle and demand and answer from Osei. Why was Tony in Kent, if not following her and breaking his word? She would write to Lydia, too. And Lady Darkefell, Tony's mother. She would write to them all, demanding answers! She would know the truth.

But now the fever that burned her from within whenever she thought of Tony, Lord Darkefell, and his lips against her mouth, his arms wound around her tightly, leaped into a fire. His hard body, his soft lips, his persuasive kisses. It seemed he was in her very blood, and her pulse pounded out his name. Tony. Tony.

Dreams of him obsessed her after that afternoon. Despite a certainty that he would not come back there, she haunted the gypsy camp every day, begging her father not to evict the gypsies until she figured out what was going on. The man didn't come back—that she saw, anyway—and the gypsies would not speak of him. And yet every night Darkefell visited her in her dreams, calling out her name as she tossed and turned in her feather bed. In those dreams he would do wicked, shameful things to her as she reveled in his lusty abandon.

There was only one way to end her fever; she must see Darkefell, and soon. If the only thing keeping him in her blood was the heat of his kisses and the sensual temptation he presented, then she would make love with him, and either quench the flames or immolate herself on the pyre of passion.

Author's Afterword

Dear Reader,

As with my last book, *Lady Anne and the Howl in the Dark*, I'd like to offer interested readers some pertinent information on the factual basis of *Revenge of the Barbary Ghost*.

First, though the Barbary Ghost legend, the Barbary Ghost Inn, and St. Wyllow village are all the author's own creations, Barbary pirates truly were a frightening fact of life in Georgian-era England and other northern hemisphere countries. The Barbary Coast is a stretch of north Africa coastline that runs along the Mediterranean Sea west, past the Strait of Gibraltar; Muslim pirates and privateers who came from this region were thus called Barbary pirates. Barbary pirates raided northern countries, including England and Ireland, right up to the late 1700s and took hostages to sell, use as slaves, or to trade for ransom.

These bold pirates even raided the ships of the new republic, the United States of America. In the very year in which *this* book takes place, 1786, Thomas Jefferson, ambassador to France, and John Adams, ambassador to England, met in London with the ambassador to England from Tripoli to express their dismay over the Barbary pirates' continuing hostility toward American ships. They received no assurance that the practice of raiding American ships would stop unless an enormous amount of tribute money was paid as a bribe, money the new republic could not afford. It would be many more years before the threat would be contained.

Smuggling is another matter explored in *Revenge of the Barbary Ghost*. As an English county with a long coast and many remote beaches and ports, Cornwall was a favored spot for smugglers, and the illicit practice of importing tax-free goods grew to astronomical proportions in the late 1700s. Taxation of "luxury" goods, such as tea, liquor, tobacco, and even fabric, put those things out of the reach of most common folk, so smuggling was a common way to not only supplement income, but to add a little joy to a grim life with some tobacco or sugar bought from "free traders."

Excise officers patrolled the coast, but though many were diligent, they often could not compete with the crafty and increasingly wealthy smugglers who did on occasion (it is rumored) use caves and tunnels along the Cornish coast to store and transport smuggled goods. More than one excise officer was charged with accepting bribes from the smugglers to look the other way.

There are many fascinating books about Barbary pirates and smuggling in Cornwall available, as well as Internet sites with much information, and both topics are wonderfully interesting details in the colorful tapestry of history. Happy reading!

Fond regards,
Victoria Hamilton

About the Author

Victoria Hamilton is the pseudonym of nationally bestselling romance author Donna Lea Simpson. She is the bestselling author of three mystery series, the Lady Anne Addison Mysteries, the Vintage Kitchen Mysteries, and the Merry Muffin Mysteries. Her latest adventure in writing is a Regency-set historical mystery series, starting with *A Gentlewoman's Guide to Murder*.

Victoria loves to read, especially mystery novels, and enjoys good tea and cheap wine, the company of friends, and has a newfound appreciation for opera. She enjoys crocheting and beading, but a good book can tempt her away from almost anything . . . except writing!

Visit Victoria at: www.victoriahamiltonmysteries.com.

Made in the USA
Middletown, DE
20 July 2021

44509778R00144